T0201597

"*The Attic on Queen Street* is [rife] with family dynamics, a murder mystery, intrigue, and apparitions from the past that just might help bring some much-needed closure to unfinished business for family and friends. . . . For admirers of White and her Tradd Street novels, *The Attic on Queen Street* will literally reveal a hidden gem, while providing a bittersweet farewell."   —Holy City Sinner

"White has created a more than satisfactory end to a fun and entertaining series while somehow tying up all the loose ends."
                                                    —Jacksonville.com

ALSO BY KAREN WHITE

The Color of Light
Learning to Breathe
Pieces of the Heart
The Memory of Water
The Lost Hours
Falling Home
On Folly Beach
The Beach Trees
Sea Change
After the Rain
The Time Between
A Long Time Gone
The Sound of Glass
Flight Patterns
Spinning the Moon
The Night the Lights Went Out
Dreams of Falling
The Last Night in London

Cowritten with Beatriz Williams and Lauren Willig

The Forgotten Room
The Glass Ocean
All the Ways We Said Goodbye
The Lost Summers of Newport

The Tradd Street Series

The House on Tradd Street
The Girl on Legare Street
The Strangers on Montagu Street
Return to Tradd Street
The Guests on South Battery
The Christmas Spirits on Tradd Street
The Attic on Queen Street

THE
SHOP ON
ROYAL STREET

KAREN WHITE

Berkley
New York

BERKLEY
An imprint of Penguin Random House LLC
penguinrandomhouse.com

Copyright © 2022 by Harley House Books, LLC
Readers Guide copyright © 2023 by Penguin Random House LLC
Excerpt from *The House on Prytania* copyright © 2023 by Harley House Books, LLC
Penguin Random House supports copyright. Copyright fuels creativity, encourages diverse
voices, promotes free speech, and creates a vibrant culture. Thank you for buying an authorized
edition of this book and for complying with copyright laws by not reproducing, scanning, or
distributing any part of it in any form without permission. You are supporting writers and
allowing Penguin Random House to continue to publish books for every reader.

BERKLEY and the BERKLEY & B colophon are registered
trademarks of Penguin Random House LLC.

ISBN: 9780593334591

The Library of Congress has catalogued the Berkley hardcover edition of this book as follows:

Names: White, Karen (Karen S.), author.
Title: The shop on Royal Street / Karen White.
Description: New York: Berkley, [2022]
Identifiers: LCCN 2021057102 (print) | LCCN 2021057101 (ebook) |
ISBN 9780593334584 (hardcover) | ISBN 9780593334614 (ebook)
Subjects: | LCGFT: Novels.
Classification: LCC PS3623.H5776 S56 2022 (ebook) |
LCC PS3623.H5776 (print) | DDC 813/.6 23/eng/20211—dc26
LC record available at https://lccn.loc.gov/2021057102

Berkley hardcover edition / March 2022
Berkley trade paperback edition / March 2023

Printed in the United States of America
3rd Printing

To Nancy Mayer Mencke and Lynda Ryan—
for sharing your native city with me,
and for proving that the oldest friends
are the *best* kind of friends

CHAPTER 1

Shadowy reflections of drooping banana leaves haunted the dirt-smudged windows of the old house. It made me think of the hidden memories of people and a past long since gone but still trapped within the walls of the crumbling structure. The roof of the front porch sagged as if weighted with the gravity of the experience of people who had once passed through the corridors before exiting through the doors and windows forever.

I stepped up onto the porch, my fingers brushing the rainbow-hued Mardi Gras beads dangling from the handrails and next to empty spaces left by missing porch spindles that lent a grinning-pumpkin look to the front of the house. Creeping vines from the overgrown front yard claimed most of the three guillotine windows that lined the porch adjacent to the front door, completing the abandoned air and haunted look of the Creole cottage I'd already set my heart on buying. This dilapidated structure was a symbol. A call to arms for me. A new place to start after an impressive and unexpected stumble and a complicated knot of bad decisions, stupidity, and an alarming amount of unwarranted confidence that had almost derailed my life. And all despite the family whose love and support I wasn't convinced I deserved.

"Nola . . ."

Despite the worry and caution in my stepmother's voice, she stopped. We had both learned over the last six years that I needed to make my own decisions. And accept the consequences.

I slowly hopscotched broken boards and patches of termite-chewed wood, the lacelike sinews as dangerous as thin ice. Spots of faded fuchsia paint clung to the front door and corbels of the porch roof, contrasting with the inevitable blue paint of the ceiling and lime green of the clapboards. A line of dusty blue bottles sat atop the sash of one of the windows, a precarious position for something so fragile. Maybe whoever had placed them there believed in taking chances.

"It needs a little work," I said. "Mostly TLC. And maybe a few gallons of paint and linseed oil." I looked down at the sidewalk where my stepmother, Charleston Realtor Melanie Middleton Trenholm, stood in her high heels—despite my warnings about New Orleans sidewalks. Her face wore the expression of someone who'd just witnessed a train wreck. I would have laughed, except she was looking at the house I wanted to buy.

She muttered something under her breath, something that sounded a lot like *Oh, no, not again.* Louder, she said, "You know, Nola, speaking from experience here, I'd say this house needs more than paint and linseed oil. A wrecking ball or flamethrower might be more appropriate."

To distract her, I pointed past a cluster of debris piled on the porch, including a discarded surfboard—not completely out of place in the eclectic Faubourg Marigny—in the direction of a tall oleander plant, its clusters of white funnel-shaped blooms drooping drunkenly in the heat. "The front and back gardens are a little overgrown but contain lots of gorgeous plants. I can't wait for Granddad to come visit and offer his expertise."

I said this with a grin, trying hard to transfer my need for her to see what I saw, the possibilities and hope that I imagined both the house and I required. The beauty and life that existed just under the surface and would emerge if we were given the opportunity to shed our old paint. I looked around again, determined to be honest with myself. Maybe it did need more than TLC and touching up. But whatever it required, I was up to the task. I straightened my shoulders and returned my gaze to Melanie. One thing I was sure of: Our foundations were strong. The house and I were survivors.

"Nola . . ." Melanie began again, but stopped. She met my gaze, her eyes warming with understanding. She'd inherited a historic house in Charleston despite a lifelong dislike of old houses. It wasn't the houses so much as the restless spirits of past residents who hadn't left and had insisted on communicating with her—a gift she'd tried to deny for most of her life but seemed to have finally come to terms with. Through the years, as the "goiter on her neck"—as she'd once called the architectural relic she'd inherited—had become less of a burden and more of the warm and welcoming home where she lived with her husband, children, and multiple dogs, she'd developed a grudging admiration for old houses. I'd even heard her describe one to a client as "a piece of history you can hold in your hands."

Now, as she looked at me with dawning perception, I knew she was seeing this house as I saw it. As a chance for me to move on with my life, much as the inheritance of her own house had pushed her forward. Kicking and screaming, for sure, but with a forward and positive trajectory. The light flickered in her eyes, and I hoped she wasn't hearing the sound of a cash register ringing in the back of her practical mind.

"Well, then," she said, carefully stepping onto the porch's bottom step, "let's have a look inside."

Relief unclenched my chest and allowed me to take a deep breath as I reached inside the rusted metal mailbox nailed to one of the square columns holding up the porch.

"Is that really a good idea?" Melanie asked. "I mean, anybody could just walk in and steal everything."

"Uh, yeah. That. Luckily, there's nothing left to steal. Anything of value has been long since stolen or otherwise removed. Anyway, Ali said it would be a good idea for us to have access."

"Who's Ali? What happened to what's-his-name?"

"Frank? He resigned as our agent. Something about how he wouldn't show me another house if you were going to be there. I'm sure it's because he recognized that you're an accomplished real estate agent and that I didn't need both of you." I spared Melanie the adjectives Frank had used to describe her—pushy, overbearing, officious, and anal retentive. The rest of his descriptions weren't repeatable in polite company.

"Good. His presence was completely redundant. I'm glad he was gracious enough to admit it."

I hid my smile as I stuck the old-fashioned iron key into the lock and jiggled it the way Ali had instructed me over the phone. "She said the owner would stop by to answer any questions. Apparently, the owner's made of stronger stuff and can't be cowed by a labeling gun." I bit my lip as I continued to jiggle the key, hoping Melanie hadn't noticed my slip.

"Excuse me? Did you look inside Frank's briefcase? It was a disaster. He should be thankful that I organized it for him."

I was spared from responding by the door opening on its own, despite the fact that I hadn't felt the turn of the key or any release from the lock. I felt Melanie's gaze on me. "That was easier than I thought it would be," I said brightly. "Ali said the lock should be the first thing I replace because it took her forever to get it open. Guess I just have the right touch."

I stepped across the threshold, hearing the delicate tap of Melanie's heels following me inside, her gaze boring holes in the back of my head. I shut the door, then turned to face her. "Remember our agreement. If you hear or see anything while we are touring this house, please keep it to yourself. I'm not the one who can talk to dead people. Except for that one time in Charleston, they don't have a reason to bother me, and I can remain blissfully oblivious if they're around. If I feel a connection to a house, I won't care if there is an army of wandering souls in its hallways—I won't hear or see them, so it won't keep me up at night. Besides, there are no old houses in New Orleans without at least one lingering spirit. It's a given."

Melanie smiled tightly. "Of course."

We turned our attention to the interior of the house, neither one of us speaking. Either the pictures Ali had e-mailed me had been taken a decade or two earlier, or someone was very skilled with Photoshop. Without furniture to hide behind, the scarred cypress floor glared up at us like an unbandaged wound. Colorful splotches of varying sizes stained the old wood, and I promised myself that I wouldn't look too closely or try to identify the sources. Especially of the ones that were definitely not water- or pet-related.

Like a woman in the throes of labor trying to imagine the happy outcome after the agony, I said, "It could be worse."

"How?" Melanie walked toward the remains of a fireplace. The woodwork had been removed with what must have been an ax, judging by scars in the surrounding drywall that were deep enough to show the studs underneath. "Nothing that a match and some lighter fluid couldn't fix."

"Oh, come on. I know you don't really believe that. Not anymore, anyway. Just think of our house on Tradd Street. And your mother's house on Legare. You helped saved them both from the brink. Even you have to admit that in the end it was all worth it."

"I might. But they were only on the brink. This one has been completely pushed over it. And then trampled on. I think it would appreciate being put out of its misery."

"Look," I said, sticking my fingers through one of the holes in the drywall. "Imagine how beautiful these walls might be if we removed all the drywall and replaced it with plaster. And refinished the floors and fixed the woodwork around the windows and doors. Just look at these high ceilings! Imagine the history in these walls."

As I spoke, her gaze traveled behind me toward the stairs with the missing balustrade, her eyes following something. Or someone. I didn't turn around. She forced her attention back to me and gave me another tight smile. "Are the bedrooms upstairs?"

"Yes. Just two, and because they have to fit under the pitch of the steeply gabled roof, they're tiny, according to the floor plan. I noticed two dormer windows outside, which should at least let in a lot of light. I might have to knock out a wall to enlarge both bedrooms, as well as make the one full bath bigger. And more functional."

"More functional?"

I tried speaking too fast and too softly, in the dim hope that she wouldn't hear me, and would be too embarrassed to ask me to repeat myself. She was highly sensitive about her age, for no reason except the fact that she was a few years older than my dad. This meant I should be safe from further scrutiny regarding the condition of the house and my sanity. "Ali mentioned that the toilet was missing. As well as a sink. But at least there's a half bath down here. Although I believe the toilet doesn't actually flush."

"You do realize that despite my advanced age I have perfect hearing, right?" Melanie moved toward the stairs, turning around to take stock. "So, this room runs the length of the house and doubles as entryway and living room."

I followed behind her, smelling her rose perfume—something she'd started wearing my freshman year in college, when I'd moved back home. "Right. The other front-facing room is the dining room, and behind it, facing the fenced-in backyard, is the kitchen."

"Which I'm sure is just as functional as the upstairs bathroom."

"No," I said, hating to admit she was right. "The kitchen has a sink."

Melanie glanced over her shoulder at me but didn't say anything.

As we climbed the stairs to the second level, the temperature changed as if the thermostat had abruptly dropped thirty degrees, despite the hot sun streaming in unimpeded from one of the dormer windows. Except there was no air conditioner. Or thermostat. Melanie didn't say anything, but I saw her shiver.

We both ducked at the top of the stairs to avoid hitting the pitched ceiling, Melanie rubbing her arms as she looked around at the laminate wood panels covering the walls. Dust motes floated in front of the filthy windows, the musky scent of old house—an oddly appealing mix of dust, ancient fabrics, and furniture polish—making me a little homesick.

This room was as long as the living space beneath us, but far less functional because of the ceiling slope. Still, it held a lot of charm, and it had the same cypress floors as the first story. While getting my master's degree in historic preservation at the College of Charleston, I'd done a lot of floor rehab, and my fingers itched to see what a little sanding and linseed oil might do to these.

Melanie's gaze focused on a closed door at the top of the stairs, her mouth opening and then shutting immediately. I walked past her and turned the knob. "It's locked, and there's no key in the keyhole. I think it's just a closet. We can ask the owner."

"Do you smell that?" She stuck her head forward, sniffing the air. "It's pipe tobacco. It's like someone just blew pipe smoke in my face."

"I don't smell anything. Just the house." Which wasn't exactly true. I had caught a whiff, but just a whiff.

She nodded, her eyes remaining on the closet door. "I think . . ."

"You promised." I gave her a warning glance before going through an open doorway that led directly into one of the small bedrooms. There were two other doorways, one to the second bedroom and the other to what must have been the bathroom.

I stuck my head into the bathroom, and immediately pulled it back. "I don't recommend you look in there." I was grateful for the lower temperature sparing us from the scent of heat-baked whatever had been left in the plumbing. I looked at the tall, sloped ceiling, at the original wooden beams and dormer window surround, and a fireplace like the one downstairs, with its mantel intact. "I think if I just reposition these walls, we could have two decent-sized bedrooms. And . . ."

The familiar notes of "Dancing Queen" being loudly hummed behind me caught my attention. I shouldn't have been surprised. Loudly humming ABBA songs was Melanie's way of drowning out the restless spirits who wanted to talk to her. I assumed they found it as annoying as the living did, which is why it worked. It was one of Melanie's quirks—definitely weird but also surprisingly lovable.

I sighed. "Fine. I've seen enough up here. Let's go back downstairs." As I turned, I spotted an unhinged door leaning against the wall. The wood tone and the opaque glass of the top panel told me it hadn't come from the house, but it didn't tell me why it was there.

Melanie stopped humming long enough to lean down to look at the iron lock and doorknob. She touched the assembly gently with her finger. "It has the initials *MB* embossed on the handle."

I leaned closer. "I've seen a few of these doors before. They're from the iconic Maison Blanche department store building downtown. When the store and the offices on the upper floors were gutted to be transformed into the Ritz-Carlton in the late nineteen nineties, a lot of the unwanted interior was scavenged." I ran my hand along the privacy bubbles in the glass, admiring the thick wood of the door, a relic from a time when even basic office doors were made with longevity in mind. Straightening, I added, "Mostly by locals wanting to keep something of a New Orleans landmark, and also by renovators who wanted a piece of history in their houses. In grad school I saw a lot of pictures of how people used some of the scavenged materials—including a lingerie display counter repurposed as a kitchen island in a house in the Quarter."

Melanie suddenly turned toward the window, her head tilted slightly as if she was listening to someone speaking. She shook her head, then began humming again, this time "Waterloo." Without waiting for me, she marched through the doorway, then down the stairs as I hurried to catch up to her, glancing over my shoulder only once.

I caught up to her in the kitchen, where she'd placed her bag on a scarred and pitted countertop with stains of indeterminate origin the color of a sunset before a storm. I decided to believe they were from marinara and spilled hurricane cocktails. We both studiously avoided discussing the elephant in the room—or whatever that had been upstairs—as I examined the peeling laminate floor, its lifted corners revealing the cypress planks beneath.

Melanie opened her bag and pulled out one of her infamous spreadsheets. "I've been looking at the comps in the Faubourg Marigny. . . ."

I held up my hand to stop her. "You know how you grit your teeth when you're with a client who wants to buy a house in Charleston but doesn't know how to pronounce the street names? They phonetically sound out 'Legare' and 'Vanderhorst' and it's like fingernails on a chalkboard? So please. Locals here call it 'the *MAR-i-nee*.' No need to put 'Faubourg' in front of it, because it means 'suburb,' so it's redundant. And while we're at it, it's a streetcar, not a trolley, and whatever you do, do *not* say 'New *Orleens*,' okay? It's all one word—'Newawlins.' Otherwise, people will have the same reaction you get when you overhear a tourist call Charleston 'Chucktown.'"

A shudder rippled through Melanie. "Got it. Since I imagine your dad and I and the twins will be visiting you a lot, it's important that we fit right in."

At my look of alarm, she quickly amended: "I mean—not too much. You'll be busy with work, as will your father and I, and the twins have school, but I just thought . . ."

I put my hand on her arm and squeezed. Melanie, for all of her quirks and idiosyncrasies, had been my mother and fierce defender ever since I'd shown up unannounced on her doorstep just shy of fourteen, lost and alone, with only the name of my father—Jack Trenholm—as a certainty in my life. Owing to her own shattered childhood, Melanie had recognized a kindred unmoored soul and taken me in without reservation or conditions and proceeded to mother me long before she married Jack and the title became official.

"I'll miss you, too," I said softly. "And you and Dad and JJ and Sarah can visit as often as you like. And Aunt Jayne and all the grandparents. Just not too often, okay? I need to do this on my own."

Melanie nodded, her lips pressed together, her eyes bright; undoubtedly she was remembering the first time I'd moved to New Orleans, as a freshman at Tulane, excited and nervous about this great new adventure. Seeing only my bright new future ahead of me. Until the susceptibility to addiction I'd inherited from both parents had finally found me and it had all gone spectacularly wrong.

I blinked my stinging eyes as I opened my backpack and pulled out my own spreadsheet on recent sales in the neighborhood, earning myself a look of approval and a little bit of surprise. I hadn't meant to show it to Melanie, not wanting her to know that, despite my adamant demands that I leave my home behind me, there were some things that I would need to hold on to. And because I'd realized that she might need to hold on to a connection to me, too.

"Let's just say that after living with you for so long, a few things might have rubbed off on me. I've found that spreadsheets can actually be useful in situations where organization of details is important. Like house searches. Or class schedules. But not the contents of my dresser drawers." I raised my eyebrows. "Or shoes."

"Um-hmm." That was the Melanie equivalent of letting me know that she was right and I'd figure that out eventually. "Anyway," she continued, "even in the condition this house is in, it appears to be structurally sound. Which is why I don't understand the listing price. It's way below market, even lower than homes in worse condition that were sold before being rehabbed. I just can't figure out why. I was wondering if maybe this house sustained major damage during Katrina and that's scared off buyers."

I shook my head, remembering all the research I'd done before accepting my new job as an architectural historian for a New Orleans–based civil engineering firm. I knew I needed to be fully armed to talk my parents out of all of their objections. "The section of the neighborhood on the river side of Rampart experienced some wind damage, but the Marigny is at a high enough elevation to have escaped the flooding. Most of the nineteenth century–style raised houses are elevated enough so that the floodwaters didn't do significant damage. I know you won't admit it, but older houses were just built better."

Melanie's forehead creased. "Then why hasn't it sold? It's been on the market for over a year, and the price is so far below market that I'm wondering if the sellers forgot a zero." She raised the worksheet closer to her face and squinted. "The average time on the market for this neighborhood is less than two months—even for those in need of rehab. And, according to my notes, it looks like this house made it to escrow six times before the deal fell through." She looked at me.

"Frank or this Ali person, if they truly consider themselves real estate agents, would have done their research and figured out why."

I kept my mouth closed, not wanting to mention that they probably had but had thought it best not to tell me. Before Melanie reached the same conclusion, I marched past her toward the back door. "Let's check out the backyard."

I threw open the door and paused. "I found the toilet and sink!" Both had been planted along the fence line, a healthy sprouting of weeds spilling out of both and trailing down to the lichen-coated bricks on the ground. Muppet-hair-like spikes of grass poked out from between the worn bricks, many of them missing corners or otherwise broken. A pine coffin, questionably repurposed as a planter, grew surprisingly hardy miniature palm trees, while an impressive amount of something green and fuzzy covered it like a five-o'clock shadow.

Melanie shuddered. "I noticed that the neighbors across the street have a coffin planter, too. Maybe they'd like a pair."

I looked at Melanie with alarm. "Do you think . . . ?"

She shook her head. "No. It's not been used for its original purpose. It's just . . . not all right."

"Actually, in the Marigny it's pretty much par for the course. Did you notice the goat with a rhinestone collar in the yard on the corner? I'm assuming that's what the homeowner uses as a lawn mower. I think the whole vibe here is cool. It's pretty eclectic, and I'm excited about the neighborhood music scene. I'd like to get back into writing music, and I think I'd be a good fit here. And my office is downtown, on Poydras, so it's an easy commute. I could even bike it."

At Melanie's look of alarm, I quickly added, "Or take public transportation. Or even Uber it if it's dark."

She relaxed. "Or you could learn to drive."

"No," I said, shutting her down. "I tried once and just missed getting killed or being sued for everything we owned. No, thanks." I still had nightmares about my first and last accident, which I'd caused as a newly permitted driver. I'd hit a car in which my dad's nemesis, Marc

Longo, had been a passenger, resulting in my parents' having to allow Marc to film his movie in our house. I was not eager to repeat the experience.

I struggled to draw a deep breath in the sticky air of the end of July in New Orleans. I glanced at Melanie, whose hair had already frizzed out into wool-scrubbing-pad proportions. "Just like Charleston," I said, trying to wipe away the look of worry on her face.

She gave me her "mom look," the one that told me she knew that I didn't believe what I'd said, either. That despite the shared tropical climate that wilted less sturdy souls, Charleston and New Orleans were merely distant cousins, with traces of a common ancestry apparent in their architecture, built to accommodate scorching temperatures and the always-present threat of hurricanes.

Their separateness was evident in their respective monikers: the Big Easy and the Holy City. The aura of New Orleans was best described as feral, Charleston's as refined and graceful. My new home embraced decay, painted it in neon colors, and put it on the front porch. In Charleston a lace doily would have been thrown over it. Charleston had palmetto bugs. New Orleans had flying cockroaches. Each city had a place in my heart. One was a place from which to return, and one a place to run toward.

"Hello? Anyone here?" A male voice came from the kitchen.

Melanie and I looked at each other. "It must be the owner," Melanie said as she delicately stepped across broken bricks toward the kitchen. "We're out here!"

I held back, as the voice was vaguely familiar. And not in a good way.

"Oh." This time the voice came from the doorway. "It's you."

"Oh," I repeated with the same lack of enthusiasm.

Melanie began to speak, then stopped suddenly as her gaze fixed on something beyond the doorway, her eyes widening just before a loud crash erupted from somewhere inside the house. An icy blast of air whipped through us, raising gooseflesh over my entire body as a woman's scream pierced the quiet afternoon.

CHAPTER 2

"Stay here." Beau Ryan, a loose end from my not-so-distant youth, blocked the doorway into the kitchen almost as effectively as I'd blocked him from idle reminiscences of my past. Despite being bossy and overbearing, he had been witness to one of the worst days of my life and the beginning of my blazing path toward self-destruction. My one-year tenure at Tulane had been a disaster, my attempts at spreading my wings translating into a free-for-all of unbridled partying without parental supervision. Not exactly a good choice, considering my genetic makeup. My parents had questioned my failing grades, but it wasn't until my roommate called them after I'd passed out on the front lawn of a frat house and had to be brought home by a stranger—not for the first time—that they realized how dire the situation had become. And that I needed to come home.

In the intervening six years since I'd last seen him, he'd apparently forgotten that I was not the type to take orders from anyone—especially him. I rushed toward the doorway, Melanie close on my heels. Our shared inability to take orders was yet another thing that bonded us. We entered the front room at the same time as Beau, simultaneously taking in the shattered blue bottles scattered like ink blots across the floor and the petite redhead with her fingers, the nails painted pink, held over her mouth.

"I didn't do it," she said through her fingers. "The door was open, so I walked in, and then the bottles on the windowsill just"—she motioned with her hands—"flew to the floor."

"Must have been a passing truck," Beau said.

"Must have been a slamming door," Melanie said at the same time.

"Jolene?" Her name easily slid off my tongue. My Tulane roommate smiled back at me. Both her name and flaming red hair made her impossible to forget. And when she spoke, I was suddenly eighteen years old and standing in my Josephine Louise House dorm room while my new roommate thrust a homemade comforter at me, explaining that she and her grandmama had made one for each of us so our beds would match.

"Nola!" She embraced me tightly, her hair-sprayed locks crinkling against my cheek, a familiar scent of perfume and powder still hugging me as she stepped back. "Just seeing your pretty face again has put pepper in my gumbo. It has been too long. I wrote and wrote and wrote, and I guess you never got my letters. And your phone number didn't work anymore. But every time Mama fries chicken, I think of you and that time you came home with me to Mississippi and you had us try that meat-free chicken. . . ."

I held up my hand to stop her, remembering how she was like a Southern version of a windup talking doll with a full repertoire of expressions and sayings that defied explanation and needed to wind itself down before stopping. "Hang on a moment." I paused as my mind sorted through the proverbial collection of elephants surrounding me, the least of which being the shattered bottles and how they'd fallen.

Jolene, wearing full makeup despite the heat and humidity, met my eyes. She appeared to be waiting for me either to agree with something as nonsensical as bottles falling ten feet from their perch or to argue. I did neither. Instead, I focused on my most pressing question. Turning toward Beau, my tone bordering on hostile, I asked, "What are *you* doing here?"

"I was about to ask you the same thing."

He was tall—and some might even say good-looking—and it bothered me that I had to tilt my head to look him in the eye. "I'm planning on buying this house." I heard Melanie's intake of breath behind me.

Beau's light brown eyes narrowed as an odd smile lifted his lips. "Well, I own this house. And you can't buy it."

"What?" Melanie and I spoke in unison.

"Why not?" I didn't bother to hide my annoyance, which had nothing to do with the argument at hand but was due to the fact that I was seeing him again and he was no doubt recalling a litany of embarrassing moments from my past.

"Because I'm taking it off the market. Now. It's no longer for sale. My grandmother and I own lots of other houses in and around New Orleans that you can buy. Just not this one."

Melanie stepped forward. "Beau. It's so nice to see you again. And I agree that this house isn't the right one for Nola. Maybe you can suggest—"

"No. I want *this* house." I wasn't sure if my conviction was due to the way I'd felt the moment I'd stepped onto the front steps, as if the house had been waiting for me like a lonely old man sitting in the dark. Or because I was still angry at Beau, for reasons I couldn't really explain, and needed to be contrary.

"Because the house isn't safe. It needs to be demolished."

"Then why is it for sale?"

Melanie and Beau shared a glance, giving Jolene time to step forward. She held out her hand to Melanie. "I'm sure you don't remember me, Mrs. Trenholm—I was Nola's freshman-year roommate. Before she transferred, sophomore year."

I appreciated her softening the actual event. Besides her red hair, her kindness was the thing I remembered most about Jolene.

Instead of shaking her hand, Melanie hugged her, no doubt recalling just how much we all owed Jolene McKenna. "Of course I remember you." She turned to me. "We still think about you every time we hear that song, don't we, Nola?" Melanie's voice skipped.

I swallowed, wishing I didn't. "Of course." I forced a smile. "Jolene—just like that Dolly Parton song. It's great seeing you again. I'm sorry I never wrote back. I just got busy and . . ."

Jolene waved a manicured hand at me. "No need to explain. I figured you were as busy as a one-armed paperhanger and you'd get back in touch when you could."

Beau shifted uncomfortably. "Look, the house isn't for sale, so let's . . ."

Ignoring him, I kept my attention on Jolene. "What are you doing here?"

"I work for Beau. Well, Beau and his grandmother, Mimi. JR Properties. They buy old houses and buildings that need work, restore and refurbish them, then sell them. I just got my master's in preservation studies from Tulane, with a certificate in sustainable real estate development. One of my professors told me about the job opening and I knew it was perfect for me." Her gaze moved from me to Beau, then back again. "So, you two know each other?"

"He's the guy who made me lose my mother's guitar in a fire."

"She's the girl who was named for the city where she was conceived."

Jolene's eyes widened.

Melanie stepped between Beau and me, possibly to prevent violence. "We met Beau back in Charleston, when he was an undergrad at the American College of the Building Arts and working in my in-laws' antiques store. He did an amazing restoration of our iron fence." She winced a little, no doubt recalling how much that had cost. It was her one holdback from completely embracing old houses—the sheer expense of maintaining them, which Melanie likened to digging a hole and throwing in the contents of your bank account.

"You forgot to mention that I was in the process of saving your life when I dragged you out of that burning house," Beau said. "I thought that was more important than the guitar."

"And you forget that I could have easily grabbed it before you dragged me out that window."

Melanie put a hand on my arm. She understood what that guitar had meant to me—the lone memento of my dead mother. But, as she often reminded me, Beau had saved my life (even though I remained stubbornly convinced he could have also saved the guitar). For that, she would always have blind spots when it came to Beau Ryan. It was easy to overlook his overbearing and bossy nature and the unfortunate circumstances that had twice placed him at the wrong place at the right time to save me from my own stupidity. And regardless of how ridiculous I knew it was, I hadn't found a way to forgive him.

"Let's focus on the house, all right?" Melanie said. "Obviously, the condition of the house is too far gone to be considered . . ."

I shook my head. "Not at all. It's so far below my budget that I'll have plenty of money to do the renovations. And my landlord has already told me that I can go month to month on my lease on my current apartment on Broadway for a year, so there's no time crunch." I looked at Jolene, seeing her as a possible accomplice. Slinging my arm around her shoulders, I said, "And I'm sure Jolene would love to offer her expertise and contacts."

She smiled, then sent a worried grimace at Beau. "I'm still new at this, but Beau works with the Preservation Resource Center. I'm sure he also has some contacts for you."

"Doesn't matter," he said. "The house still isn't for sale."

Melanie's gaze strayed toward the stairs. "Look, why don't we go somewhere to sit down and have a cup of coffee to discuss this? My feet hurt."

I knew there had to be another reason she wanted to leave. Melanie's feet would have to be bleeding and on fire for her to say that wearing heels had been a bad idea.

"There's no discussion," Beau said. "I own this house and it isn't for sale."

I tilted my head back to look him in the eyes. "Well, the MLS says differently. And I'm calling my agent right now to make an offer."

Before he could respond, Jolene said, "There's an adorable café right down the street, on Burgundy."

"Is it vegan?" Beau asked. "Assuming Nola still prefers cardboard to real food."

"I'm sure I can find something," I said, less annoyed than I should have been. He'd remembered something about me that wasn't pitiful. Which probably meant that he could recall more about me than I would have liked, but at least that part was from an earlier time, before the worst parts.

"Fine," I said. "But I'm not changing my mind."

Melanie practically pushed me out onto the porch, then hurried down the stairs to wait on the sidewalk with Jolene as I locked the door. Beau held out his hand for the key, but I ignored it, slipping the key into my backpack instead. A wind chime of blue Depression glass hanging from a rusty hook on the porch ceiling clinked behind me despite the complete absence of a breeze. I saw Beau and Melanie share a glance—Jolene oblivious as she reapplied her lipstick—but I wasn't alarmed. It was as if the house was letting me know it and I were meant to be together.

For a woman whose feet supposedly hurt, Melanie had a long and purposeful stride. It could have been because of the promise of bakery items and café au lait, but a part of me said she was trying to put distance between her and the house.

The yellow building that housed Who Dat Coffee Cafe sat on the corner of Burgundy and Mandeville, a short walk from the house on Dauphine Street—yet another sign that the Creole cottage was meant to be mine. Living with Melanie had turned me into something of a coffee snob, and—although I'd never admit it—a craver of sweet baked goods. It had started when I began eating instead of discarding Melanie's hidden contraband items when I'd replaced them with my Wasa crisps. Now I craved doughnuts like a mouse craved cheese, but I ate them in secret, which was enough to tell me that I was in full denial. But, as I'd learned the hard way, there were some vices that were better substitutions for others.

Tables sat scattered on the sidewalk outside the café, red umbrellas valiantly stretched over them absorbing the heat of the sun, potted yellow flowers wilting prettily on their centerpiece perches. The words "Wake up & smell the Who Dat" covered one of the windows, right above a painted cup of coffee with white steam curling over the cup. An A-frame chalkboard sign by the entrance informed us that *It's never too late to start your day over.*

We walked through the red wood-and-glass double doors, the warm yellow and the cluttered walls and the tin ceiling making me feel like I'd stepped back in time as the mixed scents of coffee and baked sugar made my mouth water. I heard Melanie swallow next to me. "I wasn't really hungry," she said. "But now I'm starving."

"The Who Dat coffee cake is to die for. And their banana bread. And cupcakes. Oh, gosh, there is nothing here that isn't worth the calories," Jolene said.

We placed our orders, then settled onto one of the outside tables. I resisted getting something to eat and ordered only an iced coffee— decaffeinated and with soy milk—to hold to my face in an attempt to cool off. What I really needed was to fall into a fountain. Same with Melanie, judging by the size of her hair.

"Feels just like home," she said, taking a spoon and eating a bite of whipped cream from the top of her café au lait. She'd also ordered a piece of the coffee cake—one fork, no extra plates. I was used to Melanie's proprietary attitude toward her food, but I caught Jolene glancing at the gooey confection more than once.

"Don't even ask," I warned her. "You'll end up with fork scars on the top of your hand."

Melanie took a sip of her coffee so she wouldn't have to lie.

I turned to Beau, summoning every crumb of advice from my long-suffering therapist about confronting adversity. Admittedly, she'd helped me over the worst of my issues. It wasn't her fault that I was born too stubborn to pay attention to the rest. I wished my dad were here. He had a habit of inspiring fear in males who dared circle my periphery—although the one exception had been Beau. Jack had a knack for breaking down every problem into solvable puzzle pieces. But he was currently in London, on a book tour with his latest international bestseller. It was just me and Melanie—who apparently didn't want me to buy the house. That left Jolene, who was currently placing on her head a wide-brimmed hat she'd pulled out of her enormous tote bag.

"So," I began. "The house is for sale. I want to buy it. I can give you full asking price. I don't see why this is a problem."

Melanie and Beau shared another glance. He shifted in his chair. "The neighborhood would like to build a community center. My grandmother and I feel that the house would make a good charitable donation to the neighborhood."

"So, when did you make this decision? Before you saw me or after? Because you should have pulled it from the MLS listing before I saw it. Now it's too late."

"It's just . . . not for you. If it's not demolished, I think one of the many restoration firms in the city might buy it to rehab. It's a big job."

I crossed my arms. "And because I'm a single woman you don't think I can handle it?"

Melanie put a hand of caution on my arm. "Nola, I don't think he's saying that at all. It's just that there are . . . things . . . about the house that you might not be aware of that could make living there . . . difficult. And I'm not talking about the termite damage."

"If by 'things' you're referring to restless spirits, you know they don't bother me. I've lived in a haunted house since I was fourteen, so it would be almost weird for me if there wasn't at least one or two rubbing elbows with me. I'm not sensitive to them. And Beau used to spend most of his free time hosting a podcast debunking so-called psychics, so I don't understand the problem."

I glared at Beau. "You said your business is buying old houses and rehabbing them. Not knocking them down. Obviously, the job was too much for you, so maybe you're just a little jealous that I can handle it and you can't. Fine. I graduated number one in my class in grad school, so I understand competition. But please don't be petty about it."

Jolene pulled out a monogrammed compact from her oversized purse and opened it. "My family's house in Mississippi was built in

1839, so it has a lot of memories. All old houses do. I think that's what spirits really are. I never saw any ghosts—which is a good thing, because I was raised not to believe in them—but I always had a sense that our house had mostly good memories."

Jolene finished dabbing her nose with powder and was now considering Beau with her wide green eyes; those and her red hair were the reason why her mother thought it a good idea to saddle her with the name Jolene. "I think if you won't sell Nola the house you'll be stepping in a whole pile of worms, because it *does* sound like discrimination." She smiled at me. "I've been thinking while y'all were arguing that this could be my first project, and I can get my friend at *New Orleans* magazine to do a story on a female-led team restoring a house in the Marigny. It would be like free advertising for JR Properties, as well as good PR."

She placed her manicured hands on top of the table. "And since nobody here is worried about ghosts, there shouldn't be any problem with rehabbing and moving into that house." She returned the compact to her purse and snapped it shut. "Even with its history."

Only Melanie and I looked surprised. Apparently, Beau already knew what Jolene was referring to.

"Its history?" Melanie repeated, her crossed leg bumping up and down violently—one of her many quirky habits—making the table shake.

Jolene turned toward Beau. "You didn't tell them?"

"No." He spoke through tight lips. "Because if Nola doesn't buy the house, then it doesn't matter."

"What doesn't matter?" I asked.

We all faced Beau, waiting.

He took a deep breath. "It's, um—it's what we call in the business a, um . . ."

"A 'murder house,'" Jolene finished, just as a crack of thunder shook the air and a gust of rain-scented wind picked up our red umbrella and swept it away down the sidewalk, flipping and turning like a thing possessed until it disappeared around the corner.

CHAPTER 3

Melanie, Jolene, and I sat around the small dining table in my Uptown town-house apartment on three of the five mismatched chairs, all jettisoned by previous tenants, along with a large scarred wooden teacher's desk from the sixties and a couch that was older than I was. The sun peered meekly between gray clouds, the sudden storm over as quickly as it had begun, leaving the Crescent City sodden and sweltering, steam floating up from the streets like escaping demons.

I reached over to the window AC unit rumbling next to us and cranked it as high as it would go. I was sure I looked as bedraggled as Melanie, and studiously avoided catching my reflection in the window. Jolene's hair still looked perfect, a testament to whatever hair spray she used. As a lifelong Southerner, she would have had lots of practice defying humidity. I still had a lot to learn, as my years in Charleston had taught me only to always have a hair band handy, and I had been forced into wearing my hair in a ponytail from May through September.

Since we'd returned to my apartment after our quick departure from Who Dat Coffee Cafe, Jolene had been searching through the vast number of cold-case and unsolved murders on YouTube and elsewhere on the Internet. Apparently, this was a hobby of hers that she didn't even pretend to be embarrassed about, and I didn't question it when the information gleaned proved to be a lot more enlightening than the sparse details and graphic euphemisms found in news accounts from previous decades.

"Are you sure that's the right house?" Melanie leaned over Jolene's shoulder, squinting to read the laptop's screen. For as long as I'd known Melanie, she'd never willingly worn her glasses in front of anyone.

Jolene turned the computer to face us. "This is a newspaper photo of the house from 1964—it's definitely it, right?"

I nodded. Even without all the clutter on the porch, I recognized the house. Which confirmed what we'd been searching for—it was definitely a murder house.

"And there was only one victim, and she was female?" Melanie squinted harder.

"Yes, ma'am." Melanie had asked Jolene to drop the "ma'am" and just call her Melanie, but solid raising by a Southern mama couldn't be messed with. "A young woman—Jeanne Broussard, aged twenty years. She lived in the house with her cousin Louise. They were both sales associates at Maison Blanche downtown." Jolene turned the laptop back to herself, silent for a moment as she read. "Louise found Jeanne's body on the stairs when she returned from a date. She had been strangled. There was no evidence of a sexual assault, and the perpetrator was never caught."

"Never caught?" Melanie's hand went to her neck.

"Not according to this article. I might be able to take a deeper dive if you really want to know more. I know someone who might be able to give us access to the police report." Jolene flushed slightly.

"'Someone'?" I asked.

"Yes. Jaxson Landry. He grew up in Metairie and went to Tulane Law. He's a public defender, so he knows a lot of police officers. I'm sure he'd love to help." Her flush deepened.

"Are you two dating?" Melanie asked. Marriage to my dad had apparently turned her into a hopeless romantic. Watching Hallmark movies had become her favorite pastime. I would sometimes join her to give her company, not because I actually enjoyed sappy romances and happy endings. Maybe it was because in my twenty-six years I'd already seen too much evidence that not every story had a happy ending.

Jolene shook her head. "We're just friends. We met at a Mardi Gras party last year at a mutual friend's house, and we just hang out occasionally with the same friend group. He's, um, sort of dating that mutual friend. Carly."

"Sort of?" Melanie asked.

"They break up a lot and then get back together. Just when I think I've got a chance in between the breakups, Carly starts blinking her eyelashes at him like a toad in a rainstorm and Jaxson is besotted again. They met in law school—she's an attorney in a private firm here. They've been pretty much an item since then."

"Ah, I see," Melanie and I said in unison. We'd definitely watched too many Hallmark movies together.

"So, could you ask him to dig a little more?" I straightened, thinking of the possibilities of Jolene knowing a lawyer. "While you're at it, maybe ask him the best way to fight Beau and buy the house that is meant to be mine?"

Melanie shifted in her chair, but managed to remain silent.

"Yes to the first question. And definitely no to the second. Jaxson is a public defender, not a miracle worker. I haven't known Beau for a long time, but he's as stubborn as a mule. You only have to listen to a single episode of his podcast to know that. Maybe if we had a reason why he's suddenly changed his mind, we would be able to work around it. But there have been dozens of people looking at the house since I've started working for JR Properties, and this is the first time I've heard him voice an objection." She shrugged. "I guess it's just you." She blinked her eyes a few times as if waiting for me to tell her more.

Melanie cleared her throat and sent me a sidelong glance. "I think Beau is concerned about Nola's safety." She squeezed my hand in warning. "We've known Beau for years and really consider him one of the family."

I stared at her. "Seriously? Because . . ." Melanie squeezed my hand harder, forcing me to close my mouth.

Melanie continued. "Nola has always been a bit . . . accident-prone, and Beau has been in the position more than once to help out before any harm could come to her. He probably sees the house as a hazard zone for Nola. And I'm not completely disagreeing. Maybe it would be best if we call the real estate agent back—was it Ali?—to show us more houses."

I stood, my chair scraping the floor as it slid backward. "No. I've been searching for the perfect house, and I've found it. I'm a grown woman with renovation skills and my own tool belt. Whatever dangers you and Beau are imagining"—I gave Melanie a warning look—"I don't care. It doesn't matter that someone was murdered in the house. I'm curious, sure, but that was a long time ago, and has nothing to do with me. Whoever committed the crime back in 1964 is more than likely dead or too old to cause me any harm anyway."

"Even though the house could hold bad memories?" Jolene's flawless forehead creased with worry.

"Whether there are bad memories, lost spirits, or a voodoo spell, I'm not sensitive to any of it. I love that house and I need to find a way to make it mine. I feel like I've been offered a box of doughnuts and then had the lid slammed shut on my hand right before I could take one." At Melanie's confused look, I amended: "I meant a box of tofu bars. Or vegan cupcakes. Either way, the feeling's the same."

"Not really," Melanie muttered.

Jolene carefully closed her laptop. "It's a shame the house isn't more move-in ready. I was going to beg you to rent me one of the upstairs bedrooms. My lease on the house I share with three friends on Willow Street is up at the end of the month and I need to find someplace new. You and I were roommates for a full year and I thought we made a good team. And if we can convince Beau to change his mind, we would be working together, which could be really convenient if we also lived together. I have a car," she added, as if she needed to sweeten the deal.

"Not that it matters. Nobody's going to be living there for some time. Unless they're a termite."

I'd sat back down at the table, my chin in my hands as my fingers tapped a rhythm on my cheeks as I thought. I stared at the old-fashioned pink princess telephone that had been left in the apartment despite the fact that there was no landline anymore. The cord lay coiled behind the desk, the empty wall jack staring out at the room with one-eyed wonder at this strange new world that had rendered it obsolete.

"You know," I said, "I've got three bedrooms here. Besides mine, I'm using the back one as an office and music room, but the middle one is empty. We're on fraternity row, so it can get noisy; the fuses blow if more than one hair dryer is turned on at the same time; and the three bedrooms downstairs are rented to three undergrads, so the parking situation with the single driveway can get dicey. But the rent's pretty low and it's an easy commute to pretty much anywhere, which kind of makes up for all of that. I've been looking for a roommate, but if you'd like it . . ."

"Yippee!" Jolene said, clapping her hands with perfectly straight fingers, just like the cheerleader she'd once been. "I had a feeling when I woke up this morning that it was going to be a great day, and it felt like fate when I bumped into you at the house. Beau would have something to say about how everything can be explained, but I for one would like to think that there is a wizard behind the curtain."

I grinned at her *Wizard of Oz* comment, recalling her fascination with the movie and remembering that she'd owned a pair of red sparkly pumps and had hung over her dorm bed a poster showing the yellow brick road with the words "There's no place like home."

Melanie stood and glanced at her Apple Watch and then at her phone. My dad and I had explained dozens of times that they would always be in sync, but—being Melanie—she always had to double-check that she had the right time. "I have to leave for the airport in about fifteen minutes, and I still need to finish packing and call an Uber." She gave me a worried smile. "I'm glad that at least the roommate situation is settled. I just wish . . ." Melanie stopped, as if remembering her promise, but then barreled on anyway. "I think you should look at more houses, Nola. I'd stay if I could, but I can't miss JJ and Sarah's piano recital, especially without Jack being there. I'd hoped we'd have found the right place by now—"

"I have," I interrupted her. "I know you have reservations. And I understand why. But I don't. I see so much of myself in that house. We need each other."

Melanie's eyes moistened, and I blinked rapidly because she was going to make me cry. She hugged me tightly. "You are so strong, Nola. Your father and I are prouder of you than we can ever say." She pulled away and held me at arm's length. "I'm going to trust you to make your own decisions, because you've earned it. Even if it kills me. I'm reassured that you use spreadsheets, because that's sort of like me leaning over your shoulder." She dropped her hands, tugging at the two charm bracelets I wore. They each had a four-leaf clover, and had been given to me by Melanie and Jack when I was in high school. I never took them off. "Keep wearing these, okay?"

I nodded, unable to speak.

"Well, then, I'd better finish packing." Melanie hesitated, her worried eyes searching mine, before turning and heading toward her room.

"Hmm."

I turned toward the sound. Jolene still sat at the table, her hands folded neatly on top of her laptop, her eyes narrowed, her head tilted. Even though it had been almost ten years since we'd spent any time together, I still knew what she was about to say. "Chickens pecking at your brain again?"

"You remembered." Jolene sounded surprised.

"It's pretty memorable. I can honestly say I've never met anyone else who uses that expression."

She smiled as if I'd just given her a giant compliment. "Well, those chickens have been busy, because I think I've figured out how we can work around Beau."

I liked the way she said "we," and I especially liked how she believed that Beau wasn't an unsurmountable brick wall.

I joined Jolene at the table. "And?"

"There's only one person you need to speak with who can change Beau's mind. His grandmother Mimi."

I recalled what little I'd heard about her, from both Beau and one of his ex-girlfriends whom I knew in Charleston. Assuming nothing had changed in the intervening years, Mimi Ryan lived in an old house in the Garden District, where she'd raised Beau after his parents disappeared during Hurricane Katrina. There was something odd about the house, but I couldn't remember what. But all old houses were odd in some way. They were stuffed with too many years of accumulated stories of the people who'd once lived in them to appear normal. Like a scuffed and cracked, well-worn pair of shoes that was more beautiful than when it was new, if only because the shoes showed where they'd been.

I remembered, too, that Beau's grandmother owned an antiques shop in the French Quarter. A wedge of unease lodged in the back of my brain. Something to do with a locked door in her Garden District home and with her unusual collections. And a story of a missing sister. Not that any of that mattered. If I had to put on heels and play nice to get Mimi Ryan to like me and side against her grandson in this ridiculous fight, I would. Mimi was a grandmother. I had two grandmothers who adored me. How hard could it be?

Melanie reappeared, rolling her oversized suitcase across the hardwood floor. I cringed, hoping she wasn't making grooves with the wheels. I'd never seen her pack lightly, even for an overnight trip. I never asked, but I'd always assumed she needed the extra space for her spreadsheets and shoes. I stood. "Ready?"

"I already ordered the Uber. It'll be here in—" She was cut off by the phone ringing on the desk next to her. Before I could explain that the phone wasn't plugged in and we didn't have a landline, Melanie picked up the receiver and held it to her ear. "Hello?"

The faraway crackle of energized sound and a tinny, hollow noise that could have been a voice trickled from the earpiece. Melanie's gaze traveled to the empty wall jack and then slowly rose to meet my eyes.

With a smile aimed at Jolene, she replaced the receiver in its cradle. "Isn't that strange? It must have been some latent stored electricity still in the phone. I know we sometimes have the same problem with an old phone in our house in Charleston."

Jolene nodded as if this made perfect sense before grabbing the handle of Melanie's suitcase. "Here, let me help."

"I've got it," I said. "I'll wait with Melanie outside."

"Of course," Jolene said. "Y'all will want to have some private time."

They said their good-byes while I struggled to get the suitcase down the stairs and through the front door, adding more than one dent to the already pockmarked drywall. I stood on the sidewalk, perspiring profusely, glad for the extra minute to catch my breath and wipe the sweat from my face before Melanie emerged.

Before she could slide on her sunglasses, I said, "That was your grandmother Sarah, wasn't it?" To anyone else, asking someone if they'd had a conversation with a long-dead woman on a phone that wasn't plugged in would have seemed strange. But since I'd known Melanie, "strange" had become one of those terms, like "almost pregnant" and "civil war," that defied explanation.

I saw the indecision in her eyes as she wrestled with whether to tell me the truth. But we'd made a pact when I'd fled home to Charleston after my disastrous freshman year. We would always be honest with each other. No matter how difficult the truth was to hear.

"Yes. It was." She looked at me closely. "Are you sure you want to pursue buying that house?"

"Melanie . . ." I began.

She held up her hand. "You know your dad and I support you in everything you do. But there's no reason for you to make your life more difficult right now than it needs to be. Especially when there are other options."

A car drove by, its windows down despite the heat, the heavy thrum of rap music vibrating the heavy air as it passed. "Remember how when you and my dad got together you knew there could be no sub-

stitute? That's how I feel about that house. It was meant to be mine."
I shrugged. "I don't know how to explain it."

Her lips twisted in a lopsided grin. "Yes, well, I'm used to unexplainable things."

We both turned toward the navy Camry that had pulled up to the curb. Melanie took out her phone to compare the Uber photograph to the driver and then snapped a photo of the license plate. I felt my phone buzz in my pocket as her text arrived. "I got it. Call me when you get to the airport."

The driver grunted as he hoisted Melanie's suitcase into the trunk, the back end of the car dipping slightly. Melanie hugged me, and I held on as she began to pull away. "What did your grandmother have to say?"

She pressed her lips together. "I hoped you'd forgotten."

"Have I ever?"

The driver's door shut, the engine rumbling and blowing heat into an already sweltering afternoon. "Fair point." She glanced briefly inside the car as if either wishing to be in the air-conditioning or wanting this conversation to be over. Or both. "She said the house chose you."

I widened my eyes in surprise. "I told you. See? Everything's going to be fine."

She didn't open the car door, which meant she wasn't through.

"Did she say anything else?" I held my breath.

Melanie gave a quick nod. "She said to pay attention to the things you can't see." Brief pause. "Not all of them are harmless."

I appreciated her not giving me the "I told you so" look she was so good at. "You knew that, didn't you? When you visited the house with me."

She nodded. "But I'd made you a promise. Do you want to change your mind about the house?"

"No." I spoke without hesitation. As my dad had told me more than once, life wasn't supposed to be easy. Challenges just made it more interesting. Most of the time.

"I didn't think so." Melanie hugged me again and kissed my forehead. "Your dad and I are only a phone call or quick flight away." She opened the car door, a cold blast of air-conditioning teasing my cheeks. "You've got this."

She slid inside and looked up at me. "Make good choices!" Without waiting to see me roll my eyes, she closed the door. As the car pulled away, she waved from the back window, and I waved back until I couldn't see the car anymore.

I stood on the sidewalk for a long time, looking down Broadway where the car had disappeared, feeling loneliness, optimism, and fear all at the same time, and wondering why I had ever left Charleston and everything that was comforting and familiar. And safe. Eventually I turned and headed back inside, Melanie's grandmother's words reverberating in my head as I slowly climbed the stairs. *The house chose you.*

CHAPTER 4

"Are you sure you want to drive instead of taking the streetcar?" Jolene readjusted a hanging strip of duct tape attaching the car's visor to the windshield of her grandmother's pea green 1989 Lincoln Town Car before checking her lipstick in the rearview mirror. "I figured we could kill two birds with one stone by grabbing a carload of stuff from my old apartment on the way back from meeting with Beau's grandmother. That could save us some time just in case I hear back from Jaxson and he wants to meet to go over anything he's discovered about the murder." I heard the note of hopefulness in her voice and would have mentioned it, but I didn't want to create more sweat by exerting myself.

I reluctantly closed the passenger door and buckled my seat belt. "All right. But could you please turn on the air conditioner? I'm melting and I can't get the window to go down." I flicked the window button several times to illustrate.

"That's because it's broken. And I'll turn on the air conditioner as soon as I pull out of the driveway and get going. I can't accelerate and use the AC at the same time or the engine dies."

I grabbed onto the armrest, my only consolation being that the car was as long as a block and made of steel, which offered some protection. I closed my eyes as she reversed down the driveway, the car rocking and the collection of Mardi Gras beads draped over the rearview mirror shimmying as we rolled over the rutted concrete. She backed into the street, an act of faith since it was impossible to see what was coming from the driver's seat, her petite frame making her look like a little girl stealing her mom's car. The bench seat was pulled up as far as it would go, and I shot a look at her feet to make sure they could actually reach the pedals.

"You know," I said through clenched teeth, "I don't think U-Hauls are that expensive."

She laughed as if I'd said something funny. "This trunk is bigger than a U-Haul. My grandmama never owned a car that was too small to fit eight bodies and the tools to bury them."

I slid her a sidelong glance. I remembered that her family had owned a funeral home for generations and that her references to her childhood and other family members—especially her grandmother—were peppered with remarks that might be considered bizarre or even leading if one hadn't been exposed to Jolene for any length of time.

"We'll be fine on the main roads, but when we get to the smaller streets with cars parked along the curb, we're going to have to suck in our breath so we can fit without scraping off any side mirrors."

She said this without laughing, which worried me. "I know what you're thinking, Nola, but don't look a gift horse in the mouth. Having access to a car will make your life easier. Especially for field visits. After you learn how to drive, of course. One accident doesn't make you a bad driver. You just need to try again. Just let me know when, and Bubba and I will be happy to put you behind the wheel."

"Right. But wouldn't I need a special license to drive this thing? Like one that would authorize me to drive tanks?"

"Very funny." She reached over and patted the dash. "You'll come to appreciate Bubba. Just mark my words."

That was another thing I remembered about Jolene. She always named her cars. "So, where did this car come from?" I asked, changing the subject. Even in college, Jolene had been the recipient of a wide assortment of vehicles gifted by her grandmother. Apparently, running the only funeral home in town made them a target of bereaved families looking to off-load unwanted vehicles.

"I'm not sure. My cousin Nathan drove it down for me and didn't say. I'm sure it came to us the usual way." She braked hard, making my seat belt press against my chest, as she stopped at the intersection of Broadway and St. Charles Avenue. Flipping off the air conditioner, she said, "Sorry—don't want to get hit by the streetcar if I have to gun it. There's one now, but I think I can make it. Hang on."

I closed my eyes as the car picked up speed, the tires bumping over the streetcar tracks before taking a sharp left turn onto St. Charles Avenue. I opened my eyes in time to see a streetcar rumble past, causing even more sweat to erupt on my forehead.

As if we hadn't just had a near-death experience, Jolene said, "We'll park in the Hotel Monteleone garage on Royal Street. An SAE I dated my senior year works there. He's saving money for grad school, so he works a lot of hours." She dodged a pothole deep enough that it might contain marine life, my head and its contents swaying along with the Mardi Grad beads. "It's very handy, since I can coordinate my trips into the Quarter when he's working, so I don't have to worry about parking. He makes sure to reserve three spaces at the top just for Bubba."

I nodded absently as we continued toward downtown, with Jolene dodging potholes, bicycles, and pedestrians while I clutched my armrest. I wanted to admire the historic mansions that lined St. Charles Avenue like grandes dames from another age, dressed up for the social event of the season, but instead I kept my eyes closed for most of the ride so I wouldn't be tempted to throw myself out of the car to save myself.

As promised, Jolene's old flame, Alex, quickly traded seats with Jolene as soon as she pulled into the garage, Bubba blocking the sidewalk and most of the narrow street. After a quick hello, I jumped out and stood on the sidewalk in front of the hotel, relieved to be out of the car and all in one piece.

"Come on. The shop is about two blocks this way," Jolene said as she adjusted a pair of large white-framed sunglasses on her nose and settled a wide-brimmed straw hat on her head. "I could get a sunburn standing inside my kitchen. And my mama would tan my hide if I let any sun touch my face."

I followed her, and I was surprised to find that I was nervous. At least I didn't need to worry about running into Beau. Jolene had confirmed that he was on-site today at the renovation of a midcentury ranch in Chalmette, so the coast was clear as far as he was concerned. All I needed was to win over Mimi and all of my problems would be solved. Theoretically.

The pervasive scent of beer and other not-so-sweet-smelling liquids that I'd heard referred to as "Bourbon stew" followed us as we stepped over discarded plastic go-cups and glops of stuff I didn't want to examine too closely but knew I didn't want to step on. Wanting to reassure myself, I said, "And you know Mimi well enough to believe that she'll be on my side?"

"Um, sure. Although I just said that I know her well enough to introduce you, and to even say a few good words on your behalf." She quickened her pace.

"But you know her."

"Yes. We've met several times. She and Beau are extremely close, which is why I suggested that we take your case to her."

"And she's nice, right? And she'll listen and seriously consider my point?"

Jolene didn't answer right away, which intensified the sweat dripping from my temples.

I stopped in the middle of the sidewalk, passersby walking around me like I was a rock in a stream. In any other city they'd probably have run over me and kept walking. Realizing I wasn't next to her anymore, Jolene turned back.

I crossed my arms, then dropped them, unable to tolerate the sticky sweat that pooled in the insides of my elbows. "What aren't you telling me?"

"Nothing. Really. It's just . . ."

"Just what?"

She sighed. "Like I said, they're really close, with him being raised by his grandparents since he was a little boy and all. But she is real nice." She clamped her lips closed.

"You keep saying that, which makes me think you're not telling me everything. And for someone who likes to talk as much as you do, I'm wondering why you've suddenly decided to go light on the details."

"I'm not going light on the details. I'm just busy thinking. About . . . how we should hurry in case Beau finishes up early in Chalmette and decides to stop by the antiques shop. He does their website, so he's there a lot to photograph stuff. But not his podcast—he does his podcast, *Bumps in the Night and Other Improbabilities*, from the Ryans' house on Prytania, in a little room at the top of the house. I bet it's really cool, and you should ask him for a tour someday, because—"

"Jolene, stop. Please. What aren't you telling me? That Mimi is some hateful ogre?"

"Of course not." She didn't meet my eyes, but I was distracted by the storefront where we'd stopped. Two heavy glass doors behind iron filigree crescents and vertical bars sat tucked in between two protruding bay windows with large beveled panes. The entire front of the building sat beneath a long balcony with cast-iron handrails and S-shaped wall brackets to support it.

A large black sign in the shape of a Renaissance shield hung on a horizontal pole above the door. I stepped back to read it. In gold paint in a bold old-style serif font were the words THE PAST IS NEVER PAST. Beneath those words, in smaller letters, was the word ANTIQUES. A gold fleur-di-lis punctuated the sign at the bottom, as if to remind passersby that they were in New Orleans.

A Regency-era dining table set for twelve, completely with Old Imari china and Baccarat crystal glasses, filled the window on the left.

A Venetian glass chandelier hovered over the table, its bulbs and colored crystals emitting a festive glow. But it was the other window that drew my attention. I moved to stand in front of it, an old memory pausing in my brain, of a moment with my mother, Bonnie, when she'd taken me to a carnival and let me ride the carousel. I could almost feel her hands on my waist.

"Aren't you coming?" Jolene was already reaching for the door handle.

"Coming—I was just admiring the horse. It's a 1910 Muller carousel horse. Even though it's been years, I somehow remember Beau telling me that his family's antiques shop had one in the window. I'm guessing there's not a huge market for them."

"Or Mimi Ryan hasn't found a buyer worthy of it."

"What?"

Jolene wrapped both hands around the thick brass door handle. "That's what I was trying to tell you. Mimi Ryan is the grandmother we'd all want to have. She's just a bit . . . peculiar."

Before I could question her, she pulled the door open, icy cold air blasting us in the face. "The air conditioner must be broken again," Jolene explained. "They can't get the temperature to go above fifty-five degrees in the summer."

I shivered, wishing I'd brought a sweater, which was ridiculous considering it was over ninety degrees outside. "What do you mean by 'peculiar'?"

"May I help you?" a soft voice interrupted.

An older woman with a serene smile that matched her voice stood with her hands folded in front of her. My own two grandmothers didn't comply with what people thought grandmothers should look like, but this woman certainly did. With gray hair piled up in a bun, a sweet round face with a sunburst of wrinkles at the corner of both her eyes, a stout frame, a herringbone suit, thick black stockings, and sensible shoes, she appeared to be straight from central casting. She even wore glasses on a chain around her neck, along with a strand of pearls. In her earlobes sparkled small earrings in what appeared to be the shape of an hourglass, with small gems as the sand. I wouldn't have been surprised to find on her hands flour from the biscuits I imagined she'd just put in the oven.

"Hello, Mimi." Jolene stepped from behind me, and the older woman's face brightened.

Mimi opened up her arms—no flour that I could see—and Jolene stepped into them to be embraced as if she and Mimi were old friends. "I'm so sorry I didn't recognize you—must be the hat hiding your red hair." The older woman released Jolene, then looked at me, as if waiting to be introduced. I held out my hand, then paused. I looked into her face closely for the first time, and wondered if I'd just discovered what Jolene had been referring to as peculiar. Mimi's left eye was a brilliant blue, but her right eye was a clear green, reminding me of a cat's-eye marble I'd once found on a playground when I was a little girl.

"Mimi," Jolene said, "I'd like you to meet an old friend of mine, Nola Trenholm. She's . . ."

"I know who she is." The woman smiled, her odd eyes tilting at the corners as she reached for both of my hands. Hers were soft and warm—no doubt from all that butter and flour—and she studied my face for a long moment before speaking again. "I've been expecting you. Although, to your credit, I didn't expect to see you so soon."

At my questioning look, she said, "Call it a grandmother's intuition or whatever you like, but when Beau mentioned that you wanted to buy the Creole cottage on Dauphine and he had second thoughts, I figured that if you had any brains, you'd come see me."

She dropped my hands, and I was glad, because mine had begun to sweat despite the freezerlike temperature in the building. "Actually, it was Jolene's idea. I just happened to agree." I cleared my throat, ready to give her my rehearsed speech. "I'm here to solicit your help. I have a master's in historic preservation. I can climb roofs and replace tiles, scrape off two hundred years of paint from a wall, and repoint old bricks in my sleep. I love history and old houses. I want to buy that house and restore it so I can live in it. I've even saved up the money to purchase it. But to be ornery, Beau said no."

"Wait a minute." Jolene's eyes widened. "Did y'all date when you both lived in Charleston?"

"No." I softened my tone when I noticed Mimi's eyes narrowing. "I mean, he's smart, I guess, and my friends all thought he was handsome." Mimi's eyes didn't change. I cleared my throat. "Because he is handsome, of course. But we just have opposite personalities. He's . . . bossy. Like he thinks he should always be in charge of every situation and every person and knows what's best for me, even though he has no clue."

"And you're not like that, too?"

"No. Not at all." I shook my head to amplify my argument.

"Which is why you're here arguing against his decision."

I might have stuttered in my attempt to reply, but I was saved from speaking when the door opened behind us and an older couple walked in. The man's face was chiseled with time, his eyes carrying a burden of sorrows that matched the woman's. He carried a bulky object beneath a tartan blanket, heavy enough that he had to readjust it in his arms.

"Please excuse me for a moment," Mimi said, then walked toward the couple.

I gave Jolene a look I hoped said that she had a lot of explaining to do, and her response was a shrug and a slight shake of her head that I hoped wasn't the entire apology I would get out of her.

While we waited, I looked around the shop, feeling a little homesick as I recognized the similarities to my grandparents' shop in Charleston. I'd worked at Trenholm Antiques in high school and off and on during my years at grad school. Despite my efforts to stage furniture in settings that would help customers imagine a settee or chair or highboy in their own homes, the resulting effect was more like a maze of mahogany and cherrywood interspersed with flamboyant gilt, intricate marquetry, and priceless Scalamandré silk. For a lover of antiques, the shop was an adult candy store, full of rare porcelain urns, crystal vases, bronze statues, and other objets d'art that had managed to survive wars and other human upheavals, strong despite their inherent fragility, outlasting their creators by decades.

If I closed my eyes, I could pretend I was back at Trenholm Antiques. The familiar and beloved scent of various varnishes, waxes, and lacquers used over the years and exposed to heat and moisture produced the unique perfume that my grandmother Amelia referred to as a "bouquet of old." We'd always joked that we needed to find a way to re-create that particular chemistry and bottle the smell, so that if I ever got homesick, I could just spray it in the air to at least momentarily return to Charleston.

I ran my finger on the spotless top of a Regency escritoire, admiring the intricate wood inlays, imagining the people who had once sat in front of it and penned their thoughts. It was this personal connection to old things and houses that made me love them. The exact same reason why Melanie didn't.

My gaze traveled to the back of the store, where an enormous English partners desk dominated a corner. A new and shiny iMac computer sat in the middle, a crystal pedestal dish containing foil-wrapped chocolates next to it. Comfortable modern upholstered chairs had been placed on both sides of the desk to make the process of spending enormous amounts of money as pleasant as possible.

"She's nice, though, isn't she?" Jolene whispered, taking my silence as simmering anger and needing reassurance.

"I'm not . . ." I lost my train of thought as my gaze strayed behind the desk, to what I now recognized as a hidden door, flush with the wall, with matching paint and chair molding so that it was hardly noticeable. Except for the heavy padlock—also painted a matching alabaster—I wouldn't have seen it at all.

"Is that where the most valuable items are kept?" I was curious since my grandparents kept their most expensive items on display and kept only the front and rear doors locked.

Jolene shook her head. "I don't know. I've only been here a few times, with Beau, and we never went back there."

"I know she has a collection of Frozen Charlottes and anthropomorphic taxidermy, which I don't see out on the sales floor. Maybe she keeps them in the back, along with her frozen-head collection."

"Nola." Jolene sent me a warning look. "I said she was *peculiar.* Not crazy like a betsey bug. That would be my great-aunt Thelma. Now, *she's* crazier than a—"

"I'm so sorry." Mimi reappeared at my elbow, and I saw that the couple was now standing by the desk. "My assistant, Christopher, isn't here today, so I have to speak with this couple now. Why don't you two join Beau and me for dinner tonight at the house—say six o'clock?—and we can talk it out then and hopefully come to a mutual agreement?"

I pushed back my disappointment at not getting the answer I needed, and I nodded. "That works for me."

"Me, too," said Jolene, as she reached into her bag to pick up her pinging phone.

"The address is 2505 Prytania. Just look for the black iron gate with a large half-full hourglass depicted in the middle. If you get lost, just ask for the sand-glass house."

We said good-bye and Mimi walked us to the door, then locked it behind us and turned the sign to CLOSED.

"It's a text from Jaxson," Jolene said, looking at her phone. "He has information about the murder house."

I was about to tell her not to call it that but stopped as my gaze followed Mimi and the couple with their covered burden as they approached the locked door. Mimi pulled a key from her pocket and unlocked the padlock before stepping back to allow the man and woman to move into the room beyond. Mimi's head turned in my direction, her mismatched eyes staring back at me. She acknowledged me with a brief nod, then followed the couple behind the padlocked door and closed it after her.

CHAPTER 5

We sat in the car. Jolene had found street parking on Banks Street in Mid-City, near Soule' Cafe, not far from the public defender's office where Jaxson worked. The car took up two full spaces, but she'd hit only one garbage can (twice) while maneuvering it close enough to the curb so other cars could still pass down the street. She spent a lot of time powdering her nose and fixing her lipstick in her rearview mirror, preparing for our lunch meeting with Jaxson.

"So, Jaxson is still dating what's-her-name, right?"

Jolene nodded while blotting her lipstick with a tissue. "As of this morning, anyway. Carly texted me to say they'd just had the best makeup sex last night, so all's good."

She smiled brightly. "I'm happy for them."

"Right." I unlocked my door, then pushed it open with both arms. "Do you think you could just leave the car running with the air-conditioning on while we eat? That way when you turn it off to move the car forward, it will still be cool."

"But then someone might steal it." With a shove of her hips, she managed to close her own door, then locked it the old-fashioned way, by using an actual key.

"Would that be so bad? Doesn't anybody with a small car ever die in your hometown? Maybe your grandmother could call dibs?"

Coming around the front of the car to join me on the sidewalk, she said, "Remember what I said about gift horses. Come on."

She led the way to the corner and a blue-painted two-story building with *Soule' Cafe* emblazoned on the glass door. Wooden picnic tables sat outside, with patrons crowded together eating, the scent of fried food mixed with the smell of beer permeating the entire block. I watched as heads and gazes turned toward Jolene and her red hair. I was more than happy to follow in her wake of floral perfume as an afterthought, content with not being the center of attention. I'd had enough of that over the last six years.

Many of the diners wore scrubs or other types of medical-personnel uniforms. Seeing my gaze, Jolene said, "We're within spitting distance of three major hospitals and a medical school. So if you're going to choke on an oyster or have a heart attack, this would be the place to do it." She pulled open the door. "Did I ever tell you about my cousin Wayne and the frog bone that got stuck in his gullet?"

Happily for me, she didn't have the chance to tell me more as a young man waved at us inside. We approached a simple table with four chairs, tucked beneath a wall mural—one of several—depicting the face of an exotic-looking woman with a flower in her hair. The man stood and pulled out two chairs for us.

Jolene beamed. "Thanks for meeting us, Jaxson." He and Jolene embraced, Jaxson ending it with a platonic pat on Jolene's shoulder. She kept smiling as if she hadn't noticed. "This is my friend—and new roomie—Nola Trenholm."

His handshake was firm and brief, all business, but his smile and the spattering of freckles on his nose prevented the impression from being absolute. His sparkling blue eyes and dark auburn hair—a shade that had probably been a lot brighter and caused him some pain when he was younger—made him look less like a serious lawyer and more like a mischievous boy who'd been reluctantly dragged into adulthood.

"It's a pleasure to meet you, Nola." He waited for us to take the two seats across the table before reseating himself. "I went ahead and ordered waters all around, but they have a full bar, and I can get you whatever you'd like. I have to get back to work, so just water for me, but don't let me hold you back."

"Water is fine with us," Jolene said. At my look of surprise, she smiled at me, making me wonder if Melanie had said something to her. I wanted to be angry at my stepmother, yet all I could feel was gratitude.

While Jaxson turned to get our waiter's attention, I had a chance to take a better look at him. He was tall and broad shouldered, his well-formed muscles defined beneath the high-thread-count button-down he wore. His hair, with natural highlights and auburn shades most women would kill for, was professionally cut but in need of a trim. I imagined he didn't notice that kind of thing until someone pointed it out to him. He'd loosened his tie and sat with his forearms on the table and hands clasped with restrained energy, like a football player in a huddle ready for action, his attention focused on Jolene and me. Even when a group of young women, all short skirts and long legs, walked past our table, he didn't turn to look. I decided then that despite his thickheadedness in choosing this Carly person over Jolene, I liked Jaxson Landry.

As we studied our menus, Jaxson said, "You have to come back on a Monday for their red beans and rice. I don't know what they do with the andouille sausage they put in there, but it's the best I've ever tasted. And that's saying a lot, since I was born and raised here." He gave us a winning grin that looked out of place on the face of a guy who spent his days defending accused felons. "Just don't tell my mother I said that, or she'll knock me sideways into next week. She's a bit proud of her beans and rice."

"Can you order it without the sausage?" I asked, studying the menu.

When my question was answered with silence I looked up to find Jolene and Jaxson watching me with blank expressions.

"I'm vegan," I explained.

"Oh." Jaxson nodded. "That's cool. For how long?"

"My whole life. My mom said we were vegan, so that's how I was raised."

"Was she a big animal lover?"

It was the first time anyone had asked me that, and I had to take a moment to think. I remembered us eating canned beans, cereal, and boxed frozen vegetables for most meals when I was a child. I'd once invited a school friend over for dinner and when she asked us where the meat was, my mom had explained that there wasn't any because we were vegan. Mom had always found it easier to confess that she was an addict than to admit that she was intermittently employed and struggled to put food on the table. Especially after all she'd gone through to keep me, including moving across the country and not telling my dad that I existed. Searching now for the easiest answer, I said, "I'm originally from California."

Both Jaxson and Jolene nodded, as if that explained everything.

After ordering—the tofu stir-fry for me, and the Soule' burgers with fries for Jaxson and Jolene—Jaxson leaned forward in a stance I was pretty sure he used with his clients. It showed interest, confidence, and restrained strength. If I were a felon, I wouldn't even think about picking a fight with this man. Or lying to him. "As I texted Jolene, I've heard back from my uncle Bernie about that house on Dauphine."

I nodded eagerly. "That's the house I want to buy. But for some reason, the seller—Jolene's boss, as it turns out—won't sell it to me, even though I'm a qualified buyer with all the preapproved paperwork ready to go."

He lifted auburn eyebrows. "Beau Ryan is the owner?"

"Yes. You know him?"

"Sure. New Orleans is actually a very small town. My grandparents lived down the street from the Ryans on Prytania for about forty years, and Beau and I went to Jesuit together—we both played lacrosse. And we were members of the Krewe of Bacchus, too. Great guy. We didn't keep in close touch after he moved to Charleston, and I haven't seen him much since he returned. I guess he stays pretty busy."

I tried not to grimace. "Yeah, well, I knew him when he was in school in Charleston—he worked at my grandparents' antiques store. I remember him as being very bossy." I didn't say anything about the fire, or my guitar, or any of the stuff afterward, when I'd left Tulane and returned to Charleston. It was irrelevant. Or at least it should be.

"And you think he doesn't want to sell it to you because it's a murder house?"

I shrugged. "I have no idea, and he seems reluctant to give me any reason at all. The murder took place in 1964, so I don't really see why that should make a difference. And the house was shown to a number of potential buyers before me and was still listed when I went to see it."

He nodded, absorbing my words. "And there's nothing in your background that might make Beau hesitant about committing to a financial transaction with you?"

I felt my face burn, but I didn't look away. "No."

My brief hesitation made him lean a little closer, and I had to remind myself that I wasn't a criminal and this wasn't an interrogation. When I didn't say anything else, he sat back in his seat. "You might need to see a lawyer, then. Someone who deals with housing discrimination. I'd be happy to get you some names."

"Thanks. I hope it doesn't come to that, but I'll keep it in mind. We're having dinner with Beau and his grandmother tonight, to see if we might be able to get to the bottom of this. That's why I was hoping you could give us a little more information, so that I'm better prepared."

Jolene leaned forward, her voice earnest. "Nola really loves this house. And she knows how to save it. She believes that they were meant to be together."

I sent her a grateful smile before turning back to Jaxson. "I have this affinity for old buildings. I know there are other homes in desperate need of renovation and restoration, but this is the one for me. That probably sounds crazy to you, but this one just spoke to me."

Jaxson surprised me by smiling. "Not crazy at all. I get it. It really broke my mother's heart when she decided to sell my grandparents' house in the Garden District after they died. It's where she'd grown up and it had been in the family for generations. But my brothers and I had all grown up in our house in Old Metairie, so that's home for us. Didn't make sense to move. I'd be lying, though, if I said I didn't think about maybe someday buying that house back and raising my own family in it."

I dared not look at Jolene, afraid of what I might see in her eyes. Probably something that belonged in a Hallmark movie.

Our food arrived and I pretended to get excited about my tofu while smelling their burgers and fries, and telling myself it would be rude to ask for a single French fry. I took a bite, chewed, and swallowed it down with a sip from my water before turning to Jaxson again. "So, you heard back from your uncle. I believe Jolene said he'd been with the New Orleans Police Department?"

He nodded, his mouth full. As I waited for him to swallow, I admired the eclectic décor of the restaurant—the psychedelic wallpaper and murals behind basic black tables and chairs that could have belonged in any school cafeteria, the full bar, the corner stages set up for musical entertainment—and wondered if this unique mix of mod bar and vegan soul food restaurant could exist anywhere in the world besides New Orleans.

Jaxson took a long drink of water. "He's actually my great-uncle, but he was the baby of the family and he's only sixteen years older than my dad. He never had any kids, so he was like an extra dad for my brothers and me. Anyway, Uncle Bernie was with the NOPD for almost forty years. Started as a beat cop and rose all the way to lieutenant before he retired. My family jokes that Uncle Bernie is the black sheep of the family. The whole family tree is overflowing with lawyers, judges, and politicians. I guess we needed a cop so that we couldn't be accused of not knowing the difference between right and wrong." He grinned and I could almost hear Jolene sigh.

Jaxson didn't appear to notice. "Anyway, Uncle Bernie's seen a lot over the years, so I figured he might know something about that old case. Unfortunately, a lot of evidence files for current and cold cases were destroyed during Katrina. Luckily for us, Uncle Bernie has a steel trap for a memory. My brothers and I were on the wrong end of his memory many times when we were teenagers." He grinned again, and this time Jolene's sigh was audible.

"Uncle Bernie kept his own personal notes on every case he ever worked on. Drove my aunt Betty nuts. Almost got them divorced when she organized all of those pages of notes in filing cabinets as a surprise when Uncle Bernie and my dad were at their fishing camp for a week.

"Anyway, he remembers this case. He happened to be the neighborhood's beat cop in 1964 and was the first officer on the scene. He says it shook him up, since the victim was so young—only twenty. He was about the same age at the time."

"I texted you a photo of the article. Was he able to add anything?" Jolene asked.

"Quite a bit, actually. Jeanne's parents called him regularly for a long time, up until he retired in the mid–two thousands."

"That's heartbreaking," Jolene said.

Jaxson nodded. "It is. Anyway, his notes are a little sporadic. When Aunt Betty reorganized his files, she must have misfiled some things, because there's some stuff missing, including his personal notes, which would have included his conversations with Jeanne's parents. He said he'd keep looking, but he did have enough to fill in a bit of the information that was considered too gruesome for the newspapers back in the day. He said that the cause of death was manual strangulation—no ligature marks—and according to her cousin and roommate nothing was stolen, so burglary wasn't a motive, and there were no obvious signs of rape. A clock was broken on the floor, apparently knocked off a table during the attack, but that's it. And no sign of forced entry."

"Sounds very personal," Jolene said, reminding me she'd been a true-crime-television addict back when we were freshmen; apparently, she was still a fan.

"Exactly what he thought, too. His interview notes must be with the missing file, but he remembers canvassing the neighborhood. He doesn't recall exactly—it *was* a long time ago, despite what he says about his recall of events—but he said that he probably would have interviewed everyone she might have had any contact with, including customers at Maison Blanche. She worked in ladies' lingerie and kept a clientele book—he's positive about that. Uncle Bernie said that most of the sales associates did back in the day when department stores were known for their customer service. It made things easier for the investigation, but nothing came of that, either. And her boyfriend had a watertight alibi—he was in jail for being drunk and disorderly. Apparently, he went on a bender after he dropped Jeanne off at the house following their date—and there were a number of witnesses who saw that and watched him leave."

"Her cousin, the roommate—Louise, I think. The one who found her. Did she also have an alibi?" I asked.

"He didn't say, but I'm assuming so, since he didn't mention her. Although . . ." He tapped his finger against his glass. "Uncle Bernie did mention that there was another girl, Jeanne's best friend, who was planning on moving in to help with the rent. Her first name was Mary or Mignon or Margaret, he thinks, and there was something important about her, but he couldn't recall—said he'd think on it some more. She never moved into the house, so that's probably why she wasn't mentioned in the newspaper accounts. He promised to let me know if it comes to him."

Jaxson looked at his watch, a classic, old-fashioned type with a worn leather strap. I imagined it had been a gift from his grandfather or father. Or maybe his great-uncle. It said a lot about him and the importance he placed on family. I was sure Jolene had noticed it, too. "Ladies, this has been great, but I have to get back. I'll let you know if Uncle Bernie finds out anything else. He'll probably want to tell you in person. He loves meeting new people."

"Thank you," I said. "For all of this. Please keep me posted."

"It was my pleasure. Nice meeting you. And great seeing you again, Jolene. Don't be such a stranger. I miss seeing that flash of red hair at Carly's parties." He grinned again, and it was so attractive, even *I* felt like sighing. "We gingers have to stick together, don't we?" He patted her shoulder again and then, despite my protest, paid the tab and left.

As we walked back to the car Jolene was uncharacteristically silent, no doubt replaying Jaxson's words over in her head and trying to read something into them that didn't exist. As we climbed into the car, she said, "Did you know that less than two percent of the world's population has natural red hair? And because it's a recessive gene, they say that redheads will have been bred out of the population by 2060."

It had been a long time since Jolene and I had spent any length of time together, so I was only beginning to remember her roundabout way of sharing what was on her mind. "Yes, you and Jaxson would make beautiful redheaded babies."

"I know, right?" She sighed, pumping the gas pedal a couple of times with more force than necessary before turning the key in the ignition. I hoped she was remembering Jaxson's platonic pats on her shoulder. "Maybe I should move to Ireland. Or Scotland."

She pulled the car out, then forced me to suck in my breath as she drove down the narrow street, managing to get to the stop sign without removing any side-view mirrors.

Jolene's phone erupted with what sounded like clacking from an old-fashioned typewriter. Without looking, she said, "Can you read that, please? It's from Jaxson."

"You have a separate sound for his texts?"

She blushed. "I do that for all of my important contacts. You have your own sound, too."

"So what's mine?"

"'Summertime.' Because your dogs are Porgy and Bess."

I smiled as I picked up her phone and typed in the code she gave me. "It says . . ." My eyes skimmed the message, then went back over it to make sure I'd understood it correctly.

"What?"

I made the mistake of looking up as Jolene took a sharp turn, causing two pedestrians to jump off the sidewalk. I quickly glanced down again and read the message out loud this time.

Uncle Bernie called remembers Jeannes BFF was Mignon Guidry her married name is Ryan and she goes by Mimi you can ask her about it tonight at dinner LMK if you find out anything

Our stunned silence was interrupted by a large pothole that appeared through the heat shimmer of the asphalt in the middle of the road. The front right end of the car dipped as if swallowed by the street, and then it was spit back out with a thud and the familiar *thump-thump* of a flat tire.

CHAPTER 6

That evening, as we drove down St. Charles Avenue on our way to Prytania, I found myself relaxing in the passenger seat as Jolene maneuvered Bubba over streetcar tracks while simultaneously turning the air conditioner off and then on. She was like an orchestra conductor, skillfully cuing the horns and strings to create a cohesive sound. After watching her change the flat tire all by herself—although I did help a little by holding lug nuts and handing her a wrench from the trunk—I felt a newfound confidence in my roommate's abilities. She could solve problems like an engineer, add triple-digit calories in her head, and change a tire on the side of the road in sweltering heat—all while wearing heels. If only she could apply that skill set to figuring out that wishing Jaxson Landry was hers wouldn't make it true.

I kept thinking about my friend in Charleston Meghan Black, who'd briefly dated Beau and had stayed at the house on Prytania. She'd said it was beautiful, and full of antiques as was expected, considering that the house had been in the family for generations. The antiques shop had been run by the family for almost as long. I tried not to linger on Meghan's comments about a locked door upstairs, recalling seeing Mimi—Mignon—at a similarly locked door at the Past Is Never Past earlier that day.

Meghan also said that the house had the same vibe as my home on Tradd Street in Charleston. But all old houses did, I reminded myself. The shadows of lives once lived within their walls were bound to linger. Except there was one more thing Meghan had said that I hadn't been able to forget. The atmosphere in the Ryans' house was like the one in my own family home. Only darker.

The Garden District—aptly named, due to the lush and vibrant blossoms in the manicured gardens that surrounded most of the district's mansions like frilly hoopskirts—had once been part of an old cotton plantation. It had flooded during a massive storm in the early nineteenth century, destroying the plantation but leaving behind rich alluvial soil that could grow anything. It reminded me a lot of my South of Broad neighborhood in Charleston, and at the sight of a giant crepe myrtle, with its thick, twisty trunk and a halo of small pink blossoms, I had to swallow back a lump of homesickness.

Jolene slowed the car, following my gaze. "Grandmama says those old crepe myrtles look like old ladies at the supermarket with their hair done up with pink rollers."

I was in the middle of laughing when Jolene hit the curb, the right front wheel climbing over it before bouncing back onto the street with a jolt. "We're here," she announced.

I ran my tongue over my teeth to make sure nothing was chipped or missing, then looked out my window. An Italianate house dominated the middle of a large lot with three oak trees—two much younger than the third—along with the requisite flowering bushes and trimmed hedges surrounding the base of the house. Italianate was my favorite style of nineteenth-century architecture, maybe because its asymmetrical and complex nature might have resembled my own. Its elements were borrowed from different styles and countries, all picked up along the way. Yet in this house, at least, everything had come together to form something perfect and complete. Something I hadn't quite yet managed to do.

The imposing white two-story made me smile at its audacious beauty. A large semioctagonal bay sat on the left side, while a slightly recessed smaller one had been placed on the right side. A visible wing, what others not familiar with the style might think of as an after-thought, projected from the back of the house. Closely spaced full-length windows covered the front of the first floor, which was tucked inside a wide gallery surrounding the front and sides, enclosed by wooden box columns sitting on simple, short newel posts. Small arched panels had been inserted between the columns, creating a lovely skirt for the second-floor balustrade above it. A low-pitched hipped roof sat on top, supported by elaborately detailed corbels, the effect like that of an elegant hat completing an outfit.

"Wait until you see the inside," Jolene said. "I've only been in there once, to pick up some paperwork from Beau, but it's finer than a frog's hair split four ways. Although . . ." She stopped.

"Although?"

"Well, it's definitely got some memories." She stopped again, considering her words. "Some darker than others, I'd say. There's just something about the front stairs. Like I wasn't supposed to go up them, you know?"

Darker. There was that word again. I grimaced. "Yeah. I know."

We exited the car and stood together on the broken sidewalk, the flagstones lifted by the dinosaur roots of the closest oak. Like most of the properties in the Garden District, this one was encircled by a cast-iron fence. A fleur-de-lis capped each spike, and in the middle of the front gate a forged half-full hourglass sat inside an iron oval.

Jolene opened the gate and walked through, holding it open for me. "I'm guessing that's a nod to the Past Is Never Past?" she asked.

"Maybe. Although I'm thinking it would be more welcoming if the sand was at the top instead of the middle."

Letting the gate clank shut behind us, Jolene grinned. "It's better than empty, right?"

The dusk song of chirping and whirring cicadas and other insects hidden in the lush vegetation followed us as we walked across the white-painted brick path to the carved marble steps leading to the front doors. As I reached the top of the steps, I stopped, noticing the inlaid marble design on the floor of the gallery. Finding unexpected beauty in old things was probably a learned appreciation forged by living in Charleston and working in an antiques store, but I never got tired of the sweet surprise of discovery. I was crouching down to get a better look when one of the tall, dark wooden front doors opened.

An elegant brown-skinned man with amber-colored eyes looked down at me, and his lovely eyes smiled with the rest of his face. "It is beautiful, isn't it? Most people are so busy looking ahead that they miss it." I could have sworn his eyes twinkled—or it could have been a reflection from the gas lanterns hanging above the door—as he reached out a hand. I took it, grateful for the help and not feeling awkward at all. "You must be Nola," he said, opening the door wider. "And Jolene. So nice to finally meet you. I'm Christopher Benoit."

Jolene and I shared a glance as the man stepped back into a vestibule and motioned us inside. "I'm sorry I didn't get to meet you earlier today at the store. I was tracking down a rare pair of crystal champagne urns for Mimi last seen in a dilapidated house on River Road."

"Any luck?" Jolene asked, apparently as captivated by Christopher as I was. There was something about him that was warm and familiar while at the same time . . . not. The word "strange" popped into my head, but that wasn't right, either. It was more like the feeling a person got when opening up a gift and finding it wasn't what was expected at all, but something much, much better.

"I'm afraid not," he said, sadly shaking his head, where in the overhead light I could see sprinkled gray hairs interspersed with the dark ones, all cut close to his head. "The hunt continues."

He turned and led us into the foyer. "Mimi is busy in the kitchen and will join us shortly—she loves to cook and is preparing an impressive meal for y'all tonight. She's asked me to entertain you while we wait for Beau. I hope that's all right."

I was barely listening as I stood in the grand foyer, trying to take in all of the architectural details, from the Venetian chandelier with daffodil design to the dark Cuban mahogany stair railing with tuliplike spindles. My attention was drawn to the oil portrait hung above an Italian Renaissance hall table, a pinpoint light shining on it from the ceiling like a finger pointing from heaven. The subject was a middle-aged man wearing a navy blue suit and wide tie, and he reminded me of Walter Cronkite reporting about the *Apollo 11* rocket launch in vintage news footage.

Thick light brown hair with streaks of gray sat atop a strong-boned face, handsome in a profile-on-a-coin kind of way. But it was his eyes, blue and piercing, that caught my attention. Whether or not the artist had intended it, the eyes seemed to follow me as I approached, staring directly into mine as I stood in front of it.

Christopher spoke from behind me. "That's Mimi's late husband. His first name was Beauregard, the family name given to all firstborn sons. But he always preferred to be called Charles."

"So this is Beau's grandfather?" I asked.

Christopher nodded, his arms folded across his chest. "Yes. He was a doctor. He had no interest in the family's antiques business, so it's a good thing that he married someone who did."

"I'm sure," I said. "Beau's dad was also a doctor, right? A surgeon?"

He nodded. "A very fine one."

"So Mimi has run the Past Is Never Past pretty much on her own all these years?"

"Yes. She's in her element around antiques. Happily, Adele had an interest and a great acumen in antiques. Mimi really depended on her."

"Adele?" It wasn't my nature to be nosy, but the old house full of treasures and enchanting architectural accents, along with the knowledge of the locked room upstairs, lent a mysterious air to the evening. It was like the overture from the orchestra before a theatrical performance, and I didn't want to miss any of it. Yet I'd grown into the type of person who didn't like surprises, who wanted to know everything up front so she could plan. Maybe I'd learned to be that way from Melanie. Or maybe it really was possible to learn from past mistakes.

"Beau's mother." Christopher's voice had gone somber.

"She disappeared during Katrina. Looking for Beau's sister." I knew so little about Beau's background, mostly because he didn't talk about it, which made me reluctant to ask about it. But that dark note in Christopher's voice made me want to know more. I wanted to understand the connection I felt to Beau despite all of the friction, wondering if it was because of the shared loss of our respective mothers and the holes inside us that could never be completely filled.

"Yes," he said, a finality to the one word that made it clear that the conversation was closed. "Won't you join me in the parlor?"

I pulled my gaze from the painting to follow Christopher through a set of open pocket doors into the front parlor. Jolene elbowed me gently, and I wondered if she, too, felt the eyes from the portrait following us.

Christopher indicated a pair of Biedermeier chairs upholstered in a deep salmon velvet in front of the white marble fireplace, the soft ticking of an ormolu clock on the mantel melding with the steady hum of central air. He moved to stand in front of a Georgian mahogany secretary-bookcase that contained bottles of liquor and crystal glasses of various sizes. Holding up a bottle of Sazerac Rye whiskey, he said, "May I get you ladies something to drink? I make a mean Sazerac, if I do say so myself."

A frosted crystal pitcher containing water and floating lemon slices sat on a shelf behind him. "Just water for me, please."

Jolene hesitated a moment. "Water for me, too."

"It's okay," I said. "If you'd like a Sazerac, go for it."

Christopher's gaze moved from me to Jolene. "It's got a bit of a punch, but it's still early, and we'll make sure you eat enough of the feast Mimi is preparing so you can drive home. Or Nola can drive."

At my look of horror, Christopher belted out a deep laugh. "New Orleans drivers are the worst. They'd hardly notice one more bad driver."

I grimaced. "I don't know how to drive."

"Most of them don't, either." He smiled broadly. "No worries. We'll see that you get home safely."

"The offer still stands to teach you, Nola."

We turned to see Beau standing in the doorway we'd come through.

Jolene looked at me with surprise. "I thought you said no one had ever offered!"

"I believe I offered more than a few times," Beau said, approaching the bar and placing two ice cubes from a silver ice bucket into an empty glass.

"You really should learn," Jolene insisted. "It's what my grandmama calls a life skill that you will always use and appreciate. Like potty training and playing tennis."

There was a brief silence while we all digested her words. Turning to me, she said, "I'll be happy to teach you. Or Beau can."

"The offer still stands," Beau repeated at the same time I said, "I think I'd rather eat glass."

"Nobody's eating glass," Mimi said as she appeared from the door leading to the dining room, the tantalizing smell of food drifting in from behind her. "I hope you'd all prefer crawfish étouffée instead." She smiled at Jolene and me in greeting, then looked at Beau. "Would you please join me in the kitchen? Lorda is helping me tonight, but she's spending more time talking than helping."

"We're happy to help," I said, but Beau waved us back.

"I got this. I know my way around Mimi's kitchen, so she won't have to yell at me as much. And I know how to handle Lorda." Mimi sent him a disapproving glance as she led him through the dining room, and I fought the urge to follow, if only to make sure Beau didn't put something in my food.

"Who's Lorda?" I asked Christopher.

"The housekeeper. She's been with the family forever. Lives in Chalmette with her mother, so she has to be on the road home before it gets dark. We have a guesthouse out back she uses when she has to stay late, and calls her sister to go watch their mother. Really nice lady, but she can talk your ear off on just about any subject."

"Let me guess," Jolene said. "Lorda isn't her given name, but she was probably a jabberer as a child, and because all the adults around her would say, 'Lord-a-mercy, that child sure talks a lot,' the name stuck."

Christopher laughed as he handed us our drinks, along with starched white linen cocktail napkins monogrammed with a large crimson red R. "How did you know?"

"I'm Southern. Names like Precious, Honey, and Stinky dot my family tree. I've got a natural ear for name etymology." She took a sip of her drink, her eyes widening.

"Wow. Doesn't that just take the rags off the bush!"

"Does that mean it's good?" I asked.

She nodded and took another sip. "Oh, yes. Very. It's like a slap in the face at first, and then a kiss as it goes down."

Christopher's shoulders shook as he poured his own glass before sitting down in a Chinese Chippendale camelback sofa across from us.

I would have liked to spend hours examining the room, with its hand-blocked wallpaper, fluted arches, and inlaid-glass transoms, but Jolene had started asking the questions I wanted to ask but hadn't yet figured out a way to wedge into polite conversation.

"So, Mr. Benoit . . ." she began

"Please. Call me Christopher. I'm sure with you working for Beau now, we'll see each other enough to be considered family." He smiled, the gleam of his white teeth matching the sparkle in his eyes.

"And are you family?" she asked with a bright smile and another sip of her drink, so that coming from her it didn't sound rude.

He sipped from his own drink, something amber with two ice cubes in a crystal double old-fashioned glass, then stared down into it for a moment, thinking. When he looked up again, he was smiling. "In a way. Beau's dad and I were thick as thieves growing up. Not such a common thing back in the seventies, to see a white kid from Uptown be friends with a black kid from the Treme. But my dad did all the deliveries for the shop, and learned a lot along the way. I used to ride along with him when I wasn't in school or doing homework, and he taught me all about antiques, and what makes them special. When I got a bit older, I worked in the shop, and had a real talent for selling antiques—mostly because I had a passion for them and was in my element extolling their virtues to customers. The Ryans paid for my college, probably because they knew Buddy—that's what we all called Beauregard—wasn't interested in the antiques business. Since he was their only child, I guess they saw me as their last hope."

Jolene took a long drink from her glass, then leaned back in her chair, her perfect posture having disappeared at the same rate as her Sazerac. She pressed her napkin to her lips and hiccupped. "So, what does Mimi call you?"

Christopher's expression became serious. "She calls me 'the king of lost things.' I seem to have a knack for finding missing pieces that most people can't. Because they're looking in the wrong place, mostly. Or because they're hidden in plain sight. I've discovered that a lot of people can be looking directly at something and still not recognize what they're seeing." His gaze flickered toward me before he stood. "Can I get anyone refills?"

"Yes, please," Jolene said, handing him her glass. "I'll be sure to eat lots of étouffée to soak up the alcohol." Since she usually had the appetite of a small bird, I was curious as to what she considered *lots*. "Do you live here?" she asked; her filters, not always reliable, had certainly become relaxed with alcohol.

"Jolene, I don't think . . ."

"No, I don't." Christopher's face was turned from us as he mixed Jolene's next Sazerac, and I felt as if that was intentional. As if he didn't want me to see his expression. "I rebuilt my parents' double shotgun in the Treme after Katrina, and I live there now. I have a lot of good memories from growing up in that house."

Jolene sat up at the word "memories." I'd thought that her meaning of the word was quaint until right now, when I couldn't help but wonder if Christopher had used the word on purpose.

I sipped my water and looked around the room. "The Italianate style is my favorite. I love the wide-open passages between rooms, and all the access to the outside. I hope that if it's not too late after dinner I can get a tour."

"Maybe." Christopher handed Jolene her drink and sat again on the sofa. "I understand that you want to buy that old Creole cottage on Dauphine."

I nodded. "I'm a little obsessed with it. I can't wait to get my hands on it and bring it back to what it once was. But Beau . . ."

He held up his hand. "I know. Mimi tells me everything. Hopefully we can work something out over supper." At the sound of voices coming from the dining room, he said, "Which looks like it's about to start." He stood and held out his elbow to Jolene before escorting her to the dining room, leaving me to follow behind.

My parents' dining room in Charleston was of similar proportions, with twelve-foot ceilings and ornamental plasterwork. But, as with all things New Orleans, these cornices and ceilings had more ornamentation, and bigger and more intricate moldings, and the room included a marble fireplace—even less useful in New Orleans than it would have been in Charleston. I stood for a full moment by the table, staring up at the ceiling mural, focusing on the cluster of painted grapes congregating around the center medallion from which an enormous Baccarat chandelier dangled. "Is that . . . ?"

"The Roman god Bacchus at a thinly disguised orgy? Yes. It is. Good eye, Nola." Beau held out my chair, waiting for me to sit. I was still looking up as he pushed in my chair.

From the head of the table, Mimi said, "It was done as an act of spite between my husband's father and uncle in a dispute over ownership of this house. It was a parting 'gift' from my father-in-law's brother before he moved out, and nobody looked close enough to notice the copulating cupids until it had been there so long that it had become a part of the house. It was most likely a point of pride that my father-in-law didn't paint over it, to prove that his brother hadn't put one over on him. Since I don't think whitewashing history changes anything, I've left it." She paused as she carefully unfolded her linen napkin and placed it in her lap. "I've always loved objects that tell a story." Mimi looked at me as she spoke, her eyes reflecting the light from the chandelier.

"And most people don't look closely, anyway," said Christopher, taking his place next to Jolene.

"Oh, I did." Jolene giggled as she reached for the bread basket, then apparently forgot about calorie counting as she took two pieces of corn bread and began slathering both with butter. "But I was raised not to talk about sex in polite company."

Beau walked around the table pouring wine into wineglasses, but he skipped Jolene's glass and mine without comment. Before sitting, he placed the water pitcher within easy reach in the middle of the table.

The food was passed family style—Lorda had apparently already left to beat the sunset—and I took something of everything in deference to the chef, promising myself that I would separate the andouille sausage and crawfish from the gumbo and jambalaya and eat just the rice soaked in roux, and not be overcome by the tantalizing scents wafting up from my plate. I did take a piece of corn bread, but felt virtuous by not helping myself to the butter.

I wanted to enjoy the meal, and appreciate the food, the beautiful linens with the R monogram, the Limoges china, and the heavy sterling silverware, all under a hand-painted mural of the god of wine, fertility, and partying. But the relaxed demeanor exuding from Beau, and the unspoken disagreement between us, erased any enjoyment I might have had. I kept looking from him to Mimi, waiting for one of them to bring up the subject of the house I meant to buy, but the conversation was tossed between an Italian neoclassical inlaid walnut desk that had just arrived in the store, Christopher's search for a Windsor lantern, and the excavation of a former outhouse behind Jolene's family home in Mississippi. Apparently, Jolene had forgotten her grandmother's instruction about acceptable dinner conversation, too.

After the dishes had been cleared by Beau and Christopher, Mimi led Jolene and me back into the parlor, Jolene rubbernecking to get a different view of the ceiling mural as we exited the dining room.

When the men returned, they brought a plate of homemade pralines and a pot of chicory coffee. Not wanting to appear rude, I took a praline and accepted a cup from Mimi. Chicory coffee is certainly an acquired taste, and I hadn't yet acquired it, but I figured now was the time to try. My house was on the line.

Jolene leaned over to me, her mouth full of praline, and whispered loudly while blowing crumbs, "Did you see the naked people on the ceiling? My grandmama would have her panties in a twist just knowing I even looked at it once."

I wanted to add that talking with her mouth full was also enough to ruffle her grandmother's underwear, but she was already reaching for another praline and I had more important things to talk about.

"So," I said, before the conversation could be hijacked for another discussion about antiques or the weather or Jolene's outhouse. "I want to buy the house on Dauphine. I'm preapproved by my lender, and you know I have the qualifications to restore it the right way, so there is absolutely *no* reason why you shouldn't let me." I turned toward Mimi. "Is the reluctance to sell it because you were best friends with the young woman who was murdered in the house?"

Her face didn't show surprise that I knew, either because she wasn't surprised or because she was good at hiding her emotions.

"No. And it's not so much reluctance as it is concern. Our concern stems from the fact that we are personally connected to you because of your relationship with Beau." She must have seen me shift uncomfortably in my seat, because she added, "However you define it. We have been told by others who have been in the house that there are . . . undercurrents, and a not-too-pleasant ambience inside. It's why it hasn't sold and the few buyers who made it to escrow dropped out. We don't want there to be any . . . misunderstandings if you change your mind after you move in. Because then it would be too late, and we would hate to lose you as a friend."

I frowned at Beau, not sure if "friend" was the right word for someone who had saved my life twice, literally and figuratively. Maybe my ambivalence toward him was because both of my parents, my aunt, my uncle, my siblings, and all of my grandparents loved him. Even my dogs followed him around like, well, puppy dogs. Or perhaps Melanie had been right when she told me I kept Beau at arm's length because I wasn't happy being the "rescuee" in a "rescuer/rescuee" relationship. She was wrong, of course. He'd put himself and me in those roles only by not giving me enough of a chance to save myself.

"Just to make sure I understand correctly, you don't want to sell the house to me because you believe it's haunted?"

Beau and Mimi exchanged looks. Beau started to speak but Mimi shook her head. "I suppose it depends on what you believe in. One buyer changed his mind because he brought his mother in and she said the house reeked of bad juju. He tore up the contract right then and there."

"And what do you think?" I asked, holding my steady gaze on Mimi.

"I believe that certain . . ."

"Memories," Jolene piped up, the last consonant rolling out in a sibilant hiss as her eyes closed and just before a loud snore erupted from her mouth and her chin dipped toward her chest. It was clear I'd need a plan B for getting us home.

"Yes, memories," Mimi said. "Having lived in or worked with old houses and objects my entire life, I do believe that over the years, bad—or good—memories can be absorbed by their surroundings. And some people are more sensitive to them."

"Except Beau doesn't believe in that sort of thing," I said. "At least not according to his podcast."

"Not necessarily," Beau said. "If you ever listened to my podcast, you'd know that I explore stories of supposed hauntings and residual memories to dispel rumors and to flush out the people who just want some grieving person's money. Which, I'm sad to say, is just about one hundred percent of the mediums and self-professed clairvoyants I've ever met." He paused. "Except for Melanie."

Our eyes met, and I wondered if he might be remembering that night of the house fire, when Beau and Melanie miraculously escaped—

along with three other people—from a locked attic engulfed in flames and smoke. I chose never to mention that night, and so did Melanie. But that didn't mean I never wondered what had actually transpired behind the locked door.

I took a sip of coffee and with great effort managed not to spit it back into the cup. "As much as Melanie is a mother to me, we are not related by blood. I have not inherited any of her abilities to . . . communicate with those no longer living. I've lived side by side with restless spirits since I moved in with Melanie when I was fourteen. They don't bother me, and I'm happily pretty much oblivious as far as they're concerned." I refocused my attention on Mimi.

"I love that house. We were meant to be." I left out the phone call from Melanie's deceased grandmother. *The house chose you.* "I promise I will do my best to make it the beautiful home it is beneath the mess right now. And if I hear any bumps in the night, I won't blame you."

"But what about your stepmother? What did she say?" Mimi leaned forward, keenly interested in my answer. I was too interested in making my case to wonder why.

"Nothing. I made her promise that she wouldn't say anything, and she didn't. She won't. She understands old houses. And what it means to have one pick you."

"I see," Mimi said, sitting back in her chair, her expression still guarded, but I'd seen the flicker in her eyes, the shift of decision that every child learns to recognize before the word "yes" is even spoken.

She turned toward Beau. "Then I think we should allow Nola to buy the house. If you could please get the paperwork together . . ."

"Mimi, maybe you should think on it. . . ."

"No. I've decided." To me, she said, "You will waive inspection and the contract will specify 'as is.' The other buyers signed off on that, and if you want the house in the condition it's in, then you will as well."

I could almost feel Melanie's finger prodding me in the middle of the back, but I ignored it and instead said, "Yes. That's fine."

Jolene jerked awake, her gaze registering where she was. "I know

Nola would love a tour of the house." Her accent was stronger than usual and would have needed subtitles if she'd been filmed.

Mimi stood. "Another time, perhaps. It's late." She seemed almost relieved.

Jolene stood, swaying slightly, and looked out a window, noticing that the sun had long since disappeared. She blinked several times, then hiccupped. "I think we may need a ride back. Because this dog won't hunt."

Despite my protests that I had the Uber app already pulled up on my phone, it was Beau who ended up driving us to our apartment. Jolene fell asleep in the backseat even before I could snap my seat belt.

Neither Beau nor I said anything until he pulled out onto Prytania. I tried biting my lip to stop the words, but I couldn't hold them back. "Wouldn't that have been a lot easier if you'd just said yes the first time?"

I saw his jaw tighten in the light that ebbed and flowed as we passed under the streetlights on St. Charles. "It wasn't my decision to make."

I shifted in my seat to face him. "Because of what Mimi said? Because of our connection?"

He stared straight ahead. "Pretty much. I just hope you know what you've gotten yourself into."

"I've done renovations and restorations before. I can handle it."

Beau turned his head to look at me, his eyes in shadow. "It's not the renovations that I was referring to."

I sat back in my seat and stared out the window, riding in silence for the rest of the drive while his words inside my head danced around my new mantra of *The house chose you*. I closed my eyes, wishing for a moment I could be Melanie, if only so I could tell myself that if I ignored my misgivings, they would go away.

CHAPTER 7

One week later, in the crushing heat of a New Orleans August morning, I pulled up at the curb in front of the house on Dauphine Street with nothing but my backpack and the toolbox that my very practical maternal grandparents had given me for grad school graduation. "Are you sure that's the right address?" My Uber driver looked at me in the rearview mirror, then looked back at the house.

"Yes, this is it!" I said, exiting the car. He waited for a moment, his expression dubious. "Really—this is the right place."

With a measured shake of his head, he pulled into the street and drove off slowly, as if expecting me to run after him. My phone beeped, alerting me that a charge from Uber had been made to my credit card, and I winced. I would need to find a more economical mode of transportation for the days Jolene couldn't drive me. Like a moped. Which would be a solution only if my parents didn't find out.

I stood on the street looking up at my house. *My* house. All of it. The porch, the elegant windows, the lovely shape of the roof, along with the tall ceilings and gorgeous woodwork inside. I could almost hear Melanie's mental cash register ringing in my ear as I considered

what else was mine—the rotten wood, the piles of junk, the absent
plumbing, and the toilet in the back garden.

Still, it was all mine. *Mine.* What I hoped was both the end and the
beginning of my personal journey. My own renovation and restoration.
And if the house came with memories, so did I. Squatting in abandoned houses with a drug-addicted mother could do that to a person,
no matter how many much-better years had passed since then.

Despite there being no breeze, the glass wind chime sang as I pulled
the single door key from my backpack—the only existing key to the
house, according to Beau—and stuck it into the lock. It turned easily
and the door made only a slight squeaking sound as I pushed it open.
I made my way to the kitchen, where I could lay out my spreadsheets
on the chipped Formica countertops. On the first one, under the column THINGS TO BUY, I wrote *WD-40.* I stood back admiring my handiwork, feeling as if I'd accomplished something. Until I looked around
me at the warped floors and ceiling stains and the carcass of an alarmingly large cockroach lying on its back.

"At least it's dead," Jolene said from behind me, making me jump.
She pulled a tissue from her purse and tapped her way across the floors
in her high heels to pick up the insect. She looked around for a garbage
can before giving up and dropping both the roach and the tissue on the
floor. "I guess it doesn't matter right now, huh?"

I wrote down *GARBAGE CAN* beneath *WD-40* on my spreadsheet. "Why are you here? You could have saved me an Uber fare if
I'd known you were headed this way."

"Sorry. I ran into Beau at the office and we had a conversation. . . ."

The sound of a truck pulling up in front and then idling brought
us both into the living room, the blue glass from the broken vases still
lying in the middle of the floor and crunching under our feet. From
the window I saw a big brown UPS truck, its driver standing next to
it squinting up at the house, a parcel tucked under one arm. He glanced
down at his handheld device, then looked back at the house before
giving his head a quick shake and jumping back into his truck with
more speed and agility than seemed necessary.

I ran out of the house, shouting for the driver to stop, and caught up to the truck before it had made it to the end of the block. I stood panting at the open door of the passenger side, leaning on it to catch my breath in the strangling humidity. "Is . . . that . . . package . . . for Nola . . . Trenholm?" I gasped.

"You live there?" The rise of his eyebrows punctuated his question. "I thought that place had been condemned."

"Not quite. I own it, and I'm renovating it," I said proudly. "I plan to live in it when it's ready."

He stared at me without moving, as if waiting for the punch line. Eventually, he stood and disappeared into the back of the truck for a moment before returning with the package. I was about to ask him to wait while I got my ID, but he practically tossed the box at me before returning to his seat and putting the truck in gear.

"I'll be getting a lot of deliveries here as the renovation progresses, so we'll probably be seeing a lot of each other if this is your usual route. I'll make sure the house numbers are more visible from the street next time."

He looked at me as if I'd just suggested we spend the afternoon wrestling alligators. "Maybe you should start with getting a priest over to sprinkle some holy water. Have a nice day." He sped off in a cloud of dust and exhaust, leaving me standing at the side of the street.

I stood watching the truck disappear, disappointed that the driver had left before I could think of an adequate reply. Not that there was much a person could say once their new house had been so maligned, but I would have appreciated the chance. I turned and began walking back to the house, my attention focused on the package. It was from Melanie, and because it wasn't marked as fragile, I gave it a little shake. A solid thunk with each shake told me absolutely nothing, but I shook it again just to be sure I didn't know what it was.

"I hope that's not street numbers for your house, because I've brought some as a housewarming present."

I looked up to see Beau standing on my front porch, carrying a bright floral gift bag stuffed with pastel tissue paper and trailing ribbons. Joining him, I said, "Did you wrap it yourself?"

"Sure—can't you tell?" He smirked. "Actually, Mimi did the wrapping, but the gift is from both of us."

"A peace offering for causing such a needless hassle?"

"More or less." He followed me into the house, stepping on the broken glass as we passed into the kitchen.

We put our packages on the counter while I added BROOM and DUSTPAN to my spreadsheet.

Beau glanced over my shoulder. "You might as well put 'notepad' on the list, since that's what you really need to make a to-do list."

I capped my pen and placed it carefully on the spreadsheet. "I'm sure that works for some. But I find spreadsheets . . . comforting."

He didn't smile or laugh or accuse me of joking. Instead, he simply nodded as if he completely understood my need to feel a connection to my former life. Maybe because he actually did. I brushed the thought aside, having no room inside my head for hindsight or reevaluation. Those would have to wait for later—much later.

The floorboards above us creaked. "Jolene's here," I explained. "I'm not sure what she's doing upstairs, but I hope it has something to do with figuring out how to make the plumbing work sooner rather than later."

"That's a good start. And I've already arranged for a dumpster and portable potty permit."

I stared at him, speechless for a moment. "What? Why? I don't remember asking you for help."

He held up his hands, palms facing me in surrender. "I know. God forbid that anyone try to do anything for Miss Independent. Trust me, I know better. But before your offer to buy the place, I'd pretty much resigned myself to either demolishing it or renovating it myself, so I'd already got the ball rolling before you even showed up. I'd be happy to cancel everything and let you start from scratch. But there's always a wait for permits, and I know you're eager to get started."

"Oh." I swallowed, wondering if that powdery taste in my mouth was from eating crow. "Thank you."

"See, Nola? That wasn't so hard, was it? Does that make us even over losing your mother's guitar in the fire?"

"Don't push your luck." I turned my attention to the gift bag. Beneath the tissue, and wrapped in more tissue, were four gleaming brass house numbers, along with the same numbers in cheap black and gold sticker form. "Why both sets?" I asked, holding them up.

"Mimi thought the brass ones were enough, but I figured you wouldn't want to get them destroyed by all the paint and construction mess that's about to happen. So I thought you could stick these numbers on the old mailbox for now."

I was surprisingly close to tears, which said a lot, because I never cried. Something else I'd learned during the first fourteen years of my life. Without looking up at him, I reached for the box.

"Here," Beau said, handing me a pocketknife. "Do I need to add one to your list?"

"Thanks, but I've already got one." I sounded shorter than I'd wanted to, still unable to untangle my feelings about Beau and why his kindness irritated me when even I knew it shouldn't.

I stabbed the knife into the packing tape and slid it across the top. There were more foam peanuts and Bubble Wrap than necessary, but considering that Melanie had probably stood over the UPS Store employee to make sure it had been wrapped to her specifications, this was not entirely surprising.

After cutting through all the layers, I peered inside and started laughing.

"What's so funny?" Jolene asked, tapping her way into the kitchen.

I held up the machine, already labeled with my name. "It's from Melanie. She said she was sending a housewarming present."

"But what is it?" Jolene asked.

"A labeling gun," Beau and I said at the same time. He shrugged. "I've known Melanie for a long time."

"It's an old-fashioned kind," I explained. "There are digital ones now, but Melanie likes this type, where you have to turn the dial at the top for each letter. She says the clicking noise is soothing."

A note fluttered to the floor and Jolene picked it up and handed it to me. I recognized Melanie's handwriting and I once again felt that unwelcome warmth in my eyes. Blinking rapidly, I read it in silence.

Dearest Nola,

Congratulations on your first house! It's not exactly what your father and I had envisioned, but we do understand why it is the best choice for you right now.

We are all so very proud of you. Always remember we're only a phone call and a short flight away. JJ and Sarah send hugs and kisses and have been asking when they can come visit. No pressure, of course, but fall break at their schools is early October. I just wanted to let you know that we all miss you.

With much love,
Melanie

PS Please let me know Jolene's and Beau's birthdays. I bet they don't already have labeling guns.

I took my time folding up the Bubble Wrap and gathering peanuts to return to the box so that my eyes had a chance to clear. "Well, then," I said cheerfully. "I'd better get started with my spreadsheets. Thank you both for coming."

Beau looked at Jolene. "You didn't tell her?"

"Tell me what?" I said, belatedly remembering what Jolene had said right before we were distracted by the UPS truck. About why she was there.

Jolene gave me her warmest smile, the one I'd seen her use on drivers of cars who blocked intersections as she walked across, as slowly as possible. It made me nervous. "So, like I was saying, I ran into Beau at the office this morning and we had a little conversation. We figured that with both you and me having full-time jobs, getting this house spick-and-span and actually livable could take forever. At least longer than you can afford your apartment lease. Unless you've already budgeted paying your mortgage and lease at the same time for at least a year."

She looked at me expectantly, as if she really believed that I had thought of anything past buying the house.

"Beau said if you officially hire JR Properties to help with the renovations, I can tag-team with you here to do what's needed, and to manage crews to do the things we can't do ourselves. We'll just need to set up a schedule so that our real jobs don't suffer, but Beau says you're an expert with schedules because you were trained by the best."

"I didn't . . ." I stopped, realizing that I had actually hoped she would help me, because we were friends. Still, it irked me that others were making decisions that affected my life without even consulting me. Or that they had realized before I did that I hadn't really thought things through. I might not have inherited Melanie's genes, but not thinking things through was another trait I probably had gleaned by osmosis.

"Jolene can be your project manager," Beau said. "So that you're dealing mostly with her instead of me. Or be your own project manager and use Jolene for specific things, like sourcing the appliances and fixtures. Whatever works best for you. And I'll be the general contractor."

"That's very big of you, Beau, but I can't afford to hire you and your company."

"I don't think you can afford *not* to." He looked around him as if to punctuate his point. "But I think Jolene came up with a solution that would work for both of us. It won't cost you anything except for materials, which you were having to buy yourself anyway. I'm sure that factored into your decision to buy this place."

It took me a moment to realize that the reason they were both staring at me was because they were waiting for my response. I quickly nodded several times. "Yes, of course. Of course it did."

"And unless we're not aware, you aren't a licensed contractor, correct?"

"No," I said, my voice embarrassingly low. "But I figured I could hire one for the major stuff but do most of the work myself to save money."

Beau nodded. "Glad we're on the same page. Jolene, why don't you tell her your great idea?"

Her smile faded slightly. "Do you need me to prepare it on a spread-sheet?"

"No. Go ahead. I'm sure I can manage to follow along." I crossed my arms over my chest, feeling defensive. I hated to admit that I might need help. And I especially resented that Beau Ryan might be in a position to offer that help. Again.

"So, what would you say about making this entire renovation a huge promotional opportunity for JR Properties?"

"What—like take a bunch of pictures during the renovation for your website and the occasional ad?"

Beau and Jolene exchanged a glance, which made me shift uncomfortably. "Well, sure," Jolene said. "Among other things. I'm good friends with the people over at *New Orleans* magazine, and I know we can get at least a feature story on the reno. They love stuff like that."

"Great," I said. "I guess I can handle the intrusion of a few cameras. Would that be all?"

Beau smiled without showing his teeth, the kind of grimace my little brother, JJ, used when being forced to eat a vegetable. "Not exactly. Jolene and I brainstormed a bit and there are lots of possibilities. We have a local TV station that features New Orleans businesses and will run what's basically a feature-length advertisement practically for free. Not to mention YouTube videos, and Instagram Reels, Facebook Live, and our website. Pretty much anything and everything to raise our company's profile, put it first and foremost in people's minds when they're looking to hire a home-renovation company. And we do the work for you free of charge in return for complete access to the site."

"But . . ." I began.

"You would still be in charge, calling all the shots. We'd supply the professionals needed for a project of this scope."

"But . . ."

"Nothing would be done without your knowledge or approval first."

"But . . ."

"No purchases or expenditures would be made on your behalf without your full knowledge and agreement."

"But . . ."

Jolene put a hand on my arm, silencing me. "Of course, you probably want to discuss this with Melanie and your dad first, but you and I both know they will agree that this is a logical win-win for everyone involved." She dropped her hand and looked serious. "The only thing that I would add would be to ask for final say on any shots or film of you, just in case it's not your best angle, or you'd like some photoshopping. Not that you need it, of course. It's just that we all need reminding sometimes that the Internet is forever."

Frowning, I looked around me at the water-stained ceiling, the warped floors, the fireplace missing parts. I didn't need reminding that I also had a toilet and a coffin sitting in my backyard. Yet I loved every inch of this house. My grandmother Amelia had once told me that the secret to being an expert antiques dealer was being able to separate one's head from one's heart. And that sometimes it was okay to let the heart win. I imagined it was the same feeling when picking out a wedding dress. Not that I'd had any experience with getting married—although Melanie and I had binge-watched all of the *Say Yes to the Dress* episodes—but a bride seeing her dress for the first time and knowing that it was *the one* was probably the exact feeling I'd had when I'd first laid eyes on this house.

Reason and practicality had taken a backseat to that one simple fact. *The house chose you.* And now it was time for a reality check. My excitement over making this huge step into the rest of my life had blinded me to most of the in-between stuff. My dad had once accused Melanie of going from idea to action without pausing in the middle. Even though I knew that was the crux of most of their disagreements, I had apparently learned nothing. Which is why I now found myself in way over my head. It just made it so much harder to admit it to Beau Ryan, for reasons I resisted examining too closely. Our relationship was that dark space at the bottom of the basement stairs, better unknown than faced in the glaring light from a bulb.

"Think about it," Beau said reasonably, making me resent him even more. "Call your parents, see what they say, and let me know."

I bit my lip and nodded. "Just please don't refer to this transaction— or whatever you want to call it—as you saving me from a fiasco. I could do this on my own—find my own contractor. I just underestimated, well, pretty much everything."

"I get it. I love old houses, too. It defies logic sometimes. And bank accounts." He grinned, transforming his face into something other women might find attractive.

I narrowed my eyes at Beau. "When we met, you were studying blacksmithing at the American College of the Building Arts. What happened?"

He looked surprised that I would have remembered. "Mimi and I decided I needed to expand my horizons. I still do some of the iron repair work needed in clients' houses, but only small jobs. It keeps me happy."

Jolene was examining the mangled fireplace surround, rubbing her hand over the raw wood, which seemed to have been ripped out instead of being carefully removed from the wall. "What do you think happened here?" she asked.

Beau and I didn't move, both aware our conversation wasn't finished. Feeling an imaginary finger prod from Melanie, I said, "Thank you."

"You're welcome." He grinned that grin again, making me turn away and move toward the fireplace.

Beau followed. "We only lost a part of that one fireplace surround to thieves. Luckily, they didn't take the cypress floors. That happens a lot to empty houses. Old cypress is worth a lot these days because people want authentic old floors in their new houses."

"Why wasn't more taken?" Jolene asked. "The house has been empty for so long, I'd think it would have been a prime target."

Beau looked past Jolene at me, pausing a beat before answering. "I'm not sure. Maybe they heard a police siren, or people walking by outside, and got scared off."

"Probably," Jolene said. "I wonder why they didn't take that Maison Blanche door from upstairs. That might actually be worth something."

"It's solid wood, so it probably weighs a ton, which might have saved it," Beau said. "I have no idea how it got here or why, but I could get some guys to haul it out of here."

I opened my mouth to protest, but Jolene interrupted. "Don't be so hasty. I could think of a dozen ways to incorporate the door into the reno."

"Yeah. Me, too." I wiped my sweaty palms on my jeans. "Speaking of which, I need to get back to work. First order of business is calling a dumpster rental company so I can get started clearing out the mess."

"I'll be happy to—" Beau began.

"Stop," I said, not allowing him to finish. "I can do that myself. If you'd like to recommend a company you've used before, just text me the name and number. And a portable potty company. I'm not completely helpless."

"Oh, I know," Beau said. "It's not something I could ever forget."

Before either one of us could bring up the past, the floorboards upstairs creaked. The three of us looked up. "It's an old house," Beau said. As if the noise upstairs hadn't sounded exactly like footsteps across the floor. His eyes met mine, and I wasn't imagining the challenge I saw there.

"That it is," I agreed.

Despite Jolene's insistence that she could stay and help, I convinced them both that because it was my first day as the homeowner I wanted to be left alone to get the lay of the land. And to figure out just how big this project was going to be. I hoped I had enough storage on my laptop for all the lists and spreadsheets I would need to make.

I walked them out onto the porch, where Jolene said good-bye and said she was making a coffee run before heading back to the office. I turned to Beau. "Thanks for the house numbers. That was really thoughtful."

"You're welcome—I'll let Mimi know they were safely delivered and appreciated."

I started to go back inside, but, as my father said, it wasn't in my nature to let a subject drop until I had flattened it, then beaten it mercilessly until there was no life left. "Not to sound ungrateful, but if you'd just told me that you didn't want to sell the house to me because of Mimi's connection to it, we could have settled this much earlier."

Beau paused on the front step, holding a pair of sunglasses. "I didn't tell you because I didn't know. She's been after me for a long time to have it condemned, saying nobody in their right mind would buy it, despite the interest we actually did get from prospective buyers. Now I think I understand her insistence, knowing her history with it."

"Until I came along."

He nodded. "Yeah. Until you came along."

He stepped off the porch and headed to a motorcycle he'd parked at the curb. I recognized it as the Harley Shovelhead that had been made the year his mother was born, 1977, and restored by his father. He'd had it when he'd lived in Charleston, and I knew it had survived Katrina because it had been stored at his grandparents' house in the Alabama mountains.

After putting on his shades, he kicked up the stand and sat astride the seat. "Don't even think that I'll ever ride that thing," I called out.

"Don't worry—I wouldn't think about asking you."

He grinned and started the engine, then pulled out onto the street with a sharp wave.

I stood on the steps, listening to the fading hum of the motor, remembering something else about the bike. Something Melanie had said about seeing a woman's set of wet footprints wherever Beau was, including once next to his Harley.

She disappeared during Katrina. I recalled Christopher telling Jolene and me that the night we'd had dinner with Mimi. Both of Beau's parents had been looking for his little sister, who'd disappeared the week before. There was a whole untold story there, waiting to be unearthed.

I turned around and walked back inside, shaking my head. I had enough to keep me occupied for a long while. No need to dig up the past and disturb old bones. Shutting the door behind me, I looked up at the ceiling as the telltale sound of footsteps crossed the room upstairs.

I went to the kitchen and grabbed my backpack and worksheets and headed out to the back garden to organize my thoughts without the distraction of creaking floorboards. No, there was no need to dig up a sleeping past. But sometimes, as I'd learned, the past had a way of unearthing itself.

CHAPTER 8

Two weeks later on a Saturday afternoon, on my front porch I sat on an old plastic lawn chair that had been found hidden beneath the banana tree in the backyard. I'd discovered it and a second toilet after I'd hacked the plant back to a size that was more fruit tree and less *Little Shop of Horrors*. My current sitting position could best be described as "splayed," something Melanie would definitely not approve of. The effort of lifting my water bottle to my mouth was more than I could handle, and most of the water trickled down my chin and neck in cooling relief.

Every muscle in my body ached, the raw skin on my knuckles and knees burned, and my hair, skin, and clothing were wet enough to wring out. Late August in New Orleans was just like that in Charleston: hot, humid, and unbearable. True to his word, Beau had sent a demolition crew to the house to help tear out laminate floors and Formica countertops and what remained of the derelict kitchen and bathroom fixtures; the work was interrupted for a period of time by an asbestos-abatement team to deal with that unwanted surprise. The demolition crew always showed up long after the sun had risen and were gone long before dusk. I wanted to ask them why, but it was a rotating cast of faces with none repeated. I'd made a point of asking Jolene if we could make a stop at the Ruby Slipper Cafe on our way to the house in the mornings so I could get a large box of Bam Bam Biscuits and a jug of iced coffee. But even though the guys on the crew seemed appreciative, it wasn't enough to get them to return.

I'd been working by myself all morning. After watching Jolene break off all of her nails and destroy an impressive collection of linen shorts over the last couple of weeks, I made the executive decision to relegate her to the social-media-and-publicity portion of the renovation until it was time to do the interiors and décor. Her mother was an interior designer—I'd seen photos, and her family's funeral home really was the prettiest I'd ever seen—and Jolene had a great eye, judging by my memories of our freshman dorm room. I was pretty much colorblind when it came to paint and floor finishes, and knew what I liked only after the fact. But what Jolene lacked in proper renovation attire she made up for in dogged determination. One of her recent coups was the deal she'd made with a flooring company to supply the tiles for the bathroom floors and kitchen backsplash below cost in return for free advertising on the JR website and YouTube channel and a mention in any of the print coverage. When I'd asked her how she'd accomplished that, she'd smiled broadly and said, "If you can't run with the big dogs, stay under the porch." I wasn't exactly sure what that meant, but I was thrilled to get the price cut.

My phone rang where it rested on my thigh, stuck to my skin with sweat. I opened my eyes wide enough to see that the call was from Dr. Sophie Wallen-Arasi, a professor of historic preservation at the College of Charleston and Melanie's best friend. Ever since Melanie told her I was restoring a Creole cottage in New Orleans, she'd been sending me reams of instructions on the most authentic methods for renovation, many of which—like picking berries to make my own paint—made me cringe. I'd made the mistake of mentioning I was eager to get an electric sander for the floors, and from her shocked and horrified reaction one might have thought I'd said I was going to meander naked outdoors. I declined the call before pouring the rest of the water in my bottle over my head.

"Hello, Nola!"

I waved to my neighbor Ernest across the street as he attached a leash to his brown and white Havanese dog, Belle, before attempting another walk—or "drag and carry," as he and his partner, Bob, called it. Not that I blamed Belle for her reluctance to move. It was too hot outside to do anything more strenuous than blink. Unfortunately, Belle's vet had put her on a strict diet-and-exercise regimen due to Bob's habit of bringing home tasty scraps from his job as a waiter at Upperline.

Ernest and I were both grateful for Bob's culinary expertise; I was sure I would have starved if not for the lovingly prepared meals he'd brought over. With so much work to do on the house, and with my full-time job, I didn't want to waste time eating. I always asked Ernest to join me, but he would politely decline with an implausible excuse, like the need to express Belle's anal sacs. I had no idea what that was, but I was fairly certain that I didn't want to know.

"The planters are looking great!" I called out, nearly depleting my energy reserves. On the first day of the demolition, Ernest and Bob had come over to introduce themselves and Belle, and asked if I was going to be keeping the coffin planter in the back garden. Now they had a matched pair in front of their porch, each containing artificial Christmas trees that were currently decked out in red, white, and blue for the upcoming Labor Day weekend. I was looking forward to seeing what they'd do for Halloween.

Ernest waved again, then proceeded to tug on the leash, dragging the stiff-legged Belle for several feet before giving up and hoisting her in his arms.

Beau's truck pulled up at the curb in front of the house. I considered sitting up straight and making myself presentable, but the mere thought exhausted me, so I didn't move as I watched him through droopy eyes. He aimed his phone at me, which acted as a jolt of ice water to the face and jerked me up to a sitting position. "Put that thing down unless you want me to grab it and stomp on it before throwing it at your head."

"Does that mean you don't want to be photographed today for the JR Properties website? I wanted to get you in action hand sanding the floors."

"Do I look camera ready?" I pointed to my sodden T-shirt and dripping hair.

An odd look crossed his face. "I'm guessing that's not up for discussion, so I'll hold off on candid shots." He gave me an ice-cold bottle of water before sitting down on the steps and unscrewing the top of another bottle.

"Thank you. And please give me plenty of warning when the official photographers and video people are scheduled. Melanie and Jack will want to see everything, and I don't want to give them anything to worry about."

"Yeah. About that. The people I had in mind are booked way out. Jolene overheard me telling Mimi and she had a suggestion. So I've hired Jaxson Landry. I believe you've already met him."

"The lawyer?"

"Yeah—we go way back. Great guy. He's apparently an amateur photographer in his spare time and would love to chronicle the rest of the renovation. I'm sure he'll want to make a schedule that works with you. Sound good?"

"It does. I'm just amazed that every professional photographer is booked. And what's with the rotating work crew? It's like a new group every day or so. Is there a huge building-and-renovation boom that I'm not aware of? Things would move faster if I had consistency in the crews you send. Having different people here every few days is almost like starting from scratch. I waste a lot of time going over the same things every day."

"Something like that." He didn't meet my eyes. "The guys did tell me that you're very nice to work for and they appreciate the food. Not so much the posted schedules. Lamont said he hasn't seen a potty break schedule since kindergarten."

"I learned that from Melanie. I'll try to make them bigger and more colorful next time. Maybe with cute graphics or something, to make them friendlier."

Beau raised an eyebrow. "Or not use them at all. I think the point was that they're grown men who know what they're doing and don't really need posted schedules."

I sighed. "Well, at least it's not personal. I was starting to get the feeling that they didn't like me or something, or that I wasn't working as hard as they were. I will admit to not being able to swing a sledge-hammer as hard as they can, but I did a lot of damage to the wall separating the rooms upstairs. Lamont told me he was impressed."

"Did he?" Beau asked with a smile.

"He did. And I'd like to have him return, but after three days I haven't seen him. Jorge—the young guy who I think might be completely deaf—is the only one who shows up consistently, and even he hasn't been here today. I think he said something about taking his mother to the doctor, but it's difficult to understand him. He's a hard worker and I'd love to have him back. I'd love to have anyone back. And the generator. They always take it with them when they leave, and I can't afford one right now."

Beau scratched the back of his neck. "Yeah, well, unfortunately, consistent workers and schedules aren't generally part of the renovation process. We have a lot of jobs going on and I'm doing my best to get you workers here. But you know how it is—sometimes there's a waiting period to let drywall mud set or floors dry, and I can only spare a few guys to work here for a period of time."

I watched him closely as he looked everywhere but at me. "Yeah, well, I've joined the Faubourg Marigny Improvement Association and the Preservation Resource Center. They've all been nice and friendly, and very helpful, especially after I explained that I wasn't demolishing anything original to the house, and I wasn't altering the facade. They practically hugged me when I told them I had no plan to make it a short-term rental—apparently there's an 'Airbnb epidemic' in the Marigny. But I can't get anyone to actually come inside. They keep recommending that I refer to their online videos and other resources—which are definitely helpful but don't really substitute for hands-on, you know? So, fine. People are freaked out because the house is supposed to be haunted, and yeah, someone was murdered here a long time ago. But at the end of the day it's just a house—my future home. I'm certainly not sensitive to ghosts, and I know the majority of people aren't, either. So I don't understand why it's such a problem to come inside."

Beau just nodded as if I wasn't telling him anything he didn't already know.

"I asked for a recommendation for a good electrician who understands old wiring and how to update it in a reno, but everyone is apparently booked for the next year. I've been waiting for the electrician you promised me two weeks ago, and I'm getting desperate. We need to be able to plug in fans upstairs and downstairs or the few workers I do manage to get will die of heatstroke, and then what will I do?"

He shrugged, his gaze fixed on the wall behind me, his fingers snapping a rubber band I'd noticed he always wore on his wrist. "This is New Orleans. People have strong beliefs about . . . things. Practically every block in the city has a church, a voodoo shop, and a tarot card reader, among other things. I think the workers are probably freaking themselves out and imagining things. Because you and I know that there is always a logical explanation to every supposed haunting. Just not everybody sees it that way."

I rolled my eyes, too exhausted to think of a more mature response. "Maybe I should start blasting ABBA on portable speakers in every room. It always seems to work for Melanie."

His mouth quirked. "I'm sure your neighbors would love that. Actually, some of them would probably start a sing-along on the street, complete with costumes."

"Talk about great social media exposure. I'll tell Jolene. Maybe that will prompt FMIA members to stop by and go past the front porch. Jolene just told me that she's been invited to write a column for their newsletter, *Les Amis de Marigny*, that will be like a progress report of the renovation. I hope they're prepared for some of her phraseology.

She showed me her first column before sending it in, where she described the condition of the house as a 'hot mess.' I'm assuming their readership is mostly local and no translation will be needed."

"Well, that's something." I waited for him to tell me why he was there, since he wasn't in the habit of making social visits. My phone rang, and I saw it was Sophie again. I quickly turned my phone on silent and groaned. "That was Dr. Wallen-Arasi. She keeps calling to make sure I'm doing everything the 'right' way and not going over to the dark side and using 'inauthentic' renovation techniques. At least I haven't had to lie to her so far. I'm dying to get electricity in here so I can get an electric sander and other things to make this go a little faster. She just can't know."

He looked at the overflowing dumpster next to the house, the surfboard and cracked Formica countertops peeking over the top like ocean flotsam and jetsam. "I'm assuming the Maison Blanche door is in there, too?"

I looked at him in surprise. "What? No. It's a gorgeous wood-and-glass door, not to mention a remnant of a vanished part of New Orleans history. I'm definitely going to incorporate it into the renovation." I sat up. "Actually, I was hoping I could ask you if Mimi would consider storing it at the shop, in the back room. I don't want it to get damaged during the renovation."

He finally looked directly at me. "You'll have to ask her, and she's in Mobile this week at an estate auction. Although I have to tell you that if it came from this house, she won't want to have anything to do with it."

"But it didn't—not really. It was taken from a department store and ended up here somehow."

"Mimi doesn't see it that way. She believes that objects—furniture, clothing, jewelry—contain memories of their previous owners. Or absorb the energy from violent or other extreme moments. Not that I think any of it is rational, but it's why she has to personally approve everything that goes in the store. That's why we don't carry as much inventory as some of the other shops on Royal Street."

I thought of Mimi, with her different-colored eyes set in her grandmotherly face, and the fact that she believed that objects had memories didn't surprise me as much as it should have.

"I'm just asking to store the door, not sell it. You've got that huge storage room at the back of the store—I've seen pictures on your website."

"Yeah, well, you still need to ask her. She'll be back on Tuesday."

I sat back, knowing that to him the subject was closed. I studied my now-empty water bottle, the JR Properties logo stamped across the front. "I'm curious. Who is JR? I'm guessing the R is for Ryan, and I'm assuming the company was named after a family member. I just can't figure out who."

He held his sweating bottle against his neck in an attempt either to cool off or to come up with a way to answer me. "JR is my sister. Jolie Ryan. We don't call her that, though. She's always been called Sunny. She got that nickname practically at birth because that's exactly her personality. My mother said she was born smiling. But Mimi wanted her proper name for the company, so JR it is."

I noticed he used the present tense. "The one who disappeared during Katrina."

He shook his head. "No. Not during the storm."

"But . . ."

"She disappeared the week before. My dad was out looking for her when the storm hit, and my mother refused to leave the city. I went with Mimi and my grandfather to their house in the Alabama mountains, along with my dad's motorcycle. I never saw my parents or Sunny again."

"I don't understand. Sunny was younger than you, right? She couldn't have been much more than a toddler." I waited for him to say more. Not able to let it drop, I asked, "Was she . . . abducted?" Even saying the word was hard.

"It's impossible to know. She was riding her tricycle in the driveway, and the phone rang. In the two minutes it took my mother to answer it and return, Sunny was gone."

I tried to imagine either one of my siblings disappearing, and I couldn't breathe.

"My mother was sure that Sunny would come back to the house. She kept on hoping that whoever had taken her would bring her back." He took a long swig from his bottle, emptying it. "The stupid thing is that the phone call was a wrong number."

We sat without speaking, the wind chime tinkling quietly despite there being no breeze. "I'm sorry," I said.

He looked at me with the same blank expression I gave people when they said they were sorry after hearing that my mother was dead. It made no sense to be sorry about the death of someone you never knew, and whose death couldn't have been prevented, even by the daughter she claimed to have loved most in the world.

"Not just about Sunny and your parents, but that I never asked you about it before. It's not that I don't care or I wasn't curious. It's just . . ."

"You were fighting your own battles. I know." He leaned back against the railing, quickly righting himself when it began to give way. "Which is why I was surprised to find out that you'd moved to New Orleans. Of all places, you chose here." His eyes narrowed as he considered me. "Or maybe I shouldn't be surprised. You've always been the kind of person to tackle your demons head-on."

I looked down at my ravaged nails, not wanting him to see my face. "Yeah, well, my parents say I come by my bullheadedness honestly—half of it inherited from Jack and the other half learned by watching Melanie." I shrugged. "Jack is a recovering alcoholic and so is Melanie's father, and my mother was a drug addict. Sometimes I wonder what took me so long to allow my demons to catch up with me." Still looking at my hands, I said, "I could have done it on my own, you know. Without your help. I just need you to know that."

"I do know. But if I see a moth throwing itself at a lightbulb, I'll turn off the light before too much damage has been done. I'd seen what losing a child could do to a parent. I didn't want your parents to go through it."

I chewed on my lip, wishing I could make him understand that I'd *wanted* to get sober. That I *could* have done it on my own if he hadn't intervened. But that would have made me sound ungrateful, and I wasn't. I was alive and facing my demons in New Orleans because of him. But the way I'd been raised for the first fourteen years of my life had taught me to never be beholden to anyone. Because everyone eventually demanded payback.

Lifting my head, I met his eyes. "The rain always stops. That's why you say that all the time. Because of what happened to your family. And to New Orleans. And you're still here, and so is the city."

"I guess you could say you and I are survivors. So that's one thing we have in common."

"I wouldn't go that far. It's not like we had a choice."

"Sure, we did. We always have choices. But sometimes we have to be bullheaded enough to make the right one."

Feeling uncomfortable with the conversation, I stood and stretched. "I need to get back to work. Was there anything you needed to tell me? I'm assuming there's a reason for this visit other than to remind me that I owe you."

"Fine, then. I was going to offer you a generator and water dispenser that one of my crews doesn't need right now, but if you're not interested . . ."

"I didn't say that," I said quickly. "But aren't you worried they'll get stolen if we leave them here? I need to fix the lock again because the front door keeps opening, even when I know I locked it and turned the new dead bolt. I have a strong feeling it's not the lock, but I need to do something."

"Do you really think someone is going to break in here?"

"Good point. I can't even get people I *want* to come inside."

"You know, maybe you should sign up for Nextdoor. That's a great way to find people."

I frowned. "I thought the whole idea of partnering with you was because you had the human and technical resources. I might as well be doing it all on my own. It's what I wanted to do when I first started, and you and Jolene talked me into this arrangement."

"And I'm still keeping up my end of the bargain. It's just that my guys are from New Orleans and are ridiculously easy to scare off. One guy said the house had bad juju. Whatever. I'll keep working on them. But that's why I suggested Nextdoor. Members are in your community and will know people who wouldn't be bothered by things they can't explain."

"And if I can't find anyone to work here? Then I run out of money and can't afford to pay my rent, and I'll have to sleep on an unfinished floor without air-conditioning."

"Do you really think I'd let it come to that? It's why I came today. To offer you help until we can get a reliable crew in here. I'm a licensed contractor and can do the plumbing work and some electrical work. I didn't want to insult you by offering my help."

I swallowed, feeling unbelievably grateful, yet still ashamed at how much I owed him, and how hard it was to tell him. Almost enough to make me cry. Or maybe it was the heat and my exhaustion. "You're not insulting me. It's obvious that I need help—although through no fault of my own."

His mouth turned up at one corner. "So you're saying you need my help."

"I'm saying I need an electrician. And anyone who knows how to plaster a wall, because I haven't a clue and watching videos isn't enough. And a plumber, because, well, the portable potties reek in this heat. Lastly, I really need a carpenter. I can't open the locked door at the top of the stairs, but I don't want to hack through it because I want to be able to reuse it. As a last resort I can call a locksmith, but I really don't want to damage the door and would rather just remove it intact."

"Sorry about that—I've never had a key to that door. It wasn't included when the property manager Mimi hired after my grandfather passed turned over the keys when I took over. He said the closet was just filled with junk. I meant to get it opened at some point, but I guess I forgot." He crossed his arms and looked at me smugly. "So, if you'll just admit that you need my help, I'll show up here first thing Monday morning with a sander, a generator, fans, and Jorge and anyone else on your list that I can find. And I will be here most days when I can't get a crew together for you until the job is done. You just need to say that one little phrase."

"You're kidding, right?"

He shook his head. "Nope." He stood, knocking off one of the Mardi Gras necklaces. He stooped to redrape it. When I didn't say anything, he said, "Suit yourself. The heat index is supposed to be one hundred and three tomorrow. Good luck with that." He began walking down the steps, then paused at the bottom, eyebrows raised.

"Fine," I said. "I need your help. Just as long as you know that I could do this all on my own. I'm just running short on time through no fault of my own."

Beau looked up toward the two dormer windows before quickly glancing away. "Yeah, I know. And just as long as you remember that you insisted on buying this house against my better judgment." He stepped toward his truck before turning around again. "Did you bring your guitar from Charleston?"

"Yeah. Why?" I didn't think it was worth mentioning that I hadn't opened the case since I'd placed it in a corner of the back room. Or that I didn't really consider it *my* guitar, because *my* guitar had belonged to my mother and had burned in the fire.

"Because I play, too. It's something else we have in common. Frenchmen Street is a real happening music scene. You should try it sometime. They also have open mic nights. In case you're interested."

"Why is it so important to you that we have anything in common?"

Beau's jaw tightened briefly before he responded. "Because Jack and Melanie told me you needed a friend here."

His admission hurt. Not just because it confirmed that my parents were worried about my choice to move, but because they had more or less asked Beau to be my friend. It was humiliating. "I don't need a friend. I just need a plumber. And a carpenter."

He jerked open the driver's-side door of his truck. "Don't forget an electrician."

"That, too," I yelled after him as he pulled out onto the street and drove away.

I watched his truck disappear and felt the need to apologize. I turned to go back into the house, mentally preparing myself to return to hand stripping the cypress floors. I stopped midstep, my breathing suspended in mid-inhale. My heart thudded loudly as I looked down at the worn floorboards. A single and very distinct set of a woman's wet footprints, each toe and heel clearly defined, each print surrounded by a spray of water droplets, led from the doorway to the porch steps, then toward the curb where Beau's truck had been before the prints vanished.

I quickly headed back inside, closing the door on the footprints, remembering what Beau had told me about his mother and how she disappeared during Katrina. I leaned against the door and spoke to the empty house. "I can't help you. I'm sorry."

Pushing myself away from the door, I headed to the kitchen to continue sanding, a lone thought following me as I worked, a speck of dust in the eye that defied removal. *Who was haunting Beau, and why did he pretend not to notice?*

CHAPTER 9

The following week, I stopped my bike in front of the Past Is Never Past and let down the kickstand before securing the bike with the four lock chains that had cost more than the bike but were essential if I wanted it to remain in my possession. I'd paid only ten dollars to buy it from a kid on a bench in Washington Square Park. He was only twelve years old but apparently already quite the entrepreneur, I'd noticed on my neighborhood ramblings, with his random assortment of junk with price tags crafted from torn cardboard boxes. The bike—complete with hand brakes and a banana seat—was circa 1980, but it had been kept in pristine condition, meaning it had minimal rust and the brakes still worked. I didn't ride it the whole way between Uptown and Downtown, but it was handy for getting around the Marigny and the Quarter and other nearby areas to run errands. It didn't have air-conditioning, but it had the advantage of giving me full view of pot-holes to avoid. I didn't tell my parents that I'd acquired the bike. Mostly because I didn't want them to worry, but also because there was a part of me that considered buying it retaliation for their asking Beau to be my friend.

I didn't ask questions when I handed the boy two fives—double what he was asking because he had good manners and when I approached he stood and said "Yes, ma'am" and "No, ma'am," which Jolene had taught me meant that he'd been raised right. He also had a beautiful smile, his white teeth bright against his dark skin, and he was small for his age, which made him even more endearing.

I'd since bought a few more essential items, like a small battery-powered fan, a water pistol ideal for squirting water on my face and at flying cockroaches, and a rubber bath mat that was perfect for my sore knees when working on the floors. I'd also since learned that his name was Trevor and he lived with his grandmother and nine siblings (he was number seven), and we were now officially friends and greeted each other with high fives.

I wiped the sweat off of my forehead after locking the bike, unfortunately catching sight of myself in the reflection of the store window. I'd been painstakingly removing nails and glue from layers of other flooring materials beneath the wooden floors, the generator Beau had brought humming happily in the background along with the whir of the floor fans. Although it was better to have fans than stagnant, humid air, the fans did funny things to my hair, which made me feel sorry for anyone who had to look at me. I opened the door to the shop, welcoming the icy cold blast of air-conditioning, and grateful that I was known at the shop and didn't have to worry about security being called.

"Nola, what a nice surprise." Christopher straightened in front of a Duncan Phyfe table—distinguished by its lion-paw feet and the urn pedestal festooned with acanthus leaves and rosettes—a polishing cloth in one hand. "Looks like you could use some refreshment."

"I'm sure you meant to say 'shower and a hairbrush,' but if you've got a glass of ice-cold water somewhere, I'll happily accept it."

"Would sweet tea work?"

"Even better. Thank you."

"It's slow today, so I think I'll join you if you don't mind." He exited through a door at the back of the shop that I hadn't noticed before, a regular door with a knob and visible hinges, unlike the one on the opposite side that I'd seen Mimi enter with the two customers the last time I'd been there. I turned my face up to catch the breeze from the air conditioner, watching the price tags hanging from chandeliers dancing in the draft. I stopped to examine a sterling silver English tea set, circa 1820, nearly identical to the one in Melanie's mother's house in Charleston that had been in her family for generations. Ginnette—Ginny—had served me tea from it more than once, making me feel as if I really were her granddaughter. It had solidified the sense of belonging that I hadn't known existed until I'd shown up on Melanie's doorstep when I was fourteen.

Christopher returned with two tall crystal glasses garnished with lemon slices and mint, starched linen napkins cupping the bottoms. Handing one to me, he said, "Let's sit down and give you a moment to cool off." He led me to the desk in the corner in front of the hidden door and I sat in the chair facing him across the desk.

He studied me closely. "I hope you don't mind me saying so, but you look tired. Working hard?"

I nodded, enjoying the cool slip of liquid down my throat. "My boss is almost as excited as I am about restoring my house, which means he's allowing me to work seven a.m. to three o'clock in the afternoon, so I have a few hours at the end of the day to work on the house. I'm basically working two jobs back-to-back, and the heat just takes it out of me." I didn't mention the landline phone that rang every night, even after I'd wrapped it in a sweater and thrown it in my closet. At least Jolene could sleep through it.

"Sounds exhausting. Beau mentioned that he and Jorge have been there every day this week. So you must be making progress, right?"

"Well, if you call discovering that all of the plumbing pipes are galvanized metal and there is dry rot in the kitchen wall 'progress,' then I guess you can call it that."

"Ouch," he said, wiping a drop of moisture off of the desk's surface.

"That's what I said. Jolene is blogging about it now, and posting stuff on the website and YouTube channel, which has given JR Properties lots of exposure—just not drawn any craftspeople to come join us on the project. Jolene said it's because when she filmed there was some dust on the lens, and everyone is calling it a spirit orb. She's cut out that section, but the damage is done."

I took a long drink from my glass before holding it against my cheek. "And I take that back—we did have one person come see Beau in person to apply for a job. He's a master carpenter with lots of experience. He just hasn't worked for the last ten years."

"Well, that's good, right?"

"That he's a master carpenter and eager to work? Yes. That he was in prison for manslaughter for killing his wife, not so much."

Christopher's eyes widened. "Is he saying that he was wrongly convicted?"

"No. That's the thing. He pled guilty and served his time and says he deserves another chance. Beau did some research and the guy checks out. Perfect prison record, was trusted with tools, and taught other prisoners basic carpentry skills while incarcerated. Sad story, really. He had a nice life in a cute little house in the Bywater and his own business when it happened. Lost everything. He has a son he hasn't seen since he went to prison—his wife's family won't allow it. The son's twenty-five but developmentally disabled, so he lives in a group home."

I put down my empty glass. "I hate to admit that I might be desperate enough to hire a convicted murderer, but I think I just might."

Christopher nodded slowly. "I'd trust Beau's judgment. He's always been an excellent judge of character."

I wanted to amend Christopher's opinion about Beau's judgment of character, but I chose to file that thought back in the place in my brain where I stored thoughts that should never see the light of day again. "Yeah, well, I'm still thinking about it. Beau says it's up to me." I sat up, placing my hands on top of the desk. "I was actually looking for Mimi. Is she back from Mobile?"

"I'm afraid not. She decided to head on up to Savannah and see what else she could find."

I drummed my fingers on the desk. "I have something at the house that I want to store during the renovation—a door." I nodded toward the storage room behind me. "Beau said I needed to ask Mimi for permission, but I really don't want to wait any longer. It's in the way and I don't want it to get damaged. Beau's in Lakeview getting another project started, but our helper, Jorge, is at the house now. If Jorge and I can get it into his truck, do you think you could let us put it in the storeroom?"

Christopher didn't say anything right away. "Is the door original to the house?"

I thought it was a strange question, but I was eager to save the door. "No. It's from the Maison Blanche department store that used to be on Canal Street. Nobody knows how it ended up in my house, but it's in perfect condition and I've included it on my plan to be the door to the downstairs bathroom. It's perfect because it will filter in light from the bathroom window into the main living space, and because it's smoky glass—miraculously still intact—it will offer privacy."

"Okay," he said slowly. "Just for tonight. I'll move it tomorrow to our remote storage facility so it won't be in the way here. Mimi's . . . particular about what's stored here. About how long do you think it might be?"

I didn't want to lie outright, but if we had one more time-sucking disaster like corroding pipes or hidden wood-eating fungi, Christopher and Mimi might need to find a place to hang it permanently. "Hopefully just a few months." I smiled. "If you like, I can help you make room for it in the storage room. I've built up my biceps in the last few weeks and can do a lot of heavy lifting."

"That won't be necessary. I've got the perfect spot in mind, right in the front so it's convenient to move it again. Is Jorge at the house now?"

I nodded, trying not to show my disappointment at not being allowed to see what was behind the door. There had been something so furtive about the couple whom Mimi had escorted to the back room. And something about her smile as she'd closed the door behind them. "Yes. He'll be there for another hour. I can ride my bike back and help him get it downstairs and into his truck. . . ."

Christopher was already standing and had begun flipping off the lights. "Don't you worry about it. It's just about closing time, so I'll drive down there myself and Jorge and I will get it done."

"Really, I don't mind. . . ."

"You're tired. Go on home. I'll call Jorge now and let him know I'm coming."

"You know Jorge?"

"We go way back. He was part of the crew that helped me renovate my house after Katrina. I was the one who discovered he wasn't deaf."

"Wait—what?"

"He's not. But he doesn't speak Spanish because he's Portuguese. He can understand English if it's spoken slowly. He couldn't make people understand that shouting at him in English or Spanish wasn't going to help, so he just pretends to be deaf. But I speak Portuguese." Christopher grinned.

I stood. "Great. Now I feel like an idiot. He could have just told me."

"Or you could have asked."

I met his eyes but felt no judgment. "That, too."

At the door I turned to him. "You told me that Mimi calls you the king of lost things. Did she ever ask you to search for Sunny?"

He was silent for so long, I thought he might not answer. But his gaze held mine and I couldn't look away, his eyes measuring to see how much he could tell me. Or maybe how much I could bear to hear. "No. Katrina had done its job erasing pretty much everything to do with the case, which was very little to begin with. The only evidence that Sunny didn't disappear into thin air was from an eyewitness who lived across the street who'd seen a dark car drive up when Adele went inside the house—apparently when she went to answer the phone. The back passenger-side door opened and a woman got out and put Sunny in the car and it drove away. She couldn't give a good description of the woman or the car besides that it was black, but it did have Louisiana plates."

"So the police never found out anything more?"

Christopher shook his head. "They might have, except that Katrina hit right afterward. And when Mimi and Charles returned weeks later, when they were allowed back into the city, and found both of Beau's parents missing and presumably lost in the storm, I think they gave up hope. And then Dr. Ryan died the following year, and it was all Mimi could do to just keep it all together, raise Beau, and keep the shop open. I only struck out on my own because I thought someone out there had to know *something*."

"Did Mimi at least hire a private investigator to see if they could build on that? It seems like that would be enough of a lead."

He surprised me by opening the door, indicating that the conversation was over. "She didn't. The police had closed the case right before her husband died, and Mimi said it was time to bury the past. It had been too long, and for Beau's sake she needed to stop grieving and move on."

Our eyes met briefly, as if we were both wondering why the owner of a store called the Past Is Never Past could ever think that the past was something to bury.

"Didn't you think that strange?" I wanted to add *and uncaring*, but I was already nosing into territory that was none of my business.

"It isn't my job to judge others. I'm sure she had her reasons, and it wasn't my place to question them." Christopher opened the door wider, making it clear that it was time for me to leave. Glancing at his watch, he said, "If we're going to get that door in the storage room, I've got to leave now. I've got plans tonight."

"Sorry. I didn't mean to hold you up. Thanks for doing that."

While he set the alarm and locked the front door, I busied myself unwrapping the chains on my bike, a laborious process that took enough energy to make me start dripping sweat again. At the sound of the sole of his shoe scraping against concrete I turned my head, curious as to what he might have stepped in—not an unfamiliar event in the French Quarter.

A small smear of moisture, already evaporating in the sun, could have been any spilled liquid, or rainwater dripping from an awning. Except it hadn't been raining, and the telltale dots of two toes of a footprint were still visible. And his movements seemed almost furtive. I looked away as Christopher wiped those away, too, and pretended I hadn't seen them. I waved good-bye and took off on my bike, nearly colliding with a garbage can.

I met Trevor at the previously agreed-upon spot at the corner of Royal and Canal and handed over my bike. Ever the businessman, he'd suggested the arrangement of watching my bike overnight for the price of one dollar so I didn't have to take my life in my own hands by riding the bike all the way uptown. I'd started throwing in an extra fifty cents if he promised me he'd do his homework. It was all on the honor system, and I chose to believe him. His grin was too hard to resist.

I sat on the hard bench seat next to an open window inside the streetcar, the humid breeze doing little to cool me off, and thought about the wet footprints and why Christopher hadn't wanted me to see them.

The smell of something delicious baking wafted down the stairs toward me as I opened the front door, giving me the stamina needed to climb the steps to my apartment after the walk down Broadway from the streetcar stop on St. Charles. I was huffing and puffing as I made my way into the living room, pausing in front of the window AC unit, then continued to the kitchen.

Jolene was bent over the oven to remove a tray of cookies before placing them on top of the stove to cool. Despite the obvious fact that she was baking, her hair seemed freshly brushed, and she was wearing a pink and white polka-dot romper and the shoes she referred to as her "sittin' down" shoes, meaning (as she'd explained) that they were pretty to look at but not meant for dancing. Her one concession to domesticity was an apron with the word *GRITS* embroidered on it, and underneath it, in smaller letters, *Girl Raised in the South*.

"Sit right down, Nola. You're panting like a bloodhound after the hunt."

"I feel like one. Maybe I should start running again and get back in shape."

Jolene made a face. "Or come to Pilates with me. The only running I'm going to be doing is if I have to run away from someone or something, and if my butt ever gets too big to haul ass, then I'll just have to make two trips." She removed a monogrammed pitcher of sweet tea and poured me a glass. "I hope you don't mind, but I put my kitchen things in the cabinets. I took up a lot of space, so if you have dishes or pots you need to store, just let me know and I can rearrange things. The cabinets were all empty, so I wasn't sure if you'd unpacked everything yet."

I had only one plate and cup, which I washed every time I used them, as well as a hot pot and a single warped saucepan. Melanie had wanted to make a run to Target when she was in town, but I declined. My parents had already done so much, and I needed to prove that I was capable of setting up my own apartment.

I looked around at the cute *Wizard of Oz*–themed dish towels hung on the oven handle and the matching ceramic jars on the counter. "Well, since you've gone to all that trouble of unpacking and putting things away, we might as well leave it. It's a good thing you brought your monogrammed pitcher, though, since I forgot mine."

"Oh, yes. Grandmama gave me that and my own deviled-egg plate for graduation. She said every Southern cook should have both."

"Of course." I took several gulps of tea, spotting a china serving plate loaded with already-cooled cookies. "Is there a party I don't know about?" I asked as I sat down on the kitchen stool and listened to my stomach rumble.

"No, but Jaxson said he was going to stop by after work on his way to see his parents. They live on State Street, so it's close by. He said he had something for me, although he wouldn't tell me what it was. I thought he might need a snack."

Jolene opened up a cabinet to pull out a plate, and placed two cookies on it. "They don't have any meat in them, so you can eat them, right?" She handed me the plate, and I recognized the old Wedgwood Blue Willow pattern from Trenholm Antiques.

I was too busy staring at the inside of the cabinet to correct her. "You have an entire set of china?"

"Of course. Fifty full place settings, including demitasse cups and soup bowls. My mama and grandmama and all the women in my family have always picked out their china patterns when they turned twelve. This one belonged to my great-great-grandma and I've always loved it, so I asked for it instead of a new set. I just love that it's part of my family's history."

"Me, too." I took another sip, washing down an emotion I couldn't name. I looked down at the cookies on my plate, stuffed with chocolate chips and pecans. "What kind of cookies are these?"

"They're sort of my own invention. They're basically chocolate chip cookies with pecans and sea salt. My cousin DeeDee calls them better than sex."

I was so hungry and they smelled so good that I didn't really care if they weren't vegan, since I wasn't really sure if I'd come by veganism legitimately. Nor did I care that they were stuffed with Melanie's three main food groups: sugar, carbs, and chocolate. I took a bite and chewed slowly. "Please tell your cousin that she's right. These are amazing."

Her cheeks pinkened. "Thank you." She added two more cookies to my plate. "You need to keep up your energy with all of your renovating, biking, and walking. We can't have you wasting away."

"Absolutely not," I said, picking up my second cookie. "Especially now, since I might be walking to St. Francisville to do fieldwork for a work assignment. My firm has been hired to work on a new railway line, so I have to go assess two existing historic structures on the site. The other architectural historian is already working on a project in the Warehouse District. I apparently drew the short stick, so now I have to go to St. Francisville. And since I don't drive . . ." I picked up another cookie to distract me from thinking about how I was supposed to get there.

"What? That's a two-hour drive. There's no way you're going to be walking that. Did you tell your boss that you don't drive?"

I took a bite out of the third cookie. "That's the thing. When I took the job I sort of didn't mention it. I knew that fieldwork would be a good portion of my job—I mean, it's a civil engineering firm and they have projects all over the state, so I never assumed everything would be in the metro area. But I just sort of thought that I'd always have one of the architects accompany me, and since everyone has a car, I'd just planned on riding with whoever was assigned to work with me."

"But it's just you." I nodded while Jolene put two more cookies on my plate. "Either you're going to have to learn how to drive and buy a car lickety-split, or find someone to take you."

I smiled hopefully. "What's your workload like next week? If I pay for gas and wear and tear on your car, would you consider driving me?"

"Oh, honey, I wouldn't charge you a penny. But I can't do it. I've been assigned as the project manager for a new rebuild in Mandeville starting on Monday and I've got to be there all week. We had to fit it in around your house, but since everything is on hold until we can schedule an electrician to come rip out all of your old wiring, we took the job."

I swallowed the last bite of the sixth cookie, starting to feel a little sick. "No worries. I get it. I guess I'll just have to tell my boss, and we'll figure out something." I drained my glass, trying to swallow my fear of losing my job.

The doorbell rang and Jolene froze. "Oh, my goodness. He's here."

"Is he early?"

"I don't know. He didn't give me a time—just said he'd drop by to give me something and it was a surprise."

I didn't want to point out the obvious, that if he was only dropping by, he wasn't planning on coming inside and having tea and cookies. I watched as she hurriedly untied her apron and smoothed her hair.

"Look," I said. "Why don't I go get the door while you settle down and fix him a plate?" Whether or not he wanted to come in, if I went to answer the door, he'd have no choice.

Jolene pressed her hand against her heart. "Thank you, Nola." She began running toward her room. "I've got to put some color on!"

As I passed through the living room to the stairs, I noticed the burning candles placed on the coffee table and television stand, and I almost didn't want Jaxson to come up and see them and maybe see what he missed every time he looked into Jolene's lovestruck eyes.

Jaxson was surprised to see me when I opened the door. "Jolene had something in the oven, so I volunteered to come down and let you in."

He glanced at his car in the driveway, and then at a large envelope in his hand, making it clear he hadn't planned on coming inside. As I waited for him to say something, I caught a whiff of the baked cookies and scented candles and I just couldn't face Jolene's disappointment.

I opened the door wider, silently asking the unknown Carly for forgiveness. "Come on in. It will only take a minute."

With a smile, he followed me up the stairs to the living area. A full plate of cookies sat next to the candle on the coffee table, and linen cocktail napkins had been placed on the tray holding the tea pitcher and three full glasses, each with its own floating wedges of lemon. Jolene sat in the armchair, apparently engrossed in a book, her feet in their sitting-down shoes and her ankles elegantly crossed.

She looked up with surprise, her lipstick giving her mouth the perfect rosebud shape. "Hello, Jaxson. I almost forgot that you were supposed to stop by." She casually placed a bookmark in the middle of her book and stood. "I just made cookies, and they're fresh out of the oven, if you'd like to try one."

At his look of indecision, I indicated a spot on the sofa. "Or two. They're a bit addictive. And they're Jolene's own recipe."

He seemed to waffle for a moment as he eyed the delicious confections on the plate. "Well, maybe just one. I'm having dinner with my parents and I don't want to spoil my appetite."

"Of course not," I said, sitting down next to him and holding out the plate.

Jolene placed a napkin and one of the full glasses in front of him before returning to her chair with her own glass and a single cookie wrapped in a napkin. As much as she apparently loved to bake, I rarely actually saw her eat anything.

"It's good to see you again," Jolene said. "I'm sorry I missed Carly's party last Friday—I was working late and too exhausted by the time I got home."

I sent her a sidelong glance, remembering the two of us on the night in question sitting on this very couch, wearing our bathrobes, with our faces smeared in a green goop mask that Jolene swore by, and watching a Hallmark movie. I couldn't remember which one, but it had been about a woman leaving the big city for a small town and reluctantly falling in love, and it ended happily.

"Yeah, well, I didn't make it, either." He shrugged. "We had another fight and I figured it would be best if I stayed away. I'm seeing her tomorrow night, so hopefully we'll be able to patch things up."

Jolene nodded sympathetically while watching as he took a bite from his second cookie. "These are amazing, by the way," he said.

"My cousin calls them better than sex," Jolene added matter-of-factly. "But not in front of our grandmama or she'd skin our hides—DeeDee's for saying it, and mine for listening."

At Jaxson's wide-eyed expression, I quickly added, "Aren't they delicious?" I felt compelled to add, "And she has a monogrammed iced tea pitcher and a deviled-egg plate." I wasn't sure why I'd said that, but at Jolene's warning look I stopped before I could mention the full set of china.

"I'll fix you a plate to take to your parents if you like." Jolene looked so demure as she spoke, hiding the Machiavellian plans whirring in her sharp brain. Everyone knew that in the South the plate would need to be returned in person, and with more home-baked goods on it.

"That would be awesome—thanks." He sat back on the couch, seemingly forgetting that he wasn't supposed to stay long, but the crinkling of the envelope he'd put there brought him back to reality. He pulled it out from under his leg. "I almost forgot." He stood and handed the envelope to Jolene, picking up another cookie before resuming his seat. "I saw this and thought of you. It's kind of big, but you've got a big car, and it would fit in the rear window."

Jolene opened the envelope and pulled out a rectangular window sticker and began laughing.

"What does it say?" I asked. The words were reversed and covered in a white backing, so I couldn't make them out from my vantage point.

Jaxson quoted from memory. "'Louisiana, a state where you need to pay for a decal on your car that says your vehicle is fit for the road, on roads that aren't fit for a vehicle.'" He smiled. "Made me think of you getting a flat on a pothole and changing the tire all by yourself. I figured you'd earned it."

Jolene beamed, no doubt pleased that Jaxson had thought about her. "I love it. I'll put it on my car first thing."

Jaxson placed his empty glass on the coffee table—using a coaster, which Jolene no doubt noticed and appreciated—and stood. "I hate to eat and leave, but my parents will be waiting for me."

"Sure. Let me go fix that plate for you."

"Only if you have enough," Jaxson said.

I thought of the four batches of cookies I'd seen in the kitchen. "There's plenty, trust me."

Jolene disappeared into the kitchen, and I watched as Jaxson's gaze followed her.

"I hope you don't mind, but I have another favor to ask," I said.

He reluctantly returned his attention to me.

"There's another cold case. Two actually—from 2005—that I wanted to ask your uncle Bernie about. Would it be possible to arrange a meeting?"

"Sure. Anyone you know?"

I shook my head, thinking of the wet footprints, and a little girl who'd disappeared and never been found. "Not really. Beau's mother and his little sister. And I guess we could add his father to that list, too, since his body was never recovered after the storm."

Jaxson nodded solemnly. "My family had already evacuated, so we weren't here when it happened, but it's all anybody could talk about when we finally moved back into town, and that was five months later." He paused. "Why the interest? Did Beau ask you? Because Mimi has always made it clear that she believes Sunny is gone forever and has made a point of never talking about it because she doesn't want to reopen an old wound. And since Beau's parents didn't evacuate, it's just always been assumed that theirs are two of the numerous bodies unable to be identified and buried anonymously."

"That's heartbreaking. I can't imagine. And I can't adequately explain my interest. My dad's a historic-true-crime mystery writer, so I'm always seeing possible plots wherever I go. It's either inherited or learned—but I can't seem to shake my morbid curiosity."

He tilted his head. "Wait—your last name is Trenholm. Is your dad Jack Trenholm?"

"Yep. The one and only."

"Oh, my gosh. I'm his biggest fan."

"Be careful who you say that to." I laughed. "Authors get a little worried when they hear that. No one can forget Stephen King's *Misery*."

"Ouch—yeah. You're probably right. Well, I promise that if I ever get to meet your dad, I'll keep that to myself."

"Well, my parents and siblings will be here in October, so I'll make sure you get to meet him then. And since you've been such a big help, I'll even throw in an autographed copy of his latest."

He grinned. "Not necessary at all, but greatly appreciated."

Jolene reappeared from the kitchen holding a plate of neatly arranged cookies in a precise pyramid that would have made Melanie proud; it was covered in plastic wrap and topped with an elaborately tied satin bow. I didn't bother asking if she'd tied it herself.

She walked past us, holding the plate and sending me a wink. "I'll see you out, Jaxson."

Jaxson paused at the top of the steps. "I'll be in touch after I speak with Uncle Bernie. And don't forget that I'll see you at your house around four o'clock on Thursday to take some 'in progress' photos and make a Facebook Live video."

"Thanks for the warning. I'll make sure I wash my hair and put on a clean T-shirt."

I began clearing the plates and glasses and bringing them to the kitchen. I was placing the glasses in the sink when I heard the distinctive ring of the landline phone, shrilling loudly in the now-empty apartment. Too loud to be coming from inside my closet, wrapped in a wad of sweaters.

Slowly, I emerged from the kitchen into the dining room in time to hear the telltale ring again, louder this time because the phone had been replaced on the top of the large teacher's desk. I turned to ask Jolene if she'd moved it, belatedly realizing that she wasn't there. And that I already knew the answer.

I picked up the receiver and slowly held it to my ear. But all I heard was distant static from an unknown part of the universe, and faintly, very faintly, the sound of breathing before the finality of the click of a receiver being replaced in its cradle. A dial tone began droning in my ear. Even though I was fairly sure what I would find, it was my nature to discover the facts on my own. I picked up the cord that was connected to the back of the phone, pulling it out from behind the desk until the end of it dangled in front of me.

The phone rang once, then stopped. I lifted the phone off of the desk and casually walked it back to my closet, then rewrapped it twice before closing the door tightly. The muffled sound of its ringing could be heard as I left my room, slamming the door behind me.

CHAPTER 10

On Thursday, I locked my bike to what remained of the railing of my porch. Although I'd been working at my real job since seven a.m., the usual excitement and rush of energy I would feel as I approached the house was missing, my thoughts still back at the office, where I had yet to inform my boss that I had no way of getting to St. Francisville on Monday. In my defense, he'd been out of the office Monday and Tuesday and in meetings most of the day yesterday, and he had seemed preoccupied all this morning and I didn't want to bother him. It didn't escape my notice that I might have adopted Melanie's questionable approach to problem-solving—if I ignored problems long enough, they would go away.

I'd called limo companies, asking for all-day rates for the one day I had allotted to do the job, and when they'd quoted their prices, I'd had to start mentally downgrading all of the lovely appliances that Jolene had begun earmarking for the finished house. At least we had my hot pot, so we wouldn't need a stove right away.

The loud backfiring from an old truck announced Jorge's arrival. Until I'd gotten used to it, I'd duck for cover, assuming it was yet another gunshot, which had become as familiar a sound of my new hometown as the music spilling onto the streets and the clip-clop of the tourist-carriage mules returning to their stable on Esplanade.

I waved in greeting, shouting out one of the few words of Portuguese I'd learned. *"Olá!"*

I didn't bother wondering why he was just now showing up, since I'd learned through Christopher that Jorge lived with his elderly mother and he was her sole caretaker. She didn't speak English and she was afraid of strangers, so his work schedule fluctuated as needed.

I'd accepted this since he was the most patient person I'd ever met and he was meticulous with every job assigned to him. It had been his idea to erect in the wreck of a backyard a refinishing center for all of the woodwork salvaged from inside the house; it was complete with an awning to protect the work space from rain and the workers from self-combustion under the hot sun. He'd brought his own extension cord so we could use one of Beau's fans to blow the hot air at us instead of having it simply sit on our sweltering bodies while we worked outside.

Beau's truck pulled up right behind Jorge's, followed by another truck—around the same vintage as Jorge's—with a man I didn't recognize in the driver's seat. I walked down the steps to greet Beau and the stranger as they approached me. "Hey, Nola. This is the guy I've been telling you about."

I turned my head sharply, taking in the middle-aged man who was built like the guy on the Mr. Clean cleaning products label, and dressed in jeans and the same white T-shirt. Bulging muscles not quite hidden beneath tattoo sleeves on both arms made impressive lumps beneath his T-shirt, making me think that most of his time in prison had been spent in the gym.

Like Mr. Clean, he was also bald, but instead of having bushy white eyebrows he had blond ones, and he didn't have a gold hoop earring. Or piercings of any kind. As far as I could see, at least. I'd walked down Bourbon Street enough times to know there were plenty of places to pierce on the human body, not all of them visible if a person was wearing clothes—not always a given in the French Quarter.

"Thibaut Kobylt, ma'am," the man said, his grin friendly and his handshake firm.

I flashed Beau a glance to let him know that he'd jumped the gun and that I hadn't had enough time to consider hiring a convicted felon. I also noticed that even though Beau was tall, Thibaut was at least a head taller.

"Nice to meet you," I said slowly, his name sounding familiar. "Did you say Kobylt?"

"Yes, ma'am. Beau tells me you might know my cousin Rich Kobylt. Our dads are brothers, but his dad married a South Carolina girl, and mine married a Cajun. We're both in the construction business, just like our dads."

My eyes flickered down to his pants at the mention of his cousin's name. Rich was famous—or infamous, depending on who you asked—for his low-slung pants that always revealed more of his backside than anyone really wanted to see. I was still on the fence about hiring Thibaut, but his belted jeans gave him a point in his favor.

"I see. Are you close?"

He shifted uncomfortably. "We used to be, before . . . the incident. We don't speak so much no more, on account of my incarceration."

I nodded, glad he'd been the one to mention his past. "I wasn't expecting you today. Beau and I were still discussing whether or not we needed more help." I sent a warning glance at Beau.

Thibaut looked up at the house and didn't bother to hide his laugh. "I don't know if you're pulling a funny or if you need glasses, ma'am, but this house needs help. Or maybe a bulldozer. I need to see the inside first before I decide if I should take the job."

My glance at Beau this time was more firm and insistent. "Sure," I said. "Come on inside."

We all turned toward the door, but stopped at the deep intake of breath from Jorge. *"Meu Deus,"* he said as he made the sign of the cross.

Nestled in the doorway was a small cloth bag, its sides lumpy from whatever small objects were inside it. Thibaut leaned down and picked it up. "Just some good gris-gris. Probably left by a neighbor wishing you good luck with the renovation." He tossed the bag and caught it in his hand. "I think it needs more than luck, so if you know who it's from, maybe you can ask for a bigger gris-gris."

Jorge was looking at the pouch with wide eyes. To our surprise, Thibaut began speaking to him in fluent Portuguese. Jorge visibly relaxed, and the conversation ended with Thibaut giving him a gentle slap on the back.

"It's all good," Thibaut reassured us. He began climbing the steps.

"You speak Portuguese?" I asked, pulling out the key.

"Yep. I learned it from a fellow inmate. Spanish, too. A little bit of Russian. I figured I could make my sentence about moving forward or I could make it about staying still. There ain't nothing I could say or do would bring my Rena back, but I was still here and I've got my son to think of, so I might as well make the best of it."

I unlocked the door, unsure how to respond, recalling what Beau had told me about Thibaut's son, and how his wife's parents wouldn't let Thibaut see him. Understandable, I thought, seeing as how he'd killed their daughter.

He stood in the middle of the downstairs room, his arms akimbo, his size compared to everyone else's making me think of Jonathan Swift's Gulliver in Lilliput. "Wow, you're really taking it down to the studs," he said, walking toward the wall with the fireplace. "Why all the half-assed demo everywhere?"

I exchanged a glance with Beau. "We've had different crews because of conflicting schedules, so nothing has been consistent. As for the walls, they were all cheap drywall that had been patched over varying layers of plaster. I'm trying to find someone who knows how to do plaster the right way."

Thibaut nodded. "That's smart. Too many people think they can just slap anything on the walls and floors and call them renovated, but there are those of us who know and appreciate the difference." He leaned down and rubbed his hand on a cypress floor plank. "These are real nice. Whoever has been removing the glue has done a nice job without damaging the wood." He paused at one of the gaping holes in the floor that I chose to believe had been caused by some heavy object. Not, as Beau had speculated, having suffered irreparable damage from unidentifiable liquids or a sharp instrument that could have been a kitchen knife or an ax.

"You figured out how to patch these yet?"

"We're still working on it," Beau said. "Absolutely nothing decent can be found at any of the salvage places, with all the renovations going on and the popularity of cypress floors. If worse comes to worse, we can grab some boards from upstairs and put down carpet there to hide the patch job."

Thibaut clutched his chest. "You serious? Carpet on these floors?" He shook his head. "I got some sources who might be able to help. Friends from my 'before' days."

"So," I said, trying to quell the excitement I felt at finally finding someone who understood the how and the why of historic renovation. I needed to find reasons not to hire him, because that one little problem couldn't be overlooked. "What construction skills do you have?"

He looked at me as if he knew exactly why I was asking. "I'm a master carpenter, and I took a lot of classes while incarcerated, so that I'm also a certified electrician and plumber. Beau here says you might could use me."

If he were anyone else, I probably would have hugged him.

"Can I see the upstairs?" He began climbing the steps without waiting for an answer. Beau and I followed, Jorge staying behind, possibly to keep an eye on the gris-gris that Thibaut had left on a step of a ladder.

Thibaut stuck his head into the bathroom and didn't scream or throw up, which I thought was a good sign, and then spent time studying the various cracks and mold patterns on the ceiling, clucking his tongue like an adding machine, tallying what everything was going to cost.

"Are you a roofer, too?" Beau asked.

"Nope. But I know some good ones. And honest ones—that's the important part. When I had my own business, I figured out who was who."

He continued to walk around, asking questions, before leading us back to the stairs and to the locked door. "What's in here?"

"We haven't found out yet," I said. "No locksmith has been able to unlock it without damaging the wood, and it's such a beautiful door and surround that I didn't want to break it by forcing it."

He scratched his chin, looking at the door from all angles. "Well, looks like some durn fool's nailed it shut. I've got a few ideas 'bout that." He led us back downstairs, pausing at the open wall beneath the stairs. Leaning into the space between two exposed studs, he said, "See this?"

I stood next to him to look closer. "It's a wire."

His mouth twitched. "Right. I see that college education of yours taught you real good. Yes, this here is a wire. Part of the old knob and tube wiring probably running through the whole dang house. Over time they get worn out, and when they're covered in housing insultation, *poof*. It's like a match hitting gasoline."

I stepped back, trying to distance myself before I said anything rash. "I'm not doubting your credentials, Thibaut. It's just that, well, you were in jail for murder."

"Manslaughter," he corrected.

"Still, you admitted that you were guilty."

"Yes, ma'am. My lawyer said that was best and I didn't argue."

I shared a glance with Beau. "Yes, but . . ."

Movement inside the half wall remaining between two studs had me reaching for the can of Raid I kept in every room.

"Hang on," Thibaut said. "It's a different kind of critter." He squatted down and reached for something small scrabbling at the wall before cupping his giant hands and lifting it up. "It's a young squirrel," he said. "Open the door and I'll let him get back to business."

We watched as this giant of a man gently placed the squirrel on the ground outside before it scurried away.

"So," I said. "About the job. Beau and I need to have a discussion before we can make any hiring decision."

He looked genuinely confused. "I thought I was interviewing y'all. And I haven't decided yet that I'm going to accept an offer."

I looked at Beau, who just shrugged.

Thibaut took a deep breath and looked around him. "If you don't mind me saying so, this place is a wreck. Looks like them houses redecorated by Katrina—although I think some of them were left in better shape than this. I think I saw more sanitary bathrooms than that cesspool upstairs. Can't figure out why the demo was left half done. If I didn't love old houses so much, I'd say tear it down. But I'm a big believer in rehabilitation. Buildings and people have a lot in common that way, y'know?"

If there was nothing else to convince me to hire Thibaut Kobylt, that cinched it. "Yeah. I do." I swallowed. "How about I call you tomorrow?"

"Nope. Don't got no phone. I'll just show up here at eight in the morning and we can talk then."

Before I could explain that I couldn't be there because of my real job, Beau stepped forward. "I'll be here and we can talk it out."

Thibaut nodded, then turned to face Jorge. *"Adeus. Vejo você manhã."*

Jorge, having heard him perfectly, smiled. *"Adeus."*

I waited until Thibaut got into his truck before I turned to Beau, speaking before he could. "If I decide to hire him—assuming he wants the job—you have to promise not to tell my parents about his background."

"If?" he said. "Except for that one small thing, Thibaut is the perfect guy for the job. And if you have the time and money to wait until we can find another person as qualified, fine. But I don't think you do."

"I don't. And I don't think murder has ever been called 'one small thing.'" I thought for moment. I couldn't help remembering Thibaut's enormous hands cradling the squirrel. "Do you know how he killed his wife?"

"He shot her. Found the gun covered in his fingerprints a few blocks from his house. His defense lawyer said there were other prints, too, but they were too smudged to identify. Could have been from somebody who found it in the garbage can but then decided to put it back. Not that it mattered, since he pled guilty."

Our eyes met, and I knew we were both wondering why a big man with muscles, and with every construction tool easily accessible, would choose a gun to commit his one and only crime.

A dark blue Audi sedan pulled up in front of the house, and we watched as Jaxson Landry climbed out of the car and approached us, carrying a black camera bag and a tripod. He and Beau gave each other man hugs like the old friends they were.

"It's been a long time, bro," Jaxson said. "Can't believe we haven't seen each other since you been back. We'll have to grab a beer or two and catch up." He looked at me. "Sorry I'm a little late. I had to talk a client out of representing himself. That never ends well, since I have a law degree and he doesn't. Took me longer than I expected to explain that to him."

"No worries," Beau said. "You're just in time to get a lot of 'before' footage, as well as of Jorge, who's hand stripping the staircase spindles and is about ready to start on these porch railings."

"Excuse me," I interrupted. "I'm in charge here, remember?" To Jaxson, I said, "Beau forgot to add that I will be upstairs pulling down the fake wood paneling and that I washed my hair so you can get some of that on film."

"Actually," Beau said, "I think Jaxson has enough to keep him busy." His expression changed to that of someone who was about to get a root canal. "Because I think now would be a good time to have a driving lesson."

"Excuse me—what?"

"Jolene told me about your little predicament. You won't be able to drive by yourself next week, but I've cleared my schedule on Monday so I can drive you to St. Francisville. In the meantime, I can be teaching you so that eventually you can drive yourself."

Gratitude and what I considered righteous anger warred inside me. My mouth opened and closed several times without anything coming out.

Beau looked genuinely embarrassed. "Sorry—didn't mean to spring it on you. I thought Jolene would have mentioned it."

"No, as a matter of fact. She didn't. I've barely seen her this week because of her Lakeview project. Not to mention that I don't remember asking you for your help."

"You didn't. And I got tired of waiting. What were you planning to do? Hire a limo and driver?" He laughed as if he found the thought ridiculous.

"I've been meaning to talk to my boss. I'm sure we can figure it out."

"You do know this is Thursday, right? And you have to be in St. Francisville on Monday. You're not giving your boss a lot of time to revise plans."

The fact that I knew he was right made me even more resistant. "Maybe I don't want to learn."

It looked as if Beau was trying very hard not to roll his eyes. "What was it Jolene said? It's a life skill. Like potty training and playing tennis."

Jaxson laughed out loud. "Jolene said that?"

The butterflies in my stomach at the thought of getting behind a wheel overrode Jaxson's appreciation of Jolene's comment. "I can't. I'm not ready."

"So you're scared?"

"I said no such thing! When I was fourteen I found my way, all by myself, from Los Angeles to Charleston. And I've lived with Melanie ever since. Nothing scares me anymore."

"Then let's go."

He strode to the door and opened it. "We'll start in a church parking lot. As long as it's not a potluck or bingo night, we should find a few empty ones. There are also school parking lots that should be emptying out about now, except we might have to share with other unexperienced drivers."

I wanted to resist, to figure it all out on my own. But in this single instance, we both knew that he was right. "Fine," I said, walking past him to the porch. I stopped short. "Wait—all you have here is your truck."

"Of course. Riding a motorcycle is a different kind of license. Besides, your father would kill me."

I gave him a look that I hoped he knew meant that I wouldn't oppose that reaction. "But a pickup truck? I can't drive a truck. It's so . . . big."

"Exactly. Much safer than a sedan in case you bump into someone." At my glance, he amended, "I mean, in case someone bumps into you. And in a truck you can drive over potholes instead of in them, which is a huge plus in New Orleans."

He held open the passenger-side door. "Besides, once you learn how to drive a pickup truck, you can drive anything. Well, except for Bubba. Bubba's in a class all his own."

I laughed even though I didn't want to, and even though I was sure I was going to throw up from nerves.

Beau settled himself behind the wheel. "Do I need to go over the basics? Like how to start a car and put it in gear? I'm assuming you'll want to drive an automatic transmission."

"I know how to start a car. And G is for 'go.'"

He gave me a startled look.

I grinned, aware that my lips were wobbling. "Kidding. But I have no idea what an automatic transmission is."

Beau laughed, starting the car. "Okay. That gives us a place to start."

"What if I can't do it? I tried before, remember?"

"Those guys who told you that you were a menace on the roads— are you going to let them win?"

"Do I have a choice?" I wasn't sure I was joking.

"You know what I do when I'm scared?"

"I told you, I'm not scared."

"Apprehensive, then. It's something my dad taught me. He said it got him through combat more than once."

"So that he wasn't afraid?"

He shook his head. "Nope. He was still petrified. But it wasn't about not making him afraid. It was about using his fear to make him do what needed to be done." He held out his arm to show me a rubber band I'd seen him snapping against his wrist pretty much the entire time we'd been showing Thibaut the house. I'd thought snapping it was a nervous habit, like biting fingernails or cracking knuckles, and equally as annoying. "I snap it when I need to be reminded that fear can't win. That whether or not I'm afraid isn't important. What matters is that I don't allow it to get between me and my objective." He paused. "And then I remind myself that the rain always stops."

We were silent for a while, listening to the hum of the motor. Finally, I said, "I chipped a tooth."

He turned to face me, waiting for me to explain.

"On my LA-to-Charleston trip. I clamped my teeth so hard, they hurt. But the pain reminded me that I had just survived another five minutes alone, and that was five minutes less until I reached my destination."

Beau nodded slowly, absorbing my words. "My guess is that learning to drive will be a whole lot less scary."

"Apprehension inducing," I corrected him. I crossed my arms and held them tightly to my chest. "That remains to be seen."

Beau put the truck into gear and pulled out onto the street. We traveled in silence until he turned into a large parking lot empty of cars, filled only with an obstacle course of tall light posts. Looking at the dashboard in front of me, I said, "I'm going to say thank you now, because I have no control over what's about to come out of my mouth, so I need you to know now that I'm actually feeling appreciative. I can't promise I'll still be feeling that way in thirty minutes."

I stepped out of the truck, prepared to change places with Beau, and took a deep breath, remembering one of the few things my mother had taught me. Whether you ran through a rainstorm or walked through it, you were still going to get wet.

CHAPTER 11

When I returned home, my jaw throbbing from clenching my teeth and my hands curved as if still gripping the steering wheel, Jolene was sliding cookies into her Emerald City cookie jar. It took up a lot of counter space, but judging by the rate she made cookies, it was necessary. She already had ribbon-wrapped Baggies—one with Trevor's name on it—next to it and ready to go.

I picked one off of the cooling sheet, knowing Jolene would understand why I didn't ask first. Most people would have poured themselves a drink, but I wasn't most people. I must have looked shaken, because Jolene didn't scold me. Instead, she handed me another and a napkin. "You poor thing. You look like you've been chewed up and spit out. And you're white as a sheet. Was it that bad?"

I nodded and closed my eyes, trying to savor all the sugary goodness of the cookie, but had to open them again as my body jerked with muscle memory from the sudden and frequent braking that had made up most of my driving lesson. I rubbed my neck, wondering how Beau had survived the ordeal and if his left ear hurt as much as my throat did from all the shouting.

She looked at me with concern. "Did you at least learn something?"

"I'm not sure. We're both alive and the truck is intact. And I now know that it's important to turn the steering wheel when approaching a stationary object."

Jolene smiled encouragingly. "Well, that's a start, isn't it?" The timer on the circa-nineteen-sixties oven began buzzing. I was surprised that the ancient oven still worked, much less the timer. Not that I would have noticed. Until Jolene had arrived, I had yet to open it.

She put on two oven mitts emblazoned with a likeness of Dorothy's ruby slippers and pulled out a bubbling Corningware dish. "I hope you like squash casserole. No meat, so it's vegan, right? Mama used to make this for me when I'd had a hard day. Like that time I didn't make the cheerleading squad when everybody knew it was fixed so that the mayor's daughter, who didn't know her left from her right, could be on the squad. I figured you learning to drive would feel the same."

She slid the kitchen stool over and forced me to sit down while she handed me another cookie.

"You look like you're tuckered out—you're practically swaying." After making sure I wasn't going to fall off, she said, "These are another of my creations—peanut butter oatmeal with pecans. And a little bit of this and that. We had a passel of pecan trees in our yard in Mississippi, so most of my recipes have pecans in them."

I blinked. "Why are you here? You usually aren't home until after eight."

She retrieved a full tea glass and handed it to me. "I finished up in Mandeville early, so I decided to bake some cookies and make us a nice dinner so we could spend time catching up."

I blinked my eyes again to show I'd heard her, not wanting to make the mistake of nodding and setting off my PTSD symptoms again.

"Did Beau say when he thinks you'll be roadworthy?"

"Not really. He did say that we needed to practice more. I just have a feeling that he might have learned as much as I did." I was embarrassed to admit that I had exposed Beau to cusswords he hadn't heard before, courtesy of Melanie's father, who'd been in the Army and who used interesting adjectives to describe many of the insect and plant pests that invaded his garden.

I put the cookie in my mouth. "These are so good," I said, rotating my neck, making sure it was still connected.

"Have another," Jolene said, holding out a plate. Not wanting to hurt her feelings, I took another one. "If I keep eating like this, I'll have to buy a whole new wardrobe."

"Would that be such a bad thing?" she asked, eyeing my jeans and T-shirt. "Besides, you're too thin. And I figure, since you can't drink, you should eat. No one's starving to death on my watch!"

I pointed to a lumpy paper sack on the counter. "What's that?"

"Arkansas Traveler tomatoes. Our neighbor back in Mississippi has a cousin, Sadie, from New Orleans who was visiting, so she gave Sadie a sack to bring to me when she returned home. And the fresh squash from her garden, which gave me the idea for the casserole. I'm putting the tomatoes in our salad as soon as I get them peeled."

I quickly took a swallow of tea to wash down the rest of my cookie. "Peeled? You peel your tomatoes?"

"Of course," she said, looking up at the ceiling as if I'd just admitted to being raised in a barn. "Actually, if you'd dip some more batter on this baking sheet, I can get busy with the peeling. You must be starving."

I was, but my body was still roiling with the movement of the car, making me wonder if it was possible to get carsick after the fact.

The doorbell rang and Jolene froze mid-dip. "Are you expecting anyone?" I asked.

She shook her head.

"Me, neither. I'll go. I know how to answer the door, so I'll let you carry on in the kitchen."

I had to hold on to the banister as I walked down the stairs to the door because my leg muscles were too stiff to bend. I threw open the door after peering through the peephole. "Jaxson—is everything all right at the house?"

He grinned. "It's nice to see you, too. Yes, all's good. Got a lot of pics and footage. And sorry for springing an unexpected visit. I should have sent you a text to let you know I'd be stopping by." He held up Jolene's plate. "My mother wanted me to return the plate and thought she'd share some of her lemon bars."

Despite having just eaten a handful of cookies, I salivated. I blamed a quarter century of deprivation, and almost half of that spent living with Melanie, for my newly discovered and ravenous sugar tooth. "Those look amazing." I opened the door wider. "Why don't you come in? Jolene's just taking a casserole out of the oven and there's plenty, if you'd like to join us." I had a strong feeling that my room-mate wouldn't mind Jaxson's joining us for supper. "Assuming you don't have plans, of course."

He hesitated on the doorstep a moment. "Actually, I don't. Carly had a last-minute business dinner, and my parents are going to the theater. I thought I might catch up on some files and watch a game at home. . . ."

"Don't be ridiculous. The casserole smells delicious and Jolene's about to peel the tomatoes for the salad."

"Peel the tomatoes?"

I practically grabbed his arm and pulled him inside. "That's what I said. Maybe it's a Mississippi thing."

By the time we'd made it upstairs, the table had been set with a tablecloth and three place settings, including linen napkins and silver-ware, and Jolene had changed into a floral sundress, pulled her hair up into a messy bun, and put on fresh lipstick. The only evidence that she'd been rushing was her heavy breathing as she leaned on one of the chairs.

"Jaxson—what a nice surprise. I went ahead and set a place for you, hoping you might be hungry."

"Well, if you're sure there's enough . . ." Jaxson said.

"There's plenty. And now we have two desserts, too." Jolene took the lemon bars and headed to the kitchen. She paused. "Nola, why don't you give Jaxson a tour of the apartment while I get supper on the table? It won't take but a minute." Without waiting for an answer, she disappeared into her kitchen. We hadn't lived together very long, but I was already beginning to realize that the kitchen was her domain, and I was happy to let her have it.

Turning to Jaxson, I said, "Can I get you something to drink?"

"Do you have beer? Although I'm fine with water. From our lunch the other day, I guessed that you weren't drinking alcohol for a reason. Trust me: I'm from New Orleans. I understand."

"I appreciate that. But we do have beer and wine—Jolene always wants to be ready for any spontaneous entertaining—and no need to drink water on my account. I'm fine. Hang on a sec and I'll go grab a beer from the fridge. Faubourg Lager okay?"

"Perfect."

As I slammed the refrigerator door shut, Jolene turned from where she was peeling the tomatoes, once again wearing her sitting-down shoes. "Don't forget a glass, Nola!"

I hurried out of the kitchen, pretending I hadn't heard her. She had monogrammed crystal bar glasses, including for pilsner, but I wasn't about to use one. And if Jaxson asked for a glass, my opinion of him would drop a notch or two.

He stood by the teacher's desk as I approached. "I haven't seen one of these in years. My grandmother had an old blue one that she still used when I was little. Did it come with the apartment?"

I knew before he turned around that he meant the old princess telephone that was supposed to be in my closet. "Yeah. Along with the desk. I suppose they've been together for a long time, and it didn't feel right to separate them."

He opened his beer and took a sip without asking for a glass, and I silently cheered. "So, how about that tour?"

"Right. To be honest, there's not much to see. I'm thinking Jolene just wanted us out of the kitchen. Maybe she heard us snickering about peeling her tomatoes and we've been banned."

Jaxson choked on his beer, wiping his mouth on his sleeve, earning him another point from me. "So," I said. "As you can see, there are old and original wood floors throughout, three bedrooms, and one bathroom right here in the middle. It hasn't been touched since the early sixties, so it's authentically vintage. I'll show you the cool room in the back, which is my office slash music room. There's a door from the kitchen, but let's cut through Jolene's room instead so we don't have to bother her."

My bedroom door, to the left of the bathroom, was intentionally closed, since without Melanie's eagle eye I might slip from her military-like requirements for bed making and laundry disposal. Jolene's door was open, and her bed—of course—was made and artfully arranged with about a dozen throw pillows, including a large monogrammed one in the middle. Despite having lived in the apartment for a very short time, she'd hung curtains and framed artwork, and a vase of fresh flowers sat on the antique dressing table she'd told me came from her childhood bedroom. A beautiful needlepoint rug sat under the tester bed—another piece from home—and the ancient ceiling fan had been replaced with a small chandelier and a floor fan that was discreetly hidden in her closet and pulled out each night. Framed photos of Jolene with her family and friends dotted every surface that wasn't already taken up by books or makeup or *Wizard of Oz* paraphernalia.

I'd made it into the back room, which, although not nearly as nicely decorated or put together as Jolene's room, still made me happy. Tall casement windows covered two of the walls, allowing in light that shifted throughout the day, and I'd set up a corner with my guitar and music stand to encourage a renewal of my music-writing passion. I kept telling myself that it would return when I'd finished the renovation and had more time.

"I learned the hard way to make sure to close these windows before dusk. I accidentally left them open to let in some fresh air and left a light on. I had lots of unwanted guests that night. I think I went through an entire can of Raid." I turned around to see that I was talking to myself. I walked back into Jolene's room, where Jaxson had picked up a photo of Jolene blowing out candles on a cake and sur-rounded by a group of smiling people.

He replaced the photo, pausing only a moment to look above the bed at the large poster of Dorothy's ruby slippers and the words "There's No Place Like Home" emblazoned on the bottom, then stopping for a moment longer to examine the fairy wand dangling from the chandelier.

"She's a big fan of *The Wizard of Oz*," I said.

"I can tell. And apparently has a lot of friends."

"And just as many family members. I need to start keeping a list, because it's a long one and I can't remember them all. Especially because most of them are known by nicknames. How many women named Honey can there be in a single family?"

"In the South? I don't think I can count that high." He took a sip from his beer. "But no boyfriend?"

"Not right now. She's single."

"That's surprising. She's, like, the whole package, you know? Beauty and brains. Just like Carly."

My smile faded a bit. "Jolene also knows how to change a tire and is a fabulous cook," I added.

Jaxson nodded and walked past me into the back room. "This is great. I love all the windows."

"Yeah. Me, too. It's why I chose it as the perfect work space. I haven't had the chance to really decorate it yet, so it's just a work in progress. Jolene keeps threatening to make curtains but I don't want to block the light."

He picked up the one framed photo in the room, a picture of me; my dad and Melanie; my aunt Jayne and her husband, Thomas; both sets of grandparents; and JJ and Sarah on the day I graduated from grad school. I kept it there to remind me of what I'd accomplished after a very long and difficult road, and of the people who'd help get me there. "Nice family. You look just like your dad. I probably should have seen the resemblance, since I own every single one of his books in hardcover and his face is on the back of each one."

"I've been told that more than once. I've also been told that I inherited his bullheadedness and love of solving puzzles. Can't have one without the other, I guess.

"And speaking of works in progress, I was wondering if I could ask another favor."

"Sure. As long as Jolene will let me take another plate of cookies home. I'll have to run an extra two miles tomorrow, but it's worth it."

"I'm sure she's already got a plate prepared with your name on it, so it's a deal. Do you remember the big guy you passed on your way into the house today?"

"The gentleman who looks like Mr. Clean."

"Exactly. His name is Thibaut Kobylt, and he spent ten years in prison for manslaughter."

Jaxson raised an eyebrow. "Really? And he's working for you?"

"Not yet. We're both thinking about it." At his questioning look, I said, "Thibaut hasn't decided he wants to work for me. But he's the most qualified person we've met, and Beau's background check on him didn't turn up anything negative."

"Except for the manslaughter part."

"Yeah, that. I'm desperate enough and want to extend him an offer. We agreed to come to a decision by tomorrow morning. Still, I was hoping that you might be able to access the case files—or know someone who can. If I had more time, I'd want to wait until I heard back from you, but I don't have endless reserves of time and money, and, well, my instincts tell me to hire him. The whole time we were together, I didn't get a single creepy vibe. And it's the only blemish—albeit a huge one—on his record. It's like he had this one uncharacteristic manic moment and then returned to normal. It just . . ." I shrugged. "Anyway, I want to know everything I can."

"I get it. I'll see what I can do. Just text me the correct spelling of his name and the year of the crime. Since Beau has already done some digging, he should know. And please ask him to send over any of his notes to give me a head start."

I took a deep breath. "Thank you. If my parents ever find out I hired a convicted felon, I can at least show them I did my due diligence."

"Got it." He turned his attention to my guitar. "You play?" he asked.

"I do. And I write music, too—I've actually had a bit of success selling it. I've just been on a hiatus for a while. With school and the move and now the renovation—it's a bit time-consuming."

"I bet." He bent to read the half-finished first line of a song I'd been working on for months. Turning to me, he said, "Have you had a chance to explore Frenchmen Street in the Marigny yet? The night-time music scene there is really incredible. Lots of known and new talent—and a lot of places have open mic nights that might interest you."

"Beau told me about it, but I haven't been yet." I didn't mention that although I was far enough along in my recovery to be with people in a private setting where people were drinking, I hadn't yet taken the step of being in a bar where music was played and lots of people were imbibing.

He drained the rest of his beer. "We should go—tonight. Snug Harbor is a favorite of mine. So is the Spotted Cat. Actually, they're all good. All of the music venues post their schedules up in their windows, so you can club crawl and hit the acts you want to hear."

"I love the Spotted Cat!" Jolene said from the doorway into the kitchen. I was hoping she hadn't heard our entire conversation. "The live jazz is amazing. We should definitely go tonight, introduce Nola to the music scene in the Marigny—especially since it's in her new neighborhood."

Jaxson and Jolene looked at me hopefully as Jolene put her arm around me. "It will help you relax after your driving lesson. I think you probably need it."

Jolene gave me a squeeze, then began leading Jaxson and me through the kitchen and into the dining room, where a lovely low vase of flowers sat as a centerpiece and the casserole and salad, all beautifully garnished and placed in elegant serving pieces, had been added to the table.

"Y'all have a seat. If you want something other than water, I'll go pour you something. Otherwise, that's bottled water in your glasses, so no need to worry. There's another boil-water advisory right now."

We all sat, and both Jolene and Jaxson placed their napkins in their laps, which reminded me to do the same. Contrary to what Melanie was constantly warning JJ and Sarah, eating cookies before dinner did not spoil my appetite. The "vegan" casserole was amazing, and the salad with the peeled tomatoes and Jolene's homemade dressing tasted like no salad I'd ever had before. Jaxson wondered out loud if it might be the peeled tomatoes that made it so delicious. He accepted two helpings of casserole and salad yet still had room for dessert.

Jaxson insisted on clearing the table while Jolene retrieved the lemon bars and cookies. Wanting to be fair, I took one of each, as did Jaxson, while Jolene helped herself to a small lemon bar. "I'd eat another, but I'm full as a tick and about to pop."

I was, too, but I wasn't going to let that stop me. It was alarming how quickly I'd thrown off the spartan lifestyle I'd brought with me from California to South Carolina. Excess saturated the air in New Orleans, along with the ever-present moisture and the odd mixture of scents that rose from the hot streets, steamed out of kitchen windows, and blew across the city from the Mississippi River. I equated it with the now-familiar scent of Charleston, the signature smell of the rotting vegetation known locally as pluff mud that provided sustenance to the Lowcountry marshes. It made a person either wrinkle their nose or deeply breathe in the magical scent of home. I had been in New Orleans for only a short time, but I had begun doing the latter, recognizing now the pervading perfume of my adopted city. The scent not quite of home but of a newly discovered favorite aunt.

Jaxson wiped his mouth and stood. "Is everyone ready?"

Jolene jumped up. "Absolutely." I wasn't sure if her excitement was about listening to live jazz or the prospect of spending the evening with Jaxson. "I'll drive."

"No," Jaxson and I said together.

"I mean, because your car is so big, which makes it harder to find parking," Jaxson said while I nodded.

We found street parking not far from my house on Dauphine and walked through the neighborhood streets toward Frenchmen. I was already enjoying the quiet neighborhood feel of the Marigny, far enough away from the craziness of the French Quarter and the more touristy sections of the city, but at the center of the live music scene that was at the core of the city's soul.

The night air, although still warm and humid, felt nice on the skin without the blazing heat of the sun. Although I still had the stresses of the whole driving-and-work scenario, as well as the renovation, which was moving at the speed of a herd of turtles (Jolene's words), I felt almost relaxed for the first time in a very long while. I hadn't gone out at night at all since arriving in New Orleans, afraid to admit that I might not be ready. But I was ready now, reminding myself that I was in control.

Jaxson said, "Since we don't have tickets, we'll be in the standing-room area of general admission. Unless my friend Buzz is there. He'll probably want to find us a spot in reserved seating if there is any."

"Buzz?" Jolene asked.

"An old client of mine. He's so grateful for my services that he makes sure I never pay for my drinks." He grinned.

The night got louder as we approached Frenchmen Street, with the sounds of brass instruments and people laughing forming their own chorus spilling out of the various doors along the street. Music fans carrying plastic go-cups milled up and down the street, and lines formed outside of clubs as patrons waited to be admitted.

We approached the Spotted Cat Music Club, where a large crowd waited to be let inside. Jaxson excused himself to find Buzz while Jolene and I stood at the back of the line. I felt a surge of excitement as I remembered going to various gigs at similar clubs in LA with my mom when her love for music was greater than her need to drown her sorrows in whatever substance she could find. Some of my happiest childhood memories were of my mother's face when she performed. I remembered those times now as the only times I'd ever seen her truly happy.

"The last time I was here I heard the Cottonmouth Kings," Jolene gushed. "Oh, my word—I was transported. I love that they haven't gone all commercial and still play some pretty obscure tunes. They rely on the talents of each member, so they don't just amplify the sound like so many other groups do. It's like shouting at someone who doesn't speak your language, you know?"

As she spoke, I casually gazed over the crowd, taking in the eclectic outfits and the diverse nature of the people brought together by music. My gaze passed over a couple at the front of the line, then slid back as I thought I recognized the man. "Is that . . . ?"

I stopped as Beau Ryan turned his head to the woman standing next to him, then brought her closer for an intimate and lingering kiss.

"Is that who?" Jolene asked, her petite stature making it difficult for her to see anything except for the floral shirt of the man standing in front of her.

I couldn't explain my reaction at seeing Beau kissing someone. There was no reason at all why I shouldn't call out his name and wave, then say hello and meet the woman I assumed was his date. Or maybe even his girlfriend. I'd never asked him if he had a girlfriend because it shouldn't have mattered to me. We were business partners and nothing more. I wasn't even sure if I liked him. The sight of him in a romantic embrace shouldn't have bothered me at all. Except that it did.

Grabbing Jolene's arm, I pulled her out of the line. "I'm so sorry, but I don't think I can do it."

"Is it because everyone's drinking?" Jolene asked with a sympathetic expression.

"Yes. It's too soon." I hated using my illness as an excuse, but I had to get away before Beau saw us.

Jolene and I ran into Jaxson as I led her away from the line. "I got three reserved seats," he said, his smile transforming into a frown as he looked closely at me. "Is everything all right?"

Jolene shook her head. "Nola isn't feeling well and we need to get her home."

"Sure. Hang on—let me give these tickets away."

I let out a sigh of relief as he handed them to three people at the back of the line before returning to us and leading us back to the car.

"I'm so sorry," I said during the car ride, feeling horrible and guilty, yet unexplainably happy that I hadn't been forced to speak to Beau.

"No problem. We'll do it again, all right?"

"Sure," I said, turning my face to look out the side window just as we reached my house. We'd almost passed it when I realized I'd seen a man smoking a pipe on my front porch, his head turned in our direction. When it registered that the house was supposed to be vacant, I looked back. But all I could see was the empty front porch and the wind chime swinging violently in the still night air.

CHAPTER 12

For the first time since buying my house, I considered heading directly to the apartment on Broadway after work. I told myself it was because there was nothing I could do at the house until it had been rewired and the plumbing replaced, but I knew it had more to do with not wanting to run into Beau. I had thought of nothing else since the night before on Frenchmen Street. How was I supposed to act when I saw him again? And what should I say?

I eventually talked myself into going to the house, wanting to get facing him over with before the long drive to and from St. Francisville on Monday. Besides, Jolene had left labeled, bagged, and beribboned cookies to take to Thibaut (just in case he decided to accept the job) and Jorge (because it would be rude not to include him) and Trevor (just because). She'd also left a bag of cookies and Hershey's Kisses for me (for being a friend and great roommate), which I'd eaten at my desk for lunch while doing the prerequisite online research prior to my site visit on Monday. I'd felt sick afterward, which at least took my thoughts off of Beau.

Beau had called several times that morning before resorting to texts to let me know that Thibaut had accepted the job working for JR

Properties and been assigned solely to my project. I hadn't felt ready to talk with Beau yet without asking him questions that were none of my business. Questions to which I wasn't even sure why I wanted to know the answers. It was embarrassing and confusing and I didn't have time to examine my feelings. Like I'd taken a page out of Melanie's playbook, I sent Beau a text saying I couldn't talk, telling myself I'd think about my reasons later.

When I met Trevor at our preappointed spot at the corner of Royal and Canal for the bike handover, I noticed the bike now sported a large wicker basket with plastic flowers wired to the front. It reminded me of the bike baskets my school friends had had when I was growing up. I'd been more envious of the baskets than of the bikes, but as my mother had pointed out, I didn't need a basket since we couldn't afford a bike. My little half sister, Sarah, had one and she let me put my phone in it when I took her and JJ for a bike ride around the neighborhood.

"Where'd that come from?" I asked, pointing at the basket.

"I traded it for a bag of box tops with a lady at the Laundromat. I put it on your bike, figuring you needed somewhere to put your stuff."

I smiled. "That was really thoughtful of you." I carefully placed the bags of cookies in the basket before handing Trevor the bag with his name on it. "This is from Jolene. Next time she comes with me, you can thank her in person."

"Yes, ma'am." He grinned when he spotted the handful of chocolate kisses inside the bag.

"Don't forget you're supposed to share with your grandmother and siblings. That's why you get the biggest bag."

He shuffled his feet, his smile fading. "Yes, ma'am." He tilted his head, looking up at me with big brown eyes. "But if Meemaw says I can have hers, I'm allowed, right?"

"Yes, Trevor. But she needs to say so first, before you ask."

Trevor stared at me. "You got psychic powers or somethin', Miss Nola?"

"No. But I do have a little brother about your age, so I'm familiar with how you think." I reached into my backpack and pulled out a ten-dollar bill and handed it to him.

His eyes widened. "I was only gonna charge you five," he said as he quickly took the bill.

"And I thought it was a gift!"

"It is. That's why I wasn't gonna charge you twenty."

I was still laughing as I pedaled down Royal Street, my new basket proudly adorning the front of my bike. After I carefully crossed the divided highway of Esplanade Avenue and began passing the brightly painted cottages of the Marigny, I felt a swell of pride. Not just because this was *my* neighborhood, but also because I had made it this far in my journey.

When I reached my house, I spotted Jorge's and Thibaut's trucks at the curb, as well as a black Mercedes SUV I didn't recognize. The absence of Beau's truck sent through me an alarming amount of relief that I didn't pause to examine.

I carried my bike up the porch steps and then into the front room. Until the house began to resemble a habitable home, it was easier to bring my bike inside than lock it up outside. The house was eerily quiet, with no sounds of men working upstairs and the wind chime on the porch unusually silent. I imagined I smelled the faint scent of pipe tobacco, reminding me of what I'd thought I'd seen on the porch the previous evening.

Ignoring the goose bumps that erupted on my arms at the memory, I walked through to the kitchen. A large and well-used toolbox sat on the floor, a claw hammer lying next to it, both covered in plaster dust. I stepped over the toolbox and peered out the filthy window into the backyard. Bits and pieces of woodwork in various stages of sanding and staining lay scattered on a tarp like wreckage from some horrible accident scene. Which was probably more accurate than I wanted to consider.

I abruptly turned, nearly running into Christopher, who was wearing a long, dark raincoat even though it wasn't raining. My hand flew to my mouth, muffling my scream. "You startled me."

"I'm sorry. I didn't mean to sneak up on you. I have a habit of walking quietly—most likely from working in an antiques store."

I wasn't sure that made any sense, but I had pressing questions. "It's good to see you, but why are you here? Did I forget something?"

"Not at all. Mimi asked me to stop by and see how things were coming along."

"She could have just asked Beau. He was here earlier."

"True. But she wanted me to meet Thibaut—get my take on him. From what I've seen, I like him. And it looks like he knows what he's doing."

"I guess that makes sense—since he's now an official employee of the family company."

"And he and Jorge seem to get along like long-lost brothers. They're both into juggling—did you know that? Ask them to show you their tool-juggling routine, where they throw sharp tools at each other and juggle them. Pretty amazing."

I nodded. "I can't wait to see it."

As if hearing my unasked question, he said, "Mimi has an attachment to the house, as you can imagine. She'll always have a sentimental interest in it, whether or not she still owns it. It was the first rental property Mimi and her husband bought together after they were married in 1964, even though they kept it empty for about a year before renting it, out of respect for Jeanne. Before Beau took over, Mimi handled all the rentals and would personally visit each property, but she never once entered this house. She let Dr. Ryan take care of it. She wanted to keep tabs on it, but it was too hard for her to be more involved because of what had happened here."

"I wonder why they bought it at all, but maybe she felt better knowing it was going to be taken care of, as a way of honoring her friend. I hope you conveyed to her that the house is in good hands. And will make a great home for me as soon as I can fix it up."

Christopher nodded, looking behind me toward the denuded kitchen. "Jolene stopped by the store yesterday to give me something for Beau and mentioned that your family is planning a visit in October." He returned his attention to me. "I guess they won't be staying here then."

I almost laughed. "My stepmother can be a little high maintenance and appreciates her creature comforts. Like running water and electricity. She also enjoys room service and fluffy robes. So no. Not here and definitely not at my apartment uptown. I don't want to witness the power struggle between Melanie and Jolene about the organization of silverware in the drawers and the placement of furniture. Not to mention that I don't do room service. My brother and sister might find it fun camping out on the floor in my room, though, as long as Jolene doesn't mind. I guess I need to start thinking about it. Melanie has a long list of requirements, so it might take me a while."

The floorboards above us creaked, but neither one of us looked up. "It's an old house," I said.

His amber-colored gaze remained on me, but he didn't say anything.

"I've been receiving a lot of unsolicited help from Melanie's friend Sophie, who is a professor of historic preservation in Charleston. There's only one piece of advice I've really paid attention to. She told me that each old house has its own language, and that eventually I'll learn to speak it fluently."

Christopher smiled. "I like that."

"And about my family's visit, would it be all right if I hid my bike at the store while my parents are here? I will never hear the end of it if they learn I've been pedaling through the French Quarter on a bike and not wrapping myself in Bubble Wrap. It's just easier for them to assume I walk everywhere."

"I'll ask Mimi. It shouldn't be a problem, though. She'll be back tomorrow, so I'll let you know. Or you could just tell your parents. You're an adult now, you know."

I looked at him to see if he might be joking so I could laugh, but then I remembered he'd never met Melanie and Jack. "Right," I said. "Or we can store it out of sight for the duration of their visit."

"Sure," he said slowly. "Now, as far as hotels are concerned, I highly recommend the Hotel Peter and Paul. You've probably seen it—it's right down the street in the Marigny, on the corner of Mandeville and Burgundy. It used to be a church, school, convent, and rectory, all built around 1860, but was abandoned a couple of decades ago. It was real sad seeing that happen. I grew up with some of the kids who went there. The restoration and reuse of the buildings are nothing short of a miracle. The convent has been converted into an ice-cream parlor called Sundae Best. Great handcrafted ice cream with traditional and New Orleans flavors. I highly recommend the Cold Testament Sundae. I don't believe they have any vegan options, though—but the rest of your family might enjoy it."

My mouth had actually started watering. "Right. I'll definitely check it out. Quick question: Are the guest rooms anywhere in or near the church area? Like, where there were once funerals?"

"I don't think so, but I could find out."

I shook my head. "I'll go check it out myself. Melanie sometimes has a hard time sleeping in places where those that should be sleeping . . . well, aren't."

Christopher grinned. "She might have trouble sleeping in New Orleans, then."

Anticipating my next question, he said, "Jorge and Thibaut will be right back. They've been tearing through the walls and dismantling the plumbing in the upstairs bathroom and they needed to get some air. They've got all the windows open and the fans blowing, but they recommended that I don't go up there right now."

"Good advice. Do you know if they've managed to open up that door at the top of the stairs?"

His eyebrows shot up. "A locked door?"

"I think it's just a closet, but it's been nailed shut. Not sure when, but it was that way the first time I ever saw the house."

Christopher scratched the back of his head. "Since Mimi never came inside the house, she wouldn't have known. And because rental properties often have owners' closets, the tenants wouldn't have reported it." He started to climb the stairs to get a look, then stopped abruptly and retreated. He waved his hand in front of his nose. "On second thought, I'll wait."

"Beau doesn't know, either. He said he's never had a key to that door—not that it matters, since it's nailed shut—and was told that it's full of junk. But since there are no other closets upstairs at all, it would be nice to be able to use that one."

The front door opened and Thibaut and Jorge entered, chattering in Portuguese. The difference in their heights was almost comical, but the expressions on their faces weren't. "What's wrong?" I asked.

Thibaut said, "Another gris-gris showed up on the doorstep this morning and Jorge thinks we need to get the house blessed by a priest."

Both Thibaut and Jorge looked at me expectantly. I should have anticipated that buying a house in New Orleans would be anything but normal. "Was it good gris-gris?" I asked, not even sure what it was I was asking.

"Yes, ma'am. And I explained that to Jorge, but he still thinks the house needs a priest."

I took a long and measured breath. "Please tell him that I'll think about it, but before I get anyone to bless this house, it needs floors and walls so that there's actually something to bless. And running water. Electricity would also be a bonus."

Thibaut spoke to Jorge in rapid Portuguese until Jorge nodded and let out a deeply aggrieved sigh that would have been understood in any language. I chose that moment to retrieve the two bags of cookies from my basket and give one each to the two workmen. "Don't worry—I didn't make them, so they're safe to eat." Despite Thibaut's translation for Jorge, neither man looked completely convinced. As if a woman who was proficient with a hammer couldn't also be handy in a kitchen. Which, in my case, was completely accurate. But they hadn't seen Jolene in action yet.

"Welcome aboard," I said, offering my hand to Thibaut. "I can't tell you how happy I am that you accepted the job."

His paw of a hand swallowed mine, but despite being firm, the shake was surprisingly gentle. I wondered if he'd practiced this or if he'd simply learned over the years that people expected him to give a bone-crushing shake. "Yes, ma'am. I'm not gonna lie. It was very hard to say yes after seeing the condition of this place. But then Beau told me that the house was one step away from demolition before you saw it, and I admire your determination. Some might call it stupidity, but I'm a big believer in slim chances."

"Thanks," I said slowly, unclear if that was supposed to be a pep talk or a scolding. I somehow doubted he'd ever coached a kids' sports team.

"Well," Christopher said. "I've got to get back to the shop for a late delivery. Glad to see you've got everything in hand, Nola, and it was nice to meet you, Thibaut." With a brief wave he exited through the front door, his raincoat billowing behind him.

After being told that the men were going to take a couple loads of corroded pipes out to the dumpster before calling it a day and didn't need my help, I reluctantly left. As I mounted my bike, I waved across the street to Ernest and Bob, who were taking turns pulling on Belle's leash to get her out the gate for a walk. She was lying on her belly and squashing the skirt of her ballerina tutu, with all four paws stretched out like a beached starfish. Just heavier and bigger and apparently glued to the ground.

"We got some good gumbo on the stove, if you need a bite to eat," Bob said.

"Thanks, Bob, but I've got to get home. Lots of homework to do for my real job, and my roommate is making 'vegan' spaghetti and meatballs. Basically, regular spaghetti, but the meatballs are made of vegetables and cheese."

"Yummy," said Bob, making a face. "You do know that's vegetarian and not vegan, right?"

"Yes, I know that, but she doesn't."

"Shouldn't you tell her?"

"Yeah, probably. But I don't want to hurt her feelings. She's so nice, it would be sort of like kicking a puppy."

Ernest leaned down and picked up Belle, who was starting to resemble a potbellied pig instead of a small dog, and held her close.

"It's just a figure of speech, Ernest. I would never kick a dog. I've got my own dogs at home and I love them."

Bob rolled his eyes at his partner. "We know. We've seen a lot of their photos on your phone. Well, you have a good evening, and if you change your mind about the gumbo, I'm going to freeze the leftovers." He walked closer to the fence. "Oh, and, Nola? Was there somebody at your house last night? When I got up to use the little boys' room at around two a.m., I saw that the lamp in the upstairs window was on."

I thought about telling him that I didn't have a lamp upstairs or anywhere in the house, nor did I have electricity. "No, but thanks for letting me know. I'm guessing one of the workers left it on."

"I figured." He gave an exaggerated shiver. "I hope you don't mind me saying this, but there's something about your house that's not all right. It just sort of stares at us from across the street, you know? Maybe once you fix it up it will start looking normal. And when it's all ready, Ernest and I would love to throw you a 'welcome to the neighborhood' party, right, Ernest?"

Ernest, still clutching Belle, took his time before nodding. "Right. And we can have the party at our house."

I frowned. "But wouldn't it make more sense to have it at my house so I can show off the renovation?"

Ernest and Bob shared a look. "Why don't we cross that bridge when we come to it, all right? From the looks of it, we've got plenty of time." Ernest moved closer to Bob and whispered something in his ear. Bob faced me again. "Also, Nola? I'm guessing that's your grandpa we've seen on the front porch smoking his pipe? Please let him know that secondhand smoke is a thing, and we'd appreciate it if he would smoke in the backyard?" He smiled to let me know he was just being neighborly and not antagonistic. They were good neighbors, with the free food and with the bagged dog poop they religiously removed from the sidewalks, and I wanted them to know that I appreciated them.

"Of course. I'll let him know." I waved again and began pedaling away before they could say anything else. Unless they wanted to tell me that my roof was falling in or that the downstairs was on fire. Anything except for the confirmation that my house was indeed inhabited by restless spirits who were getting bolder in letting their presence be known. I could replace old mortar in a brick wall and remove plaster ceiling medallions without a single crack, but I was ill equipped to eradicate residents who were reluctant to leave. I just wasn't sure what was worse—ignoring the problem until all hell broke loose, or asking for help.

I put my earbuds in and blasted music so I wouldn't have to think about it at all.

CHAPTER 13

On my way home, I managed to find a seat next to an open window at the back of the crowded streetcar. As I'd passed off my bike to Trevor at our designated spot, I commented on the melted chocolate on his cheek. He promised me that he'd had only one chocolate kiss after handing out the rest to his grandmother and siblings. Because his smile was so endearing, I chose to believe him.

I closed my eyes for a moment, enjoying the sticky breeze blowing on my face as the streetcar rocked inelegantly on its tracks. Across the aisle a loud conversation between two women—obviously tourists—was all about how hot it was in New Orleans (news flash) and how the trolleys should be air-conditioned. Each time one of them said the word "trolley" my toes curled tightly in my shoes. I stuck my earbuds in my ears to block them out, turning my attention to a series of texts that began popping up on my screen one after another.

The first was from Jaxson, saying he'd e-mailed all the photos he'd taken at the house and asking me to let him know what I thought. That was followed by another message from him, reminding me about brunch at Patois with his uncle Bernie on Sunday; Jaxson might join us if that was okay. The third text was from Jolene, asking me if I was on my way home and whether I had seen Jaxson's photos yet. This was followed by a string of a redheaded emojis making the *Scream* face. The fourth was from Beau and I considered not opening it, but, like pulling off a Band-Aid, I swiped my thumb across the screen.

do u have T's hammer

I read it twice to make sure I understood before I replied. No it was in kitchen i didnt move it

I waited while three dots danced on my screen, then disappeared. My thumbs hesitated over the screen, as I wanted to find out more, but I changed my mind about replying. The hammer must have been mis-placed and, because I'd been there, Thibaut assumed I had it. But I didn't. End of conversation.

I clicked on my phone's mail icon and opened Jaxson's e-mail but quickly grew frustrated trying to download pictures with no Wi-Fi. I closed it out and after a moment's hesitation I clicked on the podcast icon. I had downloaded the most recent episodes of Beau's podcast, *Bumps in the Night and Other Improbabilities*, shortly after I ran into Beau at the house on Dauphine, but I had yet to listen to any of them. I was oddly hesitant to allow his voice to follow me into other aspects of my life like a ghost that didn't know how to find the light.

Even when Beau and I had both lived in Charleston and his podcast was just starting out, I'd had no interest in listening to him discredit people who called themselves psychic. It's why he'd sought out Mela-nie in Charleston. And after the night of the fire, when we'd all almost died, he'd said that Melanie and her sister, Jayne, were the only authen-tic psychics he'd ever met, and he continued his crusade to out frauds on his weekly podcast. From what Jolene had told me, his motives seemed to revolve around exposing those who charged exorbitant fees for their services, which, to be fair, seemed valid. Yet I couldn't under-stand his dedication to the same subject after so many years.

I hit play and began listening to the intro music—something with an urgent beat produced by trumpets in an homage to New Orleans, and a haunting melody carried by violins. The music faded as Beau introduced his podcast partner, Sam Beck. I sat up straighter when a woman began speaking. When Beau had casually mentioned his partner's name in past conversations, I had assumed Sam was a guy. It took me a few minutes of listening to realize that "Sam" was short for "Samantha" and she was definitely not a guy. I didn't have to dwell on my mistake, as I quickly grew interested in their discussion of updates in recent unsolved crimes where psychics had been involved.

Beau and Sam played the "good cop / bad cop" rules of interrogation, whereby Sam offered explainable reasons for missed predictions and Beau came right out and called the psychics frauds. I found myself smiling at their banter until it occurred to me that their on-air interactions hinted at an intimacy not usually found between cohosts. I Googled Sam's name to find a picture, doing my best to tap my screen with accuracy despite the swaying of the streetcar.

The first link was for her Facebook page, her profile picture showing Sam and Beau in bathing suits on a tropical beach somewhere and telling me all I needed to know. She was the same brunette I'd seen kissing Beau at the club on Frenchmen Street, and while the revelation should have meant absolutely nothing to me, I found myself reading Sam's profile—from Memphis, communications degree from Loyola, employed at the Ritz in the PR and communications department—and in a relationship. Of course she was. I found myself scrolling down her page, looking at pictures of Sam with a large array of family and friends doing the kinds of things I had once done. She reminded me of my best friends from Charleston, Alston and Lindsey—funny, smart, kind, and fun to be around. Sam was probably someone I could hang out with, maybe become close friends with. The thought of that gave me a sour feeling in my stomach, like the one I got sitting in the dentist's waiting room.

My attention was brought back to the podcast by a drumroll followed by a spooky musical interlude before Sam's voice came on again. "And now for our weekly segment 'Name That Psychic Ability: Truth or Fiction.' Last week Beau and I had a lively discussion, and a record number of listener calls weighing in, on levitation. I gave it ten little ghosties, because I think it's a legitimate psychic phenomenon, but Beau gave it zero because he thinks it's all a load of—" The word was beeped out by a loud cymbal clash followed by the sound of a dog bark.

Sam continued. "So, now it's time to spin the wheel and choose a listener-provided topic for this week." I heard the sound of a large wheel being spun—like in *Wheel of Fortune*—clicking fast at first before slowing to a stop. "And . . . it looks like we've got psychometry on the table today, submitted by David Bishop from Texas. Good one, David. Let's have Beau read the definition so we all know what we're talking about."

"Or we could just skip it because this sounds pretty bogus. Psychometry is the ability to gain insight or information about someone by touching an object associated with that person. I'm going to go ahead and give this zero ghosties."

"Feel free to ignore him, listeners—I know I'm going to. Please call, e-mail, or text your thoughts and experiences for us to discuss in the next half of the show while we hear a word from today's sponsor." She began rattling off the phone number but was suddenly cut off as my phone shut down, the battery drained. I tossed my phone and earbuds into my backpack and listened to the women across from me continuing their conversation about trolleys and the heat, until we stopped at the intersection of St. Charles and Broadway and I got out.

There were vehicles parked along the curb on both sides of Broadway, and groups of young people walked around with go-cups. Living on the section of Broadway that was called "fraternity row" because of all of the Greek houses was pretty manageable except on the weekends, when there were endless rounds of parties. Jolene had gifted me with a set of pink earplugs and a matching silk sleeping mask since my bedroom faced Broadway. Despite telling myself I would never use either, they now held an important spot on my bedside table.

The Phi Chis across the street were holding their annual luau, and a truckload of sand had been dumped onto their front yard and driveway to go along with the theme. Palm trees were draped with paper-flower leis, and tiki torches lit the way to the backyard and pool. Jolene and I had been invited via a flyer slid through the mail slot, but despite the dubious lure of piña coladas in real coconuts and of a hula competition, we had agreed we'd have more fun at home eating popcorn and bingeing on true-crime television.

As I jogged up the stairs I was already thinking about what we should watch, not paying attention until I'd reached the top and opened the door and it was too late to retreat and hide. Beau stood next to Jolene at the dining table, an open laptop in front of them, a plate of homemade pralines next to the laptop.

It took me a moment to school my face into a neutral expression, no longer sure how I was supposed to act in front of Beau-with-a-girlfriend. The longer I considered how utterly ridiculous I was being, the more awkward I felt.

"Hey," I said, casually tossing my backpack in the direction of the sofa as I walked past, hearing it miss and smack the coffee table. "Were we expecting you?" A bolt of fear flashed through me. "You're not here for another driving lesson, are you? Because there are a lot of pedestrians out now, and it's getting dark. . . ."

"No, not that."

When Beau didn't smile, I said, "Is this about Thibaut's hammer? Because I really don't know . . ."

"No. I brought something for you in my truck—the Maison Blanche door. Mimi asked me to remove it in any way I saw fit, so I thought I'd bring it here since you have plenty of room. I figured I could find a frat boy looking for some easy cash to help haul it upstairs."

"Okay, but—"

"Mimi is very particular about her storage room at the shop. She has her own way of organizing things and doesn't want anything disturbed. Christopher knew better, so I have no idea what he was thinking, but Mimi wasn't happy when she found it in there."

"I feel terrible. I didn't mean for this to be such a problem. It just made sense because the shop is close by and I'd seen the storage room at the back and Christopher said he was going to remove it to remote storage right away—"

Beau cut me off again. "No harm done. We'll store it here, so problem solved." He turned to the laptop, ending the conversation. "Jolene was just showing me the pictures Jaxson took at your house."

"Did you look at them yet?" Jolene bit her lower lip while her fingers worried the pearls at her neck.

I felt suddenly nervous. It's not that I didn't have strong suspicions that I wasn't ever really alone in the house. There are just some things that are easier to ignore if you don't have any proof that they exist.

I shook my head. "They were taking too long to load, so I figured I'd look when I got home. Is that what you're looking at?" I indicated the laptop with my chin.

Jolene nodded. "I think your house has a lot of memories." She leaned forward and tapped a few keys before sliding the laptop so it faced me. "I've separated three of the photos that I think you'll find interesting."

I leaned in, studying the photos on the screen. The first was taken from the stairs, pointing upward from the bottom step, the sealed door at the top barely visible because of two large orbs of light seeming to hover like puffs of breath in the middle of the stairwell. I pulled back. "That could just be dust on the lens, though. Or a bug. Right?"

"It could be. Except that the pictures taken right before and after are clear—it's just this one." Jolene got closer, using her fingers on the touchpad to enlarge the picture. "There's definitely some sort of shape inside each one, although the one on the right just looks like some kind of a cloud. But this one . . ." She moved the cursor to the orb on the left side and made the image even bigger. "In this one you can almost make out a face, right?" With a pink-tipped fingernail she pointed to the screen. "Like, here you can make out two eyes, and you can see a little bit of a nose shape, and then darker lips. Definitely a face, I think."

I wanted to disagree, to say that it was only a dust mote that happened to look like a human face, just to play devil's advocate, like most people do when confronted with anything that doesn't fit into their scope of understanding. Except that my scope of understanding during the last dozen years of my life had widened so much that things like orbs and bumps in the night were now as ordinary as electricity and peanut butter and jelly sandwiches.

"And these make me feel like a raw gizzard is being dropped down my back every time I look at them." Jolene hit an arrow on the screen to show two photos of the front of the house. She expanded the photo on the left to expose the distinct outline of a woman with dark hollows where her eyes should have been, staring back at the photographer. "See what I mean?" she said, giving a shudder as if a gizzard—whatever that was—was slowly slithering down her back. Jolene slid a finger over the touchpad and slid the cursor to the second photo. "This one's almost as creepy."

I pulled the laptop closer. This photo was also taken in front of the house, but of the porch, and focused on the same spot where I'd seen the man standing the previous night. In the photo, a distinct curl of smoke wafted ribbonlike toward the porch ceiling, in the same pattern made from a burning pipe. But no man—or pipe—was visible.

"Last night," I said, "when we were driving home with Jaxson, I thought I saw a man smoking a pipe on my porch. But when I turned back, no one was there."

Beau sent me an odd look, as if remembering something, and I wished I hadn't said anything about the previous night.

I turned back to the laptop and crossed my arms. "There's really no logical explanation for any of these, is there?" I took a deep breath, confident that neither Beau nor Jolene would be surprised by my theory. "Except a paranormal one. Which is to be expected, I guess. A young woman lost her life in the house and the murderer was never caught. Whether or not you believe that sort of thing is real, that would make even me want to haunt a place."

"Aren't you scared?" Jolene asked. "I mean, I've felt cold spots in my house in Mississippi, and heard footsteps, but I always figured that was just the house reminding me that it's been through some things. But I've never seen anything like"—she waved her hands at the screen—"this. I mean, it's a full-bodied apparition, and Jaxson swears there was nobody there when he snapped the photo. I'm just wondering if . . ." She stopped.

"If what?" I prompted.

"If they're here because they need help. My grandmama would say these sorts of things happen because they weren't laid to rest properly— but she's a funeral director, so you have to take what she's saying with a grain of salt. But my cousin Earl—sweet as pie but definitely only has one oar in the water—says all wandering spirits need help moving on. I'm wondering if that's poor Jeanne in the window and she's asking us for help. Which gives me goose bumps thinking about why that man might be here."

I turned around at the sound of snapping, realizing that it was Beau pulling on the rubber band around his wrist. When he caught me looking at him he stopped, then reached forward and closed the laptop. "I suggest you delete those photos so there's no chance of them getting out. You don't need your house to become some freak show for the ghost-hunting tourism crowd. And it certainly isn't part of the brand for JR Properties. I'll ask Jaxson to delete them, too."

I studied him closely. "I thought you said you didn't believe in ghosts."

His eyes darkened. "I've never said that. I've only ever said that the majority of people claiming to be able to communicate with them are frauds. There's a big difference." He ran his hand through his hair, more agitated than I'd ever seen him. Except once. "And if you're looking for someone to talk to them, don't bother. In all the years I've been looking for someone to help find my parents and my sister, I've all but run through my inheritance. Which pretty much proves that they're all a bunch of quacks." He nodded in my direction. "Except for Melanie and her sister, Jayne. They're the real thing. But they live in Charleston, and you claim that bumps in the night don't bother you, so I suggest moving on."

I stared at him. "Is that why you do your podcast? Because of what you went through?"

He didn't say anything. Because he didn't have to.

"I'm sorry. I didn't know."

He looked away for a long moment, his attention drawn to the princess phone sitting on the corner of the desk, its cord unhooked from the wall and dangling on the floor. When he turned back to us, his face was neutral. "That's because you never asked."

"I'm sorry," I said again, because I couldn't think of anything else to say.

With measured words, he said, "I need you to understand something. Let the dead stay dead. Nothing good can come from digging up the past. Mimi agreed to sell you the house because the house's past didn't bother you. So let it go. Please."

He picked up the car keys he'd left on the desk. "I'm going to bring that door inside now. Figure out where you want it, and please prop the doors open."

Jolene picked up the plate of pralines. "I'll put these in a couple of Baggies for you and your helper. What color ribbon would you like?"

I gave her a look that turned her smile to a grimace; then she disappeared into the kitchen just as the phone on the desk rang shrilly. I watched as Beau's gaze traveled down the unplugged telephone cord before meeting my eyes, a definite challenge in his eyes. Slowly, I lifted the receiver.

"Hello? Who is this?"

The voice sounded far away, separated by space and time, filled with air and the murmur of hundreds of indecipherable words spoken in the background. And then a scratch in the atmosphere, and a gathering of molecules to form a single word came through the phone to my ear, loud enough for Beau to hear. *Adele.*

Beau shook his head, his face suddenly pale. He took the receiver from me and shouted into it. "Mom? It's me. It's Beau. Where are you?"

The dial tone droned loudly from the receiver until I took it from his hand and hung up. His eyes met mine for a moment. "That didn't just happen." He shook his head. "That couldn't have just happened." He took two steps backward before turning around and heading toward the stairs.

I moved to follow him to turn on the stairwell lights but stopped when I noticed a single set of a woman's wet footprints on the wooden treads, following Beau down the stairs.

CHAPTER 14

Bubba jerked and bucked over the potholed asphalt of Henry Clay Avenue, a street that looked like it had been attacked with mortar shells. I wanted to ask Jolene if the streets in New Orleans ever got repaved, but I was clenching my jaw so I wouldn't break any teeth. I tried to admire the eclectic architecture in the Uptown neighborhood—all styles from shotgun singles and raised Greek Revival cottages to full-on Queen Anne Victorians and everything in between—on our way to brunch with Uncle Bernie, but the wavelike motion of the car was making me seasick and I had to close my eyes.

"We're here." Jolene brought the car to an abrupt stop in front of a corner building at the intersection of Laurel and Webster. Blue French doors with, on the upper half, glass windows with a gold *P* in elegant script opened up to the sidewalk, where red bistro tables clustered to one side, under an awning. The name Patois, in matching blue, appeared in the large side windows facing the two streets.

"This is adorable, but are you sure we're in the right place?"

Jolene gave me one of her looks, probably learned from her grandmother, usually reserved for customers who wanted to choose the least expensive option for their dearly departed. "Just because he used to be a policeman doesn't mean he only eats at doughnut shops."

"You're right—sorry. I assume he lives nearby?"

"He actually lives in the Irish Channel neighborhood, but he said he'd been wanting to try Patois for a while."

"Uh-huh. Did he choose the restaurant before or after Jaxson told him I was paying?" I held up my hand before she could scold me. "I know. You're right. He's doing us a huge favor, so I'm not going to complain. I could always sell a kidney if I run out of money."

She rolled her eyes. "I need to park Bubba, so go on inside and I'll meet you there. We're a few minutes late, so Jaxson and his uncle might already be there."

"Don't take too long," I said with meaning. Even though we'd just left the apartment, I knew she'd want to refresh her hair and makeup since she was about to see Jaxson.

"Please close the door, Nola. Lord only knows what this humidity is doing to my hair, and I've probably talked off all of my lipstick." Jolene was already pulling away before my door was completely shut.

I sighed with happiness after walking through the front doors, admiring the meticulously refinished narrow-slat wooden floors, high ceilings, heavy moldings, and spinning fans. What had most likely once been a corner grocery and residence or neighborhood bar had been reborn into an iconic New Orleans restaurant in a city known for its iconic restaurants. The reappropriation of historic buildings for current use made my heart sing. The sight of the white-cloth-draped tables had the opposite effect. I could have sworn I felt the wallet in my backpack attempt an escape.

I smiled at the man at the podium in the front. "Table for four under the name Jaxson Landry?"

"Ah, yes," he said. "Follow me. The lady and gentleman are already here and have started with a cocktail."

I wasn't sure which confused me more—the mention of a lady or of drinking a cocktail at eleven in the morning. And then I remembered I was in New Orleans. The man led me to a table at the back of a side room filled with happy diners and calmly rotating ceiling fans. A white-haired gentleman with dark bushy brows, a strong Irish chin, and the heavy build of a linebacker stood as I approached; in front of him was a double old-fashioned glass filled with what looked like bourbon on the rocks.

I held out my hand. "I'm Nola Trenholm, and you must be Bernard Landry."

Instead of shaking my hand he took it, cupped it between his own hands, and squeezed gently. "It's so very nice to meet you, Nola. And please call me Uncle Bernie—everyone does. In fact, I can no longer remember how many actual nieces and nephews I have." He grinned, exposing perfectly white dentures.

"And this young lady," he said, indicating the striking-looking woman with dark blond hair, "is Carly Mouton."

She stood, too, and shook my hand. "I'm Jolene's friend. She's told me so much about you."

"Likewise," I said, deliberately not mentioning that our conversations were usually about Carly and Jaxson.

"Jaxson had a big case dumped on him, so he's working even though it's Sunday," Carly explained. "He asked me to drive Uncle Bernie. I hope you don't mind."

Bernie shook his head. "Not that I need a chauffeur. I'm perfectly fine driving myself. It's not my fault the streets are narrow and people park on both sides and that tourists jaywalk."

Carly raised her eyes to the ceiling as she helped Bernie back into his seat. Talking about bad drivers made me think of Jolene. I needed to warn her that Carly was there instead of Jaxson, so she'd be prepared, but she must have found a parking spot nearby—or parked on top of three smaller cars—because she appeared at the table, her lipstick fresh and her nose powdered.

"Carly!" she shouted with an enthusiasm that even I believed. "It's so great to see you! Did you come with Jaxson?" I saw the disappointment in her eyes as she glanced down at the table for any sign of him.

"Sadly, no. He had to work. But it's been so long since I've seen you, and I've been dying to meet Nola, so I jumped at the chance to bring Uncle Bernie."

Carly made the introductions and I watched as Jolene smiled at Bernie. "I can see where Jaxson gets his good looks," she said.

Carly turned to Jolene with a surprised expression. "You never mentioned that you thought Jaxson was good-looking."

Jolene casually placed her napkin on her lap. "Haven't I? Well, he has auburn hair, which probably makes me partial."

Jolene pointed to Carly's cocktail glass filled with something pink and garnished with a lime. "What are you drinking?"

"It's awesome. It's called a What-a-melon and it's got watermelon vodka and God only knows what else but it's amazing." She waved her hand in the air and a waiter appeared. "Can you please get two of these for my friends?"

"Just water for me," I corrected. I turned to Jolene with a meaningful look that I hoped would remind her of the night Beau had had to drive us home. She'd sworn off alcohol for life the following day and, to my knowledge, hadn't touched a drop since, but Carly's presence might be called an emergency.

"I'll have one, please," Jolene said. "Just one, though."

Our waiter handed us menus and I didn't even pretend to look for vegan items, focusing instead on the right-hand column listing the prices.

"Do you come here often?" I asked Bernie.

"Never been. I'm a bit of a foodie, though, and I've been reading about Patois for a while, but never had a chance to come. The wife's more of a meat-and-potatoes kind of gal, and a heck of a good cook, but she doesn't like going out to eat. Especially anyplace that's pricey like this."

I waited to see if he might laugh, but he was already perusing his menu. When the waiter returned, Bernie ordered the grilled hanger steak and eggs (the most expensive item on the menu) and another bourbon on the rocks. Jolene ordered the heirloom garden salad, and

I ordered a cup of the seasonal gumbo, mostly because it was one of the cheapest things on the menu.

"Is that all you're going to eat?" Bernie asked. "At least get an appetizer or you'll leave hungry. And that's a sin in this city and should be an arrestable offense." He looked back at his menu. To the waiter, he said, "I've read great things about your pancake appetizer, so you can bring one of those for her to start." He indicated me with his chin. "And you, Carly?"

"I'll have the same salad Jolene's having." She paused, glancing at her menu again before saying, "Actually, since I can afford the calories, I'm going to change that to the duck pâté to start, and then the shrimp and grits." She smiled at the waiter before thrusting her menu at him like a challenge.

"And add a side of biscuits for the table, if you wouldn't mind," Bernie said as he handed the waiter his menu.

I eyed Jolene's glass as she took her first sip from her cocktail, and for the first time since becoming sober I felt a strong need for a drink. If the restaurant's drinks hadn't been so expensive, I might have been even more tempted.

We continued our small talk after the plates of food were delivered and I discovered that what Patois considered a pancake appetizer with blueberry compote was actually a dinner-plate-sized piece of fluffy heaven with a dollop of whipped cream on top. When I raised my spoon to eat my gumbo, Jolene stopped me. "Did you ask them to make it vegan and take out the sausage?"

Carly let out an inelegant snort, which was at odds with her silk blouse and perfect hair, which looked like it had never met humidity. "Don't you mean vegetarian? Because that's no meat. Vegan is pretty much anything animal related, including dairy. And the way Nola attacked that pancake makes me think she couldn't be vegan."

Jolene speared a piece of lettuce with her fork, glancing at me with a glint in her eye that matched her grin. "I know. But I didn't want to hurt Nola's feelings by explaining the difference."

I had made the mistake of taking a sip of my water, which now came out my nose as I laughed and choked at the same time, the sound accompanied by Jolene's attempts to stifle her own snorts and giggles. We sounded like a two-sow band in a pig trough and the mental image made me choke/laugh even harder. Carly stared at us as if we'd gone a little crazy.

Carly's phone, placed faceup on the table, rang with the old eighties anthem "Everybody Wants You" and she snatched it up before it had reached the second line. Her smile grew as she listened for a moment. Lowering her phone, she said, "It's Jaxson. He just wanted to say hi to everyone, but I need to talk to him. Would you all excuse me? I might be a while, so I'll take it outside." She picked up her drink but left most of her food uneaten.

The waiter returned to clear our plates. "Will the young lady be returning?" he asked, indicating Carly's mostly untouched food.

"No," Jolene said at the same time I said, "She's done. Please put it in a to-go bag." I wasn't going to let the food go to waste and it would fit easily into my backpack.

As soon as the plates were cleared, the waiter handed us more menus. "Dessert?" he asked with a hopeful smile.

Both Jolene and I shook our heads without even looking, but Uncle Bernie said, "I read that I need to try the Black Forest dessert. And give me a nice big portion and extra plates and forks so I can share." He held up his empty glass and shook it. "And another one of these, please. Ladies?"

"We're good," Jolene and I said in unison. "Just water. With lemon," I added.

The waiter hid any disappointment as he took away our menus, which, if I'd had the kind of money to be a big tipper, would have made me add extra to his tip.

"So," Uncle Bernie said, brushing invisible crumbs off the white tablecloth. "Let's talk cold cases. Jaxson said you needed me to do a little digging on a new employee." He rubbed his hands together. "I'm not gonna lie. I love this stuff. Keeps me mentally active in my retirement, ya know?" He tapped his head. "I've still got it, and I want to keep it."

"Great," I said. "Even though it's not a cold case. Thibaut Kobylt admitted killing his wife. I just wanted to know if there might have been anything in his past that should make me reconsider hiring him."

Bernie laced his thick fingers together, his blue eyes unblinking. I wondered if he'd perfected that stare over years of being in the police force. "Well, to answer your question, I don't think you need to have any worries about Mr. Kobylt. Everything I've read, with the exception of the murder rap, points to a real stand-up guy. He coached basketball for developmentally delayed children for six years, along with being a class parent for Greg—his son—throughout elementary school. He also dressed up as Santa Claus each year for a big community Christmas party for disadvantaged kids."

He held up his hand as I sucked in my breath to prepare for a rebuttal. "I know what you're about to say. Sure, there are serial murderers who also did good deeds at some point in their lives, but I also read through the testimonies of neighbors and friends of the Kobylts who'd known the family for years. That's usually where you'll find the truth in cases like this. They were a loving family, always doing things together. Going to church every Sunday, that sort of thing. And every Saturday he and Greg would mow the lawns and take care of a little maintenance for several of their elderly neighbors without charge."

"Yet he killed his wife," I reminded him.

"But did he?" Bernie paused, bushy eyebrows held aloft.

"Well, he said he did, right?"

"He did plead guilty when he was asked by the judge. But there is nothing in the written record where he says independently that he killed his wife. Yeah, I know that doesn't mean anything in a court of law. But the facts say that the family had lived in the neighborhood with the same neighbors for fifteen years, and they never saw him have an angry outburst. Not once. From looking through the interviews with the neighbors, I found there were lots of varied opinions about who might have killed Mrs. Thibaut, but not one of them thought it could have been her husband."

Uncle Bernie's wooden chair creaked beneath him as he leaned back and the waiter placed his dessert in front of him, along with a fresh drink. Two extra plates and forks were slid in front of us, along with fresh glasses of water and a bag containing Carly's boxed-up meal. I casually opened my backpack and slid it inside, happy that Uncle Bernie was focused on this dessert.

"You're forgetting one important thing, though," I said. "The gun. When they found it inside a garbage can a few blocks away, his handprints were on it."

Bernie nodded, chewing slowly. "That's true. And I'm sure that's why everyone thought this was a cut-and-dried case. But here's a guy who by all accounts was a gentle giant and loved his family and the people in his community and they loved him. If a guy is going to snap once and only once in his life, why murder? And why his wife? Sure, we don't know what goes on behind closed doors, but in fifteen years no one ever heard a harsh word between Thibaut and wife. And then one day—bam." He accented the word with a thump of his fist on the table, making our plates rattle.

He put another bite of dessert into his mouth and chewed, then washed it down with a swallow of bourbon. "So, in answer to your question, I don't expect you to have any problems with him working for you. Even his parole officer told me he was the nicest guy he'd ever met—in both his personal and professional life. I'd just be curious to know the whole story. Not that it matters, of course. He's moved on. But to tell you the truth, I'd like to keep digging, just because I need something to keep me busy. And also because I don't quite believe that he did it. And if he didn't, then who did?"

"Well, that's a story that will keep me up at night pondering," Jolene said, adjusting herself in her chair so she wouldn't have to look at the cake.

"Me, too. Beau said that Thibaut's wife's family won't let him see his son, so it's like he's still being punished." It unsettled me, like I'd just read a book where the last pages had been removed.

I took a sip of water and turned my attention to Bernie. "You mentioned cold cases—plural. Were you able to turn up anything new about the Jeanne Broussard case?"

"I do believe I did. Jaxson might have mentioned that there were some case notes missing from Jeanne's file, but I found them. Can't blame it on the wife, though. This file was sent by a friend in the records department after I retired, because it was related to one of my cases. She found it accidentally, because it had been misfiled. It contains a copy of the coroner's autopsy report, and I guess when these notes arrived my wife filed them away according to her own system."

"Was there anything interesting about the autopsy?"

"You could say so." He leaned forward, close enough that I could smell the bourbon on his lips, and almost whispered. "Jeanne was in the first trimester of a pregnancy. An out-of-wedlock pregnancy in 1964 was a big deal, especially for a single woman. Especially for someone related to the Broussard family. They were and still are a pretty big deal around here."

"Sounds like a motive," I said.

"It sure does." He scraped his plate before noticing that Jolene and I hadn't had any of the dessert. "I'm so sorry. Let's order another—"

"No," I said quickly. "We're both too full." I stupidly patted my belly to make sure he understood. "Do you think that's enough information to reopen the case?"

"It might be. I've got to do a little more investigating first. I've got my Wednesday-night poker group with a bunch of us old-timers on the force meeting this week, and I'm going to ask them if they remember anything. And I'm going to make some calls to see where Jeanne's boyfriend is now. He had an airtight alibi, but he might have more to say now."

"He's probably dead," Jolene said. "I mean, how old would he be?"

"My age." Bernie's expression didn't change.

Without missing a beat, Jolene said, "Well, gosh, I thought you would be much younger than that. Maybe it's because you look so much like Sean Connery."

Uncle Bernie grinned broadly, raising his dark eyebrows so that I could actually see a slight resemblance to the late James Bond actor. "I used to get that a lot when I was a bit younger."

"I might have a clue for you," I said without thinking. "I believe that the killer may have smoked a pipe."

"Really? What makes you say that?"

"I . . ." I closed my mouth, quickly making up something that I hoped would sound plausible. "Mimi told me that at the time she was preparing to move in with Jeanne and Louise there was a frequent visitor to the house who smoked a pipe, but she doesn't remember his name. I just figured since we have nothing to go on, that's something, right?"

"It's something. It could take some time looking through old files and records, but I'm retired. All I've got is time." He laughed loudly, causing several heads to turn our way.

"Well, thank you. I hate to think of poor Jeanne not resting in peace."

"Why do you think she's not?" Bernie asked, his face blank.

I shrugged. "Just a feeling." I signaled to the waiter to bring the check while Uncle Bernie drained his glass, the ice clinking at the bottom.

"There's actually something else, Nola. I know you didn't ask me, but Jaxson reminded me of the Sunny Ryan case—I suppose because he and Beau have seen each other recently. I wasn't part of the investigation at the time, but of course we all knew about it—it was a huge news story. We might have had a better chance of finding Sunny if Katrina hadn't hit right afterwards and diverted all of our resources. It took a while before we could get back to thoroughly working older cases. Anyway, one of my old poker buddies was one of the detectives assigned to the case."

Carly chose that moment to reappear. Her cocktail glass was full, she having apparently taken the opportunity to stop by the bar at the front of the restaurant for a refill—and probably charging it to the table, since she conveniently hadn't brought her purse when she stepped outside. "Sorry to have taken so long. Jaxson and I saw each other just a few hours ago, but we still had a lot to say." She smirked in that "cat that got the cream" sort of way. "His whole family is heading to their beach house next weekend and he's asked me to go. You have such great fashion sense, Jolene—you're going to have to come shopping with me to pick out a beach house wardrobe. I definitely need a new bikini, for starters."

"Of course." Jolene smiled. "I can't wait."

Bernie stood while Carly settled herself back in her chair, looking surprised at the empty spot on the table in front of her. "What happened to my food?"

Jolene and I exchanged a glance, long enough to communicate that there was no way we were going to tell her it was in my backpack, but not long enough to concoct an alternate story.

"A couple of flies landed on it, so I asked the waiter to take it away. Would you like to order another meal?" Uncle Bernie looked so sincere, even I almost believed him.

Carly slung back her drink, then placed the empty glass on the white tablecloth. "Never mind. I rather like having a liquid brunch. Less calories." She giggled, then stood abruptly, causing Bernie to attempt to stand again, but his knees must have still been in recovery mode from Carly's recent reappearance, and he made it only halfway. "Please excuse me—I need to go powder my nose. I'll be right back."

Eager to hear what he'd been about to say regarding Sunny's case, I turned back to Bernie, just in time to see him signing a credit card receipt and handing the folder back to our waiter.

"Wait . . ." I began.

Bernie waved him away. "I hope you didn't think that I expected you to pay for our meal. The wife would never forgive me." He laughed, but his eyes were serious, and I had the feeling that he had seen my every twinge throughout the food-and-drink ordering. Even though he was long past retirement, he couldn't stop being a detective. Leaning forward, he said, "And you can keep the doggie bag—I promise I won't tell."

The three of us were still laughing when Carly returned to the table and we all stood to leave. "What's so funny? Did I miss something?"

"Nothing at all," Jolene said as she pushed in her chair. "Just talking about how we're going to be having leftovers tonight for supper."

"I'll go get the car if you can wait with Bernie. I'll be right back," Carly said before heading out with Uncle Bernie, leaving Jolene and me to snicker like schoolgirls as we followed them out of the restaurant.

As soon as Carly stepped off the curb I turned to Bernie. "What were you going to tell me about Sunny's case?"

He took a step closer, casually glancing around us as if expecting eavesdroppers. "My buddy—the one who'd worked on the Sunny Ryan case—said that the reason the investigation was stopped was because of pressure from higher-ups, from the very top. At the time, the superintendent was real good friends with a lot of prominent New Orleans professionals and businessmen—read into that what you will. Rumor was that the push to stop the investigation came from Dr. Charles Ryan."

"Wait—Dr. Ryan? You mean Beau and Sunny's grandfather?"

Carly pulled up to the curb and jumped out to open the passenger door before helping Bernie inside. She said good-bye to us—with a promise to call Jolene and set up their shopping trip—then returned to the driver's seat.

Bernie rolled down his window. "Yes. I don't think it's widely known—at least outside of certain circles—but you might want to ask Beau. And I'll see what else I can find out." He smiled. "It was a pleasure meeting you girls. Don't hesitate to let me know if there's anything else I can help you with. There are lots of other restaurants I want to try."

"The pleasure was mutual. And thanks for lunch. I didn't intend for you to pay for it."

"I know. Thanks for allowing this old man a few hours of good food and excellent companionship."

Jolene leaned in and kissed him on his cheek, and I could have sworn he blushed.

"You watch it, Jolene," he said with a smile. "My missus is very territorial. But I won't tell if you won't."

He was still laughing as Carly drove away, the window slowly rolling up.

"That's really odd," I said, staring after the car.

"What? That Carly is a little late getting her hair highlights?"

"No. That Dr. Ryan wanted the investigation into his granddaughter's disappearance halted. It doesn't make sense. I need to find a way to ask Beau about it." I remembered the wet footprints that seemed to follow Beau, and for the first time in my life I wished I could speak to the dead. From my experiences living with Melanie, I'd discovered that no restless spirit lingered because it wanted to. Even if I couldn't communicate with ghosts, it seemed wrong to allow them to exist in torment until someone came along who could. "I wish Melanie was here." I hadn't meant to say that out loud.

"We all miss our mamas, no matter how old we get, don't we? Don't worry—she'll be here with your whole family in October. I can't wait to meet everybody."

Happy to follow along and redirect my thoughts, I said, "I'll be sure to invite Jaxson over to meet Jack. He's a big fan. And I won't tell Carly if you won't." I nudged her with my hip, making her laugh as she led the way to Bubba.

CHAPTER 15

On Monday morning as I waited for Beau to pick me up for the drive to St. Francisville, I sat not so patiently at Jolene's dressing table while she French braided my hair. Since I'd be working outside, doing lots of walking and snapping pictures, I'd planned on the old standby of scraping my hair back in a ponytail and forgetting it. Which actually worked out perfectly, since my only brush had somehow gone missing from my backpack and I'd been making do with my fingers and a small comb.

Apparently, Jolene had other, Machiavellian plans to butter me up (her words) by feeding me homemade French toast and something that smelled and looked like bacon but that she swore was vegan. This had started us laughing for a full five minutes, and by the time the laughter had died down I was sitting at the table with a full plate in front of me, as well as a cup of coffee—a new habit I'd picked up since Jolene had moved in—and she was showing me clothing options for my trip to St. Francisville. Which was why I was wearing her sapphire blue cap-sleeve blouse, which she swore was the exact color as my eyes.

"You've got the most amazing cheekbones and your face is perfectly symmetrical. If I didn't like you so much, I'd hate you." She lifted my hair. "See what happens when you do more than a sloppy ponytail?

You accentuate all your gorgeous features. I think you could stop traffic, so be careful when crossing the street."

"You know, Jolene," I said to her reflection in the mirror, "it's called fieldwork for a reason. It's typically done in boots and jeans, no makeup, and a baseball hat."

She tugged on my hair, winding it and tucking it and putting it through other movements with which it was unfamiliar. "You poor, sweet darlin'," she said, slowly shaking her head. "I'm going to give you a pass because you spent the first fourteen years of your life in California and weren't raised to know any better. But there's a difference between dressing casual and looking like something the dog keeps under the porch."

I gave her the look I usually reserved for Melanie when her parting words were "Make good choices." "It's not like it matters. Nobody is going to be seeing me."

"Except for Beau."

I looked up sharply, but Jolene remained focused on the back of my head. "He doesn't count. He's only driving me as a favor. It's not like I asked him."

The ticking of her Cowardly Lion wall clock filled the silence for a full minute. "I saw him with that girl, too," she said. "That night we went to Frenchmen Street." She raised her eyes to meet mine in the mirror. "I've been waiting for you to tell me, but I guess I'd have to wait for hell to freeze over, so I'm bringing it up first."

"There's nothing to tell."

She stared me down in the mirror. "I wasn't born yesterday. I see that look on your face. It's the same face every member of our club wears, which is how I recognize it."

I turned in my seat. "What are you talking about? What club?"

"The Mooning Hearts Club." She tugged on the bottom of my braid to turn me around but I didn't budge. "For those of us strong, smart, and independent women with advanced degrees and good jobs who find ourselves somehow braying like lost sheep after an unavailable man."

"I'm not braying over anyone. And sheep don't bray—they baa."

She forcefully turned me back to the mirror. "That's how I know I'm right—because you're trying to change the subject."

"I'm not—"

Ignoring me, she said, "It's not a club any of us are proud to belong to or admit to membership in. Our mamas would be ashamed, because they brought us up to be better than that." She wrapped an elastic band around the bottom of the braid before moving in front of me and leaning against the dressing table. "Do you know what a come-to-Jesus meeting is? Because you and I are about to have one, you understand?"

I nodded, not because I did, but because she looked so serious.

"What exactly happened between you and Beau in Charleston after you left Tulane?"

My eyes heated, threatening tears, but I blinked them away. No one knew the story except for my parents and probably my grandparents and Aunt Jayne. Considering all the advantages and chances I'd been given in my relatively short life, I had failed spectacularly to meet anyone's expectations, including my own. For so long I had blamed genetics for my addictive tendencies, but it had taken four years of therapy to understand that everything was a choice and I alone had been responsible for making some very, very bad ones.

"I was so mad when I was sent home," I said quietly, the Cowardly Lion staring at me as he ticked away the minutes. "I thought that I could get clean and sober when I was ready to, and on my own terms. And I told myself that I would, that I could, that I was stronger than my mother. That I was better than my father because I didn't need anyone's help. So it just got worse. Melanie blames all of her gray hairs and wrinkles on me, and she's probably right. I certainly didn't try to make her life easy. My uncle Thomas is a detective with the Charleston police and was able to save my butt more than once, but it was obvious to everyone except me that I was spiraling out of control.

"It was Beau who removed me from a really bad situation and brought me to my parents. After I partied at a bar downtown and blacked out, Beau rescued me. One of the bartenders was a friend of Beau's and had seen us together, so he called Beau. Beau arrived just as

I was being led to a pickup truck by a group of five very inebriated guys. I know I should have been grateful. And I was. I just couldn't quite reconcile my gratitude with the inherent sense that I could have extricated myself from the situation without any help—especially his.

"He was the one who talked me into rehab. He was the only one who could reach me." I clenched my eyes, trying to describe my feelings, and knowing I'd make a mess of it because I wasn't even sure about them myself. "So I hate him for it. Because now I'm beholden to him for the rest of my life." I chewed on my lower lip, then blurted out, "But I love him, too. And I don't think it's a real love, but something buried in the gratitude for saving my life. Twice. He saved me from that fire, too, when I was in high school."

Jolene continued to lean against the dresser, her arms now folded across her chest, and her head shaking slowly from side to side. "Sweetheart, while you're wrasslin' in your head about your feelings for Beau, just know that he's crazy for you. There is no man in the world who would do what he's done if he didn't have strong feelings for you. Sure, he's got a girlfriend now, but I can guarantee she's just a stand-in because you've hung out your Unavailable sign for so long, he got tired of waiting."

"That's ridiculous—" I began, only to be interrupted by the doorbell. I stood abruptly, glad to end the conversation. "He's here, so I've got to go. . . ."

For such a small and slender person, Jolene was very strong. She forced me back into the chair. "Let's just put a little mascara on, and a little bit of color. . . ."

She was reaching for her makeup tray when I managed to free myself. "I do not need mascara or color. I need to go."

"Hello?" Beau's voice came from the front room.

I looked accusingly at Jolene. "Why isn't he waiting in the car like I suggested?" I hissed.

"I texted him that I would keep the front door unlocked for him and to just ring the bell when he was on his way up. Just in case we needed more time to get you ready."

"It's fieldwork," I enunciated carefully before heading toward the door, then pausing. "But thanks for the braid. It looks really nice and will keep me cooler than a ponytail."

She beamed. "You're welcome. Are you sure about that mascara?"

"Very," I said as I headed out of the room. "I just need to grab my backpack and spreadsheets. I'll be right there," I called out.

When I came out to the front room, Beau and Jolene were chatting while each held a brown paper lunch bag decorated with curling ribbon. "Is that . . . ?"

"Your lunches. I thought instead of you eating that awful drive-through food, I'd make you a homemade lunch just like my mama used to make: pimento cheese sandwiches on white bread, a small bag of Zapp's Voodoo potato chips, a dill pickle, and some of my cookies, all wrapped in thermal bags so it won't spoil. I don't want y'all going hungry—at least not on my watch!"

She handed me my bag, and I could see my name written on the front in calligraphy. "That's really thoughtful—thank you, Jolene."

"You're more than welcome," she said, ushering us to the door at the top of the stairs. "Just take all the time you'll need—I'll leave the front light on in case you're late."

I turned to say thank you, but she'd already closed the door behind us.

"That was nice of her," Beau said.

"Very."

"Got your spreadsheets to keep you on schedule?" He might have had a grin on his face, but I didn't look.

"Of course." I followed him slowly down the steps.

He held my door open as I hauled myself up on the running board of his truck and pulled myself into the passenger seat, and then he settled himself behind the wheel.

"Do you want me to move the garbage cans in the neighbor's yard?" I asked.

"Why? They're next door, and nowhere near your driveway."

I closed my door and shrugged. "Jolene usually asks me to. Just to be safe."

He grinned. "I think I'm good, but thanks." He backed up out of the driveway and onto Broadway without running over a curb or hitting anything stationary, then headed down the street, neither of us speaking.

He kept glancing over at me, as if waiting for me to say something, which eventually became unnerving enough that I had to speak. "Do I have anything on my face?" I licked my finger and rubbed at the corners of my mouth. "Could be syrup. Or powdered sugar. Jolene made French toast this morning."

"No, nothing on your face. I think it might be your hair. Did you do something different?"

So much for stopping traffic. "Jolene braided it."

He nodded. "That must be it. It's, um, different."

I wasn't sure if his comment had been meant as a compliment, so I remained silent.

"I hope it's okay if I take some business calls while I drive. It's hands-free in Louisiana, so they'll be on speaker."

"No problem. You're doing me a favor, so whatever you want to do is fine with me." I reached inside my backpack and pulled out a book. "I brought some reading material of my own."

"Anything good? Any juicy parts you can read out loud?"

I read the title. "*A Field Guide to American Houses: The Definitive Guide to Identifying and Understanding America's Domestic Architecture.* Is that juicy enough?"

"Oh, yeah. Practically porn."

"For some of us," I said, opening the front cover.

We drove in silence for a short distance; I found it difficult to concentrate, reading the same paragraph over and over. There were things I wanted to ask him, to clarify some of the information I'd gleaned from Uncle Bernie, but I couldn't quite settle on a posture or tone that wouldn't give away the awkwardness I had been feeling since my conversation with Jolene.

I hadn't had the chance to argue with her that Beau's saving me had nothing to do with any feelings for me. His choice had been to either rescue me or watch a burning house collapse on top of me. And, not wanting to feel as if he'd wasted his efforts, he felt compelled to save me again several years later when I was on my way toward self-destruction. Even though I'd never asked to be saved. So instead of talking, I kept staring at the little black letters dancing up and down like ants on the white page, until I had to close the book and lay my head back so I wouldn't throw up inside Beau's truck.

"So," Beau said, breaking the silence. "I'm curious. I know you work for a civil engineering firm as an architectural historian, but I have to confess, I have no idea what that is. I was kind of expecting you to show up dressed as Indiana Jones and wearing a funny hat and carrying a whip."

I was glad he was annoying me, because it made it easier to talk to him. "Well, then, I guess that explains the strange looks you keep giving me. For the record, Indiana Jones was an archaeologist. I will be working with archaeologists sometimes, depending on the job, but I just look at old buildings." I returned to my book. "I'm relieved that you're not wearing a tool belt and pants that ride too low in the back. Nobody wants to see that."

He laughed out loud. "You might be surprised."

I was irritated to feel the heat in my cheeks, the awkwardness returning. I turned my head toward the window so he wouldn't see.

"I'm curious, really. What do you do besides look at old buildings?"

I felt relieved to talk about something that I knew about and wasn't personal. I figured that with a two-hour drive, we should be able to find enough subjects like that. Such as the best way to eat an Oreo. Or if the toilet paper roll end should be dangling face out or toward the wall.

"In a nutshell, I work in an advisory capacity. When my company is hired on a project, I'm used to survey the site and any existing structures for their historical significance and make a recommendation to the National Register of Historic Places if I identify anything noteworthy. Sadly, just because I believe that a building or structure should be recommended doesn't mean it will be saved from demolition."

"Ouch."

"Yep. I've actually had several 'screaming into a wad of paper towels' moments in the ladies' bathroom already and I haven't even been in the field yet. That was just from reading about the projects of my predecessor to get me up to date. I should probably save Jolene's brown paper lunch bag to breathe into, just in case."

"Good idea. So, what are we doing today?"

I sent him a sharp glance. "*We're* not going to be doing anything. You're going to be making phone calls and doing your own stuff, probably in your truck or in a Starbucks. Assuming there's one in St. Francisville. The population is less than two thousand, but it has a really cute downtown, so there's likely to be a café or restaurant where you can park yourself.

"Meanwhile, I'll take my camera, clipboard, and spreadsheet to the site and basically take notes on every structure I see and snap tons of pictures. I plan to throw in a few extracurricular pictures of the quaint downtown, with its shops and businesses, as a sort of impact statement."

"Very devious of you, Nola. I don't think I've ever seen that side of you before."

"There're lots of sides to me you haven't seen," I said, immediately wishing I hadn't, since I felt my cheeks warm again at all sorts of implications that I knew were completely one-sided and therefore doubly awkward. *Oreos and toilet paper, Oreos and toilet paper,* I reminded myself.

"Anyway," I continued, "when I'm done in the field, I'll need to head to the state archives to study maps, deeds, newspapers, and other records connected to the site. A lot of stuff I can find online, but there's always buried treasure to be found in the archives—one of the most important things I learned in grad school. Then I write my report and submit my recommendations. And then I step away. I'm usually not involved in the project after that point. Which can be a good thing."

He signaled to exit onto Interstate 10 toward Baton Rouge. "You seem the type to take it personally."

I looked at him, my mouth half-open to speak, but unable to form

THE SHOP ON ROYAL STREET   173

a single word, as angry that he'd assumed something that was star-tlingly accurate as I was curious how he would know.

As if reading my mind, Beau said, "You're a musician. So am I. We feel things a little harder than most. It's the price we pay."

I looked away. Outside my car window, the city of New Orleans passed by beneath the interstate's overpasses, the massive spaceship-shaped Superdome looming over Poydras Street and the abbreviated cluster of high-rises of the Central Business District. The CBD abruptly ended at Canal Street, the city then spreading out into the French Quarter and toward the river and the roof peaks of St. Louis Cathedral. Even in its skyline, the Crescent City showed its partiality for fun and frivolity, happy to leave the business side of life tucked back in a far corner, yet always reminding itself of its spiritual side.

"Maybe," I said. I didn't like to talk about myself, especially on any topic that might wind its way to my sad, lost mother. Turning back to Beau, I said, "How well did you know your grandfather Charles?"

Leaning one arm on the window frame and steering with the other, he said, "Not too well. I was seven years old when he died. Why do you ask?"

"I had lunch yesterday with Jaxson's uncle Bernie."

"I know him well. Growing up, I got my hide tanned by him more than once and for good reason. Jaxson and I were like hell on wheels. It's a good thing Bernie never had kids of his own, because we wouldn't have survived without his focused attention."

I thought of the mild-mannered Jaxson, with his red hair and freck-les. "I can't believe Jaxson could have been that bad. You, I'm not so sure."

"I guess it might surprise you, then, that Jaxson was the instigator. It's his fault I broke my leg when we were in fifth grade. He dared me to jump off a moving streetcar, so I did."

I turned to him. "You do know that wasn't his fault, right? You were the one stupid enough to take a dare like that. Why did you do it?"

His face became serious, his hands gripping the wheel a little bit tighter, and I knew that we had accidentally made a turn into a dark

corner where the light wasn't allowed. I opened my book again, ready
to pretend to read.

"Because he told me he knew my parents were both dead. He'd
overheard his grandmother talking to Mimi. I knew that, of course,
even though nobody wanted to say it out loud, as if that would make
it true. But nobody wanted to tell me because they knew that hoping was what got me out of bed in the morning. I mean, what kid
wants to believe both his parents are dead? I used to make up all sorts
of scenarios in my head—like they were spies and the government had
to give them new identities and they couldn't tell me; or they'd been
taken to Texas with a lot of the Katrina evacuees but had amnesia and
couldn't remember who they were, so they stayed there."

He shrugged as if retelling another story of a childhood escapade,
but I'd seen the tightening in his jaw, the bobbing of his Adam's apple
as he swallowed. In all the years I'd known Beau Ryan, I'd never seen
him vulnerable. He was always so in charge, the one who knew all the
answers. The one in control. Which was why I'd decided long ago that
we were incompatible as friends or anything else. I was still wrestling
with whether I should mention the set of wet footprints I'd seen more
than once that seemed to be following him, but I was saved from making the decision by his phone ringing.

"Excuse me. I've got to take this." He pushed a button on his steering wheel, and his conversation faded into the background as I studied the passing views of Old Metairie and Greenwood cemeteries on
both sides of the car. Tall monuments and sculptures on the above-
ground tombs sat time stained in white and gray, watching the passage
of years from their lofty perches. I was a self-proclaimed taphophile—
a cemetery enthusiast—and loved exploring old cemeteries and reading the epitaphs, imagining the lives lived between the two dates. I
knew that Melanie hated cemeteries because she didn't have to do
any imagining, as too many of the dead volunteered to tell her their
stories.

I looked over at Beau, his conversation having ended, the steady
thrum of tires against concrete once again filling the silence. As if

sensing my gaze on him, he turned and met my eyes for a moment. "But that's not why I jumped."

We traveled down the interstate for what seemed like miles before he spoke again. "I jumped because Jaxson said he knew where Sunny was, but he'd only tell me if I jumped."

I sucked in a sharp breath. "And did he know?"

Beau shook his head. "No. He was just being a stupid kid who was mad because I wouldn't let him ride my new bike. He's still apologizing, and I'm not going to let him forget it. He was grounded for a month and had to mow our yard all summer. Got the worst sunburn of his life, which Uncle Bernie said would be a good reminder each day of why we should never dare our friends to do stupid things."

"That's pretty harsh. But he seems like he learned his lesson. I mean, he grew up to be a public defender."

"True. Not that he had much of a choice about whether to do something good with his life. His brother is a priest. His mother starts every other sentence with 'My son the priest.' Hard to compete with that."

"I bet."

"So, what were you saying about my grandfather Charles?"

I opened my mouth to tell him what Uncle Bernie had said about his grandfather being responsible for the premature closing of Sunny's case, but stopped. What if he didn't know? If he didn't, I was certainly the last person in the world he'd want to hear it from.

"Just that he was good friends with the higher-ups at the NOPD." I watched Beau's face to see if that meant anything.

"From what Mimi has told me, my grandfather knew pretty much everyone in New Orleans. He was even good friends with Governor Edwin Edwards—before he was sent to jail, of course. But my grandfather was the doctor that everyone who was anyone went to."

"Well, then, it would make sense that he'd know the head brass in the police department."

"The mayor, too," Beau said. "According to Lorda, they all sat beneath the Roman orgy in the dining room at least once. It seemed to be a bucket-list item for lots of people in my grandparents' circle."

The mental image made me grin. "He also mentioned something about Jeanne. The coroner's report was filed separately from the rest of her case files, so this is the first time he's seen it. Apparently, she was pregnant when she was killed."

"Wow. Well, that's a smoking gun. I'm sure Uncle Bernie is already digging into it."

"He is, as a matter of fact. I was thinking about asking Mimi if she knew anything about it. She was Jeanne's best friend and about to move in with her, so I'm thinking they must have been close."

Beau looked at me for a long moment before turning back to the road. "Why is it so important to you that you find out what happened to her?"

"Curiosity, I guess. She was murdered in my house. And I get the sense that there's something . . . restless there. I'd hate to think that she wasn't at peace because her murderer was never identified. Not that I can ask her, but if I were in her position, I'd haunt the heck out of the house where my body was found before I could rest in peace."

"That's not always the reason why restless spirits remain earthbound."

"How would you know?"

After an almost imperceptible pause, he responded with a shrug. "I talk to a lot of people on my podcast who've had ghost encounters—some of them actually believable. And there seem to be as many reasons for a haunting as there are ghosts."

I sighed and leaned back in my seat, watching the blur of the passing landscape. "Sometimes I wish I could be like Melanie and just ask them."

"No, you don't." Beau's phone rang again, and while he was on the call I closed my book, all pretense of reading gone, and thought instead of Jeanne, and all the reasons she might have for lingering in the place where she'd been murdered.

"Nola?"

I jerked my head in Beau's direction, realizing he'd been talking to me while I was daydreaming about ghosts. "I'm sorry—what?"

"I was saying that I saw you at the Spotted Cat last week. I was wondering why you didn't say hello."

His question caught me by surprise, and since I didn't know the answer, either, the various attempts to respond got jumbled in my throat and all that emerged was "Righto."

"What?"

I wondered if Beau could hear my panicky breathing as my mind went into overdrive. "That's just a thing we historic preservationists say. It sort of means 'Yep' and 'Sorry' at the same time. In other words, I'm sorry, but I didn't see you, or I would have said hi and asked to be introduced to your friend."

"That's too bad." He leaned forward to flip on the stereo, and for the remainder of the drive we listened to his playlist of classic jazz, nearly identical to my own, which didn't completely surprise me, since the one thing we'd had in common back in Charleston was our love of the same music. We drove without speaking until we were past the WELCOME TO ST. FRANCISVILLE sign. I was just about to relax when Beau lowered the volume on the stereo and said, "If you didn't see me, how would you know I was with a friend?"

The GPS piped in, saying we'd reached our destination. "Oh, look. We're here!" I grabbed my lunch bag and backpack and slid out of the truck, feeling like a kid being dropped off at school. Looking some-where past his head, I said, "I'll text you when I'm done." I slammed the door shut.

I began to walk away, hearing behind me the mechanical whoosh of an automatic window being lowered.

"Nola?"

I turned to see Beau with his elbow resting casually on the window frame, his face oddly serious. "I figured it's not just your hair that's different." He paused, as if waiting for me to respond. "It's your shirt. It matches the color of your eyes."

Our gazes met, the silence drowned out by the whirring of cicadas in a nearby loblolly pine and by a passing eighteen-wheeler. "Thank you," I said. And before he could say anything else, I headed out into an overgrown field, with no direction in mind except away.

CHAPTER 16

I sat on the curb with my baseball cap—which I had hidden in my backpack so Jolene wouldn't see it—pulled low over my forehead, and I was nearly drowning in a puddle of my own sweat and reeking of insect repellent. I thought it might be close to three thirty in the afternoon, but I lacked the strength to look at my phone for confirmation. I had even had to swallow my pride and ask Siri to send Beau the message that I was done and ready to be picked up because I didn't have the energy to lift the phone. I had seen Melanie resort to verbal texting, since she was a complete failure at texting with her thumbs, and I had laughed at her and called her a boomer. Oh, how the mighty had fallen.

At the honk of a car horn, I looked up and saw Beau's truck. He got out and took my backpack and helped me stand, none of which I asked for or needed, as I could have stood on my own if I'd had an extra fifteen minutes or so.

"Thank you," I said through dry lips as he opened the passenger door and helped me inside. I stopped him with my hand when he reached for the seat belt. "I think I can manage the buckle," I said, although it took me three tries to lift my arm to reach it, and then another two to manage clicking it shut.

After he'd seated himself behind the wheel, he leaned over and turned all the AC vents in my direction and turned the fan on high. I pulled off my soaking hat and eagerly stuck my face in the powerful airflow like a dog with its head out a car window.

When I finally leaned my head against the headrest, he lowered the fan speed. "I hope you had a successful day, because you look like something the cat dragged in. Backwards. In the rain."

I glowered at him. "Are you taking lessons from Jolene now?"

He grinned and handed me a tall foam cup with a lid and straw. "The nearest Smoothie King is in Baton Rouge, so I got you the next best thing. Sweet tea from the Magnolia Cafe right here in St. Francisville. Great place for lunch, by the way, if you need to come back. Don't tell Jolene, but I was still hungry after I ate my packed lunch, so I ordered a French dip po'boy and it was pretty amazing. Lots of vegan options, too."

He winked but I didn't have time to laugh because I was sucking down the sweet tea like a honeybee stranded in the desert.

"I also bought a large ice-cold bottle of water that I stuck in my cooler in the back for when you need it." At the sound of me slurping the bottom of my cup, he said, "Which sounds like now." He reached behind us into the backseat, then handed me the water.

"Thanks," I said, holding the cold plastic against my neck. "You're a lifesaver." Our eyes met at my choice of words, but I quickly turned away.

"You're welcome." He started the truck and pulled out onto the street. "By the way, Jaxson called. He stopped at the house to get more photographs and video footage, and he said that Thibaut was working on getting that sealed door opened and should be done today. He didn't have time to wait but said to let you know just in case you wanted to stop by on your way home."

I shook my head. "I'm too tired—it can wait until tomorrow. I'm planning on working from home tomorrow to start organizing my notes and photos to begin my report. I can go to the house when I'm done."

"Great," he said with enough enthusiasm that it made me worried. "Why is that great?"

"Because I already planned to stop at an empty parking lot on our way home today so you can practice your driving again."

"Again? I still haven't fully recovered from the last time."

"All the more reason to get back in the saddle and try again."

"You never said a horse was an option for learning to drive."

"Because it's not. Practice makes perfect. I'm sure you've heard that a few times."

"Maybe a couple." I pressed my head back against the headrest and sat up quickly when I realized that was what JJ used to do before starting a tantrum. At least now I knew how he felt. "Do you enjoy torturing me?"

He kept a straight face. "Maybe just a little."

I turned toward my window so he couldn't see me smile. "Thank you for driving me today. My boss says he doesn't think I'll have to do any fieldwork again for at least a month. Hopefully, that gives me time to become competent enough to get my driver's license."

His eyes rounded, and he opened his mouth as if to say something before closing it abruptly. "Maybe. We just need to make sure we practice enough. There are still some rudiments of driving you need work on."

"Like what?" I crossed my arms.

"Oh, I don't know. Maybe obeying traffic lights and stop signs? Staying off sidewalks and avoiding immovable objects, like light posts? That sort of thing."

I shifted uncomfortably in my seat. "Maybe I can ask Jolene for some lessons so I don't have to bother you."

He looked at me with raised eyebrows. "Really? So you can add picking off pedestrians with your bumper to your skill set?"

"Right. Good point."

"And I don't mind teaching you. It's actually kind of fun. I admire your determination."

While I digested that and tried to work out the proper way to say thank you, he said, "Everyone needs a bright spot of humor in their day. Perks me right up—better than caffeine, even."

My phone beeped with a text, interrupting my mental list of things I wanted to say to Beau. "It's Mimi," I said, opening the screen.

Are you free tomorrow night for dinner? 6:00?

"I've been summoned to your grandmother's house for dinner—I'm thinking it's about the Maison Blanche door."

"Possibly, although she hasn't mentioned anything to me. I can drive you."

"Really, Beau, I don't need you to drive me everywhere. I'll just take an Uber."

He sighed heavily, as if he'd argued his point more than once, which he had. "I know you don't need me to, but I thought we could meet at your house on Dauphine to check out the closet, since I'm curious, too, and then head to Mimi's house. It's not that far, and I'm going that way anyway."

I wanted to protest, but he was right. "Sure," I said, returning to my phone. "I'll let her know I'll be there. Assuming I survive another driving lesson."

The following morning, I stood to the side of the running lanes at Audubon Park, my hands on my legs, gasping for breath. The cooler air of fall was still just a tiny dot on the horizon despite it being mid-September, the humidity, hovering somewhere around seventy-eight percent, making the three miles I had just run seem more like fifteen. I still had a few years to go until I hit thirty, but at the rate I was panting, it seemed time to go ahead and start scouting out nursing homes.

Although it was almost seven thirty in the morning, the park was empty except for a few perky Uptown mothers pushing running strollers and holding phones to their ears as they multitasked their way around the park. Classes at Tulane and Loyola weren't scheduled to start until the following week, which I knew would mean a running path crowded with much younger and more spritely runners. I stood and sucked in a deep breath and wondered if they would ask me to leave.

I opened the fitness app on my phone and hit the share button to send my morning's stats to Melanie and my aunt Jayne. Despite being the mother of two elementary school–aged children and much older than I was, Jayne usually beat me in time and distance, which was fair since she'd been running for almost as long as I'd been alive. Melanie usually "forgot" to wear her tracker and had to manually input her data, which I found highly suspicious, but I let it ride because it was Melanie.

With my hands clutching my waist, as if that might pump more oxygen into my lungs, I paused to admire a preening snowy egret on the edge of Bird Island in the middle of the lagoon, and enjoy the cackles and caws of the hundreds of birds nesting in the rookery's trees. The melody of a song I'd started working on when I'd first moved to New Orleans and seen the island began playing in the back of my head. I needed to write it down before I forgot it, but each time I tried, the music stopped.

Turning my back on the lagoon, I began my cooldown walk toward the main entrance, passing the bronze statue of the woman holding a bird and standing on a pedestal in the middle of a fountain, a pair of mallard ducks cruising under the jets of water spraying from two bronze statues of children sitting on turtles on the perimeter. I stopped on the path near the fountain to change my playlist from running music to acoustic guitar to accompany me on my walk to my apartment.

Movement caught my attention and I looked up to see a dark-haired man about my age sit down on one of the benches. He smiled at me before bending his head to his own phone, and I smiled back in reflex even though I could hear both Melanie and Jack warning me to never smile at strangers, especially good-looking young male strangers. But this guy looked oddly familiar, and he must have recognized me, too, since he'd smiled. Or maybe he was just being polite. I wondered if we'd passed each other before while walking around Uptown, or if maybe I'd known him during the year I'd been at Tulane. Or, since he was wearing running clothes and was in the park, maybe we had just passed each other on the path and that was why he looked familiar.

The man looked up again as I was staring. Embarrassed, I gave him a quick smile and walked away toward the park's main entrance, on St. Charles Avenue, and then, instead of walking home, I picked up my pace and did a short jog through Tulane's campus to Freret Street, and then back to my apartment on Broadway. It wasn't that I got weird vibes from him, or that he was acting creepy or threatening in any way. And it definitely wasn't because he was odd-looking in that white-van-driving-predator kind of way. It was just that he'd seemed familiar, and I couldn't figure out why. And a stranger appearing enough times to seem familiar was what most people would call a strange coincidence. Except my dad's well-known motto was "There's no such thing as coincidence." And in my twenty-six years, I'd already learned that he was right.

I spent the rest of the day working from home, organizing my photos and notes from my day in St. Francisville and starting my report. I even remembered to book an appointment at the state archives in Baton Rouge to finish my research. I'd resigned myself to hiring an Uber for the trip, or risking my life with Jolene. She'd already offered to drive, but it was scary enough driving with her on city streets. The thought of her flying down the interstate with Bubba was enough for me to open my wallet for a rideshare. The one thing I was sure of was that I wasn't going to ask Beau. I owed him enough as it was, and my offers for reimbursement for gas and wear and tear on his truck fell on deaf ears.

I was so busy working that I'd forgotten all about the man in the park when Beau picked me up before heading to Mimi's for dinner. As we drove down St. Charles Avenue past the park and the main entrances to both Tulane and Loyola, I caught a brief glimpse of a dark-haired young man across the neutral ground on the opposite side of the street from us. He wore a backpack and was riding an expensive-looking ten-speed bike and passed by too quickly for me to get a good look at his face. Yet I was sure it was the same guy. Something about his jawline—or maybe it was his brow line—seemed so memorable. I turned to look, watching as he took a right through the gates of Audubon Place.

"Who was that?" Beau asked, following my gaze.

I shrugged. "I don't know. I'm guessing he's a student at one of the universities, because he was wearing a backpack. I think I saw him at the park this morning, but I can't be sure. It's just that he seems so . . . familiar. Like I've seen him before, but not in a way that I should know his name. Like maybe we were in the same class freshman year, but I think I've seen him since. I just can't remember when."

"Could just be a coincidence."

Our eyes met. "Except there's no such thing as coincidence," we said in unison. Beau had been around my dad enough to have learned the Jack Trenholm mantra.

"He rode his bike into Audubon Place, if that means anything," I said.

"Well, if he lives in a house there, his family probably has money. Or he could be a tutor or visiting a friend. Who knows? He might not even be the same guy." Our eyes met again before I quickly glanced away.

Jorge was gone by the time we pulled up in front of my house, but Thibaut's truck was still there, the windows all the way down so he wouldn't combust from the heat when he returned to his truck. The wind chime was conspicuously still as we walked up onto the porch, but a faint whiff of pipe tobacco drifted past.

"Do you smell that?" I asked.

"Smell what?" Beau gave a perfunctory sniff of the air before opening the door. "I don't smell anything but rain."

I walked past him into the house. "Thibaut?" I called out.

"Back here."

We found him in the kitchen, pulling his head out from inside a wall, corroded pipes scattered around him on the floor. He smiled broadly at us. "I'd greet y'all proper with a handshake, but I know where these hands have been and it ain't pretty." He nodded toward the hole in the wall. "I was hoping I could just replace a section of the piping and save you the trouble of all-new kitchen plumbing and a new wall, but that dog just won't hunt. It's all got to be torn out and started again from scratch. The upside is that you'll get a brand-new kitchen and you won't have to worry about nothing leaking or breaking for a long time."

He motioned us toward the back door. "Come over here and let me show you something. When I got here this morning, this door was wide open. Now, I might be more forgetful than I used to be, but when it comes to leaving a job site, I don't take no chances. I lock up everything real tight; then I go back through and double-check everything. And I know I not only locked this door last night before I left, but I also rechecked it and it was definitely locked—both the door handle and the dead bolt."

Holding up his hand, he said, "Now, don't get ahead of yourselves and think we've got ourselves a few ghosties opening doors around here, because that's what Jorge says and it's why he's calling his priest tonight about doing a blessing. But this is definitely man-made."

He opened the door and pointed at the dead bolt. It was one of the first things I'd installed in the house before I realized that the house wasn't a target for visitors, either the wanted or unwanted kind. Long gashes and scratches marred the surface of the bright stainless steel as if it had been mauled by some wild animal. Or attacked with a very sharp knife. Beneath it, the original brass drum-style doorknob and the backplate with the simple old-style keyhole hadn't been damaged at all. The lock was different from the one on the front door and the key had been missing, which was why I'd installed the dead bolt. Thibaut had found the key when he removed the old water heater behind the louvered door in the kitchen, where it had apparently been kicked and forgotten years before. He pulled at a ring of keys he'd attached to his tool belt. "And the only key is right here, and it went home with me last night."

"And you're sure you locked it?"

"Give me a Bible and I'll put my hand on it and swear that I did. Hard to forget, because I have to take it off the ring to turn it, and I remember doing that. And I've still got the key, so I definitely put it back and didn't drop it nowhere."

"I believe you. It's just that if you have the only key, and the door was definitely locked but was unlocked without any tampering, that means that . . ."

"Someone has another key," Beau and I said in unison.

Our eyes met briefly before I turned back to Thibaut. "And you haven't made a copy, and to your knowledge no one else has, either?"

"No, ma'am. Not since I've been here. Before I found the key we just kept it unlocked, and now it's just me and Jorge, and I always get here first and leave last, so I unlock and lock all the doors."

"Was anything missing?" I asked.

He shook his head. "We always take our tools with us, and there's nothing here worth stealing except for these floors, so nothing we could tell."

The mention of his tools reminded me about his missing hammer. "What about your hammer—did you ever find it?"

"Yes, ma'am. That was real strange, too. It just showed up on the front porch here the next morning when I got here for work. And I *know* I didn't leave it there. I wasn't even working outside, and I re-member leaving it in the kitchen, and when I went to get it, *poof*—it wasn't there. Really freaked Jorge out and I gotta admit I was a little bothered by it, too. But at least whoever it was gave it back. It's not like it's expensive or anything, but just the bother of it, ya know?"

I nodded, thinking of my missing hairbrush and making a mental note to stop by a drugstore before birds began mistaking my hair for a nest.

"It could be the neighbors playing a joke to welcome you to the neighborhood," Beau suggested, his tone lacking conviction.

"The neighbors across the street are organizers of the Krewe of Barkus parade during Mardi Gras, where the dogs are all in costumes, as well as a lot of their humans, so that says something, right?"

Beau and Thibaut stared silently at me for a moment before Beau said, "It definitely says something. I'm just not sure what."

"Whatever." I blew a tangled knot of hair off my forehead. "But my point is that it's not inconceivable that a neighbor could have done it for whatever reason. Maybe they just needed to borrow a hammer and you weren't around to ask."

"Sure thing," Thibaut said, nodding his head enthusiastically. "Me and Jorge were upstairs working on pulling out that plumbing, so someone could have easily come through the unlocked front door and then returned it at night when everything was locked up tight."

"Great," I said. "Glad we solved that mystery." Before anyone could contradict me, I said, "I'd like to see the closet. Beau said you finally managed to pry the door off." I headed toward the stairs, Beau and Thibaut following.

"Sure did, but not without a lot of resistance from the door. It was like someone from the other side was hanging on to it just as hard as I was pulling. I managed to remove it in one piece, but I'm afraid I did some damage to the wood surround. Don't worry, Miss Nola—I'm a master carpenter and I'll fix it so it's as good as new."

"Thanks, Thibaut." My steps slowed as I approached, the damaged door lying against the wall, the frame splintered in places, the remaining nails bent in all directions, as if they'd been caught in a tug-of-war between two equally fierce opponents. I looked nervously at Thibaut's bulging biceps, then into the black chasm of the unlit closet. Although it was at the top of the stairs, across from one of the dormer windows, no sunlight penetrated the black interior. It looked like a giant mouth swallowing any light that attempted to cross its threshold.

I'd left my phone in my backpack downstairs, so I turned to Beau to ask him to shine his phone flashlight into the closet, but I found he wasn't behind me. Instead, he'd stopped halfway up the stairs, looking down as if studying something on the ground, and snapping the rubber band on his wrist.

"Beau?"

It took a moment for him to look at me, and when he did it seemed as if he was fighting to keep his eyes focused just on me. It reminded me of a birthday party for JJ and Sarah where we'd had two performing clowns (Melanie's idea, of course). While one juggled, the other made balloon animals, and JJ kept putting his hands over his eyes because it was too hard for him to keep them focused on one thing. Except here, there were no balls flying in the air and no distracting colorful balloons. Just Thibaut, me, and an empty closet that might have been sealed since the sixties.

Beau slowly climbed the rest of the steps before pulling out his phone and aiming the light into the closet while I held my breath. I almost expected it to throw the light back at us, or at the very least reveal some horrible creature from my childhood nightmares staring back at us.

Instead, we were greeted with the smell of mothballs and by heavy coats and long-sleeved dresses neatly hung. Several hatboxes sat on the upper shelves, and rain boots and evening shoes from a different era were placed carefully on a shoe rack on the floor. "Can you lower it a bit?" I asked.

The beam shot across the pristine wooden floor, and I was excited to know that we would have a sample to match when we redid the rest of the floors. I leaned closer to get a better look, automatically cringing as I inspected the corners and the edges near the walls for the carcasses of cockroaches or rodents or both. But only a heavy coating of dust lay undisturbed across the floor, except for a trail of a woman's high-heeled shoe prints starting at the back wall of the closet and heading toward the doorway until they disappeared. There was no dust on the prints, as if the person who had made them had left just minutes ago. It almost seemed as if whoever she was had been inside the closet for decades, waiting to be let out.

"Well, don't that beat all?" Thibaut said. "I swear those weren't there earlier, but no one's been in the house."

"Maybe she's the one who took your hammer," I suggested.

He nodded, ignoring the fact that there was only one set of footprints and they exited the closet without entering, but it was clear he thought my idea was as stupid as I did.

"Is that a Mr. Bingle?" Beau directed the beam of his flashlight to a space between two hatboxes to illuminate what looked like a stuffed animal. He stepped forward, avoiding the footprints, and pulled the toy down from the shelf.

I could see now that it was a plush toy in the shape of a snowman with an upside-down ice-cream-cone hat, a red bow tie, and red-and-white-striped gloves, with a candy cane in one hand, and what appeared to be wings made of holly leaves. "What on earth is a Mr. Bingles?" I asked.

"Bingle," they said in unison as if I'd just mispronounced the name of the Saints quarterback.

"Jingle, jangle, jingle: Here comes Mr. Bingle," Thibaut sang off-key.

"Something like that," Beau said, looking at the toy. "Mr. Bingle was the Maison Blanche Christmas icon—a part of most people's childhoods. At least from the forties until the late nineties, when the Maison Blanche building was sold, and the trademark for Mr. Bingle, too." He grinned. "I had one when I was a kid—no idea what happened to it. But if this is an original from the sixties or earlier, it could be pretty valuable, especially in this pristine condition." He thrust it into my hands. "You definitely shouldn't leave it here since we have proof of at least two break-ins."

The stuffed snowman looked up at me with bulgy blue eyes, its button nose and yarn-sewn smile almost cute enough to make me overlook the fact that it had come from the dark closet with the unyielding frame and disembodied footprints. Almost.

"All right," I said, gingerly holding it away from my body. I looked back inside the closet. "I'll go pick up a few storage boxes and come back with Jolene to clear everything out of here and remove it so nothing gets damaged. Then we can go through everything back at the apartment and see if there's anything worth donating. Or maybe selling to one of the local vintage shops. I mean, it all belongs to me now, right?"

"Oh, yeah," Beau said a little too quickly. "Possession of everything in the house transferred to you upon closing. Even Mr. Bingle."

"Great," I said, looking anywhere but at the doll, unwilling to look into the bulgy eyes again.

"Don't make no sense why it would be nailed shut, but that's all that was in it. Jorge and me didn't touch a thing."

The first taps of rain hit the window and the roof. I'd bought enough pails to put under the leaky parts of the roof and had emptied them out after the last storm, so they were ready. Thibaut had reached out to his trusted roofer and scheduled a roof replacement, but they'd already pushed us back twice, citing existing jobs taking longer than expected. I was frustrated enough to look for an online roofing course so I could at least figure out how to do a patch job to get us by for a while, even though Beau had warned me that putting on my own roof would be a lot like performing brain surgery on myself. Still, I considered it an option. Nothing could go into the house until the roof was replaced, and I didn't want my parents to see the house in its current condition when they arrived in October. With their experience at renovating an older home, I knew they would understand. But I needed something tangible to prove to them that I had succeeded in outrunning my demons.

I was about to ask Beau if he needed to see anything else while we were there, but I was distracted by the sound of him snapping the rubber band on his wrist. "We should get going," he said, moving his gaze from the window to the closet, then dragging his eyes back to me. "Looks like the sky is about to fall in."

The sky cracked above us as a gust of wind pushed at the house, the lightning chasing the rain as it began pummeling the roof. The barest scent of cologne tiptoed through the air, the woodsy scent of pipe tobacco slithering silently behind it.

I looked at Beau, whose head had turned back toward the gaping closet, his nostrils flared. "Do you smell it now?"

"Smell what?" Thibaut asked just as a blinding bolt of lightning lit the sky and something nearby—possibly a transformer—exploded and extinguished all streetlights, throwing us into an eerie darkness and an odd quiet.

"Why isn't the generator on?" I asked, loudly enough to be heard over the rain.

"I have no idea," Thibaut said, heading down the stairs. "But I'm fixin' to find out."

A new, overpowering smell that reminded me of my grandmother's hair spray, now mingled with the strong scents of cologne and pipe tobacco, almost choked me. I coughed, finding it hard to breathe. "Beau," I said, grasping his arm, wanting him to tell me that he smelled it, too.

I felt his arm around my shoulder just as a huge crack of thunder sounded above us. At the same time, a brilliant flash of blue-white lightning illuminated the upstairs hallway with bright light and showed us the clear image of a woman with a bouffant hairstyle and a high-waisted dress looking back at us with opaque, brooding eyes, a secretive smile on her lips, before we were plunged back into darkness.

CHAPTER 17

I clutched Mr. Bingle on my lap as Beau and I sat in his truck in front of the house on Prytania, the rain cascading down the windshield with a violence that still couldn't erase the image of the woman with the sad eyes who had disappeared as soon as Beau aimed his flashlight.

We hadn't spoken on the fifteen-minute drive, except for me repeating the same unanswered question. "You saw her, right?" I said again. Despite the blasting air-conditioning, sweat beaded on Beau's forehead.

His hands still gripped the steering wheel and I noticed he was wearing two rubber bands instead of just one. He followed my gaze and slid one off. "Here," he said, handing it to me, his voice straining to sound normal. "I got one for you. It's blue, and it reminded me of your shirt, so I figured you'd like it. I was going to wait until our next driving lesson, but I thought you might want it sooner."

I stretched it between my thumbs, testing it, not sure what I should be focusing on—the fact that he remembered the blue blouse or that I might have need of the rubber band now. I decided on the latter. "So you *did* see her."

He dropped his hands from the wheel and met my eyes. "I saw *something*. But there was nothing there when I shone my light in the corner, and nothing showed up in the photo I snapped. When Thibaut got the generator running again and we could see in full light, the corner was definitely empty. No one was upstairs, and no one could have passed us on the stairs if they had come from downstairs. I think the storm and the power outage freaked us out a bit. And the lightning created weird shadows that looked like a person standing in the upstairs hallway. This is a common thread in all the stories I discuss in my podcast."

"Are you listening to yourself? I'm not just anyone with a casual belief in ghosts. I lived with a psychic medium for more years than I can count right now, and I know what a shadow is and what a ghost is. I can't talk to them, but I have seen them when they are strong enough to allow being seen by ordinary people like me. And I know you saw her, too, so stop trying to deny it and instead tell me why you won't admit that she was real."

His nostrils flared as he took two deep breaths, his chest slowly rising and falling with each one. It's what my dad did when he caught Melanie in his office with her labeling gun. Instead of answering, he said, "Why is it so important to you?"

His question surprised me. "Because if I have a ghost living in my house, there's a reason she's there, and chances are she'd rather not be. I always thought it was a real gift that Melanie and my aunt Jayne could release earthbound spirits by figuring out what tethered them here. I'd feel guilty moving into the house and carrying on with my life with her unhappy spirit lurking around."

"A gift, huh?" His voice was sharp

"Well, Melanie used to call it a curse, but I think she's finally come to terms with it. She and my aunt actively work on cold cases for the Charleston police now—on the down low, of course. They've helped bring closure to a lot of families."

When he didn't say anything, I said, "I think the ghost might be Jeanne. She was murdered in the house and her killer was never caught.

I hate to assume, but since I can't ask her, that's the best I can do. And there's another spirit, too. A man. I saw him once, on the porch. He wears cologne and smokes a pipe. Melanie once got involved in a case where the spirit of the murderer was locked in the same place as the victim, unwilling to let the victim go. Melanie said it was one of her hardest cases, because one of the reasons the murderer was reluctant to be sent into the light was because she wasn't ready to face retribution. I'd hate to think that's what's happening here." I paused. "If I keep digging into Jeanne's case and end up solving it, maybe she'll find her own way without guidance. I could ask Melanie when she's here in October, but that's a long time off. Or I could hire someone. New Orleans is full of psy—"

"No." He shook his head. "Sorry. I didn't mean to shout. It's just that I've had a lot of experience with them. They're all thieves and liars. And even if they don't take your money, they steal your hope."

I studied him in the growing dusk, the rain slashing at the roof and windows of the truck. "You talked to psychics before, didn't you? When you were trying to find Sunny."

He didn't respond right away, like a child caught in a lie. "Yeah, a lot. But just one was legit. And that was enough to tell me that it wasn't something to dabble in if you don't know what you're doing. Because chances are you're not going to get the answers you're looking for, and you don't know who's going to respond." He reached to pluck at the rubber band on his arm but stopped when he saw me watching. He dropped his hands to rest on his thighs. "It's like opening a door that you can't close."

I waited for him to say more. When he didn't, I said, "Melanie can. She thought you could, too."

His jaw tightened. "Well, even if she's right, I'm not interested." He flipped off the ignition. "We should go. Mimi will be waiting."

I'd obviously touched a bruise, and I was almost as eager as he was to change the conversation. I was just a client, and personal conversations were for closer relationships. Like with girlfriends. "What should I do with him?" I indicated Mr. Bingle on my lap.

He looked at it and frowned. "It might be valuable, so we need to hide it. It would really tick me off if someone broke in to steal it." He unbuckled his seat belt and rummaged on the floor of the backseat before retrieving an empty reusable grocery bag from Rouses Market and held it open. "Dump him in here and stick it under your seat."

I held up the bag. "It looks like it's never been used."

"It hasn't. I just drive around with it in my truck so I can forget it every time I shop. Just like everyone else."

"I actually use mine. Melanie taught me a trick of setting a reminder on my phone when I schedule my grocery trips on my calendar each week. Works every time."

He looked at me for a moment, then said, "Just put him in the bag and shove him under the seat. We're late and I'm not in the mood for one of Mimi's lectures on punctuality."

I leaned over to see the space beneath my seat but stopped when I spotted a piece of scarlet lace protruding onto the floorboard. Acting first instead of thinking, I pulled it out of its hiding place before I realized it was a handful of red lacy items. I held up the scanty double-D bra for less than a second before I dropped it back on the floorboard. Unwilling to put Mr. Bingle next to it, I swung the bag over my shoulder with my backpack and waited for Beau to open the door. As Beau held an umbrella over us, we raced to the front doors.

After leaving the umbrella to drip on the porch, he let us in with a key. We were greeted with the spicy aroma of cooking food, making my stomach rumble despite the certainty I'd had after seeing the apparition that I would never want to eat again. Not wanting to drip on the floor, I placed the Mr. Bingle bag on the entry mat, covering it with my backpack.

"We're here!" Beau called out, poking his head into the empty dining room. When he returned, he said, "We must be eating in the breakfast room, since there's only the three of us."

"The three of us? I thought Mimi only invited me."

"True, but I live here." He grinned. "Follow me."

We started walking across the black-and-white-checked marble foyer, but I paused, feeling again as if the eyes of Beau's grandfather Charles were following me from his portrait on the wall. I began walking toward it, but Beau called me back. "It's unnerving, but you get used to it after a while. You can look at it later—Mimi's waiting."

His fingers were icy cold against my bare arm, and when I looked at him closely, his flushed face was dotted with sweat. "Are you feeling all right?"

"I'm fine. I've been working a lot, so I'm pretty exhausted. I think it's just catching up with me."

We continued walking toward the back of the house. I tried to keep up while also admiring the architecture and restraining myself from walking into interesting rooms with elegant furniture and with antique converted gasoliers hanging from intricate plaster medallions. As much as I regretted not getting another chance to study the Bacchus mural in the dining room, just walking through the house was as much of a treat.

I slowed my steps as we passed the window-lined room that jutted off the right side of the house. The walls not filled with windows were paneled in rich mahogany and hung with fishing trophies. An old medical bag sat next to an antique tobacco chest atop an olive-wood Italian chest, a framed Audubon print above it. This was undoubtedly Charles's domain, hardly touched in the twenty-one years since his passing. The room seemed like a shrine to a man who might or might not have called a halt to the investigation into his granddaughter's disappearance. I must have lingered too long, because Beau tugged on my elbow, pulling me away and into the kitchen at the back of the house.

"You're late." Mimi wasn't smiling as she turned, holding a covered soup tureen in mitted hands, from a large stainless steel six-burner stove. "I know it's not Monday, but I was in the mood for red beans and rice. Nola, you can just pluck out the andouille, although I don't know why, since that's the best part. Collards and corn bread are already on the table, although I'm sure everything's cold by now."

"I'm so sorry . . ." I began.

Mimi walked past me to a rear sunroom next to the kitchen; it was filled with knickknacks and wildlife prints and the floor was covered with a sisal rug. A round antique table sat in the middle, with four mismatched chairs wearing the same leafy linen print seat cushions. The table was fully set with a more casual but no less elegant china pattern than we'd used in the dining room. Fresh flowers matching the flowers in the china pattern spilled over a silver epergne in the center of the table.

"It's not your fault," she said, placing the tureen on a black iron trivet on the table. "Beau knows better and should have picked you up earlier."

"But we had an incident at the house—"

She cut me off. "No need to say any more about it."

She turned back to the kitchen, and I followed, determined to be of use, but I was distracted by the view of the brick-paved sitting area tucked beneath towering fuchsia crepe myrtles and a giant old oak outside. The empty areas between chairs and loungers were populated with two large potted citrus trees and random pots filled with succulents and bougainvillea. It was as charming as it was eclectic, and I wanted to snap a picture to show Melanie's dad, a master gardener who had redesigned the garden at her house on Tradd Street more than once. If the differences between the two cities could ever be explained, it would be in pictures of their respective gardens.

I felt a small pang as I looked at it, imagining finally getting to the point in my own home restoration to put in a garden to replace the old coffin and banana tree. *If* I ever got to the point—I was learning it wasn't a simple matter of fixing the plumbing and stripping wood.

"Where's Lorda?" Beau asked.

"The streets are already flooding," Mimi explained, "so she left early. It's supposed to rain all night and it's going to get even worse. I'm surprised you didn't have any problems. Even in your truck, I worry." She held the back of her hand against Beau's forehead. "You're burning up. Have you taken anything?"

"I'm just tired. Really. As soon as I eat something, I'll feel better."

"You need to at least take something. I've got a bottle of Tylenol in the medicine cabinet in the upstairs-hall bathroom." She frowned. "I'd go get it myself, but my knees are aching because of all this rain. Can you manage the stairs, Beau?"

He sat down heavily, his eyes looking glassy. "I'm fine. I don't need anything."

"If you tell me where to go, I'll go get it," I offered.

"Thank you, Nola. That might be best. Just head up the stairs to the next floor and follow the hallway to the right. It will be the second door past the alcove with the stained glass window."

"No problem. I'll be right back." I headed out of the kitchen the way that I'd come—mostly. I ended up mistakenly taking a detour that meant I missed seeing Charles's study, which was probably a good thing since I wouldn't have resisted going in. I eventually found my way to the front foyer and the elegant staircase, deliberately ignoring Charles's portrait. I climbed the stairs slowly so I could feel the smooth mahogany banister beneath my hand and enjoy the view of the foyer below, the close-up examination of the cornices and center medallion above. But somewhere in the middle of my ascent, I felt the pull of the portrait again, and found myself turning around to face it.

One of my dual undergrad degrees had been in art history, and I knew the moving-eye technique was a thing. But that didn't explain the feeling that I got that the eyes in the portrait had actually lifted to follow me up the stairs. Turning my back, I ran quickly to the top.

A warm patina of age that couldn't be manufactured, regardless of how much money people were willing to spend, covered the wooden floors of the hallway, which was lined with hand-loomed rugs from the Far East of a kind that was normally seen under plastic at house museums. Even in the house where I'd lived for almost ten years I hadn't seen floors and rugs this pristine. With two small children and three dogs—sadly, now two—Melanie had given in and removed all the rugs in the house, planning to put them back when JJ and Sara were older, and the dogs better behaved. She was in the habit of telling Porgy and Bess that they were the reason we couldn't have nice things, and then feeling bad for scolding them, and handing out treats.

Having been a docent over the years at several historic homes in Charleston, I found myself walking along the edges of the rugs, trying to hurry while also admiring the art prints and paintings, which displayed an eclectic taste curated over decades if not over a century. The wall on my right was lined with four closed doors, with an alcove window in the middle. I tried to remember if it was the second door before or after the alcove. Or the first. My wandering through the house and general nosiness had distracted me from recalling the simple directions. I studied the closed doors. I could either waste time by finding my way back to the kitchen and asking, or just methodically open doors, starting with the first.

One at a time, I turned the knobs of the first two doors, revealing large bedrooms, both furnished with antiques and wearing a sense of occupancy, including bedside tables with books and a framed New Orleans Saints poster. It had been signed, but already feeling as if I were trespassing, I hastily closed the door without getting a better look and moved past the stained glass window.

Knowing I now had a fifty-fifty chance of opening the right door, I quickly twisted the next knob, and was surprised when nothing happened. The doorknob plate had an empty keyhole like the other doors, so I tried again, thinking it had to be stuck. While turning the knob, I gave it a bump with my hip. The door didn't budge, but something hard and heavy fell from the top of the doorframe, hitting the rug, then bouncing onto the wooden floor. I squatted to retrieve an old-fashioned brass key from beneath a demilune accent table, then held it up to the light from the window. The metal felt hot in my hand as a tremor went through me and I recalled something Meghan Black had once said, something about locked doors and unusual artifacts stored in the house on Prytania.

My gaze bounced from the key to the lock, then back to the top of the doorframe. I doubted that I'd be tall enough to stand on my tiptoes and replace the key from where it had fallen. If the door was locked, it was locked for a reason, and by process of elimination the next door was the one to the bathroom where I'd find the Tylenol for Beau. If I were thinking like my dad, I would move on to the next door, and then find another way to learn what was beyond this one. Like just asking.

Or I could be like Melanie, who jumped from thought to action without pausing in between. It's what usually got her in trouble, and something my father had cautioned me against more than once, even using Melanie as an example. But maybe I was more like Melanie than I thought.

I shoved the key in the lock and turned it, moving it noiselessly until I heard a click. I pushed the door open, the hinges giving only a brief and noisy protest. I smelled dust and the familiar scent of old things as I stared into the completely black space. My fingers fumbled along the wall until I found a switch, and after a brief hesitation I flipped it on.

A Murano glass chandelier came to life in the middle of the ceiling, casting mottled blue and white light over the room. Wooden shelves lined the walls of the room, each crammed with an assortment of what looked like flea market items—children's toys; lamps of all types and sizes; shoes for men, women, and children; a pair of cheerleading pom-poms; a full golf bag. An entire shelf was devoted just to women's purses. There was too much to focus on, and I tried to take it all in and identify what exactly I was looking at. In one corner a mannequin wore a beaded and feathered Mardi Gras queen gown, its bodice covered in purple, gold, and green sequins. On the adjacent shelf sat a collection of hats, mostly baseball caps but also one lace christening bonnet with delicate pink ribbon ties.

Between two tall windows on the far side of the room, both with drapes closed to the light, stood a massive curio cabinet, each shelf covered with a morbid collection of naked pixie-faced porcelain dolls. A shudder tumbled through me, propelling me back against the wall. I was all too familiar with Frozen Charlotte dolls, Victorian portents of doom meant as a warning for wayward children. My family had been haunted by one after it had been dug up from the collapsed cistern in the backyard; it proceeded to show up randomly throughout the house until we reunited it with its previous owner in a Magnolia Cemetery grave.

At the time of its discovery, Beau had laughed at the odd proclivities of late nineteenth-century people, calling them "crazy Victorians," and mentioned that his grandmother had a collection of Frozen Charlottes. Now, seeing said collection in person, I wondered if the same adjective could be used to describe the kind of person who owned at least one hundred of these dolls. And why someone would even want to.

I averted my eyes to study the rest of the room. It was smaller than the other two and might have once been part of the bedroom next to it and used as a dressing room or sitting room. Tucked inside a small circle surrounded by the crowded shelves sat a Queen Anne chaise longue covered in red brocade and flanked by two cane-backed black walnut chairs and a low table upon which rested a child-sized pair of pink gingham sneakers and a matching gingham hair bow. An old Sony tape recorder with toothlike silver rectangle buttons sat on a corner of the table, a white cassette inserted in it, the name Adelyn Wallace written on it in black marker.

I recognized the tape recorder because my father still used one for his writing, finding the pressing of the buttons as reassuring and comforting as Melanie found the clacking of her labeling gun. The habit of clinging to old technology was one of the idiosyncrasies of old people that I had learned to be patient with, like their insistence on using phrases like "record a show" or texting in complete sentences.

I stepped closer to the table, my curiosity admittedly leading me into trespassing. But my dad, in his search for facts, had long since taught me that sometimes it was easier to ask for forgiveness than for permission. Completely ignoring the fact that I wasn't researching anything, I hit the play button.

For a full moment the only sounds I could detect were the soft whirring of the recorder turning and the background hum of central air. Then, almost imperceptibly, came the sound of whimpering and the high-pitched voice of a child saying over and over, *I'm cold. I'm cold.* But no, not a child. A woman. A woman speaking in a child's voice. The child/woman stopped speaking and the ambient sounds of a room were added to by the shifting of fabric, like the movement of a woman's dress as she leaned closer to the recorder. Then, in a low, terrified whisper, came the words *Uncle Freddy.*

With a trembling finger, I hit the stop button, missing it twice before I could press it hard enough to stop the chilling voice. I stepped toward the door, unwilling to turn my back on the macabre tableau and disembodied voice. My shoulder grazed a shelf, knocking off a small stuffed sheep. I quickly picked it up, eager to get out of this chamber of horrors or whatever it was, and settled it back on its perch, prepared to turn and run.

But I couldn't. I froze, staring at the hairbrush on the shelf next to the sheep, separate and random like the rest of the objects displayed on the shelves. Except this object was glaringly familiar. I picked it up, recognizing the faded brand name on the handle, and even the shade and length of the hair in its bristles. It was undoubtedly my missing hairbrush, the one I kept in my backpack but had gone missing at some point that I hadn't been able to recall. Yet here it was in a room full of random personal items and a curio case full of Frozen Charlottes.

"Nola?"

At the abrupt sound of Beau's voice shouting from somewhere outside of the room, I dropped the hairbrush, the smack of it hitting the bare wooden floor like a gun firing next to my ear. I stood immobilized, unsure about everything except that I didn't want him to find me in the odd little room with dark curiosities and the eyes of sightless dolls.

I forced myself to replace the hairbrush on the shelf and flip off the light before retreating from the room.

"Nola?" he called again from the bottom of the stairs. "Are you lost?"

"Nope!" I called back, my voice sounding surprisingly normal.

"Just admiring the beautiful architectural details of the house and all the art." With a trembling hand, I managed to lock the door before placing the key on the floor in front of it so it would appear as if it had fallen. Which, technically, it had.

Then I threw open the last door, relieved to find that it was, in fact, a bathroom. I swung open the medicine cabinet above the sink and grabbed the red-capped Tylenol bottle before walking quickly back down the hallway to the top of the stairs. Holding the bottle aloft like a proud Olympic torchbearer, I forced myself to walk slowly down the steps.

"Thank you," Beau said at the bottom of the stairs as he took the bottle, his face even more flushed than before. "We thought you'd gotten lost."

"I might have," I said, practically jogging as I tried to keep up with his retreating form as he walked toward the kitchen, the words *I'm cold* echoing in my ears as the penetrating gaze from the man in the portrait chilled the back of my neck until I passed out of its sight.

CHAPTER 18

I wasn't sure if it was my imagination that Mimi was looking at me more closely than usual, her bicolored eyes more penetrating. Or it could have been just my guilt over having trespassed so blatantly. As I sat down in the chair Beau had pulled out for me, I had to bite my tongue to keep from blurting out all my questions about that weird room, including why I had found my missing hairbrush amid the detritus of other people's lives.

"I'm sorry I took so long," I said, helping myself to a steaming bowl of white rice. "I was admiring the architectural details of your house, as well as the artwork." I passed the bowl to Beau, who placed it on the table without taking any. "Whoever picked out the art has an incredible eye," I continued. I'd learned in my recent past that when lying it was best to keep as close to the truth as possible. I was hoping to also butter Mimi up in the hope that it might save her opinion of me in case she discovered I'd been snooping.

Mimi lifted the lid from the tureen and I ladled red beans and sausage on top of my rice. I was grateful for the sausage, as I could focus on removing it and not meet Mimi's eyes. Beau waved his hand at Mimi, indicating that he didn't want any, his plate conspicuously empty.

"Really, Beau," Mimi said. "Go on up to your room and lie down, at least until the Tylenol kicks in."

He looked at her through slitted eyes, as if opening them further would allow in too much light. "I will. I just wanted to ask you one question while Nola is here."

What little appetite I'd had when I'd first sat down fled. He must have seen me leaving the room. Or heard me drop the hairbrush. Or he could just tell I'd been up to no good by looking in my trespassing face.

Mimi raised her eyebrows in a mildly interested expression. "And what might that be?"

"The Maison Blanche door from Nola's house. Was it worth getting Christopher so upset that he almost quit?"

My single bite of rice and beans stuck in my throat. I quickly swallowed a gulp of water. "That was my fault. I was the one who asked him to store it for me. I didn't realize . . ."

"It wasn't for you to realize," Mimi said calmly. "Christopher understands that I have strict rules about my storage spaces. They each hold specific and meticulously researched objects and it's important to me to keep them separate."

"He told me he was going to move it to an off-site storage area before you returned from your buying trip to Savannah, so he knew it was temporary." I was trying to make sense of her anger at Christopher. Even Melanie, whose adherence to order and organization bordered on OCD, could always be reasoned with when her plans were thwarted.

"I realize that," Mimi said, her gaze locked on mine. "And it was my fault because I returned home early without warning. But it never should have been in there in the first place. Christopher has worked with me long enough to understand my rules."

Beau had his elbows on the table, his hands on either side of his head as if holding it in place. "Just so you know, Mimi, I stand with Christopher on this one. Please don't ever make me choose sides again."

Mimi's bosom rose and fell, her eyes soft as she regarded her grandson. "You just need to understand, Beau, that there are some things on which I cannot compromise. And that is one of them." Her eyes slid to me, and I wondered if I was imagining the accusatory look in them. "No matter. We had a customer today in the shop, a young man, who asked us if we had anything from the former Maison Blanche building on Canal Street. Since the door doesn't belong to me, I wrote down his name, address, and phone number and told him I'd be in touch if I came across anything." She smiled at me, which worried me more than anything else. "He said he would pay anything to get a relic from the old department store. His address is on Audubon Place, so I imagine he has the funds if you were interested in selling your office door."

"Audubon Place?" I asked.

"Yes. It's off of St. Charles Avenue, opposite Audubon Park," Mimi explained.

"I know. I . . ." I started to mention the man from the park I thought I'd seen on the bicycle, turning into the street. "Never mind. But whether he can afford it or not, it's not for sale. I already have a spot for it, and I love the sense of history it will bring to my house."

"I knew that's what you'd say. He insisted on giving me his information anyway. Just in case you change your mind, I've written it down. Remind me to give it to you before you leave."

Beau slid back his chair and stood, leaning heavily on the table. "I'm going to go upstairs and lie down."

I stood, too. "Do you need help?"

He waved me away. "I'll be fine. Just need the Tylenol to kick in, that's all." He headed back toward the kitchen, his steps slow, then headed toward the front of the house.

When I sat down again, I found Mimi looking at me with a strange expression. "Why do I suddenly smell pine trees and cinnamon? It's like Christmas in here. Were you in a holiday shop or something?"

I sniffed the air, smelling only the smoky andouille and spicy red beans. "No. I haven't been anywhere today except to stop by my house to see what was behind that sealed door at the top of the stairs. It was a bit disappointing, because it was just stuff you normally find in a closet. Well, and an old Mr. Bingle doll."

Her eyebrows rose with mild interest. "Really? A Mr. Bingle? I haven't seen one of those in years."

"Well, that was my first. Anyway, we sometimes smell roses inside our house in Charleston even in the middle of winter, but that's . . ." I stopped, unsure if she'd want to hear about our resident spirit.

"But that's what?" she prompted.

"Louisa. She used to live in our house back in the twenties."

"Ah." Mimi nodded, a small smile on her lips. "A ghost."

"I've never seen her, but I've definitely smelled the roses more than once. I can't communicate with her, but . . ." Once again I stopped midsentence. These were topics I never talked about with other people. But somehow as I sat with Mimi in an old house and with the vivid memory of the room upstairs, they didn't seem out of place.

"But your stepmother can," Mimi finished. She picked up the bread basket full of corn bread and offered it to me.

I took one piece to be polite, knowing that I wouldn't be able to swallow a bite. "Yes. Melanie can. I didn't realize you knew her."

"I don't. But I know of her, of course. Her reputation carries in the same societies I travel in—the world of antiques and old houses. Both areas are very ripe for hauntings. Assuming you believe in that sort of thing." She delicately buttered a piece of corn bread before taking a bite.

"I wasn't really given a choice. I've known Melanie since I was fourteen, so it's not like I could remain oblivious." I plucked out another piece of sausage and placed it on my soup plate to give me something to focus on besides reasons my hairbrush would be in the room upstairs.

"I understand Melanie and the rest of your family will be visiting in October."

I looked at her with surprise.

"Christopher mentioned it. He said he'd recommended the Hotel Peter and Paul. Excellent choice, especially if your stepmother has high standards."

"Yes, she does." I felt uneasy at the thought that they had discussed my family's visit in any kind of detail. It made me wonder why they had.

"But I'm sure they'll be visiting your house, even if they won't be staying there." Mimi sipped her wine, a pleasant smile gracing her face.

"Of course. They're very proud of me."

"As they should be. You're quite young to be buying your own house and taking on such a massive renovation." She carefully placed her glass back on the table. "You know, Nola, that JR Properties is in the business of buying up old homes and renovating them. We have a slew of other candidates with far less work that are available. And might even be further along toward being finished by the time your family visits."

I placed my hands in my lap, no longer pretending to eat, and met her gaze. "I've found my house. I know it won't be easy, but I've discovered that the easy path is rarely the right path."

She nodded and looked down at her plate as if in defeat. "How very true. And how astute you are to have figured that out already, at such a young age."

Half of my mouth turned up in a reluctant grin. "Kicking and screaming, for sure, but I eventually figured it out."

Mimi stood and picked up our plates, waving me back when I stood to help. "I've got it. Would you care for some coffee?"

I didn't, but I still had a lot to talk to her about and I needed the excuse to linger. "Yes, please."

"Good. I've already got a pot brewed, so it will just be a minute. Have a seat on the sofa by the window and I'll be right with you."

I did as instructed and settled myself into soft cushions covered in cotton damask and an eclectic mix of throw pillows. I leaned against a pale blue one with a honeybee embroidered in gold, listening to the rain hit the window glass like the tapping of invisible fingers. Mimi returned once to remove the food from the table, the second time bringing a tray with a coffeepot and two cups, along with a plate of pralines.

She sat down next to me and poured coffee in both china cups before sitting back. "I invited you tonight to discuss the Maison Blanche door, but it seems as if we've already covered it. Although I do think you should call that gentleman who was interested in it. From what I've heard about the renovation so far, it would seem you could use the money right now. Artifacts from the department store still show up from time to time, so you could just wait until the rest of the house is finished."

I took a sip of my coffee, only to allow myself time to respond with something more dignified than an eye roll. "I get what you're saying, Mimi. But I feel as if that door was meant to be a part of the house. And who knows when another door might show up? Besides, it's meant to go on the downstairs bathroom, so it's important that we have the door now."

Despite her compressed lips, Mimi managed a smile. "All right, then. I understand. I hope it helps you to know that I have already apologized profusely to Christopher. It wasn't his fault at all. He did plan to move it before my return, and then I came back early. My only excuse is that I was in a terrible mood because I'd been at an estate auction where I'd been outbid on the one thing I'd gone to acquire, a complete set of Chippendale dining chairs. And then, after setting my heart on two Paris street sketches from a lesser-known artist, I lost on that bid, too. It's no excuse, I realize, but I was in a foul mood when I returned to the shop and jumped at the first thing I saw to be unhappy about.

"Which brings me to my next point. Christopher mentioned that you will need a place to hide your bicycle when your parents are here. It would be my pleasure to store it for you in the off-site storage room for the duration of your parents' stay. Although"—she took a sip from her cup—"it seems to me that you should just tell them. Nothing has ever been gained by deceit."

My gaze shot up to meet hers at her word choice. I wasn't completely sure I was imagining a challenge in her eyes. It was almost as if she knew that I'd found my missing hairbrush, but I couldn't ask her about it without implicating myself.

"I'll think about it," I said as I reached for a napkin and a praline. "I love this fabric on the sofa and matching curtains. Is it new?" I nibbled at the praline while forming my next question, half listening to her response about finding the fabric years ago and hanging on to a clipping of it in her handbag until she found the right piece of furniture for it.

I smiled, crumpling my napkin in my hand before leaning forward. "I had breakfast with Bernard Landry last Sunday. He's the uncle of Beau's friend Jaxson, and a retired police officer."

"I know who he is," she said, her expression suddenly guarded. "He was the first officer on the scene when Jeanne was found. He was the one who was sent to interview me, since I was supposed to be moving in with Jeanne and Louise. He thought I might know something that would help with the investigation. I didn't, of course, but I told him everything I knew that might have been of some help. We sat on the front porch with my parents and Charles. I remembered then thinking how lucky I was to have found Charles. We weren't even engaged then, but he stayed right by my side during the whole ordeal."

I nodded, listening to the constant drumming of the rain outside and beginning to worry about how I was going to get home. "I don't mean to pry, but since the murder occurred in my house, I feel as if it's my responsibility to find out what really happened. So I can rest easy, and Jeanne can rest in peace."

She was already shaking her head before she spoke. "I don't have anything else to add to my original statements. Jeanne was my best friend, and I was going to move in with her and her cousin Louise. But I never got the chance."

I savored another slow sip of coffee, trying to find the right way to frame my next question. After gently returning my cup to its saucer, I said, "There's one piece of information Bernie shared with me that I'm not sure was well-known at the time. Were you aware that Jeanne was pregnant?"

Mimi's face blanched as she stared back at me. "Pregnant? No. That can't be right. She was . . . no. That wasn't like her at all. I can't . . ." She shook her head, unable to finish her sentence.

"I'm guessing, then, that she didn't confide in you."

Mimi shook her head again. "Of course not. That's why I find it so hard to believe. It's just so unlike Jeanne. She was very devout, and she and her boyfriend, Angelo Benedetti, were saving themselves for each other. I know that's a foreign thing these days, but back then many of us were very serious about it. Including Charles and me. Which is why I can't believe . . ." She shook her head. "It's not possible. It must be a mistake."

I just nodded, not wanting to argue with Mimi's memories. "Do you know if Angelo is still alive?"

"I don't. He moved away, and we lost touch."

I nodded. "What about Louise? Have you kept in touch?"

"No. I was mostly just friends with Jeanne. We were friends, but only because of Jeanne. After Jeanne died, we didn't keep in touch. I do know that Louise got married and moved to Metairie but I believe she's now in a care home. Dementia, I think. Her daughter apparently found her asleep in her bedroom after having left a grilled cheese on a burner on a lit stove, and that was a few years ago, so I can only imagine her mental state now."

"That's very sad. Bernie might still want to try and talk with her. He's very gung ho about digging into cold cases. I guess it's something to keep him busy and his mind active in retirement."

"Most likely." She placed her empty cup on the tray and smoothed her pristine skirt, signaling that our conversation was over. Except I had one more question.

"Bernie also told me something about another cold case." I bit my lip, then blurted it out before I could change my mind. "It involves the disappearance of your granddaughter, Sunny."

Mimi took a deep breath and closed her eyes. "Please don't. For over two decades we have tried to find answers. I still think I see her on the street, and try to imagine what she might look like now. I have only been able to continue with my life by recognizing that she is truly gone. And I don't appreciate you bringing this up now."

Mimi stood, her hands clasped in front of her. "It's late . . ." she began.

I stood, too. "Bernie told me that he found something new, something that wasn't with the rest of the case file."

She bent to lift the tray and began walking with it toward the kitchen, almost as if she knew what I was about to say. I followed her, my inherited bullishness making me unwilling to let it go. She set the tray on the counter and, with her back to me, began placing the cups in the sink.

"Bernie said that the reason why Sunny's case file was closed quickly was because your husband, Charles, asked that it be closed. He was friends with some of the higher-ups on the force and had some clout. But that doesn't tell me why."

For a moment, she didn't move. Then she reached over to the faucet and calmly turned on the water. "That's because it isn't true. Charles had friends in the police force, but he also had enemies who would be all too happy to smear his name. He loved his grandchildren. He never would have done such a thing." She began soaping up a sponge and cleaning the dishes as if we were talking about nothing more important than china patterns or dog breeds.

I waited for her to rinse the cups and put them in the dish rack. Then she turned around to face me. "I don't know what Bernie is up to, but I have a strong suspicion that he has a lot of time on his hands. For years he hinted around about writing a book about various unsolved cases. I can't help but wonder if his renewed interest is because of that. I'm just sorry he dragged you into it."

I swallowed down the lump in my throat. "I'm sorry. You're right. My curiosity has led me to overstep, and I can't apologize enough. I won't bring it up again."

Her shoulders softened and she gave me a genuine smile. "Thank you, Nola. I knew you'd understand. And I'd hate something like this to get between us. I rather like you, you know. And I know that Beau does, too. He would be as disappointed as I would if you were no longer a part of our lives."

She walked to the window and peered out. "I imagine Beau is still sleeping and I don't want to wake him. It's too dark and wet for me to drive, so I think it best that you stay here tonight. I've got plenty of room and clean sheets in the guest room."

I hoped I succeeded in hiding my look of horror at the thought of sleeping anywhere near the creepy room. I would have rather swum home. "That's so kind of you, but I need to get back. I've still got some work to do before I head into the office tomorrow, and my notes and computer are all at home. I'll call an Uber—I'll request a large SUV to get over the potholes."

"Only if you're sure, Nola. It's no trouble."

I was already opening the app and requesting my ride. "See— there's one just five minutes away, so all's good." I headed to the front of the house, Mimi correcting me only once as I tried to go the wrong way. I quickly picked up my backpack and stepped out onto the porch. I held up Beau's umbrella. "Tell Beau I've got his umbrella and I'll have it with me the next time I see him to give it back."

A large black SUV slowed to a stop at the front gate, its headlights refracting through the thousands of raindrops falling from the sky. "Thank you so much for dinner, Mimi. And I hope Beau is feeling better tomorrow."

"Anytime, Nola. I love to cook for guests, so I'm always looking for an excuse to have people over." She shoved her hands inside deep pockets in the skirt of her dress. "Before I forget—here's the name and contact info of the man who was interested in buying any Maison Blanche artifacts. Just in case you change your mind."

I took the piece of notepaper and read the name—Michael Hebert— before sticking it in the back pocket of my jeans. "I won't, but thanks."

I took a step, then quickly turned back. "One more thing. Did Jeanne's boyfriend or anyone else that hung around her or the house smoke a pipe?"

She thought for a moment. "Not that I can recall. Why do you ask?"

"Just wondering. Sometimes I think I can smell pipe tobacco."

"How curious. Could be someone walking or driving by the house."

There was something in her eyes I couldn't quite read. "Probably,"

I said. "Thanks again." I opened Beau's umbrella and stepped off the porch before running toward the SUV.

It wasn't until I was climbing the steps of my apartment that I realized I didn't have the bag with Mr. Bingle inside. I knew I hadn't forgotten it. I had placed my backpack over it when I arrived, but when I picked up my backpack before leaving, it wasn't there. It was inexplicably gone.

Before I had time to think about the implications, I heard the landline phone ringing upstairs. I ran up the steps to pick it up before Jolene could, which would have left me to explain one more thing I couldn't understand.

CHAPTER 19

The following morning, I stumbled from my bedroom in search of coffee. I was still relatively new to the concept of needing caffeine first thing, but it was a habit I was happy to form. Mostly because it meant pairing it with freshly baked muffins or whatever concoction Jolene whipped up each morning.

Although it wasn't yet seven o'clock, Jolene was already sitting at the dining table with her laptop open, a plate of lemon poppy-seed muffins sitting next to two steaming mugs of coffee. I had no idea what time she woke up, but no matter how early I emerged from my bedroom, she was up and fully dressed—including shoes and jewelry and makeup—with perfect hair. And her bed was made. I was beginning to think she actually never slept, which would explain so much.

The coffee mug closest to her depicted the glowing green palace of Oz. The second mug simply had the word *NOLA* printed in bold black letters against a white background and had a black handle. It had been a gift from Jolene and I loved it for both its simplicity and also its double meaning.

She turned to me with a bright smile. "Good morning, sleepyhead," she said cheerfully.

I grunted, then shuffled to the table. My cup was still hot. As I took my first sip, I contemplated her through the rising steam. "How did you know I was awake and ready for coffee?"

"I've learned to wait until you hit the snooze button the third time. Then I get up to fill your cup and return just in time for you to emerge from your cave."

I raised my eyebrows, the move using up most of my energy. There was something in her use of the word "cave" that I should probably have been offended by, like an unspoken comparison to a Neanderthal, but it was still too early to form words. I'd never claimed to be a morning person, and waking up before noon had been one of the hardest parts of adulting.

She watched as I took several happy sips from my mug, then helped myself to a muffin; she slid a napkin toward me as a reminder about crumbs. I mumbled my thanks as I demolished the muffin in two bites, then washed it down with more coffee.

"If you keep feeding me like this, I'm going to be as big as a house and it will be all your fault."

"You know, Nola, I'm just as happy to whip up one of those green shakes you used to drink if you'd prefer."

I felt a moment of completely irrational panic. Of course I could survive again on veggie shakes with protein flakes. But why would I want to? I was like a person who'd only ever tasted white chocolate suddenly being given a chunk of dark chocolate. With almonds. There was no turning back. "No, thanks. I prefer to be the guinea pig for all of your culinary creations. I wouldn't want you to feed something to Jaxson that wasn't up to par."

"That's not why I do it, and you know it. Besides, Jaxson is dating someone else, so it's not like it matters." She smiled grimly, like the bridesmaid who'd just watched someone else catch the bouquet. She reached down into her monogrammed tote bag, pulled something out, and placed it on the table next to me. "Look what I found. No need to look like your head got stuck in a wind tunnel."

For the second time that morning, I was at a loss as to how to respond. My hairbrush, the exact same one I'd seen on the shelf in the odd room in Mimi's house, sat on the table next to me. "Where did you find this?"

"In your backpack. I wasn't being nosy, but I needed a look at your worksheet showing the interior renovation work schedule and there it was—right on top! I'm sure you looked for it there, but sometimes we all suffer from situational blindness, where our brain tricks us into thinking we're not seeing what we're looking for. From my experience, it's mostly men who suffer from this affliction. And by the way, I don't think scheduling potty breaks should be included on a spreadsheet. It's a little much, don't you think?"

I was only half listening to her, wondering how my brush had gone from the shelf to my backpack. I cleared my throat. "No. It wasn't in my backpack. I emptied everything and searched every pocket and corner. It definitely wasn't in there."

"But maybe—" Jolene began.

I cut her off. "I saw it last night. At Mimi's house. It was in a locked room upstairs that was filled with shelves stuffed with all sorts of random personal items that looked like they belonged to a bunch of different people. But it was definitely my hairbrush."

"That's probably why Mimi gave you the key, so you could find it. I mean, that's how you got into the locked room, right?"

I managed to meet her eyes. "Mimi didn't give me the key. Neither did Beau."

"But you said it was loc—" She stopped, shook her head. "Oh, Nola. What did you do?"

"Nothing—I swear. I was looking for the bathroom and I guess I bumped the wrong door too hard and the key fell from the top of the doorframe. What was I supposed to do?"

She gave me the same look Jack usually gave Melanie when she impulsively jumped from idea to action without pausing in between to think. "At least tell me you didn't touch anything and that you returned the key."

"More or less. But I think the main thing here is how my brush made it into—and out of—their creepy little room."

"Good point, but it's not like you can ask them, is it? And by 'their,' you're assuming Beau knows about it, too?"

"Well, shouldn't I? He lives there. I can't imagine he doesn't know. And it's not the only weird thing. Beau and I took a Mr. Bingle doll from that attic room at my house. It could be valuable, so we didn't want to leave it there, and I brought it in from Beau's truck for the same reason." I purposely neglected to mention the lacy bra that I found under the seat and that contributed to my decision. "But I didn't realize until I got home that I didn't have the bag. And I explicitly remember placing it on the floor beneath my backpack. It definitely wasn't there when I left, because I would have seen it."

"Maybe you left it in Beau's truck and just don't remember?"

I shook my head. "Definitely not. I placed it in a Rouses Market shopping bag and brought it inside, then put the bag with my backpack so I wouldn't forget it when I left. But I did forget, because it wasn't there."

"Did you call Beau?" she asked, a small dent between her brows.

"No. He was sick last night and went to bed early, so I just texted him. But I *know* I brought the bag in with me. And this whole thing with my hairbrush is just . . . not right."

"Wait and see what Beau says. Maybe he took the bag with the doll up to his room when he went to bed early."

"That's a possibility, I guess. But my hairbrush . . . It's all so strange."

"Like I said, talk to Beau. There's a logical explanation somewhere. Sometimes you just got to hang in there like a hair on a biscuit." She turned back to her laptop. "I was just updating our YouTube page with Jaxson's latest video. I'll add some commentary, but I have to say that Thibaut and Jorge are a bit of a comedy team—sort of like the Two Stooges. Jorge does a great job of pretending to nail-gun his sleeves to the wall and Thibaut is an expert faller—like, off of ladders and down the stairs. I'm going to suggest that Jaxson use a tripod, because otherwise the camera shakes too much from his laughing."

"Seriously? They're funny?" I moved to stand behind her and

watched as Thibaut waved at the camera as he walked closer, and tripped over his own feet, taking the camera with him.

"I'm serious. And Jaxson and I aren't the only ones who appreciate their little routine—we've got over thirty thousand followers already. Which is something, because home-improvement videos are huge. I guess the comedy part adds something fun to the usual renovation video."

"That's good, I guess. I mean, hopefully it will turn up some new clients for Beau's company, since publicity is basically how I'm paying him. Are the commenters local?"

Jolene scrolled down. "Mostly—at least the ones who say where they are. There's actually one guy who comments a lot, and he says his home is in New Orleans. He must have his notifications set for alert, because he always comments as soon as I post a video." She was silent for a brief moment as she moved the cursor down the screen. "Yep! First comment on the video I sent not ten minutes ago. Michael Hebert."

I leaned closer to read his comment. Love seeing the progress of this reno. Can't wait to see what you might find hidden in those walls!

Straightening, I said, "Why is that name so familiar?"

"Well, maybe because Hebert is probably the third most popular name in New Orleans. And Michael has been popular since the archangel Michael got his wings. Although, come to think of it, the name is familiar to me, too. Not as in I think I know him; it's just that I recall his name being called—like in roll call for a class. Maybe I went to grad school with him or something. Which would make sense, since he's obviously interested in old-house renovations."

"I'll be right back." I returned to my bedroom to retrieve the jeans I'd worn the day before, which were helpfully still on top of the pile of clothes where I'd tossed them. I fished out the piece of paper Mimi had given me, then returned to the dining table.

I placed it in front of Jolene. "Same spelling?"

She nodded. "Where did this come from?"

"Mimi gave it to me. It's the name and contact info for the guy who walked into the Past Is Never Past looking for Maison Blanche artifacts—like doors and other fixtures. She didn't mention that I had one, but promised to be on the lookout."

"Well, if he lives on Audubon Place, he can certainly shell out a lot of money for your door."

I snatched the paper. "*Et tu, Brute?* Mimi said the same thing. It's *my* door and it's staying in *my* house." I looked down at the address again. "What's so special about Audubon Place?"

"Well, it's private, for one—they've got a security hut and a No Trespassing sign at the front. They actually hired Israeli commandos to guard the twenty-eight homes right after Katrina, which didn't endear them to the rest of the city but worked, because none of the houses got looted. It's some of the most prime real estate in New Orleans, all worth well into the millions and mostly built in the last decade of the nineteenth century and first part of the twentieth century."

"I wonder why he's looking to buy old department store fixtures."

"Same reason why we would if we hadn't found the door in the house, Nola. My guess is, he's restoring a house."

"Would make sense, I suppose." I grabbed another muffin, remembering to eat this one over a napkin. "I saw a guy yesterday at the park after my run. He was about our age and I was pretty sure he was staring at me."

"In a disturbing way?"

"Not really. I think I've seen him on my runs before, but this was the first time I got a close-up of him. He sat on one of the benches by the fountain, but didn't say anything even though he smiled at me. Maybe he just wanted to cool off, too. It's not like I'm the only person allowed on those benches."

"You know, Nola, he could have been just wanting to meet you."

I rolled my eyes. "Right. Even you've accused me of stealing clothes from Goodwill to go running in. I highly doubt that. Anyway, when I was in the truck with Beau later, I was pretty sure I saw the same guy on a bicycle, and he turned into Audubon Place. I know this is a huge leap, and it could all be a huge coincidence . . ." I let the word trail away.

"But there's no such thing as coincidence," Jolene said slowly, voicing the unspoken words in my own head. Closing her laptop, she stood. "There's one way we can find out. If you can do a power walk today instead of a run, I'll come with you. I've got an idea."

"Would you like to tell me your idea first? Just in case it involves me speaking to strange men?"

"Trust me, Nola." She began walking toward her bedroom. "Don't forget your hairbrush. You might want to use it before putting your hair in a ponytail. If it was Halloween I'd stick acorns in it so you could go as a squirrel's nest."

"Very funny," I said to her closed door. After grabbing another muffin, I retreated into my bedroom to throw on my running attire.

Despite it taking me less than five minutes, Jolene was already changed and waiting by the door. She looked like an advertisement for Lululemon, her leggings, jog top, and head wrap in a matching floral pattern of soft pinks and greens. Her hair had been pulled back into a high ponytail and she'd put on fresh lipstick.

"Seriously, Jolene? I thought we were going to exercise in the park, not going to a cocktail party."

"Good to know, since you look like you're dressed to panhandle and I'm not even sure that's legal here. Seriously, Nola. How old are your shorts?"

I looked down at my USC shorts I'd been wearing since tenth grade. They were faded to a mottled blue, with a quarter-sized hole on a side seam, and hem threads dangling like fringe from the bottom. "High school. But they still fit and they're comfortable."

Her eyes widened. "Well, bless your heart." She opened the French door at the top of the stairs and motioned for me to go first.

We speed walked down Freret to cut through campus, which we found preferable to dodging full garbage cans and broken sidewalks on

Broadway. When we reached the park, Jolene stopped me and grabbed my T-shirt. Before I knew what she was doing, she'd tied it in a knot at my waist.

"There," she said, swiping her hands as if she'd just put out a fire. "Now you don't look like you're pregnant with all that bagginess. There's nothing wrong with showing off your figure, even in workout clothes. The secret is to let your clothes be tight enough to show you're a woman, but not too tight to show you're not a lady."

Despite myself, I snorted. "Very funny. Did your grandma teach you that?"

"Actually, no. I read it in a book. But it's accurate either way." She began walking, pumping her arms as if she were preparing to take flight, and I had to jog to catch up to her. "Okay, you be on the look-out. Use a secret code if you spot him."

"A secret code?"

"Yes. Like 'Hairy toad.'"

"'Hairy toad,'" I said slowly. "And then what do we do?"

"You just keep looking. If we don't see him, then we'll go to plan B."

"But I don't even know what plan A is!"

"Don't worry, Nola. We'll figure it out. It's good for your brain not to always have everything planned in advance. Keeps you creative."

"Fine," I breathed, unable to carry on conversing because I was panting too heavily.

We went around the path three times without spotting him, or any male older than four and younger than seventy. We stopped at the fountain where I'd seen the man before; I put my hands on my knees as I gasped for breath before using the knot on my T-shirt to wipe the sweat from my face.

"No luck?" Jolene asked. She had delicate perspiration beads on her forehead, her makeup still perfect, her ponytail sleek and bouncy, soft curls forming around her headband.

I shook my head. "This is the usual time I go running and when I know I've seen him. He must not be running today."

Jolene turned toward the exit of the park. "I guess it's time to turn to plan B."

I trotted after her, still gasping as I tried to catch my breath. I needed to lay off the muffins. I thought of Jolene's offer to make my green smoothies but quickly pushed it aside. In typical Melanie fashion, I decided I'd think about changing my diet when the renovation was done and I wasn't so stressed.

"Where are we going?" I asked as we jogged across St. Charles Avenue.

"To Audubon Place."

"I thought you said it was private."

"It is. But my best friend and sorority sister from undergrad, Mary-Swan, lived here—and her family still does. I'm in the habit of bringing them baked treats, so I'm on the approved-access list and the security guards know me. Plus, I practically lived in her house during exam weeks. It was a quiet place to study. And it had a chef's kitchen where I could bake off some stress."

With only a couple of bats of Jolene's eyelashes, she and I walked through the gate, slowing our pace so I could marvel at the various architectural styles of the palatial homes set amid towering oak trees on a wide boulevard, a manicured park in the middle separating each home from the neighbor across the street.

"This is very SOB," I said, admiring a white stuccoed mansion with a red terra-cotta–tiled roof.

"Pardon me?"

"South of Broad. In Charleston. It's where you find historic houses like this. My family's house on Tradd Street is SOB. Melanie inherited it and it's been a love-hate relationship ever since. She swears that as much as she loves it, she still has dreams where she uses a flamethrower to solve all of her renovation problems."

"Ouch. I can see now why you turned to historic preservation."

"Eventually. I used to want to be a professional musician and song-writer. But there was something about bringing derelict houses back to life that carried special meaning for me. I guess I found the parallels to my own life irresistible."

"There's still time," she said gently. "My grandmama didn't know she wanted to be a funeral director until my granddaddy died. People kept telling her to sell the family business, but she's as stubborn as a mule under an apple tree and wouldn't budge. And now her funeral home is rated number one in the state and people agree that her customers look better when she's done with them than when they were alive."

We stopped in front of a Queen Anne Victorian with an inviting wraparound porch and leaded glass front doors. "Is this it? I didn't bring the paper with the address, but I think this is the right one."

"I didn't, either, and I only glanced at it once." Jolene bit her lip. "And this is the main reason why I don't like to exercise—there's no way to carry your pocketbook with everything you need."

"It was just a piece of paper, Jolene. There's plenty of room in your bra top."

With a sidelong glance she led us next door to a Spanish Renaissance mansion with a green tiled roof, and deep porches along the first floor. "I think this is it."

"Does it really matter?" I asked. "I can only hope that your plan B doesn't involve knocking on a door unannounced."

She looked at me with genuine shock. "Dressed like this?"

I rolled my eyes. "That wasn't my point. But seriously, why are we here?"

"Don't you want to meet your mystery admirer? If it's the same guy who wants to buy your door, it would give you a good excuse to set up a meeting, even if you have no plans to sell it. I figured if he lives here and goes running in the park, we might catch him going or coming."

"And then what? Light myself on fire so he'll stop to chat? Or just let him know that I'm stalking him?"

"That would be plan C. I haven't quite worked that out yet."

"Can I help you?"

We both whipped around at the sound of the male voice behind us.

Without thinking, I shouted, "Hairy toad," cringing immediately at the perplexed expression on the man's face.

"Michael? Michael Hebert?" Jolene blurted, pronouncing it the French way, with a silent H and T. "It's so great to see you again—it's been, what? A year? Two years? Whatever—it seems like forever ago."

He stood on the street, holding his bicycle, looking at us with interest. He was even more good-looking close up, his dark hair more chestnut but brightened with sun-streaked highlights, and hazel eyes looking dusky green, most likely owing to his green polo shirt. He smiled, but his confusion was evident. His eyes narrowed for a moment. "Wait a minute—preservation technology? Or was it environmental law? I seem to remember a redhead in one of those classes. We were a pretty small group, though. I'm sorry—I don't recall your name. . . ."

Jolene extended her hand. "Jolene McKenna. I was pretty shy back then, so I kept to myself. I decided to stay in the city and now work in the preservation field. What about you?"

Michael kept glancing at me, as if waiting for an introduction, but I didn't want to interrupt whatever plan C was. "I still live here." He indicated the Spanish Renaissance house. "With my aunt and uncle." He shrugged. "My sister moved away, but there's something about New Orleans that won't let go of some of us, you know?"

"I most certainly do," Jolene said with a sympathetic nod of her head. "Just like my friend here, Nola Trenholm. She's from Charleston, but after just one year of undergrad at Tulane, she knew she had to come back."

He turned to me, and his gaze didn't register surprise, almost as if he'd expected to see me. It was a look of familiarity, as if he already knew who I was.

As if reading my thoughts, he said, "I've seen you before—running in the park. We must go at about the same time, because I've seen you there a lot."

"Yes." I nodded eagerly. "That's probably it. I thought you looked vaguely familiar, too."

He grinned, his teeth white against his tanned face. "I noticed you were admiring the architecture on the street. I take it you're into old buildings, too?"

"Oh, yes. I have a master's degree in historic preservation from the College of Charleston, and I work as an architectural historian for a civil engineering firm here in New Orleans."

"And she just bought her own house in the Marigny and is restoring it," Jolene added.

"That's amazing," he said without looking away. He also didn't volunteer anything about himself.

"I work with JR Properties," Jolene interjected. "We buy and renovate old houses and sell them."

When he still hadn't said anything, I asked, "What about you?"

It took him a moment to answer. "Oh. I work for my uncle on various projects. Right now I'm also the research assistant for one of the preservation professors at Tulane. It's a good gig and it's convenient, since I'm just next door."

He smiled again, which made me forget that he really hadn't told us much at all.

"I have an idea," Jolene said in a tone of voice that always made me nervous. "I'd love to host a little dinner party at our apartment and invite some other preservation-minded friends so we can compare notes and get to know each other."

"That sounds great," Michael said, looking directly at me.

"Wonderful. As soon as I figure out when, I'll send you a text. We're on Broadway, so not too far."

"I'll look forward to it." He pulled out his phone. "You'll need my phone number. Give me yours so I can call you so then I'll have yours, too."

"Oh, right," Jolene said, then proceeded to give Michael my cell number. "Just let it ring—we didn't bring our phones with us."

"It was great running into you," he said, not making any attempt to move.

"Definitely," I said. "The historic-preservation community is a small one, so we have to stick together." It sounded incredibly stupid even to my ears, but there was something about Michael Hebert that left me a little tongue-tied.

"So," Michael and I said in unison.

"I meant, excuse me," he said looking directly at me.

I found myself inexplicably blushing, reading something into his expression that was probably my imagination. I found his elusiveness added to his allure and made him oddly compelling. Maybe it was his New Orleans accent, or the fact that he lived in an old house and loved historic preservation. I couldn't help but draw parallels with my own story. It didn't hurt that he easily could have been a contender for *People* magazine's sexiest man alive.

I looked at him expectantly.

He smiled. "This is my house and you're kind of in the way. I don't want to hit you with my bike."

"Right. Gosh. Sorry!" I jumped out of the way, landing on Jolene's foot and eliciting a small *oof* from her.

"Looking forward to seeing you again soon," he said with a wave before leading his bike up the driveway.

Jolene grabbed my arm and began pulling me back down the street toward St. Charles Avenue. "Do I have toothpaste on my nose or something?" I asked.

She looked at me. "No. Why?"

"Because Michael kept looking at me in a weird way."

Jolene sighed heavily before resuming her arm-pumping power walk, causing me to jog to catch up. "Because you're a beautiful woman, and because you didn't stop blushing from the moment he appeared. I can't smell pheromones, but if I had an infrared camera or whatever those things are that can photograph things that are invisible to the human eye, I'd bet you were showering him like an April rainstorm with them."

"I was not," I said, jogging faster to overtake her. When she'd caught up to me, I said, "Did you really remember him from your classes?"

"No. It was just an educated guess. My daddy always told me, if it looks like a duck, waddles like a duck, and quacks like a duck, it's probably a duck." She held up her manicured nails and, starting with her thumb, counted off her points. "He was standing on Audubon Place with a bike and a backpack and I thought I'd remembered his name from grad school, so I made an educated guess."

"Purely Machiavellian. Who would have thought?"

"Hey, it got you a date, right?"

"It's not a date. It's simply the possibility of a small gathering of like-minded people."

"Really, Nola, you have so much to learn." She pulled out her phone from a hidden pocket on the outside of her leggings, the vibrating now audible, and looked at the screen.

"I thought you didn't have your phone."

She gave me an innocent smile and batted her eyelashes before looking down at her screen, her smile quickly fading. "It's from Beau. He wants to know if I'm with you and why you're not answering your phone."

Her thumbs flew over the screen as she typed, the beep of a reply sounding immediately after she hit SEND. "He says there's a problem at the house and he needs to talk to you." Jolene looked up. "He asks if you could meet him there within the hour. I can drive you—I need to pick up the hatboxes and other stuff from the closet anyway."

"He doesn't say what it is? Or any response about my Mr. Bingle question I texted him about this morning?"

She shook her head. "That's probably one of the things he wants to talk about."

"Fine, I guess. I just need to call my boss and tell him I'm working from home today." I leaned closer to see her phone. "Did Beau say anything about his fever? Is he better?"

She tapped something on the screen and waited a moment before shaking her head. "Not even a bubble. Typical. He could be texting from a hospital, for all we know. Maybe you should call Mimi."

"No," I said a little too quickly. "I don't feel as if she'd want to talk to me right now, and I've got too many questions that still need sorting in my mind first." I picked up my pace.

We started moving at a slow jog, Jolene's ponytail bouncing with a perkiness I don't think I'd ever felt. "I'll pack up a few bundles of my muffins for you to bring with you. That should help smooth any ruffled feathers."

I nodded, even though I had a strong feeling that ruffled feathers were the least of my problems.

CHAPTER 20

After four failed attempts to parallel park in between Thibaut's and Jorge's trucks at the front of the house, Jolene finally gave up and parked two blocks away. With her sun hat on her head and with her white sunglasses and heels, she looked as if she were heading to a ladies' luncheon instead of going to a house under construction. "You know we'll be carrying stuff down from the attic and putting it in the car, right? That's a lot of steps in high heels."

"I'm sorry to have to say this twice in one day, Nola, but bless your heart. It must have been divine intervention that led us back to each other, because there is so much I need to teach you. There are three able-bodied and very strong men in that house who wouldn't let us lift and carry all that stuff even if we wanted to. And by the way, your hair looks nice."

"I brushed it."

"Well," she said. "That's a start. I don't want you setting your goals too high. Do you have a choker-length strand of good pearls?"

"Yes," I said slowly, trying to catch up to where her mind was running. "Melanie gave me her grandmother Sarah's when I graduated from high school. Why?"

"My grandmama always says that a string of pearls looks good with everything except a thong bikini. She keeps a whole drawerful of pearl chokers and matinee length—she gets them from Walmart—for those unfortunate customers who aren't properly accessorized to go meet Jesus."

"That's good to know," I said as we reached my front porch. I grabbed the door handle but was stopped at the sound of a dog barking inside. I whipped the door open and froze. A small, fluffy gray and white dog sat in the middle of the room, apparently keeping Thibaut, Jorge, and Beau at bay where they stood—or sat, since Beau, still looking flushed, was on the floor with his head against the wall, a blue thermos that I knew belonged to Jorge sitting next to him.

"Whose dog is this?" I asked.

Thibaut made a move to walk toward me, only to back away when the dog snarled, the large man's hands held up as if he were being arrested. It was uncharitable of me to think he might be familiar with the pose, but I couldn't help it. I looked closer to make sure the dog wasn't foaming at the mouth. It definitely wasn't rabid, nor did it look very threatening, due to its short, floppy ears, big dark eyes, and round black nose and how when he sat, his back legs and rear end made a tripod.

"We don't know," Thibaut said. "Jorge and I were upstairs tearing out the dry rot so we can get started on the wiring and he just walked in. He's been down here ever since and won't let us leave."

"Is he—or she—wearing a collar?"

Thibaut shrugged. "We don't know. It won't let us close enough to find out."

To Jolene, I said, "Are these the strong, able-bodied men you were referring to?" I shook my head as I knelt. Looking directly into the button eyes, I patted my thighs. "Come here, sweetie."

A pink tongue came out, so it looked as if the dog might be smiling as it stood and trotted over to me, its beautiful plumed tail wagging. He jumped into my lap—it was definitely a he—toppling me over and covering my face with licks.

I felt his neck and didn't find a collar. I didn't expect to once I got a close-up view. His fur was matted in balls and his ribs poked out from beneath his skin. He was either lost or abandoned, and when I looked into his big dark eyes, it was clear that he no longer considered himself homeless.

Jolene approached and the dog bent his head into her hand to be petted. "Isn't he just the sweetest thing? He thinks you're his mama."

Thibaut poured water from a bottle into a paper cup and brought it over with hesitant steps. The dog didn't complain as the giant of a man knelt next to him and brought the cup to the dog's snout. It began lapping up the water, spraying my face and legs with little droplets and making me laugh.

"I think you just got yourself a dog," Thibaut said, stroking the dog's head.

"Oh, no, no, no," I protested. "I can't—"

"Of course you can," Jolene said. "He looks just like the dog you had growing up, General Lee. I figured you loved him a lot, because you've got more pictures of him in your room than people." She straightened and began counting things off on her fingers, starting with her thumb. "Obviously we need to take him to a vet to see if he's chipped, and put up flyers in the neighborhood—which can wait until tomorrow. On our way home, we can stop at a pet store and buy food and a bed and other important supplies, like cute bandannas and a couple of sweaters, because it will eventually get cold. I was hoping he was a she, because I love painting my mama's dog's toenails and putting bows on her ears, but I'll get over it. Lastly, we'll give him a bath with the flea shampoo we're going to buy, and make an appointment with a groomer. I'd do it myself but I left all of my dog-grooming equipment back home in Mississippi."

We all needed to take a breath after listening to her. "I didn't say I wanted to keep him."

Thibaut grinned. "I don't think you got much of a choice."

"I didn't say you had to keep the little guy," Jolene said in that tone that always made me nervous. "We just need to make sure he's taken care of while we wait for his owners to claim him."

Beau, who hadn't said a word yet, grunted before closing his eyes and leaning back against the wall.

Jorge began talking rapidly in Portuguese. When he was done, Thibaut said, "Jorge's mother made some of her special broth for Beau. He's not sure what's in it, but she always gives it to Jorge when he's sick and he swears it's like a miracle cure after the first day of taking it."

I raised my eyebrows, the dog now resting his head comfortably on my chest. "What about the first day?"

After a brief exchange in Portuguese, Thibaut said, "Well, I'm not sure how to translate that exactly, but he says it makes you really relaxed and sleepy so you don't realize you're feeling so bad." He scratched his neck. "Not really sure if these are the right words, but he also said something like that first day is definitely not the time to have a discussion with your ex-wife."

"What does that mean?" I asked.

"It's not a literal translation—but I think he said it loosened the tongue."

Jorge nodded. *"Não pode mentir."*

Thibaut's eyes widened. "Oh, okay. Well, that's interesting."

"What did he say?"

"It means that you can't lie."

We all looked over at Beau, including the dog, who stopped licking my chin and neck long enough to turn his head.

Jolene walked over to Beau and put the back of her hand on his forehead. "How long has he been like this?"

"Well, when he got here this mornin' he didn't look so good, but said he was fine. He went upstairs and took pictures of that closet and hallway, but he still didn't look so good. He said he didn't take any Tylenol because he was fine, so Jorge here jumped in his car and came back with his mama's broth. Says she always keeps a batch in the freezer just in case." He jerked his head in Beau's direction. "He's been like that ever since."

Jolene unscrewed the thermos lid and took a sniff. "Smells like cherry Kool-Aid." She stuck her finger inside and tasted it before screwing up her face. "Oh, my word. That's a grain-alcohol punch."

Jorge said something in Portuguese to Thibaut. Turning toward us, Thibaut said, "It's his mother's special recipe. She uses the Kool-Aid to make it taste better and the grain alcohol to make the patient forget they were ever sick."

Jolene screwed the lid on before turning back to Beau. "Does anything hurt?" she asked Beau.

Shaking his head, he slurred, "Nothing hurts. I feel pretty good." He gave her a drunken smile.

Not trusting his judgment, Jolene prodded the lower-right side of his abdomen, eliciting a loud giggle. "No pain there, then?"

He gave her another loopy smile. "Nope. I liked that. Do it again."

Jolene stood, her hands on her hips. "Well, he's just pitiful. At least it's not appendicitis. My guess is it's just some kind of bug he picked up and it needs to run its course. But that's not going to happen if he won't stay in bed."

She frowned, and I could almost hear the cogs in her brain spinning. "I make an excellent chicken soup and we have a couch. My car is big enough to lay him down in the backseat with the dog for company, and the trunk is big enough for hatboxes and probably whatever else is in the attic." Jolene wagged her finger at me. "I told you that a big car is an asset."

"Only if you know how to drive it. Besides, don't you think Beau would be better off at home?"

"Absolutely not. Trust me. I've nursed people before and I know what I'm doing."

"But did they survive?" I asked, not entirely joking.

In the end, Thibaut and Jorge were able to fit all the contents of the closet in Bubba's trunk, since—as Jolene reminded me—her grandmother had never owned a car that couldn't carry eight bodies and the tools to bury them. The men wouldn't let us carry anything, and they even managed to put Beau in the backseat without dropping him. I placed the dog next to him for company, then jumped in the passenger seat up front.

"You should probably call Mimi to let her know where Beau is," Jolene suggested.

"Good point. Although I'm not ready to talk to her until I've spoken with Beau about the hairbrush and Mr. Bingle. She might bring them up."

"Then text her. That's what we Gen Zs do best, right? She might actually think it's weird if you call."

"True." I texted Mimi that Beau was staying at our apartment because he was still feeling under the weather and that Jolene was going to make him chicken soup. I made it clear that both Jolene and I would be there and that he would be sleeping on the couch, but I left out the part about the thermos from Jorge and the mystery ingredients.

I waited a few moments for her to respond, and when she didn't, I tossed my phone into my backpack. "I hope she calls his girlfriend, Sam, so she doesn't worry."

"Or not," Jolene said, a purely wicked smile gracing her innocent face.

I awoke to a rough tongue lapping my cheek. I sat up in the pitch dark, disoriented for a moment as I imagined I was back home in Charleston with Porgy and Bess, who'd slept on my bed since they were puppies. Except they weren't puppies anymore, and I wasn't in Charleston. And the stray dog, albeit bathed and bandannaed, had been given strict instructions to stay in the cute blue dog bed with the Tempur-Pedic bottom—Jolene's insistence—on the floor by my bed. He'd apparently disagreed and had waited until I was asleep to assert his place next to me.

I gently pushed him away, then stood to place him back in his own bed. I hadn't named him yet, because I wasn't going to keep him. I couldn't. I loved dogs, and even made Melanie and my dad FaceTime me with Porgy and Bess. But I wasn't in any kind of position to take care of a dog or any other living creature. Taking care of myself was still a relatively new concept. I continued to feel as if I were walking on ice, not quite steady and taking it slowly, being careful not to slip or fall through a hole. I wasn't even sure if I could handle a goldfish yet.

I stopped, still holding him in my arms, listening. Yes, there it was. The sound of a man's voice, speaking quietly and pausing at intervals. I put the dog back in his bed with a stern warning to stay, then quietly let myself out of my bedroom. The scented night-light that Jolene had placed in the little hallway that was between our bedrooms and separated the bathroom from the dining area illuminated the lower half of the teacher's desk and a man's feet.

By a quick process of elimination—necessary, since I was still half asleep—I realized the man was Beau. I took a step closer, then froze when I saw the dangling cord from the landline telephone bounce across the shaft of light. Beau was talking on the disconnected phone. Either he was sleepwalking or I was losing my mind. Or both.

I could never remember what to do with a sleepwalker. Wake them up? Don't wake them up? Lead them back to bed? I began to step backward toward my bedroom to let him sort it out himself, but a single word made me freeze again. *Mom.*

My lips opened, a barely audible *tick* sounding as I peeled my suddenly dry tongue from the roof of my mouth. I wanted to move away, disappear into my room, but my feet seemed glued to the floor, unable to move even if my brain insisted on it.

"I miss you."

An odd sound, like invisible ions rushing through space, crackled and popped in the air between us. A language that was more of a song, or an emotion, than words danced from the receiver. I'd heard it when Melanie's grandmother Sarah had called on the same phone. Completely indecipherable to me and most people, but somehow understood by Melanie. And Beau.

"Can you help me find her? I know she's alive or she'd have told me. I've been searching for so long and I can't do this on my own."

The same rushing noise came at me again, making my ears ring. I heard Beau lean against the desk, the wood creaking. "Not her." His voice sounded defeated and tired, and I wanted to go to him and put my arms around him. But I remained frozen to my spot. "Not her," he said again. "I want her too much."

The room seemed to zing and buzz with electricity for a moment. Then silence fell, as if the person on the other end was waiting for an answer. Then Beau's voice, still a little slurred: "She's dangerous. I can't afford to lose my focus. I can't ever let that happen again."

The silence fell like a shroud. Then, like it was a whisper without a source, I heard a single word. *Nola.*

Something soft and wet tickled my ankle. I yelped, imagining a large cockroach or a rat—neither too far from the realm of possibility in any building in New Orleans.

The receiver slammed down into the cradle. I stood, motionless, only the sound of the dog's licking giving us away.

"Nola?" The light reached only up to his knees, but I felt Beau looking at me.

"How did you know it was me?"

It took him a moment to answer. "The dog." The desk creaked as he stood, and the movement made me suddenly nervous. "And your scent. It's . . ." I felt rather than saw him shrug. I waited for him to say something like how I smelled like hair detangler or sawdust. Or dog shampoo. Instead, he said, "Intoxicating."

He swayed toward me, his feet stumbling as he struggled to balance himself.

I reached forward and wrapped my arms around his bare chest. After Jolene had dumped out the contents of the thermos and made him eat her chicken soup, she'd put him to bed on the couch in the living room, becoming more than a little bossy when she told him that she didn't care if he normally slept naked as a jaybird—he was keeping his britches on in our apartment. Thank goodness, since I was currently pressed front to front against him.

"Let's get you back to bed."

He began walking in the direction of my room, and it took all of my strength to redirect him back to the couch. Either he was sleepwalking or Jorge's miracle cure took a long time to work itself through.

After fluffing his *Wizard of Oz* pillow (borrowed from Jolene) and covering him with a blanket, I affixed the brand-new leash to the equally new collar and took the dog outside for a potty break. So far, he hadn't had any accidents, which meant that he'd been house-trained at some point. I tried not to feel sad knowing that he had another home and that someone was probably looking for him right now. Which was why I wasn't going to name him. Because I didn't want a dog.

When we returned, I navigated my way up the stairs and into the apartment from the glow of the streetlight shining through the stairwell window. I unhooked the dog's collar and he immediately jumped up on the armchair instead of heading back to his bed. After thinking for a moment, I slid the coffee table across the rug to block the door at the top of the steps just in case Beau decided to sleepwalk again.

His phone lit up and vibrated on top of the coffee table. I glanced down and saw there was a text message and photo from Christopher. It was only one word: Jeanne. Without slowing down to think first, I held my finger down on the message to open it up and fill the screen.

It showed a screenshot of a black-and-white photograph of a woman from sometime in the sixties. Her dark, wavy hair was puffed up in a bouffant style, her shoulders were bare, and her delicate collarbones were decorated with a strand of pearls. She was looking off to the side, as if the photographer had asked her to peer into her future. Unable to stop myself, I let my eyes slide to the message bubble.

This is Jeanne Broussard. Is this the woman you saw? Tell Mimi. It's going to get worse. LMK if you got more pictures today

The screen went black but I continued to hold the phone, staring at it as if an explanation of some sort would magically appear. But I had a feeling that I didn't need one.

Stealthily, I replaced the phone on the table, then crept toward the sofa. I lowered my head close to the pillow, holding my own breath to listen to Beau's breathing, hearing mostly the dog licking himself in places I didn't want to know about. I began to straighten, but Beau's strong arm reached around my waist and pulled me down on the couch, holding me tightly against him.

I braced my forearms on his chest, trying to see his face. "Beau? Are you sleepwalking?" I couldn't hide the hopefulness in my voice. Because if he was, he wouldn't have seen me reading his text.

Instead of an answer, his fingers gently took hold of my face and pulled me closer. With the shadow of my head blocking any ambient light, I couldn't see the intention in his eyes, but I could feel it in the length of his body. In the trembling of my own as I lowered my barriers for one dangerous moment. When his lips touched mine, a burst of light seemed to explode behind my eyes—or was it in the room?—illuminating everything I'd been feeling for Beau much longer than even I wanted to admit.

I felt myself slipping and falling, losing myself in the warmth and the pleasure and the mindless joy of lips on lips and skin on skin, the mere fact horrifying me. I lifted myself up on my hands, for all the reasons I'd be kicking myself for the next day. They had nothing to do with him having a girlfriend and everything to do with how I knew what it was like to want something outside of myself so much that I would sacrifice everything I loved to have it. And Beau Ryan could easily fit into that category if I slipped just once and allowed him in.

"I'm not Sam," I whispered, praying that he was sleeping, that this had all been a dream playing out in his potion-addled brain.

"I know." The two words rumbled in his chest beneath me, and in the darkened room I saw the reflection of the streetlight in his wide-open eyes.

And then, just as suddenly as I'd found myself grabbed and hauled on top of him, Beau's arms fell from my waist and the light in his eyes went away as his breathing returned to the steady rhythm of sleep.

I waited to make sure he was sound asleep before carefully sliding off the couch. The dog jumped down from the chair, but instead of coming to me he leapt onto the bottom of the couch, at Beau's feet, and curled up as if he planned to be there for the long term.

I should probably have been insulted, but having lived with dogs since I was fourteen, I knew better than to assume anything when it came to dog behavior. He was staying with Beau for a reason, perhaps to make sure he didn't get up and wander. Or maybe to protect him from things only he and Beau could see.

After a gentle scratch behind the dog's ears, I retreated to my room. I left the door open a crack so I could hear if Beau stirred, then lay awake for another hour as I snapped the rubber band against my wrist in a vain attempt to forget the feel of Beau's lips on mine as I recalled the photograph of Jeanne Broussard and imagined I could hear the phone ringing and a disembodied voice calling my name.

CHAPTER 21

The following morning, after hitting my snooze button three times, I dragged myself out of bed, tangling myself in the sheets and toppling on top of the empty dog bed. Stumbling across the room, I threw open the door and entered an alternate universe. The dog, wearing a blue and white paisley kerchief, had his head stuck in the food bowl Jolene and I had purchased the night before, except someone had used a white paint pen to write the word *Mardi* on it. Judging from the curlicues and heart over the I, I assumed it hadn't been Beau.

The dog didn't even look up from his food—showing me where his priorities lay—but I barely had time to notice since I was busy looking at a freshly showered and perky Beau sitting at the table with a steaming cup of coffee and a plateful of homemade biscuits in front of him. Matching jam and honey jars in Jolene's china pattern with the handles of delicate silver spoons protruding from the tops sat next to his plate.

He stood when I appeared, but Jolene was faster. She bolted from her seat with my cup of coffee before anyone could say, "Good morning," and dragged me into her bedroom before quickly shutting the door behind us.

"Honestly, Nola. Are you trying to scare him away? You look like death on a cracker."

She handed me my mug and I gratefully blew on it before taking the first sip. I looked up at her over the rim, needing the smell of the caffeine to carry me through until the next sip. "I thought he'd still be flat out on the couch. Why is he up? And why does the dog's bowl have a name on it?" There were other questions I should probably have been asking, but my brain settled on the first two.

Jolene grabbed a pink ribbon from her dressing table and began wrapping it around my head as she spoke. "Beau is up because my chicken soup is a guaranteed cure for any ailment—except for heart-break. Then it's just like a soft puppy that will give you comfort if not a cure. And your dog needed a name, so I picked Mardi—like in Mardi Gras. Isn't that adorable?"

I just blinked at her as she stepped back to admire her handiwork, then reached up to make an adjustment. I took a larger sip from my mug. "I don't have a dog, remember? We're supposed to be putting up flyers today, and taking him to the vet to see if he's chipped."

She disappeared into her closet, her voice muffled as she slid hangers on the metal rod. "I've already printed the flyers and I'll give you a stack to bring to Jorge and Thibaut. Between the two of them they can cover the Marigny in less than an hour, starting with the neigh-borhood hangouts like Horn's and Who Dat Coffee Cafe. I figured I'd take a picture of Mardi before his grooming so his owners might rec-ognize him." She reemerged from the closet, holding a pale pink brushed-cotton robe and wearing a triumphant smile. Holding the robe open, she began guiding my empty hand into one of the sleeves, knowing I wasn't caffeinated enough yet to protest even though I blinked hard several times.

"The dog grooming is my treat," she said. "An elderly lady who I used to bring meals to always had me take her Yorkie to At Your Bark and Paw and they did the best job. Not that I'll have Mardi's nails painted, but besides a general de-matting and cut, his ears and tail could certainly use some shaping."

"I don't really think—"

She tightened the tie around my waist, cutting off my words. "There—that gives you some shape. Your rock concert T-shirt was too baggy and didn't show off your figure."

"That's the point," I mumbled. "It's for sleeping. And I don't know why you're doing this. Beau has a girlfriend, and I'm not interested."

With a short laugh, she pinched my cheeks before gently leading me over to the pier mirror in the corner. "Now, then. Don't you look prettier than a basketful of peaches!"

I studied my reflection, focusing on the huge bow she'd tied at the top of my head. "I don't know about peaches, but I look like a five-year-old." I lifted my hand to remove the ribbon but she took my arm and led me to the door. "I made biscuits, and I just finished cubing a whole mess of fresh fruit, so I'll bring the bowl out in a minute if you want to get settled at the table."

She pried my empty cup from my fingers. "I'll go get you a refill."

"Good morning," Beau said jovially, pulling out a chair at the table. "You must have stayed up late last night. I figured you'd be up way earlier than seven o'clock. Did Mardi keep you awake?"

I listened for any hint of memory of the night before beneath the jovial banter, but couldn't detect any. For the second time that morning, I was sure I'd stepped into the twilight zone. "No. And his name isn't Mardi. It's whatever his family named him before he got lost. I was up last night because I heard you sleepwalking."

He shook his head. "Must have been Jolene, because I haven't sleep-walked my entire life."

I met his eyes to see if he was telling the truth. He simply smiled, then picked up the fruit bowl that Jolene had just put on the table. She placed my full coffee cup in my hands to save me the trouble of reaching for it. Then she sliced open a biscuit and covered half of it with honey and the other half with homemade jam. The honey and jam had been delivered—along with all of the fresh fruit—from a cousin's cousin, or a neighbor's cousin, or someone's long-lost cousin who lived within a twenty-mile radius of her parents in Mississippi. It seemed

Jolene's mother knew just about everybody who had any reason to travel to New Orleans and didn't mind dropping off bags of home-grown and homemade treats for her daughter. The night before I'd overheard her talking to her mother about someone's ex–in-law's aunt who made dog clothes, and Jolene had promised to call back with measurements.

"Nice hair bow," Beau said before taking another bite of his biscuit.

"It wasn't me, either, last night," Jolene said as she seated herself next to me and cut a small corner of biscuit to put on her plate. "Must have been Mardi, exploring his new home."

"This isn't his new home, Jolene. Unless you want a dog. Because I can't. Not now."

"We've got so many critters at my mama's house, if I said I was getting another dog, they'd disown me."

I sighed heavily, not yet willing to let go of my coffee cup to eat, and allowed my gaze to travel to the living room. The coffee table had been moved back to its place in front of the couch, and the pillow and blanket had disappeared, along with Beau's phone. Stacked on the floor were the eight hatboxes we'd brought from the recently opened closet.

Seeing my glance, Jolene said, "While you were sleeping, we brought up all the clothes and boxes from my car. We went through the pockets to see if there was anything you might want, but all we found was a receipt for a purchase of paregoric from the pharmacy that used to be in the Maison Blanche building. I thought that would be something for your scrapbook so I put it on your dresser. We put the clothes in the front terrace room for now. I've got a friend in the Quar-ter who owns a vintage clothing shop as an option for what to do with them if you're not sure."

I nodded, finally feeling awake enough to put down my mug and stab a sliced strawberry with my fork. While I chewed, I casually looked at the pink phone to see if it looked any different, as if it might show some sign of what had happened the previous night. I could barely look at Beau, recalling all too clearly the feel of his naked chest beneath my fingers, and the spark of light that had threatened to combust something inside me and burn all of my resolve to ashes. Maybe he hadn't been sleepwalking at all. Maybe I had simply been dreaming.

"We haven't gone through the hatboxes yet, so I figured we could do that tonight while watching Investigation Discovery," Jolene continued. "I thought I could make jambalaya and maybe invite Jaxson over since Carly is out of town on a girls' trip and he sounded lonely when I called." She kept her eyes on her plate, as if she knew what kind of look I was giving her.

"Sounds like a plan," I said. "Unless we hear from Mardi's owners and have to drive him somewhere." As if already recognizing his name, Mardi finished licking the bottom of his bowl, trotted over to me, plopped himself down on the floor by my chair, and commenced to stare lovingly up at me.

Beau's phone vibrated on the table and he looked down at the screen. "Christopher needs me to stop by the shop. I'd be happy to take an Uber, unless it's not too far out of your way to the job site, Jolene."

"Of course. I can drive you, too, Nola, so you don't have to take the streetcar." She smiled sweetly at Beau. "It only takes her fifteen minutes to get showered, dressed, and ready." Her tone made it clear that she didn't mean it as a compliment.

"You can just drop me off at the shop, too. I can walk to my office from there since I didn't get a chance for my morning run." I didn't add that I wanted an opportunity to talk with Christopher about the text he'd sent Beau. To tell him that I'd seen her, too. And even ask him what he'd meant by *It's going to get worse.*

Jolene stood to clear the dishes, shooing us both away when we offered to help, telling us to stay and finish our breakfast. As soon as she'd finished placing another biscuit on each of our plates and scooping out more fruit, she took the serving pieces and headed back to the kitchen.

"Mimi called me this morning," Beau said.

The dog began pawing at my leg, begging to be petted. I welcomed the opportunity not to have to look in Beau's face, since just the sound of his voice brought heat to my cheeks.

"Yes?" I said, focusing on the soft underside of Mardi's ears.

"She said you forgot the Mr. Bingle doll when you left the other evening. She had Lorda bring it to me at the office to give to you. I was surprised to hear that you'd brought it inside to begin with."

I swallowed, remembering the red lacy bra and having zero interest in mentioning it then. Or ever. "I brought it in because I thought it might be safer than leaving it in your truck. And I definitely didn't forget it. I placed it under my backpack when I arrived, and it wasn't there when I left or I would have seen it." I found my eyes drifting down to his lips before I quickly jerked them back up.

"Well, Mimi said the bag was inside the front doorway with Mr. Bingle inside. You just forgot—we all do every once in a while."

"But . . ." I stopped, noticing the set of his jaw that meant the conversation had ended. I knew I'd brought it inside the house and that it wasn't there when I left. Someone was lying, and I had no idea who or why. Especially since the doll and bag were safe and back in Beau's office. Clearly, it was a subject that I should drop. But I was too much my father's daughter to stop digging just because someone said I should.

"Mimi said she could smell pine and cinnamon when we were having supper. Maybe she could have been smelling the Mr. Bingle doll? Maybe you were sleepwalking then, too, and had taken the doll out of the bag and she smelled it. . . ."

"Really, Nola. I don't sleepwalk." He stood and began gathering our empty plates. "I'll clean up here so you can go ahead and get dressed."

I hated being dismissed almost as much as I hated it when people who thought they knew more than I did tried to argue with me when I knew better. It was why I'd resented his presence at my grandparents' antiques shop in Charleston, especially when he'd been made my direct supervisor. That, and the fact that he always insinuated himself into situations where he thought I needed saving, had soured our relationship from the start. Yet it had done nothing to quiet that heat and longing I felt for him. There. I'd admitted it to myself. I wouldn't call Beau my kryptonite, but it wasn't too far off the mark. The closer I got to him, the more I lost a part of myself. I almost relished a fight with him, if only to erase the memory of the night before.

"Did Mimi also mention what I learned from Uncle Bernie about your grandfather?"

A plate clattered on top of the pile he was stacking. "Yeah. She did. And I happen to agree with her. Uncle Bernie has too much time on his hands and is most likely writing a book, like he's been threatening to do for years. Nothing like a bit of sensationalism to sell a book, right? And now that you own the house, he's got access to the scene, too. But there's not one shred of verifiable evidence to back up his accusations, regardless of what he says. Because it didn't happen. My grandfather loved Sunny and me. He would never have stopped the police from searching for her. You didn't know him—we did. And Mimi and I would both appreciate it if you wouldn't mention it again."

"I get it. But hear me out this one time and then I'll drop it, but I need to say this to you. What if there is some element of truth? Shouldn't you at least ask Bernie if you can see the evidence? Even if it doesn't put your grandfather in the best light, wouldn't you want to know?" I remembered the scattered words from Beau's phone conversation the previous night. *I know she's alive or she'd have told me. I've been searching for so long and I can't do this on my own.* Softening my voice, I said, "What if your sister is out there but doesn't know she's lost?"

His eyes met mine and in that one unguarded moment I knew that he had been thinking the same thing. Then the hood fell over his eyes again. "Go ahead and get dressed. We're running late enough as it is." Carrying the pile of plates and the two little jars of honey and jam, he disappeared into the kitchen.

Jolene dropped us off at the shop on Royal Street, making Mardi wave his paw good-bye as I stepped from the car. This, of course, meant I needed to lean in and scratch behind his ears. "Tell them not to cut his ears or tail too short," I said, not sure why I cared, since he wasn't my dog and would be going home to his rightful owners shortly.

"And don't forget these," she said, handing me a Saks Fifth Avenue shopping bag filled with her wrapped and beribboned biscuits with calligraphed name tags and the stack of flyers. "I made one for Christopher, too. Y'all have a good day, and Mardi and I will see you later!" She waved his front paw again before rolling up her windows, then narrowly missing a parked car on the other side of the street as she pulled away.

Beau opened the door to the shop and I was once again hit by the freezing chill of the space, recalling how Jolene had said no one had been able to fix the thermostat problem despite numerous attempts. Christopher was speaking to a customer in the architectural-remnants part of the store. I couldn't see whom he was talking with, but the conversation sounded animated, like two *Star Wars* enthusiasts meeting at Dragon Con.

Not wanting to interrupt, Beau and I stood uncomfortably next to each other, each pretending not to be aware of the other by watching the blowing price tags of the chandeliers.

Unable to take the silence any longer, I said, "Are you feeling all better now?"

He nodded once. "I am. Thank you."

"I washed Jorge's thermos but forgot to bring it with me. I'll make sure he gets it back tomorrow."

Beau nodded again while running his hand over the smooth casing of an ancient phonograph.

To fill the quiet, I said, "Thibaut mentioned you were at the house yesterday to take pictures of the upstairs landing and closet. I thought Jaxson was in charge of all of the publicity photos and video."

His head snapped in my direction, causing me to take a step backward. He hadn't raised a hand or said anything, but the look in his eyes was . . . dangerous. "Am I not allowed to take pictures for myself?" His voice didn't sound like his. It reminded me of the voice he'd used on the phone the night before. A voice full of desperation.

"Nola?"

I turned around to find Christopher and the customer with whom he'd been speaking. "Michael," I said with genuine surprise. "What are you doing here?"

Michael Hebert smiled, and I saw again how his hazel eyes—now green because of his shirt—were fringed with thick, dark eyelashes. "I was about to ask you the same thing," he said while walking toward us. Almost reluctantly, he turned his attention to Beau, an odd expression on his face. "You look familiar. Have we met? Michael Hebert." He stuck out his hand and the two men shook.

Beau narrowed his eyes a bit. "Beau Ryan. And you do look familiar. Did you go to Jesuit?"

Michael shook his head. "No. I was sent up north for boarding school. But I went to Christian Brothers before that."

"That could be it—or maybe I've just seen you around town. Or if you're in the renovation business, maybe at a conference or preservation meeting."

"That's a strong possibility. I work for my uncle Robert Sabatier."

"Oh." Beau's expression shifted slightly from one of guarded friendliness to one almost of hostility. "Of the Sabatier Group?"

"Yes. He's the founder and CEO."

"I see," Beau said, the two words stiff, as if they'd been yanked from his mouth.

Christopher approached, cutting through the tension that suddenly clouded the air. "Were your ears burning, Nola? Michael and I were just talking about you—although not by name." Turning to Michael, he said, "Nola is the woman I mentioned who is renovating the house on Dauphine that your uncle had been interested in buying."

"Ah, I see. I didn't realize when we met that your house in the Marigny was the same one. What a coincidence."

Beau and I shared a quick glance. "Right," I said. "What a coincidence." But when I looked back at Michael's handsome face, his pleasant smile made me forget everything my father had taught me about coincidences.

"Mr. Hebert has been looking for anything related to the downtown Maison Blanche store. He's been here a few times but hasn't found what he's looking for yet." Christopher sent me a meaningful glance.

"What sort of things are you hoping to find?" I asked.

"My uncle and I are building new retail space on Magazine Street and we're trying to find authentic old New Orleans trim and finishes to mix with the contemporary look of the structures. Not just from commercial buildings, but also from old houses. Like leaded glass or stained glass windows, mantelpieces, cabinets, doors. That sort of thing. And anything that can be linked to Maison Blanche is always a selling point."

"I bet," Beau said, his tone definitely not congenial anymore.

Christopher sent Beau a warning look before turning back to me. "I mentioned to Michael that someone I knew was restoring a home in the Marigny and might have some salvaged artifacts that the owner might not want to keep. I was going to give you a call so you could decide if you wanted me to handle it, but since you two know each other, I'll let you take it from here."

"What exactly are you looking for?" Beau asked, his voice struggling to sound amiable.

Ignoring Beau, Michael turned to me. "Are you free for dinner tonight? We can talk about it then."

Forgetting the plans I'd made with Jolene, I said, "Yes, I am. That would certainly make it easier." I felt Beau's eyes on me, but I didn't look at him.

"Great. I'll pick you up at seven, if that works for you? And have you been to Antoine's yet?"

I hadn't, but I knew about it, of course. The venerable French-Creole restaurant was world famous as the birthplace of oysters Rockefeller (known for their rich sauce, hence the name), its celebrity patrons, and its food. It also had a strict dress code. The only thing that kept me from wincing was knowing that I had Jolene as my superpower when it came to making myself presentable.

"I don't think so," I said, as if I'd forget. "But seven o'clock is perfect. Shall I meet you there?"

"My aunt would scold me if I didn't pick you up at your door.

You're on Broadway, right? I have the address." He looked at his watch—a Rolex, of course—and grimaced. "I'm running a bit late for a meeting. It was good to meet you, Beau—or remeet you. And, Christopher, please keep me posted if anything comes in that you think I might be interested in seeing." Unexpectedly, he took my hand and kissed it. "Something else my aunt taught me." He grinned his rather spectacular grin. "I'll see you at seven."

With a quick wave, Michael left, allowing in a refreshing burst of warm outside air.

"How does he have your address?" Beau asked.

"Long story short, Jolene and I bumped into him on Audubon Place. She, uh, wanted to show it to me since I'd never been. Lots of great architectural styles." I wasn't sure why I didn't want to tell him the whole story, about how I thought I'd seen Michael watching me, and how he'd been to the Past Is Never Past at least once before to ask for Maison Blanche artifacts. Maybe because I saw an opportunity to separate my past from my present, and my personal life from my professional life. I needed to build a boundary around myself and manage who crossed it. Hopefully leaving Beau on the other side.

"Is that really a good idea, Nola? You have no idea who he is, but you're going to dinner with him?"

"I don't really think you have any right to concern yourself with my choice of dinner companion." My gaze slid from his eyes to settle somewhere in the middle of his nose, since every time I looked directly in his eyes I remembered last night. The feel of his lips on mine, and the brief spoken exchange.

I'm not Sam.

I know.

His jaw tightened. "Duly noted. But you might want to do your research on the Sabatier Group beforehand so that you're fully prepared. They consider older buildings as something to bulldoze and replace. I thought you might like to know."

Cutting off my reply, Beau turned to Christopher. "I got your text and the photo. Do you have a minute to discuss it now?"

"Sure thing," Christopher said.

Beau handed me the Saks bag full of flyers and baked treats from Jolene after retrieving the one with Christopher's name on it. "For Jorge and Thibaut."

"Right," I said, taking the bag and remembering the photograph I wasn't supposed to have seen. The black-and-white photo of Jeanne Broussard. I'd have to find another time to ask Christopher what he'd meant about "it" getting worse. It was my house, after all.

Beau opened the door, but I turned back to Christopher. "I wanted to apologize to you for that misunderstanding with Mimi about the door. I didn't realize that it was a trickier ask than I thought it would be."

"No worries. And no apologies necessary. You're not to blame at all—it was just a misunderstanding. By the way, Mimi already told me that she's given you permission to store your bike during your parents' visit. We'll just need to coordinate as we get closer to the date."

"Great. Thank you."

I could feel Beau's impatience as he stood holding the door open, waiting for me to leave. I had nothing else that would allow me to linger or take part in the conversation about Jeanne, so I exited onto the sidewalk. It was too hot and the walk was too long, so I bent my head to my phone to open the Uber app.

"Just remember, Nola. There's no such thing as coincidence."

I whipped around in time to meet Beau's steady gaze, then watched him shut the door and turn the sign to CLOSED.

CHAPTER 22

When I returned from work, I'd already prepared Jolene by text to let her know we'd have to postpone our girls' night in. I'd even brought her a candy bar that I'd bought from Trevor—a new endeavor, of which my newly discovered sweet tooth heartily approved—to soften the blow.

I was barely through the door before I was greeted with soft music playing on Jolene's Bluetooth speakers and met with a stemmed glass full of sparkling water and by a very enthusiastic and groomed Mardi. I'd be lying if I said I wasn't happy to see him, too, even though it was important we didn't grow too attached since he wasn't my dog.

I dropped my backpack at the door, and bent to be bathed in doggie kisses with much fresher breath than before his grooming appointment. Mardi looked more like an enormous guinea pig now with his fur clipped marine short, but his adorable face remained the same, albeit cleaner and trimmed, his plumed tail nearly reaching the back of his head—although it was hard to tell because it was wagging so ferociously.

"What's all this?" I asked as I stood and took the glass from Jolene.

"I have prepared all battle stations, but we've got to hurry. I've already filled the tub with my scented bath beads. Your robe is behind the door—you can leave your dirty clothes on the floor and I won't yell at you." She looked at her Apple Watch and pushed a button. "You have exactly fifteen minutes to soak before you pull the plug and use the shower to wash your hair. I bought some hair products for you and they're on the side of the tub. If you're confused about how to use them, let me know. Same goes for the razor. I replaced your old one because I don't think you've ever changed the blade. Or actually used it. I think you and Mardi could have a contest for the fuzziest legs. Anyway, it's the pink one with the triple blades."

"I really appreciate this, Jolene, but I only asked to borrow a dress and maybe a pair of shoes. I don't really need—"

"Fourteen and a half," she said, tapping on her watch's screen and sounding more like a drill sergeant than my roommate.

"Fine." I allowed her to hustle me into the bathroom, taking my glass and placing it on the side of the sink.

"Fourteen minutes," she said, heading toward the door.

"So, what's the story on the dog? Is he—"

My question was cut off by the door snapping shut.

Two hours later I stood in the middle of what could be described only as a hurricane landfall. Debris in the form of shoes, clothing, underpinnings, makeup, curlers, and shapewear of types I didn't even know existed lay scattered around Jolene's bedroom like the innards of a burst piñata. An exhausted Mardi lay on his back, snoring loudly with his paws in the air—each nail painted a different color because he'd had the misfortune of being an available shade tester.

Jolene stood back like Michelangelo must have once done from his *David*. "You look stunning, Nola. Truly. And I'm not even going to take credit, because all I did was bring out your natural beauty. Granted, it took some digging, but I knew it was in there. When you were growing up, did you ever have one of those large Barbie heads where you could put makeup on it and fix the hair?"

"No, I can't say that I did."

"Well, I actually had two, but the first one was short-lived, because I burned off the hair by accidentally using a curling iron that was too hot. It was my favorite toy and I learned a lot of my beauty skills that way. I know they still sell them at Walmart. Or I could bring mine from home if you want to practice—it's still on my dresser and Mama knows not to touch it. Not that I need it anymore, since you're a good substitute for that Barbie head."

"Gee, thanks." I looked at myself in the mirror, wondering if my family would even recognize me. I felt as if I were wearing the disguise of a normal person, of a woman who didn't have issues or a past she was ashamed of. Just a regular girl dressed up and wearing makeup and going on a date with a boy.

She dabbed powder on my nose and straightened my strand of pearls around my neck. "I think you're just about ready."

I glanced at the Cowardly Lion clock and jumped out of my seat. "He'll be here any minute. I'll go wait for him outside."

Moving fast enough that I could later swear in a court of law that I saw only a streak of red hair, Jolene plastered herself in front of the door, her eyes widened in horror. "You will do no such thing. When he rings the doorbell I'll let him in, but even if you're all ready you just sit right here for ten minutes. He's Southern. He expects you to be late. And believe me, you are worth the wait."

She reached over to adjust the scoop neckline of the spaghetti-strap cocktail dress in the same blue shade as my eyes. The silk skimmed my curves instead of clinging to them, and the neckline was relatively modest, but the push-up bra Jolene had insisted I wear made it more eye-catching than I was used to.

I instinctively reached up to readjust it, but she grabbed my arm. "Stop messing with the dress, because I'm not going to be there to reach across the table and fix it for you."

"I'm not . . ." The doorbell rang and we both froze. I tried to reach for the doorknob, but she blocked me.

Grabbing hold of my hand so I wouldn't bolt, she pulled me toward the dressing table and grabbed a tall can of hair spray. "Close your eyes and don't breathe for thirty seconds, all right? This is your only weapon against humidity and I swear by it. I teased your roots enough to make them cry, and this will keep your hair from looking flat as a flounder."

"I don't—" I had to close my mouth as she began spraying.

When she was done, she pushed me toward her closet. "Go look on that top shelf and find a nice scarf to drape over your shoulders. I'm letting you pick because I have to believe you're not color-blind and can find something that matches. If not, remember that white goes with everything."

She gave me a shove before sprinting back to the door. "Do *not* leave this room until I come get you, you hear?"

I would have rolled my eyes, but she had already darted out the door, closing it behind her. After emerging from the closet with a pale blue fringed wrap, I heard Michael's voice in the apartment. I moved toward the bedroom door but stopped. It wasn't that I was afraid of Jolene. I just wasn't ready for her to punish me by withholding baked goods. Or my morning coffee.

After I waited for what seemed an eternity, Jolene slipped back into the room, closing the door quickly behind her as if I were a wayward puppy trying to escape. She handed me a slim evening bag that she'd already stuffed with the essentials—lipstick and powder, my house key, and two breath mints—and said, "Just remember two things: With great cleavage comes great responsibility; and don't order anything green, leafy, or that will get stuck between your teeth."

She started to open the door but hesitated. "Actually, there's one more thing. Try to forget about Beau tonight. Maybe this is what's meant to be."

Before I could ask her if she would feel better if she wrote it all down for me, she'd shoved me out into the hallway. I stumbled into the living room, where Michael stood with his back to us, studying a watercolor of my house in Charleston, which had been painted by my friend Alston as a going-away gift. Michael wore a dark jacket and dress pants, and when he turned, I saw that the color of his tie matched my dress.

He smiled in that devastating way he had, which made me wonder if he knew it and used it on purpose. "You look gorgeous, Nola."

"Thank you. Although I have to admit that I had nothing to do with any of this—" I choked on the last word as Jolene poked me in the back with her finger.

"That's a beautiful house," he said, indicating the painting on the wall. "Is that your family home?"

"It is," I said with a surge of pride. "It's really the reason I became interested in historic preservation."

"I bet. Is it haunted?"

I gave a little laugh to show that I didn't take his question seriously. "Why? Do you believe in ghosts?"

"I'm not sure. I've never seen one. But I do know that I'm afraid of them."

Jolene put her arm around me. "You're lucky you asked her out on a rare free night on her full calendar," Jolene said. "Mardi and I are looking forward to a quiet night of getting to know each other."

She stooped to pat the little dog, who'd followed us out of the bedroom. Michael crouched down, showing the dog the palm of his hand as he was taught to do when meeting an unfamiliar canine. Instead of approaching him to give a sniff, Mardi lifted his upper lip and snarled. Granted, the impression of a shaved ball of fluff trying to show aggression wasn't as intimidating as Mardi would have liked to think, but Michael stood quickly, pulling his hand back from biting distance.

"I've never had that happen before," he said. "Dogs usually love me. But I'm sure he'll get used to me."

"I doubt it," I said.

Michael looked at me with a confused expression.

"I mean, Mardi's not my dog. We just found him and we're trying now to locate his owner, so he won't be here long enough to get used to anybody."

"Right. Makes sense." Michael glanced toward the terrace room with the stacked hatboxes. Seeing his gaze, Jolene hurried over and closed the door, even though it was a French door consisting mostly of glass. "Don't look in there—it's a mess. We just emptied out a closet at Nola's new house and we're storing most of it in there until we have the chance to go through it all and decide what we want to do with it."

"It's not a lot, though, considering," Michael said. "When my uncle was trying to buy it, Mimi Ryan said it was full of junk and wasn't ready to sell yet. Although we learned from word of mouth that she was trying to sell it off list. It had only made it onto the MLS right before you snapped it up, before we even had a chance."

"Really?" I remembered Christopher telling me that Mimi hadn't set foot in the house since the murder of her friend, and then it had been rented out for years, so I wondered why she'd said that. Of course, if the outside porch and backyard were as cluttered as they were when I first saw the house, saying it was cluttered would have been a valid assumption Mimi could have made whether or not she'd actually seen the inside.

"It was definitely full of junk when I bought it. I think we've filled two whole dumpsters and are working on the third. Seems the more we tear out, the more we see needs to be torn out. I should have my head examined for wanting to restore a house in a city where there are two kinds of termites."

"Well, I for one am glad that you did decide to restore it." Michael extended his arm toward the door. "Shall we?"

We said good-bye to Jolene and I scratched Mardi's neck and ears before leading Michael down the stairs.

"What's that perfume you're wearing?" he said as we reached the bottom.

It was Jolene's, and I had no earthly idea what she'd spritzed on me. I recalled the big bottle of perfume that held pride of place on my little sister's dresser and said the name of it before I could think twice. "Little Princess," I said. I did an internal eye roll as soon as I said it.

I heard the smile in his voice as he said, "Who knew? And where does one find it?"

We'd reached the bottom of the stairs and he'd reached around me to open the door. With my height and the addition of Jolene's borrowed heels—not too high, since, according to Jolene, the higher the heels, the lower the morals—I could almost look Michael directly in the eye.

Knowing there was no way out, I said, "Probably Walmart. Why would you want to know?"

I stepped outside and I heard his car keys jingle as he pulled them from a pocket. "I like to bring a small gift on a second date."

I paused by the passenger side of a black Mercedes sedan while he opened the door for me. "But we haven't even been on our first date yet."

He grinned that grin again as I situated myself in the soft leather seat. "Yeah. But I'm an optimistic kind of guy."

By the time we'd parked the car at the Royal Orleans hotel in the Quarter and walked next door to Antoine's on St. Louis Street, I felt as if I'd known Michael a lot longer than a few days. We had so much in common, including our love for old buildings and historic architecture, and how important our families were in our lives. Our conversation almost sounded scripted, since everything fell together like puzzle pieces, yet still spontaneous and warm. Not that I would compare Michael to a dog, but it was the same feeling I'd had when Mardi had first approached me. It was exhilarating to talk with someone who knew nothing about me except what I wanted to tell him. For the first time in a very long time I felt as if I weren't being judged with preconceptions.

I had passed the iconic two-storied structure of the famed Antoine's a multitude of times but had never been inside. Just from reading about the history of the city, I knew its premier eatery contained a labyrinth of fourteen dining rooms all decked out with New Orleans lore and antique memorabilia from the carnival krewes that for generations have held official functions at the restaurant.

The maître d' knew Michael, addressing him as Mr. Hebert, and escorted us through the building to a dining room lit with antique chandeliers and filled with white-cloth-covered tables.

As we settled into our seats and were handed menus, our server asked if we'd like a cocktail to start.

Although always prepared for this question and my answer, for the first time in years I hesitated. I knew it was because I was nervous. It had been a long time since I'd had romantic feelings. I'd been too busy rebuilding my life and graduating from college and grad school with honors. I deliberately left Beau out of the equation. Feelings for him were taboo, just another complication in an already complicated life. Yet he always seemed to loom on the periphery of my consciousness, a dark specter I couldn't exorcise. The kiss the night before had only clouded my feelings further. Just one glass of anything stronger than water could soothe my nerves and help me forget.

Seeing my hesitation, the waiter said, "May I suggest the French seventy-five? We make it here exactly like Harry's Bar in Paris, where it was invented."

I could almost taste it, the champagne bubbling in my mouth before sliding down my throat; the tingling in my limbs as the gin slowly relaxed my muscles and my nerves melted away. The confidence I'd feel to go with the dress and heels. To feel like everybody else again.

"Yes," I found myself saying. "I'd like a glass."

"And I'll have a Glenlivet twenty-one on the rocks, please," Michael said as if everything were normal. As if something monumental hadn't just happened. As if I hadn't just decided after several years that I was now strong enough to have one drink and stop.

As we opened up our menus, I said, "I should have offered to give you my phone number for you to call me in case you needed to cancel." I grimaced. "But you already have it. Jolene gave you my number when you asked for hers when we ran into you in front of your house."

He smiled. "Good. Because it was your number I really wanted."

My face heated as I bent my head to focus on the menu, and I was barely aware when the drinks arrived. "To new beginnings," Michael said as he held up his glass.

"To new beginnings," I said as I clinked my glass with his and took a sip.

As we shared our appetizers of escargot bourguignon and oysters Rockefeller I found myself relaxing, making the one drink last and telling myself that was all I needed. But when our main courses arrived and Michael ordered a bottle of wine, I didn't say no.

We talked about our families, and our love of dogs, and how I didn't mind having siblings much younger than me. I didn't mention Melanie's extracurricular activities or my dad's job, since Michael hadn't recognized his name. Nor did I talk about my birth mother, or how I'd ended up in Charleston. In the soft glow of the cocktail and wine, I felt confident that we would have all the time in the world to get to know each other better.

"I'm curious," I said. "You mentioned that you were raised by your aunt and uncle. How did that happen?"

"My parents are missionaries. Apparently very dedicated ones, to leave the raising of their children to other family members." Michael shrugged as if it didn't bother him, but I could tell otherwise. I knew the look.

"And then you were sent up north for boarding school. Did you want to go so far from home?"

"Not really. Neither did my sister, Felicity. I don't think Aunt Angelina wanted us to, but Uncle Robert said it was important to spread our wings. They hadn't been able to have their own children, so they treated Felicity and me as if we were theirs."

I took a sip of my wine. "How are they related to you?"

"Aunt Angelina and my dad, Marco, are brother and sister. They were very close growing up. Their mother, Marguerite, had lost a sister when she was younger, and I think she was a bit overprotective of them when they were children, so they grew up relatively isolated, but had each other as best friends into adulthood."

"My siblings are only twelve right now, but I imagine I would feel the same way about them if I should ever need someone to take over raising my own children. So I'm guessing you see your aunt and uncle almost as your real parents."

"Pretty much. We were raised by them since we were really young. And we didn't want to leave them for boarding school at all, but it wasn't up to us. Our biological parents were insistent that we experience life outside of New Orleans. It was part of the agreement when our aunt and uncle took over as guardians. I think they wanted us to plant new roots up north. I've always wanted to ask them why, but we don't see them, and we only get a package and a short letter every Christmas and birthday." He took a sip of wine.

"I'm sorry. I know that hurts, regardless of what kind of good they're doing as missionaries." I touched my glass to his. "Here's to absent parents, and to the other parents in our lives who love us as if we're their own."

He looked at me with his beautiful eyes, and a welcome warmth flooded my chest. "I couldn't have said it better." After another sip he said, "In some ways it worked. Felicity fell in love with the Northeast, and while we both decided to stay there for college, she now lives and works in Manhattan, for Sotheby's. I decided I wanted to come back, and my uncle offered me a job with his company." He shrugged. "So here I am."

"A love of old things must run in your blood, then," I said. I lifted my glass to take another sip but found it empty. Our waiter rushed over and refilled my glass before I could protest, although at this point I was feeling too good to really want to say no.

"I think it does. That's why I'm so interested in finding remnants from the Maison Blanche store. My uncle wants the new condos he's building to be ultramodern, but I think adding historical elements will really make them stand out."

"It would make them meaningful," I said. "And not like all that cookie-cutter stuff being built nowadays." I had started sounding less like myself and more like an undergrad explaining why they wanted to study historic preservation. Sort of like someone saying they wanted to go into retail management because they liked to shop.

The waiter cleared the table in preparation for bringing out our Baked Alaska. I went to lean forward, but my elbows missed the edge of the table and I simply bobbed my head. Either Michael hadn't noticed or he was just being polite. "Like my door," I said.

"Your door?" His eyebrows rose with interest.

I nodded. "Um-hmm. I have a door from one of the upstairs offices that used to be above the retail space at Maison Blanche. There were lots of doctor and dentist offices up there, and they even had a pharmacy. The door has that pitted glass and original hardware with an *MB* on the doorknob plate and it will make the perfect bathroom door in the new house. Assuming I ever get an actual bathroom." I held my napkin to my lips to stifle a hiccup.

"You're so lucky to have it. Where did you find it?"

"In my house! On the first day I walked inside. It was right there in the upstairs room, leaning against the wall. Mimi wanted to put it in the dumpster. Can you imagine?" I might have swayed in my seat and had to grab hold of the edge of the table to steady myself. Fortunately, Michael didn't seem to notice.

"No, I can't. But I'd love to see it sometime."

"As long as you understand that you can't have it. It's not for sale." I gave my head an exaggerated shake.

"I get it. If I'd found it first, I wouldn't want to sell it, either."

"It's kind of a pain to store it, though. I didn't want it to get damaged during the renovation, so I had it stored at the Past Is Never Past—the Ryans' antiques shop on Royal Street. But Mimi sort of threw a fit—she is *very* particular as to what goes in her storeroom, apparently—so I had to move it to my apartment."

"I'd love to see it . . ." Michael began, just as the football-shaped Baked Alaska was wheeled to our table and then flambéed tableside. After the commotion of the preparation, and the exclamations of how amazing the dessert tasted, and the embarrassment of knocking my wineglass over and onto my dress, the conversation was forgotten.

KAREN WHITE

I excused myself to go to the ladies' room to try to blot out the wine from the dress while Michael paid the bill. When I'd returned he escorted me back to his car, because I wasn't used to wearing heels and my feet hurt, and I found myself leaning more heavily on his arm than when I'd arrived. I wasn't drunk. I'd had only one cocktail. And a glass of wine. Or was it two? Most of a glass had ended up on my dress. But I hadn't had that much to drink and I was definitely not drunk. I could remember what I ate and what we'd talked about. What Michael's long fingers had looked like wrapped around his drink; how both sides of his face creased when he smiled, and how I'd told him that when he grew old they'd be permanent.

I definitely wasn't drunk.

When we reached my apartment, Michael walked me to the door. Jolene had helpfully turned on the single-bulb outdoor fixture, where a large moth—at least I hoped it was a moth—was currently tossing itself against the glass.

"I had a wonderful time tonight," he said.

I could barely focus on his words, my brain too busy wondering if he would kiss me and if I should let him. If I wanted him to. And there, in the tiny dark recesses in the way, way back, the thought of how his kiss would compare to Beau's.

After a pause, when I realized he was waiting for me to answer, I said, "Me, too. I loved everything about it. Especially that Baked Alaska."

He chuckled. "I love a girl with a healthy appetite and who loves sweets as much as I do."

I closed my eyes and tilted my chin, my eyelids pink from the bulb above us, the moth continuing its endless battle with the light. *Clack, clack, clack.*

Michael leaned forward, the faint scent of his cologne and soap making my nerve endings jump to attention. He leaned a little to the right and his lips landed on my cheek, where they lingered only briefly.

He stepped back and took my hands as I opened my eyes, hoping he couldn't see my disappointment. "Good," he said. "Because I'm hoping you'll go out with me again. What are you doing tomorrow night?"

I laughed. Recalling the list of things to remember Jolene had given me while she'd been getting me ready, and how a girl should keep a boy guessing and never appear too eager, I said, "I don't know—I'll have to check. Why don't you call me tomorrow and see?" I didn't offer to call him, because that had been another part of Jolene's tutelage—something about how her mama would have yanked her bald headed if she'd learned that Jolene had ever called a boy. Or texted. It was the same thing in her estimation.

"Do I have to wait that long?" he asked, the sides of his face creasing in the way I'd come to really like.

"Yes. Although tomorrow is just an hour away."

"Until then," he said. "I hope I can wait that long."

He watched me while I fumbled for my key and let myself in. Then I pressed my back against the door and closed my eyes as I listened to his receding footsteps, the car door snapping shut, and then the sound of the car backing up and driving away.

I felt myself swaying and opened my eyes in the darkened stairwell. I flipped on the light, then grabbed onto the banister as I hauled myself upstairs, still hearing the incessant *clack, clack, clack* of the moth outside as it repeated the same damaging action again and again without learning a thing.

CHAPTER 23

I'd barely made it to the top of the steps before I heard the car returning and footsteps pounding up the walkway toward the door. I stumbled down the steps, missing the last two and twisting my ankle in my haste to reach the door before he did. I threw the door open, ready for the good-night kiss that Michael must have been wanting as much as I had been.

Beau stood in a circle of light on the bottom step, apparently as surprised to see me as I was to see him. "Nola?"

It came out as a question, so I stepped forward, out of the shadowed entranceway and onto the front step. "It's me. I just borrowed Jolene's dress." A small giggle erupted from my mouth without permission.

"I can see that." He gave me an odd look that might have had something to do with how I was swaying on my feet. "Are you all right?"

I gave him a vigorous nod, my hair moving despite Jolene's magic hair spray. "Uh-huh. My feet hurt a bit 'cause I'm not used to wearing heels."

His eyes traveled down the length of me to Jolene's shoes, pausing for a moment at the stain in the middle of my dress before meeting my eyes again. "I hope Michael appreciated the effort."

"He did." A loopy grin I couldn't seem to control settled on my mouth.

Beau's attention moved above my head, toward the moth still flinging itself against the light. After a flash of inspiration, I reached inside to the wall and flipped off the light. "There. Problem solved."

"You should probably turn off the inside light, too, or he'll find that one, and probably bring his friends."

"Good point." I reached inside again and flipped off the second switch, throwing us into darkness except for the glow of the streetlights and the lights from other houses. A late-night crowd gathered at the corner bar across the street, a low murmur of conversation and laughter teasing our ears.

"I thought you were Michael."

"He just left." I pointed down the street as if Beau might need clarification.

"Good. This probably could wait until tomorrow, but I thought you'd want to know. I wasn't going to ring the doorbell if your bedroom light was off."

A flash of warmth went through me at the mental image of Beau looking up at my window at night. The loopy grin settled on my face again.

"Do you want me to tell you now or should it wait? You seem . . . tired." Beau sounded uncertain and he was still looking at me with an odd expression, as if he hadn't seen a woman wearing a dress and heels before.

"Might as well since you're here." I leaned against the doorframe because my ankle was starting to throb.

"There might have been a break-in at your house tonight. The neighbors across the street called me because they couldn't reach you."

"That's terrible," I said, still leaning against the doorframe, with my foot rubbing the sore ankle. "Unless it was just a ghost. There are two, you know. Well, at least two that I've seen, but I'm not a psycho." I giggled. "I mean, a psychic. Like Melanie."

He took a step closer. "Are you sure you're all right?"

"I'm fine. Fine. Did they take anything?"

"Not that I could tell. And there were no signs of a break-in at all, unless they used a key to the back door like they did last time—assuming it's the same people. And assuming it happened at all, since nothing was taken. But all of the trim we've been keeping in the backyard was definitely rearranged. Like someone was looking for something in particular. I'm just not familiar enough with what was back there to determine if something is actually missing and call the police."

"Let's go, then," I said, moving forward. I missed a step completely and would have landed flat on my face if Beau hadn't caught me.

"I guess I don't need these." With a flick of each foot, I kicked the shoes off, listening as they landed somewhere in the bushes next to the front steps. I immediately regretted doing that to my sore ankle, but as soon as I put my bare foot on the ground it felt a little better.

I began hobbling toward the truck, and Beau quickly took hold of my elbow. "Are you sure? Like I said, they didn't get into the house, and it's not clear if anything was taken. This can definitely wait until tomorrow."

"*Pfft,*" I said. "It's been such a wonderful evening that I'm not ready for it to end. You and Michael are like bookends, you know? And I'm the lucky girl in the middle." Beau opened the passenger-side door and helped me inside, but before he could close it I reached up and pressed my index finger to his lips. "I wonder which one of you is the better kisser."

He pulled back, but the expression on his face told me it had nothing to do with what I'd just said. "Have you been drinking, Nola? You reek."

I pulled at my dress to highlight the large stain. "No, but my dress has. Jolene's going to kill me." The lie came so easily, I didn't even need to think about it. "She made me some tea to calm my nerves before the date, and I wonder if she might have added some of Jorge's mom's secret ingredient because it worked so well for you. Although I hope I won't be baring my chest and throwing myself at you, since that seems to be a side effect." I let out what could be described only as a guffaw before pressing my hand over my mouth.

After a brief pause, he closed the door and then climbed in behind the wheel. I curled up on my seat and leaned my head against the window, intent on watching the city flash by as Beau drove. But the blur of lights made me nauseous, so I closed my eyes, and the rumble of the engine lulled me into a deep sleep.

"Nola? Are you awake? We're here."

I jerked out of a dreamless sleep to find Beau shaking my shoulder from the driver's seat. I looked out my side window to find Bob standing in his front yard with Belle as she strained on her leash to go back inside. Belle was reluctant to go potty outside if it was dark. Or wet, or cold, or hot, or anytime other than the two days a year in New Orleans when the weather was balmy with no humidity.

I opened my door and nearly fell out, barely catching myself. I definitely felt more clearheaded after my nap, but not completely stable. I blamed it on my ankle. I waved to Bob, who dared lift a hand from the leash for a second to wave back.

"Everything okay?" he asked. "Sorry to bother you, but we saw someone at your house, and it definitely wasn't your grandfather. We thought you'd want to know."

"Thank you," I shouted back. "And I appreciate you keeping an eye out on my house. Doesn't look like a break-in, though."

"Good. By the way, Nola, your grandfather still comes out every night to smoke his pipe on the porch, and I hate to say it, but we can smell it over here. And your workers keep leaving that upstairs hall light on. Please ask them to stop or we're going to have to buy blackout shades."

"Will do!" I said, giving him a thumbs-up that he probably couldn't see. "Good luck with Belle," I said, limping toward Beau.

"Your grandfather?" Beau asked. "Smoking a pipe?"

"I have no idea what he's talking about."

I made to move forward, but he held on to my elbow, stopping me. "But you've smelled it, haven't you? The pipe tobacco."

The ambient light from the night sky and the streetlamps illuminated his face and made his eyes glow like those of a cat. "Yep. Pretty much every time I come here. I think I saw him once. When I drove by after that night I saw you on Frenchmen Street. I thought I was imagining it, because when I looked back, *poof*! He was gone." I swallowed back a hiccup. "Michael said that he's not sure if he believes in ghosts but that he's afraid of them anyway. I think I'm the opposite—I definitely believe in ghosts, but I'm not sure if I'm afraid of them. Not all of them, anyway. Some of them are nice. But not all of them." I leaned closer to whisper, although I wasn't sure who I was afraid might hear. "Like that awful ghost who tried to burn us alive in the attic—remember?"

I leaned far enough that I fell into him. "Kind of a hard thing to forget," Beau said. "Nola, are you—"

I spoke before he could finish the question, knowing neither of us wanted to hear the answer. "I had a really nice time tonight," I said instead. My eyes were at mouth level, so I reached up and touched his lower lip with my finger. "You have really nice lips. I like the way they taste, too. They're like fire, but with a gentle burn."

He abruptly set me away from him. "Nola, stop. What are you doing?"

I met his gaze, feeling all of a sudden unbearably sad. I shrugged. "Wishing you were someone else, I think." I took a step back, then proceeded to climb the steps to the porch. My ankle gave way, but Beau caught me. With something muttered under his breath, he swung me up in his arms and brought me to the top of the steps. He set me down for a moment while he fumbled for the key, then swung me up again to bring me inside before dumping me unceremoniously on the bottom step of the stairwell.

The generator had been removed when Thibaut and Jorge closed up for the day, meaning we had only Beau's iPhone flashlight to see by. I reached for my phone in my purse, realizing that I had neither.

I sat on the bottom step but turned myself sideways so my back wouldn't be to the upstairs hallway and the black maw of the doorless closet. Rubbing my ankle, I watched as the beam of Beau's flashlight bounced off the doors and walls like ghostly orbs as he checked the locks on the front windows. I imagined that Ernest and Bob were having a field day looking at the light show from across the street and wondering if they should call the police.

"I need to go look outside," Beau said. "Are you okay here?"

Not wanting to be alone, I jumped up, wincing at the pain. "Nope. I'll come with you."

He watched me hobble for a few steps before coming over and scooping me up again. "There's something about you, Nola Trenholm, that drives me crazy while at the same time makes it impossible to stay away from you. And I'm only saying this now because I don't think you're going to remember any of this in the morning."

"Why do you say that?" I said, pushing my index finger on his nose.

"You tell me." With more force than I thought necessary he plopped me down on the step heading to the backyard and shone the beam of his light on the rows of crown molding, bead board, mantels, spindles, and doors. "Can you see if anything's missing?"

I shook my head, then stopped, my vision spinning for a moment. "It's too hard to tell. But someone really messed stuff up. Like they were looking for something in particular. Isn't that funny? Everyone is so ready to tear down old buildings, but when they need that hand-crafted banister or carved mantel, they scavenge through old houses like grave robbers digging up bones."

"What do you think they were looking for?" Beau carefully stepped through the debris of the amputated limbs of my house and stopped in front of me.

I shrugged. "I bet if anyone knew I had a Maison Blanche door, they'd be all over it. Michael wants it. Too bad I'm not selling. I could probably do a lot with the money." I pulled myself up and moved into the kitchen.

Following me inside, Beau said, "Really? Sounds a little bit like too much of a coincidence, don't you think? That you'd be on a date with Michael—who has admitted to having an interest in your door but whom I presume you have told it isn't for sale—while at the same time your house was being ransacked?"

I looked at Beau, trying to process the words coming from his mouth but concentrating mainly on the one word. *Coincidence.* It took me longer than it should have to find the words to respond. "Oh. I get it. You're trying to make me focus on something else so I don't ask you about your grandmother and her weird little room on the second floor of her house on Prytania."

Even in the dim glow of his phone light, I could see the shock on his face. "What? How did . . ."

"That night I had to go up and find Tylenol for you. I accidentally entered the room. And I saw my hairbrush. My *missing hairbrush*, which miraculously reappeared in my backpack the following day! I won't even get started on the Mr. Bingle doll. I want it back. Before it disappears into that weird locked room at your grandmother's house and I never see it again."

Only the sound of our heavy breathing interrupted the silence in the room as we stared at each other, all the words we'd just unleashed tumbling soundlessly onto the dusty floor. We didn't drop our gazes before his phone light dimmed until it was extinguished completely.

"Damn," Beau muttered under his breath at the same time the sound of footsteps began descending the stairs. They were delicate, like high heels, and definitely those of a woman. And then, just as suddenly as they had started, they were followed by those of a man's heavier-soled shoes and the pungent smell of pipe tobacco.

"You hear that, don't you?" I whispered.

Beau didn't say anything, but I felt his eyes on me. The footsteps continued, moving down the stairs, moving toward us.

"You hear it. I know you do. And you smell the pipe tobacco, don't you?" My voice had risen a notch. "Beau, admit it. Melanie told me what happened in that attic the night of the fire. How you were the reason why the door opened to let everyone out. So admit that you can hear them. That you can talk to them. Ask them what they want and why they're still here." I was shouting now, but I didn't care. The temperature in the room had dropped and I shivered, seeing my breath rise like smoke in the dirty light of the windows.

"Stop it, Nola. Just stop it. You're drunk. I can tell. We've been down this road before. Just admit it."

I jerked back as if I'd been struck. "I'm not drunk. I will admit that I had a drink, but that's it. And I can handle it. I've learned from past mistakes, and I now know my limits. And I'm definitely not drunk."

"Nola." His voice came out as a loud whisper. "Listen to what you're saying. It's bad enough that you're lying to me, but lying to yourself is dangerous. Don't do this. Don't undo all of your hard work." He paused, as if reloading his gun. "Don't disappoint your family."

I stood, ignoring the throbbing in my ankle. "There you go again. Trying to swoop in and save me when I don't need saving, and I certainly didn't ask for your help. I had one drink, and you're trying to make me out to be some horrible lush who can't control herself. I'm stronger than that. And if you really cared enough to pay any attention, you'd know that."

The footsteps had ceased, the temperature dropping even further. Beau's gaze slid behind me but I didn't turn around. He grabbed my arm and began dragging me in the direction of the front door.

I wrenched away from him. "Go ahead, Beau. Admit it. Admit that you can communicate with spirits."

With his gaze still focused behind me his eyes widened, and for the first time I felt a tremor of fear. Even though the look in his eyes wasn't of fright at all but of something else I couldn't name.

Shifting his eyes back to me, he grabbed my arm again, his fingers sliding down to my wrist, where I still wore the rubber band he'd given me. I hadn't taken it off. He snapped it against the skin on the inside of my wrist. "Use this. Every time you feel the need for a drink, snap it. To remind yourself that you're stronger than the pull of a drink."

I yanked my arm away from him. "I told you—I don't need your help or anybody else's. I had a drink—so what? I can handle it. I'm a grown woman. And don't talk to me about lying to myself when you're doing the exact same thing. Maybe there's some kind of therapy group for psychics in self-denial you can join. Anything, really, that will make you stop looking for problems in other people and focus on fixing yourself first. And you can start with the wet footprints that follow you around everywhere—even I can see them. Why don't you ask her what she wants? Or do you want her to wander between worlds indefinitely because you're too stubborn to tell the world that you can talk to dead people?"

I stumbled toward the door and threw it open, managing to make it down the front steps before realizing I didn't have my purse with my phone and couldn't call an Uber. I looked across the street to see if Bob might still be outside with Belle, but the front yard was empty and the windows all dark.

I now stood in the middle of the street, barefoot and without a wallet. I felt Beau approach from behind. "Do you need a ride?"

Even though there wasn't a hint of gloating in his voice, I couldn't look at him. "No. But I need an Uber. I'll pay you back."

"You don't need to—" he began.

I cut him off with a quick turn of my head.

He lifted his phone, and after a moment he said, "It will be here in three minutes. I'll wait until it gets here."

"There's no need. I can handle it."

"Clearly."

I was too angry to look at him while he retreated to the porch to wait. He stayed there without speaking until the car arrived and I slid into the backseat. Even though I kept my face straight ahead, I felt Beau looking at me as I passed by, snapping the rubber band on my wrist until the skin had been rubbed raw.

During the entire drive uptown I fought sleep, focusing on the unnamed expression I'd seen on Beau's face as he'd stared at something behind me inside the house. I'd made it to the intersection of St. Charles and Napoleon Avenue when I finally succumbed to sleep, my last conscious thought the realization of what it was. *Recognition.*

CHAPTER 24

I awoke the following morning to the kind of headache that could be described only as clashing cymbals inside my head, and there was an eerie silence throughout the apartment. It wasn't until I'd dragged myself to the bathroom and swallowed two aspirin that I also noticed the lack of smells of coffee brewing and something baking in the oven. Even more telling was the empty dog bed and the glaring absence of Mardi's new metal name tag jingling against his collar.

Recalling that Jaxson was supposed to come over the previous night for dinner, I tiptoed to Jolene's bedroom and peered inside. The bed was neatly made and the blinds pulled up, but the lingering scent of her hair spray told me she'd been there at some point that morning.

Worry hurried my pace, my ankle still hurting enough to make me limp. I started to call out Jolene's name, but I froze with my mouth open. In the center of the dining table sat a severed head on one of Jolene's serving platters, with rainbow-colored brain splatter surrounding it. I screamed, slamming myself against the old desk while reaching behind me for the pink phone, dropping it on the floor in a loud clatter of jangling metal and plastic.

The sound of my cell phone ringing startled me enough to stop screaming. It also gave me the chance to get a better look at the table's centerpiece and realize that although it was a head, the brain matter was confetti, the head hadn't been severed, and it wasn't even human. It was a giant plastic Barbie head with flowing blond hair and a pretty ribbon tied in a bow on top.

I held my hand to my heart and took several deep breaths that might have contained cusswords directed at my absent roommate, and I waited until I was confident I wasn't about to have a heart attack before I went in search of my phone.

My phone stopped ringing as I gingerly approached the table and its Chucky-like centerpiece, noticing a folded note next to a wrapped plate of banana nut muffins.

Good morning, Nola!

I didn't want to wake you with a text, which is why I'm writing this note. I needed to go home for a few days—something I didn't decide on until the early hours of this morning.

I'm sorry I didn't have time to freeze some meals for you, but I'm hoping your date with Michael last night will at least lead to another date so you won't starve to death! ☺ Just in case, I made you some muffins.

I hope you don't mind, but because I know you're crazy busy with work right now, I took Mardi with me. Selfishly, too, I needed the company and a furry shoulder. Let me know if you get any calls from those flyers we posted and I'll bring him right back. I only plan to be gone for a few days anyway.

I can't wait to hear all the details of your date with Michael. Please promise me that you won't go through the hatboxes without me—we'll do it the first night I'm back (unless you have another date ☺).

Also—surprise! Your own Barbie head! On his way over last night, I had Jaxson stop at Walmart to get one for you. That way, you can practice while I'm gone. Help yourself to any of my makeup in my room and the bathroom. Just don't use any heating tools on the hair because I can promise you it won't end well.

Call me if you need anything, and I'll see you soon. And Mardi sends you kisses.

xoxoxoxo,
Jolene

PS I already primed the coffee maker for you, so all you have to do is push the start button. I figured you could at least manage that before your first cup. ☺

Jolene's handwriting on the monogrammed stationery was exactly what I expected, with teacherlike straightness and closed loops. Even the excessive use of smiley faces didn't surprise me. It was more what she hadn't said that worried me. That and the crinkled blotches at the bottom of the note that looked like they might have been tears.

My cell phone started ringing again. I found it more than a little alarming that I had no recollection of where I'd put my phone, or even of coming home the previous night and getting myself into bed. I had a strong suspicion that I had slept with my makeup on, which was offense number one in Jolene's book of beauty tips.

I followed the sound to the coffee table in the front room, where someone—presumably Jolene—had placed my evening bag after finding it wherever I'd dropped it the night before. I opened it and quickly grabbed the phone, noticing with surprise that it was Jaxson calling.

"Good morning!" His cheery voice aggravated my headache and I hoped the aspirin would kick in soon. Next time I'd have to remember to take the aspirin and a large glass of water the night before. I didn't have time to think about the words "next time," because Jaxson was speaking again. "Did you get your present from Jolene?" The sounds of people talking and dishes clinking came through the phone.

"Sure did. And I think it just took at least five years off of my life."

"Oh, man. She didn't leave the head in the middle of the table, did she? I told her not to do that because you wouldn't be expecting it, but she said you weren't prone to flights of fancy and would know immediately what it was."

"Did she? Well, then, she apparently thinks I'm a lot more solid than I actually am, because I screamed like a mule whose butt got stuck in a pepper patch."

"You're starting to sound like Jolene now," he said, laughing.

"Wow. You're right. Not that there's anything wrong with that, of course. It's just that my family might need a translator when they come visit in October. Speaking of Jolene, is she okay?"

"Have you spoken with her?"

"No. I just got the note. And the Barbie head. If it had been from anyone besides Jolene, I might have taken it as a threat. She took my dog, too. She said she needed a furry shoulder."

"Your dog?"

"*The* dog. Mardi. You know what I mean." It didn't escape my notice that Jaxson might have been trying to change the subject. "Is she okay?" I repeated.

"I'm not sure. She seemed fine when I left last night around ten."

I rolled my eyes since he couldn't see me. "Fine" for a man could mean anything from a splinter in a finger to hair being on fire. "So she didn't say why she needed to go home?"

"No. She didn't say anything."

I rolled my eyes again just because I could. And because it was clear I was speaking with a man, because "didn't say anything" could have a thousand meanings if being translated by a female. "So I'm guessing you didn't call to ask me about Jolene."

He cleared his throat. "No, actually. I'm calling for Uncle Bernie. We're finishing up our breakfast at the Camellia Grill and were hoping you might be willing to meet us in about half an hour. I can drop you off at work afterwards so you won't be late."

"Uh, sure. I can do that." I was disappointed that they hadn't invited me for breakfast, too, since I suddenly had a craving for the iconic Camellia Grill's chili cheese omelet. But it did explain the noises in the background. "I just need to throw on some clothes, and if I jog, I can be there in time."

"Actually, we were hoping you could meet us on campus, which is a lot closer to you. That way we can talk in privacy." The word "privacy" piqued my interest. The Camellia Grill had all communal counter seating, which could have been why they decided it wasn't a good meeting spot.

"Sure. Any specific spot in mind?"

"Are you familiar with the paved terrace on the academic quad behind Gibson? There are lots of benches where we can sit and talk."

"I know it well," I said. During my freshman year, I'd often fallen asleep on one of the benches nestled beneath the sweeping oak trees, as it was an obvious spot to stop between classes, especially if I had a hangover. And sometimes it was a good spot to unobtrusively take a sip from whatever I carried in my backpack that day. "I can be there in thirty minutes."

"Just one thing, Nola. If you talk to Beau, don't mention our meeting."

He'd hung up before I could ask why.

The campus bustled with students on foot and on bike, reminding me of the excitement and anticipation that I'd felt as a student here. And all that I'd missed. I quickly pushed away that last thought, reminding myself that my missteps had led me to where I was in my life now, which wasn't such a bad place to be at all.

By the time I'd made it to Gibson Hall, the in-between-classes crowd had thinned, making it easy to spot Uncle Bernie and Jaxson on one of the pretty metal benches placed in front of a bed of red and purple flowering plants. I remembered my eighteen-year-old self reading the plaque about the student to whom the terrace and gardens were dedicated, a beloved daughter whose favorite colors were red and purple and whose name was Leigh.

Jaxson stood, and I quickly approached Uncle Bernie so he wouldn't have to pull himself up with his cane. Instead, I kissed him on his cheek in greeting and sat down on the adjacent bench while Jaxson reseated himself next to his uncle. "Did you enjoy your breakfast?" I asked. The two banana nut muffins had been delicious but probably not as filling as an omelet would have been.

"We certainly did, young lady. I should have brought you some coffee to go, because you look tired."

I wondered if he might have been referring to the smeared mascara under my eyes. Just as I'd feared, I'd passed out on my bed wearing full makeup that by morning was equally distributed between my pillow-case and my face, but not in its original locations. Not having the time to search through Jolene's arsenal of skin-care bottles for makeup re-mover, I'd simply used a washcloth and soap to scrub my face, but with minimal results. I'm sure there was some sort of beauty-school-dropout purgatory Jolene would send me to when she found out. Despite my best efforts, I knew I resembled a cross between an Andy Warhol paint-ing of a clown and Edvard Munch's *The Scream*.

"I'm fine. I had a cup before I left. So," I said, putting my hands on my knees and leaning forward. "What's this James Bond secrecy all about?" I said it lightly, but from the expressions on their faces it was clear that whatever they had to tell me was serious stuff.

Bernie flexed his thick fingers on top of his cane. "When we saw each other last, I mentioned that every Wednesday is poker night with my buddies I knew when we were on the force."

"Yes. And you were going to find out if any of them remembered Jeanne's case. And Sunny's."

He and Jaxson exchanged a glance before he turned back to me. "One thing at a time. Regarding Jeanne's case, we were able to locate Angelo Benedetti—her boyfriend at the time of her death. He moved to Biloxi within a year following the murder, and has owned and op-erated a popular Italian restaurant since the sixties. He married and had three sons and they all work at the restaurant."

"Did he have anything to say about Jeanne?"

"Yes, he did. Said he was still pretty heartbroken even though he's been married to his wife for about fifty years now."

"Did you ask him about the pregnancy?"

"I did. He called me a liar. If we'd both been younger men, I think he might have given me a face-planter."

"I'm guessing that means he and Jeanne . . ." I wasn't sure how to phrase it with someone from his generation.

"Never had sex," he finished for me. "He swore that the two of them were saving themselves for marriage and that he was a virgin on his own wedding night."

"And you believed him?"

"I did. And what could possibly be the reason for him to lie now? We already know that he had a rock-solid alibi for that night, and now we know that his murdered girlfriend had a pregnancy that he apparently had nothing to do with."

"Which leads us to unknown person number three."

"Have you gone through the hatboxes from the closet yet?" Jaxson asked. "It's probably a long shot, but who knows?"

"Not yet. And Jolene asked me to wait until she gets back from Mississippi to go through them. But I plan to as soon as she does. I'm guessing it's going to be just a few days, and I think it might be a bit of a mental-health break, so I don't want to press her."

Jaxson turned away, but because of his fair skin the growing flush on his neck gave him away.

"Let me know if you find anything, if you would," Uncle Bernie said. "I'd like to update the fellows in my poker group." He contemplated me with steady eyes beneath his bushy brows. "And now we need to discuss Sunny Ryan's disappearance."

He and Jaxson shared a quick glance before Bernie continued. "I've been told, very strongly, that I am not to dig any deeper into the Sunny Ryan case. That comes from up high, and the warning is clear. If I were a younger man, I'd take on the challenge. But I'm not."

"What do you mean, 'from up high'? People in the police department?"

"Higher. Even higher than the mayor and the governor."

"Higher?" I knew I sounded naïve, and maybe I was. I watched a lot of true-crime shows, but those stories were always about other people and other lives that had no connection to me. But this story was about the missing sister of someone with whom I shared a relationship, whether or not either one of us wanted to admit it. The evidence that Bernie had found tying Beau's grandfather into an early halt to the investigation made it impossible to forget and let go of even if I'd wanted to. Mimi's abrupt denial and dismissal only made it harder.

Charles Ryan had been a doctor, and he'd died the year after Sunny and her parents disappeared. Up until that time, he had been the landlord of my house. It was a slim connection at best, but one I couldn't ignore, even if there wasn't enough substance there to grasp. Or maybe I just didn't want to ignore it. I could guess what Bernie meant by "higher," but I didn't want to say it out loud. Because that would mean dragging a world that I had always kept behind a television screen into my living room.

Jaxson glanced around as if to make sure no one was close enough to hear. In a subdued voice, he said, "There are people in this city who answer to no one, who have their fingers in every kind of enterprise, both legitimate and not. They are power brokers and influence peddlers and exist in all corners of society. And they are ruthless, and will stop at nothing to get what they want. Unfortunately, as soon as one is brought to justice, his—or her—place is filled with two or three more. It doesn't mean we don't keep trying, even though a lot of people think that because it's the way it's always been it can't be changed. I happen to disagree, but I'm just a lowly public defender."

"But Sunny was just a little girl. How could she possibly have anything to do with organized crime or any other sort of profiteering?"

"Are you familiar with Carl Jung and his theory of synchronicity?" Uncle Bernie peered at me over his glasses, and I felt as if I'd just been called on in class.

"Vaguely. From a psychology course I took in undergrad. Something to do with connections."

He cleared his throat and quoted, "'The simultaneous occurrence of events which appear significantly related but have no discernible causal connection.' I had that on a poster in my old office and now I have it hung in my office at home, which is why I still remember it in my old age. To me, it's the basis of all solid detective work. If two separate events occur at the same time with no apparent connection, don't assume that they're not connected."

My phone buzzed with an incoming call, and when I looked at the screen I saw it was from Beau. I quickly hit DECLINE. "So you're not going to keep looking."

"No," Bernie said. "And neither should you. The threat is real. We can't win. Trust me, I know. And it's dangerous. If they can make a child disappear, imagine what they'd do to anyone questioning them or their actions. I've seen bodies of people who got in their way. I don't want you, or Beau, or Jaxson to end up like that."

"So that's it, then. Case closed. And if Sunny Ryan isn't dead and is out there somewhere, she most likely doesn't know her real name or that she has a brother and grandmother who miss her and would love to have her back."

"Unless you have a connection we don't know about and can ask Charles Ryan directly, I suggest we all walk away from this investigation."

Bernie looked genuinely regretful. I reached over and squeezed his hand resting on the brass pelican at the head of his cane to hide my disappointment and to let him know that I didn't blame him. "You're right. Nobody else should get hurt. But that doesn't mean I'm not going to keep thinking about it. Who knows?" I shrugged. "Maybe we'll get sent a clue from beyond. Because otherwise we don't have a chance in hell of figuring out what really happened."

Jaxson looked at his watch, then stood. "We should leave now if you want to get to work on time. My car's parked on Freret, so we can stop for a caffeine infusion at the PJ's in the Percival Stern building on the way."

"That would be great, thanks." We each took hold of one of Uncle Bernie's elbows and helped him stand.

Bernie looked at me again with his piercing blue eyes. "You're a smart girl, Nola. Like your daddy. I've read all of his books, you know.

And I happen to agree with him that there's no such thing as coincidence. Just this once, you need to pretend that there is."

There were too many unrelated pieces of information floating around my brain, touching, then ricocheting off one another, bringing back my headache. We began walking slowly toward the coffee shop, my thoughts tumbling over themselves, and I was unable to stop myself from wanting something a lot stronger than caffeine.

CHAPTER 25

It was almost lunchtime before I realized that I hadn't received any calls or texts all morning, belatedly remembering that I had turned off my phone during my meeting with Jaxson and Uncle Bernie. I flipped it on and was immediately deluged with forty-four texts. Almost half of them were from Jolene with pictures from her "day of beauty" with her mother and grandmother (both redheads); twelve were from Beau, which I immediately deleted without reading because I wasn't in the mood to be scolded by someone who needed to look in the mirror; and the rest were from Michael, as well as a missed call from him.

Without wanting to waste time reading his messages, I quickly hit REDIAL. He answered on the first ring.

"I was starting to think you were ghosting me." His voice sounded even sexier over the phone.

"Sorry—I turned my phone off for a meeting this morning and forgot to turn it back on." I probably shouldn't have admitted that, but I already felt that we were beyond the game-playing stage.

"I was hoping you might be free for dinner tonight. I know I shouldn't be asking for a second date so soon after the first, but I'd really like to see you again."

I smiled. "Glad to know we're on the same page. Can I make a suggestion?"

"Of course."

"I could really go for a chili cheese omelet at the Camellia Grill. I've never had one, but I've sat next to enough people who have and it's time to try it."

"That's my favorite place. I don't know if we can beat the Baked Alaska from last night, but their chocolate, cherry, and Oreo freeze is pretty good. So's their pecan pie."

"I guess we'll have to get one of each and share."

"Sounds like a plan. Pick you up at six?"

"Perfect. But can you pick me up at my house? I need to go there after work to see where we are with the renovations. I've got spreadsheets tacked up on most of the walls and I need to make sure the guys are filling them in each day so I can track our progress and make plans for the next steps."

There was a brief pause. "Spreadsheets?"

I sighed. "I'll explain later."

"I'll look forward to it. How about I pick you up at five thirty so you can give me a tour? Let my uncle know what he missed out on."

I felt a small swell of pride. "I'd love to show you around. See you at five thirty."

My phone rang just as I hung up with Michael. I immediately hit DECLINE when I saw it was Beau calling, then silenced it and got back to work.

When I met with Trevor after work on our corner of Canal and Royal, he looked disappointed that I wasn't carrying an extra bag. "Sorry— Jolene's out of town." I made a point not to mention the banana nut muffins since I hadn't brought them, needing to make them last until Jolene returned. I took hold of the bike's handlebars. "Did you find the item I asked about?"

"Yes, ma'am. It wasn't easy, neither. It's gonna cost you." He reached into his backpack and pulled out a rumpled brown paper lunch bag, the creases gone soft with use, and handed it to me.

I didn't open the bag fully but peeked inside, satisfied to see a silver flask at the bottom. "Where'd you find it?"

"Some drunk college kid in Jackson Square. He was trying to get money to get his palm read, so I saw an opportunity." He grinned, his white teeth flashing.

"You're a smart boy, Trevor. How much do I owe you?"

"It cost me twenty, so I'm thinking forty for my trouble. And you might want to wash that thing before you use it. I saw the guy puking right before I bought the flask from him."

"Lovely. Don't worry—I will." I pulled two twenties from my wallet. "Thank you."

"And an extra five, 'cause I added two candy bars at the bottom of the bag for you and Miss Jolene."

I took out my second-to-last bill, which happened to be a five, and handed it to him.

He tilted his head, creasing his brow. "How come you want that for, Miss Nola?"

"For the same reason everybody else who has one does, I guess."

"To get drunk?"

His words startled me. "No. Of course not. It's just that sometimes, like when I'm at work or someplace where I want something to drink and it's not easily accessible, a flask can come in handy."

"Uh-huh." Trevor looked at me as if I'd just told him that Santa was real. I hoped the disappointment in his brown eyes had just been my imagination.

I looked at him over my sunglasses. "And don't look a gift horse in the mouth. I could have gone into any store and bought one, but I wanted to give you my business." Eager to regain my footing, I said, "How's school?"

He scuffed the toe of his sneaker against the pavement. "It's good, I guess."

"You guess?"

Trevor's narrow shoulders moved up in a shrug. "My teacher says I'm smart 'cause I got a curious mind, but says I need a computer at home so I can look up stuff. She must think I'm Jay-Z or somethin'."

"I'm sure she didn't mean for you to buy one. There are computers to use at community centers and libraries, too, you know. For free. But you can always work and save toward getting your own." I pulled out my last bill, a twenty. "How about you put this in a special place for your computer fund? We can both start thinking about ways to earn some extra money, okay?"

"Yeah?" Half of his mouth quirked upward.

"Yeah." The hopefulness in his eyes made me think of something else. "Do you have a library card?"

"A what?"

"Well, then, that's a place to start. You need a card to access the public computers at the library. Maybe your grandmother can take you to get one?"

His smile fell. "No, ma'am. Meemaw can't get around so good."

"All right. You and I will go together. Do you have any free time tomorrow?"

"Yep. All day."

I thought of my brother, JJ, who spent most Saturdays on a baseball field, since he belonged to two travel teams, and Trevor's answer hurt my heart. "Well, that makes it easier. Let me figure out my schedule and I'll let you know. And make sure you ask permission from Meemaw to go with me. Sound good?"

He nodded, not in the way of eager anticipation, but more like someone who was used to being disappointed.

"I promise, okay? And be thinking about ideas for earning extra cash for that computer."

His face brightened. "Okay."

We fist-bumped and I began pedaling down Royal Street, almost too busy thinking about ideas for Trevor to see the passenger door of a minivan opening. I swerved, barely missing a collision with the young woman who was stepping out of the vehicle. Her eyes were shaded by large sunglasses, and she didn't turn her head as I hit the opposite curb because she either didn't see me or pretended not to.

I managed to stay on my bike, but my backpack was knocked out of my basket and onto the ground, the bag with the flask sliding out of the unzipped top and skidding to a stop a few feet away. I quickly retrieved it and returned it to my backpack, annoyed enough now to go back and tell the woman to be more careful next time.

Walking my bike to where the minivan was parked, I realized it had stopped in front of the Past Is Never Past. The woman now stood on the sidewalk as a man opened up the back of the minivan and retrieved a small tricycle, its handles festooned with red, white, and blue streamers, the front wheel twisted and misshapen, the tire flattened. I began to approach, then halted as the woman lifted a tissue under her sunglasses and dabbed at each eye. The man closed the hatch, then put an arm around the woman's shoulders as he carried the tricycle toward the door of the shop.

I crossed the street, curious to know why a child's broken trike was being brought into the high-end antiques-and-architectural-remnants shop. I was in the process of chaining up my bike when Christopher opened the door and stepped outside. "Nola. This is a nice surprise."

He crossed his arms over his chest, almost as if to block my way. Looking over his shoulder through the window, I spotted the man, woman, and tricycle heading toward the back of the shop.

"Yes, um, I was on my way to check on my house, and I was nearly killed by that woman opening her door without looking. I just wanted to tell her to be more careful."

Christopher didn't move. "I'm sorry. People do need to be more aware of bicyclists in this city."

I made to move around him, but he took a casual step to the side, effectively blocking me. "And I know Mrs. Ward didn't mean any harm. She and her husband have suffered a horrible loss and I don't think now would be the best time to approach her."

I peered past him again through the window, spotting Mimi in the back with a ring of keys as she faced the hidden door, unlocking it.

The couple stood behind her with the warped tricycle, Mrs. Ward's head on her husband's shoulder as he continued to keep his arm around her. I returned my gaze to Christopher's face. "I didn't think you fixed children's toys here."

"We don't." He didn't smile, his amber eyes watching me closely. "Is there anything I can help you with? Did Jolene send anything?" His lips turned up, as if to erase the peculiar scene I had just witnessed.

I looked again through the window just in time to see the couple and Mimi disappear behind the door, the door itself disappearing into the wall. "Sorry, no. She's out of town." Unable to hold back my curiosity, I asked, "What's behind that door?"

For a moment, it looked as if he might be about to deny its existence. Instead, he smiled again and said, "That's Mimi's domain. She stores special items in there."

"And that's where you put my door?"

"Yes."

Seeing as I was getting nowhere, I began unchaining my bike. I straightened, an idea percolating in my brain. "Is there any chance you could use help dusting or polishing? Or emptying the trash? Maybe someone for just a few hours a week? I know a kid who's trying to make some money."

"Yeah? How old is he?"

"Twelve. He's a great kid, very industrious and extremely smart. He's trying to buy a home computer. I remember you telling me that you and your dad got your interest in antiques by starting here, doing stuff like that."

"What's his name?"

"Trevor." I realized that I didn't know his last name.

Christopher nodded. "Tell him to stop by and ask for me. I'll see if we can work something out."

I smiled. "Thank you. I will." I started to turn away, but paused. "Christopher, can I ask you something?"

"I suppose that would depend on what it is."

"I accidentally saw that text you sent to Beau. The picture of Jeanne. I saw her, too, you know. And it was her."

His amber eyes showed no surprise.

"I wanted to ask what you meant about telling Mimi and saying it would only get worse."

He opened the door of the shop and stepped inside. "I've got to go. I have customers waiting."

"It's my house, Christopher. Shouldn't I know?"

"Not unless you have the power to do something about it."

"Like Beau?"

He shut the door and turned away.

I pedaled the rest of the way to the Marigny, watching for parked cars with open doors, and thinking about what Christopher had said.

The front door stood partially open, so no one noticed me. Jaxson was there filming while Michael stood to the side watching Thibaut toss a measuring tape into the air as Jorge leapfrogged over his back and caught it before landing safely on the ground.

Everyone turned toward me as I clapped. "That was amazing, guys! Where did you learn that?"

Thibaut approached and shook hands with Michael, introducing himself and Jorge. "Jorge's people were circus folks back in Brazil, so he comes from a long line of acrobats. I'm just a big guy who's a sturdy base for any of the crazy things Jorge can think of. And I know how to juggle—something I learned in prison."

Jaxson glanced at me. "Don't worry—I can edit that last part out." Turning toward the two men, he said, "Great job. I swear, every time we post something like this on the YouTube channel we get about another five hundred followers. It's crazy. And Jolene says that the number of calls they're getting at JR Properties has almost tripled since last month. Who knew?"

Michael moved to stand next to me. Aware that all three men were watching us, he only lightly touched my shoulder. "It's good to see you again. It's been a while."

I laughed, feeling almost giddy—not a familiar emotion for me. "It's been, what? Eighteen hours?"

"Only that long? It felt like much longer." We grinned at each other like idiots.

Jaxson approached with an outstretched hand. "Jaxson Landry, official documentarian for this renovation. Public defender when I'm not doing this."

"Michael Hebert." The two men shook hands. "With the Sabatier Group."

"Oh," Jaxson said. "You're the ones who are trying to build those high-rise condos in the Treme, right?"

"Yes, that's us. My uncle's company, anyway. We're still having discussions with the historical society and community leaders, so it's holding us back a bit, but we're hoping to come to an agreement soon."

I regretted not taking Beau's suggestion to find out more about the Sabatier Group. Granted, I hadn't had a lot of time, but I knew a large part of my reluctance was because Beau had suggested it. The other part was that I was afraid of what I might find. My relationship—if it could be called that so early in the game—with Michael was too new to go digging for anything that might skew my perception of him.

"Well, good luck with that," Jaxson said. "From what I hear, there's a lot of opposition."

Michael shrugged. "Yeah, well, it wouldn't be called progress if there wasn't any opposition. We're used to it. I don't doubt that we will be able to come up with a plan that works for all interested parties." He smiled, then put an arm around my shoulders. "Why don't you show me around? I'm dying to see what's been done so far."

With the conversation effectively ended, Jaxson said his good-byes, but turned back at the door. "Have you heard from Jolene?"

I nodded. "She's enjoying being at home with her family. She said she might take some vacation time and do some working from home, so it could be a couple more days. Unless I need her to bring the dog back." As much as I missed Jolene, the absence of the little dog, even though I'd known him only a short while, hurt more than I wanted to admit. "I can keep you posted, or you could call her."

"Right." With a wave, he let himself out.

To Michael, I said, "Just give me a moment, all right? I want to go over the worksheets with the guys first."

I turned to where I'd thumbtacked the "potty and snack break" spreadsheet to the wall, and when I looked behind me to address why nothing had been marked down, Thibaut and Jorge were jogging up the stairs.

"Guys!" I said. "We need to talk about this."

Thibaut had already disappeared upstairs as Jorge peered over the banister. He spoke in a barrage of Portuguese that might have been simply telling me that he didn't speak English before shrugging and following Thibaut out of sight.

Michael laughed, taking my hand. "Come show me the house. I can't wait to see what you've done."

I led him into the dismantled kitchen. "Not a lot, as you can see. We're trying to get some structural, plumbing, and electrical issues taken care of before we can do any actual renovation or reconstruction. It's very frustrating, but I want to do this right."

"I somehow knew that's what you would say. I admire your patience. As much as I can love a building's historic charm, when it comes to making a structure livable, I find myself sometimes leaning toward the quickest and least expensive."

I paused to look up at him. "But you consider that a flaw, right?"

He hesitated only a moment. "Absolutely. One of my very few." He grinned and opened the back door into the yard, where the bits and pieces of woodwork had been straightened since the intrusion the previous night.

"We think we might have had a break-in last night, but luckily nothing was stolen. I think they were looking for something in particular—maybe a spindle or something that might be a match for one in their own house. Who knows? I hate leaving all of this outside, but with all the work going on inside, I don't want it lying around where it can get damaged."

"A break-in, huh? But nothing was taken? Could have just been more curiosity than anything else. Did you file a police report?"

"No, since nothing was missing. I figure the police have better things to do."

He leaned down to look at one of the mantelpieces that had been stripped of years of paint and lay naked under the tarp. He rubbed his hand over the smooth top, stroking it like a lover and doing funny things to my nerve endings. "This is beautiful. Really beautiful." He straightened. "If you ever change your mind about keeping this house, let me know. I've got lots of buyers who'd love this kind of stuff in their new houses."

I suppressed a shudder. "Sorry, but never."

We went back inside, and as I locked the door I said, "We think someone has a key to this door, too, but since nothing's been taken, we don't know for sure. The lock is original to the house, so I guess it wouldn't be unheard-of that someone who once lived here might have hung on to a key and wanted to take a look to see what was going on."

Michael nodded, then headed toward the stairs. "Can I go up?"

"Sure. Just more naked rooms and unfinished cypress floors—and no, I'm not selling those, either. There's one huge room I'm going to divide into two bedrooms, and a bathroom that has been completely gutted. Just count your blessings that you didn't see it in its original state."

He'd already climbed the stairs, stopping at the top. "What's this?"

After throwing a furtive look in the corner where I'd seen Jeanne's ghost, I stared ahead into the dark chasm of the doorless room. "It's just a closet that was locked and nailed shut for some reason. We found a bunch of old clothes that Jolene has taken to a vintage clothing boutique to try to sell. We also found a bunch of hatboxes and a Mr. Bingle doll."

"Wow—I remember Mr. Bingle! It's probably a collector's item if it's old. What about the hatboxes?"

"Don't know yet. I'm waiting to go through them when Jolene returns. I want to do it now, but she asked me to wait. We just stacked them in the front room at the apartment with the Maison Blanche door so they're not in the way. Which is good, because it allows me to forget about them and not peek."

Michael stepped inside the closet and flipped on his phone light. "Any idea who would have sealed it up?"

"None. Neither Mimi nor Beau knew anything about it. Beau didn't have a key and Mimi didn't have any knowledge of its existence."

Facing him, I said, "There was a murder here, you know. Back in the sixties. Mimi's best friend, Jeanne Broussard, was strangled to death on the stairs. They never found out who did it. But it traumatized Mimi enough that even though she and her husband owned the property as a rental, she never set foot inside it."

"Really? Do you remember the year?" He stood in the closet, his face in shadow, so I couldn't read his expression. Or know if I'd only imagined the change in his voice.

"Nineteen sixty-four. Why?"

He flicked off his light and stepped back into the hallway. "I'm a fan of true crime. Can't get enough of those shows and podcasts. I thought I might Google it later. Strange that it was sealed up like that if it only held old clothes and Mr. Bingle."

"Agreed. We'll just have to wait until Jolene gets back to see if there's anything in the hatboxes, although judging by what we already found, I'm guessing nothing more than old hats." I tugged on his arm. "Come on. I'm hungry. We can talk about our favorite true-crime shows, and I can tell you what I know about Jeanne."

We said our good-byes and made our way down to the front steps. "Hang on," I said. "I need to ask Thibaut something. Could you see if my bike will fit in your trunk? If not, I can leave it inside."

I headed toward the stairs, aware suddenly of the change in temperature, of my breath condensing and rising toward the ceiling like expelled spirits. I could hear Jorge and Thibaut talking in Portuguese in the upstairs room, but they sounded very far away. I placed my foot on the bottom step but found my way blocked by an unseen force, an invisible wall that opposed any forward motion.

The scent of pipe tobacco filled my nostrils and my lungs, making me choke and cough. I tried one more time to move forward, but it was like pressing against a concrete wall.

Strong invisible hands gripped my shoulders and shoved me backward, toppling me off the bottom step and sending me skidding into a wall. Goose bumps covered my skin, my teeth chattering as the temperature continued to plummet. I slowly backed toward the door, the sudden and powerful scent of hair spray—now recognizable to me—filling my nose. I realized that this was a battle I couldn't win by myself. I needed reinforcements, but of the two people whom I knew could help, one lived in Charleston, and the other one I never wanted to see again.

CHAPTER 26

Jolene ended up staying away for a full week. She'd planned to come back on Thursday, but then a tropical depression blew into the Gulf. Since we were smack-dab—her term—in the middle of hurricane season, she thought she and Mardi would be safer in Mississippi than in New Orleans if the storm became a full-blown hurricane.

She invited me to come stay with her, too, but I declined, saying I was too new an employee at work to be asking for time off. Which was true. But there was also Michael. We saw each other every day, our relationship growing as we discovered we had many things in common, including a love for old houses, true-crime shows, running, and listening to jazz.

We'd even gone to Frenchmen Street one night. We hadn't run into Beau, even though I looked for him. I wanted him to see me having a good time and in control. Part of me wanted him to see me with Michael, to show him that I wasn't the lonely, confused girl whom he'd once known.

Michael had also taken me to an empty parking lot to help me practice my driving skills—or lack thereof—but as he'd already admitted, he was short on patience and I didn't want his jaw to get locked in place or his teeth to crack from clenching them, so we stopped after an hour. He promised that we could try it again if I asked, but I wasn't in the habit of torturing people, so I hadn't.

The torrential rain from the storm—which didn't become a hurricane or even warrant a name—meant that any progress on my house had to be halted. It became clear that the roof could no longer be patched, as had been our hope to buy us more time—and allow me to find the money—and the entire roof needed to be replaced now instead of later. While I juggled estimates from roofing contractors, Thibaut and Jorge went to work on another JR Properties project until the roof was finished.

I missed seeing them each day, but the bonus was that I didn't have to have any interactions with Beau Ryan. He'd at last stopped calling and texting me. I knew I'd have to ask him about Christopher's text and its implications. And tell him that I'd been pushed from the steps by either a man or a woman—I was no longer sure which. If I didn't want to wait until Melanie's visit in October, I would have to talk to him at some point. But not right now. Because if I forced him to tell me that he had the ability to communicate with the dead, I would have to answer his own questions. Questions about things that weren't any of his business, but that his insertion into my earlier life made him believe were.

If he did ask about my drinking, I would tell him that I was drinking again, but only socially. That despite his warnings, having a few drinks while out with friends didn't constitute a backward step, at least not for me. I could stop when I wanted to. I was displaying a willpower that he hadn't given me credit for or had simply overlooked. He also hadn't taken into consideration that I was in a better place in my life now, with a new and exciting job, and I now owned a house that I was excited about restoring. It's why I'd been avoiding him. Because I knew he would have an argument for everything and I was enjoying my new life too much to have him bring me down.

I was easily distracted from the whole Beau dilemma by Michael's invitation to the annual fall soiree at the New Orleans Museum of Art fund-raiser at the Besthoff Sculpture Garden. It would be a night of dining and dancing under the stars and oaks and guaranteed to be romantic.

Without Jolene, I wasn't sure I could handle the hair and makeup, much less figure out what to wear. In desperation, I began practicing on the Barbie head, attempting to use all the same makeup products that Jolene had used on me. The result was a Ronald McDonald look-alike who had run into a sprinkler. In a final act of desperation, I FaceTimed Jolene.

I had the camera pointed at the Barbie head when I called, eliciting a small scream when she answered. I felt slightly justified after the horror she'd put me through when she'd left the head on the table.

"Help! I'm supposed to be going to a dinner and dance at the sculpture garden tomorrow night and I don't have a clue."

"I'd say this is an emergency situation. I'm coming first thing in the morning."

"I'm not that helpless, Jolene." I hoped I sounded sincere. "You don't need to come back early on my account. I'm sure we can just FaceTime."

"I need to come back anyway. Mama is about ready to get me out of her hair. They're still doing all that excavating in the backyard for the pool and they think they've discovered a buried cemetery, so there's all sorts of people halting the progress, and I think Mama's going to pitch a real hissy fit and I'd rather not be here to witness it."

"Wow—a cemetery. I can't wait to hear more, but I really can't say I blame your mother for being upset. But if you think you're ready and your mother is okay with it . . ."

"I'm already packing as we talk. I've been making a little pile of things to bring back for you that I thought you might like to have. Do you have your own set of heat rollers?"

"What? Like, for asphalt?"

"Lordy, girl. Sometimes I wish you were joking but I know you're not. I'm adding my old set to the pile. What about a clay mask?"

"I have no idea what you're talking about. Unless you're talking about something that's been excavated from your yard?"

"Never mind. I'm just bringing all of it. Don't worry—help is on the way. I'll leave first thing tomorrow morning, so I should get there by around noon. What time is Michael picking you up?"

"Six thirty. Will that be enough time?" I'd meant it sarcastically.

"Barely. I'll text you with my ETA when I leave so you know when to draw your bath. I'll add the bath salts and oil, so don't try it on your own, okay?"

"I wouldn't dream of it."

She reached down and lifted up Mardi, making him wave his paw. He seemed to smile as if he recognized me. "Did anybody call yet?"

"Nope. And you never told me if he was chipped or not."

Jolene buried her face in Mardi's neck and I had the suspicion that she was hiding her face for a reason. "I forgot," came her muffled answer.

"What? How could you forget?"

"I got distracted buying those cute bandannas and squeaky toys. And the doggie Halloween costumes were already out and it took me forever to choose one. I actually bought three, and I'll let you pick. Or he can change outfits throughout the day. Plus he'll need one for the Barkus parade. . . ."

"Stop right there. If he belongs to someone, we can't keep him, okay?"

She held her hands over Mardi's ears. "Don't say that in front of him. It hurts his feelings."

"Jolene, I'm serious. . . ."

As if she hadn't heard me, she asked, "Hey, did you see on the news last night that Past Posh was robbed?"

"Why does that name sound familiar? And are you talking about New Orleans news? Because I thought you were in Mississippi."

"I am. But my mama's second cousin Bedellia—you know, the one who brought us all of those pecans from her tree and I made that pie for you?—she saw it on the local news and because she knows I'm best friends from growing up with Andrea, the owner, she called to let me know. It's the boutique where I sold all of those clothes from your attic. Most of the clothes were still hanging by the door, because she was in the process of determining prices and giving them tags. Everything on the rack was taken, and her cash register emptied—although there wasn't a lot in there, thankfully."

"That's awful. Was anybody hurt?" I asked.

"No, thank heavens. It happened at night, after closing. But Andrea's pretty shook up. Since she just lost all that merchandise, she was wondering if there was anything in the hatboxes we wanted to sell."

"I wouldn't know. I've been waiting for you to get back like you asked."

"I was hoping that's what you'd say. We can do it this weekend."

"After we take Mardi to the vet to see if he's chipped," I reminded her.

"Vets' offices are usually closed on weekends. We'll have to wait until Monday."

"Fine. I'll see you tomorrow. And thank you."

"No thanks needed, Nola. I love doing it for you. There's just one thing to take care of before I get there."

"Sure—what?"

"Take a tweezers to your eyebrows before I have to get a hedge clipper involved."

The party started at seven o'clock, just past sunset, which meant that the light had already started to dim by the time Michael pulled his car into the driveway. Dimmer lighting hopefully would hide any glaring makeup mistakes or spotlight my attempt at an updo, which I'd decided to label a "messy bun" if anyone cared to ask.

When Jolene tried to leave that morning, her car wouldn't start. Her cousin Ace, who fortunately owned a repair shop, had it towed and put up on a lift, but he needed a few parts and wasn't sure how long it would take to get them. As glad as I was that Bubba hadn't conked out in the middle of nowhere between Jackson and New Orleans, I found myself wondering if I'd put on too much blush as I waited outside on the front stoop for Michael to pick me up.

As he approached I walked down the steps, feeling slightly unsteady on a pair of borrowed heels from Jolene's closet. It had nothing to do with the two glasses of wine I'd consumed to still my nerves while getting dressed. Michael and I hadn't known each other for long, but I knew tonight would be special. And as I walked toward him, I knew that right now we were on the cusp between the before and the after of our relationship.

"You look beautiful," he said, taking my hand.

"Thank you," I said, hoping he wasn't saying that just to be nice. "It's Jolene's dress. I wasn't sure if it was a good color on me or not."

"Lavender is definitely your color. But I also think that you would look beautiful in anything. Or nothing." He grinned, gently squeezing my hand. "Speaking of Jolene, when does she get back?" Michael's fingers rested lightly on my lower back as he guided me toward the car. I felt the heat from his hands through the silk of my dress as if I wore nothing at all.

"I doubt it will be before Sunday. Her car needs multiple parts. At least she's related to a mechanic, so she doesn't need to worry about it being fixed properly."

"That's a relief." He opened the door and I sat down, then lifted my legs together before pivoting forward as Jolene had instructed. Leaning inside, he said, "I know that you miss her, but at least we'll have your apartment all to ourselves tonight." His lips met mine, and I melted back into the soft leather. Michael was an expert kisser; sometimes, like now, though, I wondered if he might be *too* expert. Beau's kiss, on the other hand, although not lacking experience, had felt as if it had been meant only for me, all other recipients forgotten as soon as his lips met mine.

Which was ridiculous since he'd been practically asleep at the time and the whole experience had been just an aberration. And I shouldn't have been thinking about Beau at all. I smiled up at Michael, his green eyes framed by those enviable black lashes. "Something else to look forward to."

The Sydney and Walda Besthoff Sculpture Garden was located on the grounds of the New Orleans Museum of Art in City Park. During my abbreviated previous tenure in New Orleans I'd visited the museum once, but a torrential downpour had cut my trip short. My sudden departure from the city meant that I'd never made it back to the garden's ten acres filled with works of art nestled neatly among lagoons, centuries-old live oaks, and meandering footpaths.

The night air at this time of year couldn't be described as cold by anyone from north of the Mason-Dixon Line; the slightly cooler temperatures and lower humidity made the outdoor event bearable. Michael had bought tickets that included reserved seating at one of the white-cloth-covered tables, and his jacket was shed almost immediately and hung over the back of his chair.

Lights twinkled from trees and around the dance floor and the food and drink tables. The food was provided by the Brennan Group's long list of amazing and award-winning local restaurants, with live music delivered by a popular local band. Most important was the dance floor, since it was my belief that real men knew how to dance. My research into this was limited, having been based solely on my dad and Cooper Ravenel, a Citadel cadet I'd once dated, but dancing proficiency was a solid criterion Michael would need to meet before I could consider us "serious."

Michael seemed to know everyone and made sure to introduce me proudly as "Nola Trenholm, historic preservationist" instead of as his girlfriend, which—to me and apparently to him, too—sounded very high school.

I was already light-headed from the wine and a glass of champagne someone had pressed into my hand and I needed to eat. After a round of meeting people and chatting, I tugged on Michael's arm. "I'm starving. Can we eat now?"

"Sure, but first we need to cast our votes." He began leading me toward a large crowd surrounding a bar area. "It's the Love Cocktail Challenge—they have it every year. Ten of New Orleans's top bartenders try to win first place by creating a signature love-inspired cocktail."

Michael led me into the midst of the crowd, high-fiving a couple of friends while I smiled and followed in his wake. He lowered his head closer so that I could hear him over the din from the crowd. "The themes are forbidden love, love/hate, lust, unconditional love, and un-requited love. There are a few others, but those are my favorites just because of the names. Last year I tried them all and regretted it the next morning. I think this year we only sample them. We put a token in the little banks for the ones we like. Pretty simple, huh?"

I started to remind him that I needed to eat something, but he was already moving forward in the crowd to get us cocktails. The claustro-phobic crush of bodies held me back, my hand slipping from Michael's as he disappeared in front of me, shoulders closing the space where he'd just been. I stayed rooted to my spot, happy to sway like jetsam in the waves of people.

While I waited, I found myself in conversation with a woman named T'ish (spelled with an apostrophe—or "comma to the top," as she explained—between the *T* and the *i*) who told me she was a tour guide and a native New Orleanian, as if her accent hadn't given her away. She was telling me that her son was getting married in the spring and that the reception was being held at the sculpture garden, when Michael reappeared, two drinks in each hand.

I introduced him to my new friend and then followed him to our table, where he set down our drinks. "Having fun?" he asked.

"So far! It's so beautiful here at night. After we eat, can we go walk through the gardens? I love the way the lagoons reflect the light. It's almost magical."

"Absolutely. One of the late-night food trucks is going to be Nola's Snowballs, so make sure you save room and we'll eat them while we walk." He bent down to kiss me. "Did I mention how beautiful you are tonight?"

"You might have. But I don't mind hearing it again."

He kissed me again, slower this time, our eyes open. Straightening, he said, "I'll go fight the crowds again and fill up some plates of food for us—unless you want to pick your own?"

"I trust you. And my feet thank you. I'll keep an eye on our drinks."

"Go ahead and try each one—they're all different. And then we'll cast our votes and get four more."

I gave him a thumbs-up. "Sounds like a plan."

As I waited, I sipped on one of the drinks while my foot tapped to the music from the Boogie Men, an amazing and entertaining ten-piece horn-based dance band, and watched as dancers executed a mixture of swing and modern moves. I waved to several of the people I'd met earlier as they passed by my table, some stopping to chat, while I grew hungrier and eager to join the swaying couples on the dance floor.

I'd picked up the third cocktail and started sipping it when I felt someone pull out a chair next to me. I turned, expecting to see Michael, and my smile faded quickly when I saw it was Beau. An unexpected and unwanted jolt of *something* zapped through me when our eyes met, and I quickly took a sip from my drink so I had a reason to look way.

"Hello, Nola."

"Beau," I said, keeping my voice pleasant. "What a surprise to see you here."

He looked pointedly at the drinks on the table and the one in my hand. "What are you doing, Nola?"

"I'm enjoying myself with Michael at a fund-raiser for the museum."

"That's not what I meant, and you know it."

I looked over his shoulder, eager to spot Michael on his way back.

"Why haven't you been answering my calls and my texts?"

I schooled myself to meet his eyes again. "Because we have nothing to talk about. Jolene is my project manager and she and I are working on getting estimates for the roof replacement. Your involvement isn't needed."

He took a deep breath. "That wasn't what I was calling about."

"And I don't need you to babysit me, either. Are you going to go tattle on me to my parents now?"

"Why? Do I need to? I'm sure you've already told them that you're drinking again."

I took a defiant swig of my drink, if only to hide the wave of guilt flashing through me. "Why would I? I'm an adult."

"Then maybe you should act like one."

I stood, my folding chair wobbling. I would have walked away, but he grabbed my arm. "Stop. Please. There's something you need to know. It's important."

Something in his eyes made me sit down again, but I made sure I kept my hands in my lap just in case I needed to get away.

"Go ahead." I kept my gaze focused behind him.

"Jaxson called me. He thought I should know about what his uncle Bernie told you about my grandfather. And Sunny."

"Mimi told me to drop it, so I have. Is there anything else?" I allowed the impatience to be heard in my voice.

"Yeah. There is. He shared with me what his uncle Bernie discovered that implicated my grandfather. The information that he has not shared with anyone else because he was warned that it could be dangerous. To him and anyone else who finds out."

"So don't tell me. I don't want to know."

"But you need to hear it. Because it involves Michael."

I pulled back, wishing my head didn't feel so muddled. "What? But that's impossible—Michael was just a kid when Sunny disappeared." I started to stand again, wanting him to leave and the conversation to be over.

"Because he's a cop, quitting went against Uncle Bernie's instincts. On a hunch he did some under-the-radar digging in an ancestry database, looking for connections that nobody had thought about. And his instincts turned out to be spot-on." He took a deep breath, leaning forward as if afraid I might try to leave again. "Michael's maternal grandmother was Marguerite Hebert, but her maiden name was Broussard. The sister of Jeanne Broussard. The same Jeanne Broussard who was murdered in our house." He paused, as if to let his words sink in. "Has Michael ever mentioned that to you? That Jeanne was his great-aunt?"

I sat down hard, needing another drink almost as much as I needed to think clearly. "No. Why would he? Maybe he doesn't even know that he's related to Jeanne. She died in 1964, so it's not like he would have ever met her. It could just be a—"

"Don't say it, Nola. Don't say it, because you and I both know that you don't believe it."

"But it's just as ridiculous to say that something that happened more than six decades ago could have anything to do with your sister. Or with Michael."

"Not him, Nola. His family. New Orleans was and is full of powerful people in powerful places. Jeanne and Marguerite's father, Antoine Broussard, was one of them. He was either related or closely connected to the mayor and several other city officials since Prohibition."

I shook my head, as much to disagree as to clear it. "Okay, but how does that relate to Michael? He and his sister were raised by his father's sister and her husband. His father is a missionary, for crying out loud. Obviously, they're not connected with anything the Broussard family might have been involved with over the years."

"How can you know for sure? Marguerite married Carl Hebert, who became Antoine's business partner. They owned a lot of real estate in the city, including most of Poydras Street. Think about it, Nola. Michael's grandfather Carl and his great-grandfather Antoine were very rich and very influential." He paused. "And my grandfather Charles Ryan was the Broussard family doctor."

I picked up another cocktail and took a deep drink, the melted ice slipping down my throat along with the gin. Slamming it down on the table, I said, "So what? If you go back far enough, we could probably find out that you and I are somehow connected. Or, God forbid, even related. New Orleans is a small enough town that I would be surprised if we didn't find those kinds of connections wherever we look within families that have been here as long as the Broussards and the Heberts." I stood. "I've heard enough. All Bernie has really accomplished is digging into Michael's family tree, which anybody could do just by checking out one of the ancestry websites. It proves nothing because it means

nothing. And it certainly doesn't have anything to do with Michael."
I tried to send him a steady glare, but my feet wouldn't stay put. "You
know what I think, Beau? I think you're jealous of Michael and you're
trying to ruin it for me. Just like you did before."

Beau stood, too. "Answer me this: Has Michael once mentioned to
you that his great-aunt was the woman who was murdered in your
house? You told him about Jeanne, didn't you? So that would have been
the perfect opportunity for him to tell you, right? I think it's naïve to
think that Michael didn't know the connection, don't you? Unless he
has already told you that he was related to Jeanne. And that his uncle's
offer to buy your house was a random thing. Then I'd be willing to
say that it could actually be a coincidence."

I could only stare back at him. Because he and I both knew that it
couldn't be.

"There's something else you need to consider, Nola. What if Mimi's
wrong? What if my grandfather really did put a halt to further investigation into Sunny's case? What if there's some connection, some
business dealings with the Broussards and my grandfather, that forced
him to do something so abhorrent?" He leaned closer. "And what if
Michael knows what that is?"

I looked up to see a young woman wearing a red sundress approaching us. I stared for a moment, wondering where I'd seen her before,
and then I remembered. It had been while we were waiting in line to
get into the Spotted Cat. Beau had been kissing her. Samantha was her
name. Sam. Beau's girlfriend and podcast partner.

I turned abruptly and walked quickly toward a path partially hidden
under the wide branches of ancient oaks. I ducked behind one of the
enormous trunks and rested my hand on the gnarled bark, attempting
to ground myself and make the world stop spinning, unsure if it was
from the alcohol I'd consumed on an empty stomach or from Beau's
words, which I couldn't dismiss any more than I could the unsettling
belief that what he had told me might be true.

CHAPTER 27

For the remainder of the evening, I ate and drank and danced, eagerly attempting to drown the doubts that Beau had inserted into my already foggy brain. Michael turned out to be an excellent dancer, and I made a mental note to thank both of my grandmothers in Charleston for forcing me to take dancing lessons when I was in high school. I'd since discovered that it was another one of those life skills that would carry me forward, much like good manners. And potty training.

Yet no matter how many times Michael took me out on the dance floor, and I allowed the swirling lights and the voices of people to pulse around me, I couldn't completely forget what Beau had told me. If I'd learned anything in my recent past, it was that denial was about as useful as a broom without a handle. When I'd made the decision to move to New Orleans, my dad gave me a plaque as a reminder of where I'd been. It was on a bookshelf in my room where I'd see it every morning when I woke up. *Denial isn't just a river in Egypt.* I would ask Michael tomorrow about what Beau had said. I just wanted this one night to be perfect.

As promised, Michael bought us snowballs and we ate them while we walked and kissed beneath the branches of the oak trees. I had long since shed my shoes—although I couldn't recall exactly where—and had voted twice for my favorite cocktail, since I liked two of them equally and had even gone back for seconds of each to make sure. Michael pulled me into his arms and I rested my head on his chest as we slow danced, listening to the sounds of the dwindling crowd and the chorus of frogs.

He gently kissed the back of my head. "Are you ready to leave yet?"

I smiled up at him and nodded. Taking my hand, he led us back to our table, where he'd left his jacket and I'd left Jolene's purse—her shoes nowhere in sight.

"Why don't you sit down and I'll go look for them?" Michael suggested.

I pulled on his arm. "I'll call lost and found tomorrow. Let's go home."

With his arm around me, I walked barefoot back to the car, barely feeling the rocks and the grass beneath my feet. In the car, I tucked my legs beneath me and began singing the last song from the party, "Beyond the Sea," making up notes and lyrics for the ones I couldn't remember.

"We'll *meeeet* behind the *storrrre*, and shop like *beforrrrre* at half-price *saaaales* . . . we'll go *saaaailing*." I snorted, and Michael laughed, and then I was laughing, too, unable to stop. We continued singing and laughing the entire drive until we turned onto Broadway, quickly sobering as we approached my block. The blue flash from the roof light of a police car guided us to where it was parked in my driveway. No lights were lit in the downstairs apartment, but the windows in my apartment upstairs glowed like a lighthouse.

I scrambled out of the car and ran to the front steps without waiting for Michael. I pushed open the slightly ajar door and rushed up the stairs, stumbling twice because the walls wouldn't keep still. A dog barked, and when I threw open the door at the top of the steps, a gray and white fur ball threw itself at me, followed by a tongue bath on my face and neck.

I put Mardi back on the ground as Michael came up the stairs behind me and we both took in the scene. Jolene sat on the sofa with a
throw blanket held in place on her shoulders by Jaxson, who was sitting
next to her. She wore one of her pretty high-collared nightgowns, her
bare toes peeking out from under the ruffled hem. A uniformed police
officer sat in the chair across from them with a notepad and pen writing something down. Another police officer stood in the doorway
leading to the front room, the remnants of a smashed Barbie head
scattered in the doorway, a clump of blond hair still clinging to a part
of plastic scalp lying near a chair leg and a set of full lips sitting on the
base of the floor lamp.

My brain didn't seem capable of making any sense of the various
optical stimuli making me feel oddly as if I were inside a Rorschach
test. "What . . . ?" was all I could force out of my mouth.

Jaxson said, "There was an intruder tonight and Jolene managed to
fend him off with a large Barbie head."

"Oh, my gosh. Jolene! Are you okay?" I ran over to her and sat
down on the couch on the other side of her, dislodging Jaxson's arm
with my own hug.

"I'm so sorry, Nola. I promise to get you another one. But when
Mardi started barking, I knew it couldn't be you. And you'd left Barbie
on my dressing table, so it was the only thing I could think of to use
for a weapon."

I blinked hard. "I don't care about the Barbie—are you hurt?"

She shook her head. "I'm fine. I don't know why everyone is making such a fuss. I just wish I'd hit him harder so he would still be here
when the police arrived."

I put my hands on my head to stop it from spinning. "Jolene, you
could have been seriously hurt—or worse. Thank goodness you
weren't. Did you get a good look at him?"

"No. It was dark, but it's like he didn't think anybody was home,
because he was making plenty of noise. Ace was able to fix my car
sooner than we'd thought, so I drove straight here even though I knew
I'd be too late to get you ready for the party. By the way—I love what

you did to your hair." She smiled. "Anyway, I had to park Bubba on a side street because there was a party at the frat house next door and they were blocking our driveway. So I guess the intruder just assumed nobody was home. The guy went directly to the front room—I know because I jumped out of bed just as soon as Mardi started growling. I grabbed the Barbie, flipped on the light, and that's where I found him. I didn't even think—I just rushed him and then bashed him over the head. He ran toward the stairs and I chased him, but he kept going."

"Jolene!" I glanced over at Jaxson, whose bed-head hair was a dead giveaway that he'd been jerked from a sound sleep. "Were you here when all of this was happening?"

"No!" he and Jolene said in unison.

"I called him right after I called the police," Jolene explained. "I called Beau first, since he's closest, but when he didn't answer I called Jaxson. I didn't want to bother you, but I didn't want to be alone while I waited for the police."

"Bother me?" I shook my head. "Oh, my gosh. This could have been so much worse." I hugged her again. "I'm so glad you're okay."

"Are you Miss Trenholm, the roommate?" the police officer with the notepad asked.

"I am."

"And where were you tonight?"

"I was at the sculpture garden for a NOMA fund-raiser with . . ." I realized that Michael wasn't in the room. We all seemed to suddenly become aware of the sound of Mardi emitting a low and continuous growl and we turned in unison toward the doorway, where Michael still stood, his entrance being checked by our vicious guard dog disguised as a marshmallow.

"Mardi, come," I said, patting my knee.

With one last look at Michael, Mardi trotted toward me, then lay down at my feet.

"With Michael Hebert," I finished, sending Michael an apologetic smile. He crossed the room to stand next to the couch, his hand rubbing my back, the dog giving him a warning look before lying back down. "Did Mardi at least get a chunk out of the guy's leg?"

Jolene looked at the little dog. "I didn't want him to get hurt, so I closed him up in my room when I rushed out with the Barbie head." With a bright smile, she said, "All's well that ends well, right?"

"Right," I said. I looked up at Michael, but he was looking at Mardi, a deep V between his brows.

For the next hour we answered questions for the police, and then waited for them to dust for fingerprints and bag up the remains of the doll head to see if they could find any trace evidence. As they stood to leave, Jolene said, "Can I get you nice officers a piece of pecan pie? I made it last night, so it's fresh. If you don't have time to eat it right now, I can make you some to go."

"Thanks, but no," the first officer said. "It's unlikely the intruder will come back tonight, but make sure you put the chain on your front door since the dead bolt has been tampered with, and call a locksmith first thing. You might also consider investing in an alarm for the entry points." Then they left, promising to keep an eye on the apartment and to be in touch with any news.

Despite their insistence that they should stay, Jolene and I assured Jaxson and Michael that we'd be fine alone. It was as if by unspoken agreement we decided that we needed to prove to ourselves that we were strong enough—and brave enough—to get through what was left of the night together.

After promises to keep our phones on and close by, we let the two men out the front door, Michael turning back for a quick good-night kiss and a promise to call in the morning. Jolene and I not only set the chain but piled furniture and frying pans in front of both the front and back doors so that if anyone succeeded in getting past the lock, we'd know about it long before they made it up the stairs.

We went to bed—after I had removed all makeup while Jolene supervised—in our respective rooms, with our doors open and Mardi on high alert in case anyone should dare try again to breach our defenses. Before Jaxson left, he put Bubba in the driveway to alert anyone who might be watching that the apartment wasn't empty, and then Jolene and I turned on every light just in case. I somehow even remembered to take two aspirin with an entire glass of water.

As tired as I was, I tossed and turned, disjointed thoughts darting in and out of my head like angry bees, Beau's accusations about Michael swirling around the unasked questions about why an intruder had been in our apartment. Nothing made sense. I kept checking my phone to see if Michael had texted me, to give me an excuse to text him the single question that wouldn't leave me alone, but my phone remained dark and silent.

Eventually, I gave up all pretext of sleeping and sat up in my bed, holding my phone and staring at it as if I could will a text to appear. Or make it ring. Mardi stirred in his bed, then looked at me with such a pitiful expression that I had to pat the mattress only once before he leapt up and settled next to me, his head resting on my leg. Instead of closing his eyes, he kept staring at me as if waiting for me to do the one thing I didn't think I could.

The muffled sound of the unplugged phone ringing in my closet made both of us jump, then freeze, as we stared at the closet door. It didn't ring again, but it didn't need to. I knew what I had to do. With steady fingers, I began to type.

Did you know your great-aunt Jeanne Broussard was the woman murdered in my house?

I stared at my phone, willing Michael's response to arrive, or the phone to ring. He'd promised to keep his phone on and nearby in case I needed him. Maybe my question didn't qualify. Maybe he was waiting until we could meet in person to talk about it. Maybe denial was more than just a river in Egypt.

Giving up all pretense of trying to sleep, Mardi and I went into the back room, where my guitar hung on the wall, my pitiful attempts at writing a song still on the music stand. I held the guitar in my hands for a long time, loving the familiar heft and smoothness of the wood, and longing for the calmer mind and clarity of thinking it had once given me. But the notes didn't come, and my phone remained silent. I ended up staring out the window and watching the sky shift from purple to pink as the sun rose, and I was no closer to answering any of the questions that chased me into a new day.

I opened my eyes to the smells of coffee and something baking in the oven. And a wet nose pressed against mine. Two large round eyes attached to the wet nose looked back at me. It took me a moment to get my bearings, eventually realizing that I was lying on the floor of the back room, with my head on a dog bed and a blanket tucked around both me and the dog, whose bed I was sharing. On the other side of the door, in the kitchen, Jolene hummed "Over the Rainbow" until she was interrupted by a male voice asking her a question.

I jumped up from the floor, scattering the blanket and my phone. Gathering up my phone, I threw open the door. I'd been about to say Michael's name, but I paused as I spotted Jaxson, dressed casually in shorts and a golf shirt, standing on a stepladder by the door leading to the back staircase from the kitchen. Jolene was fully dressed, including heels, and pouring coffee into my mug.

"Good morning, Nola," Jaxson said brightly from atop the stepladder. "Hope you were able to get some sleep after such an eventful night."

Jolene pressed the mug into my hand. "Give her a moment to drink this before she can respond." To me, she said, "I already fed Mardi and took him outside, so no worries. I gave him part of one of my biscuits, too, since he gave me that look of his that makes it impossible to say no."

I nodded gratefully, took two sips, and was fortified enough to look at my phone. Nothing. Not a text or missed call. No voice mail. I opened up my texts, just to make sure I'd actually remembered to hit the SEND arrow. I had. There it was—the one simple question. Sent at three fifteen a.m. With no response, and it was now almost noon.

Maybe he was sleeping in because of the late night and because it was Saturday. Maybe he'd gotten ill during the night. Maybe he was on his way over now, too eager to see me in person to waste time sending a text.

"Everything okay?" Jolene asked.

I pasted on a smile and nodded. "Just waiting to hear from Michael." I looked over at Jaxson. "Did he say anything to you last night when you left?"

"No. We said good night and we each got into our cars and drove away. Why?"

I took another sip of coffee in an effort to appear normal, the aspirin and water taken the night before having apparently done their job. "I haven't heard from him yet. Something must have come up." Eager to change the subject, I asked Jaxson, "It's good to see you, but what are you doing?"

"Installing a security alarm. I'm putting one on the door at the front of the house and at the top of the stairs, too. You can turn them on and off with your phones—I'll show you how as soon as I'm done."

Jolene grinned. "He was at the Home Depot first thing this morning. And the locksmith has already come and gone—he replaced the front lock and rekeyed both doors. Jaxson says to consider it a housewarming present. With new locks, an alarm system, and Mardi, we're all set."

"Thanks, Jaxson. That's really nice. I appreciate it." I didn't comment on Jolene's mentioning Mardi as if he was meant to be a permanent member of our household. Nor did I question Jaxson's presence, since Jolene and I hadn't yet discussed her abrupt departure to Mississippi, which I knew was directly related to him. I had other immediate problems I needed to deal with.

I put down my empty coffee mug. "It looks like a beautiful day outside. I think I'm going to go for a run. Don't put this away—I'll be back shortly to have more coffee and at least two biscuits." I quickly disappeared into my room and changed into my running clothes before shouting good-bye and jogging out the door. I didn't want Jolene to guess the true purpose of my outing or she would have barred the door.

Instead of taking the shortcut through campus, I ran down Broadway, watching for Michael's black Mercedes heading my way. I thought of what expression I'd wear and what I'd say when we spotted each other and I laughed at how we each must have read the other's mind. Except I didn't see him as I ran down the length of Broadway and the short distance down St. Charles and reached the gated entrance at Audubon Place.

The guard was the same one who'd waved me in with Jolene. After a prolonged hesitation and a promise that I was just going to run in and out, he let me in. As I jogged down the street, I had the sudden realization that despite my seeing Michael almost daily since we'd met, he'd never once invited me inside the house where he'd grown up and still lived. With increasing dread, I slowed my pace to a walk until I was once again standing in front of the Spanish Renaissance mansion with the green-tiled roof. No cars, including Michael's Mercedes, or his bike sat in the driveway or at the curb in front of the house. The curtains on the front windows were closed, giving the house an abandoned appearance.

A man walking his poodle approached me before stopping next to me. "Can I help you?" His tone was more suspicious than friendly.

I turned to him with a wide smile. "I was on my run and decided to stop by and say hello to Michael Hebert. We're good friends." To show that I wasn't an ax murderer or someone staking out a potential robbery, I bent down to scratch the poodle behind his ears. It was a risk, but I'd never met a dog that didn't love me, and this one was no exception.

The man's face softened. "They're not home. Robert and Angelina decided to take a last-minute vacation to their house in the North Carolina mountains and I believe they planned to take Michael with them, because Robert asked me to collect their mail and newspaper while they were gone. They left very early this morning. You could try calling, but the cell service there is pretty much nonexistent."

"Oh," I said. "I guess he forgot to tell me. Do you know when they expect to return?"

"Robert didn't say. They usually go for three months during the summer, but I've never known them to be gone in September. My guess is it will be just a week or so."

I reached down to pet the poodle again in an attempt to hide the stinging in my eyes. "Well, thank you. I'm sure Michael will reach out when he gets back." I stood quickly and waved before taking off at full speed, eager to outrun my own stupidity and gullibility, and the simple truth that no matter how far I ran, I could never escape the fact that I was just like my mother.

CHAPTER 28

I ran all the way back to the apartment, my chest throbbing, the sweat obliterating my sight, my fists clenched so tight I lost feeling in them. But nothing could erase the complete and utter disbelief and hurt that gripped me like a vise.

I immediately disappeared into the shower and stood beneath the scalding water until there was no more hot water left, then continued while the water turned cold and I had no more tears left to shed.

I turned off the faucet and stood shivering in my towel with dripping hair, wanting to never leave the bathroom. Because if I did I'd have to try to figure out what was really going on with Michael, and if everything I'd felt for him had been only manipulation on his part. The humiliation was soul crushing and spirit crumbling, and the need for a drink left me crumpled on the floor next to the door, sobbing into a towel with dry tears.

"Nola?" Jolene's voice and gentle knock sounded from the door. "Did you fall in?"

Despite everything, I laughed, although it came out more like a snort. "No. I'm just not ready to come out. It might be a while."

"Oh, sweetie. Did something happen with Michael?"

"Yes." The word came out as a sob.

"All right, then. Let me just get comfortable here so we can talk about it. Jaxson left, so it's just the two of us."

I listened to the sound of her getting settled on the floor on the other side of the door.

"I'm ready when you are."

My lips twitched. "You know, Jolene, the reason why sometimes people want to lock themselves in the bathroom is because they don't want to talk to anyone."

"Well, it's a good thing we're not just people and I'm not just anyone. And you don't have to come out until you're ready, and you don't have to say anything, either. Sometimes when your heart is hurting the best thing is just to be next to someone who cares." A fluffy paw emerged from the crack beneath the door. "And a dog."

I touched it with my finger, then rested my head against the door, the crying having zapped the last of my strength and energy. We sat in silence for a long time, only the sound of Mardi's snoring coming from under the door.

I eventually managed to summon the strength to speak. "I'm pretty sure that Michael's been lying to me this whole time. That he only pretended to care about me because of something to do with my house. He's ghosting me and now he's hiding out in the mountains so I can't confront him. I really want to hate him, but I can't." I clenched my eyes, which somehow made it easier to admit out loud the one hardest thing to accept about my own stupidity. "Because I was really and truly falling in love with him."

I waited a moment, expecting her to come back with some platitude either about how all men are scum or about how it's his problem and not mine and I could do much better. Instead, she said, "I've got a big car trunk and we're doing a lot of excavating at my house in Mississippi. I also own a shovel and know how to use it."

"You're kidding, right?"

It took her a long second to answer. "Maybe. I just wanted you to know that you have options, and as your friend I'm here to help."

"Thanks, Jolene. I appreciate that." I turned around, leaning my back against the door, my bruised heart feeling a little lighter just at the image of Jolene and her shovel. It almost made me smile.

"If it makes you feel any better, Michael pulled the wool over my eyes, too. And to think of all the makeup and hair we wasted on him. Just goes to show that if it has tires or testicles, it's bound to cause you trouble."

"Does that include Jaxson?"

I heard her heavy sigh through the door. "Sadly, it does."

I could hear her breathing. Knowing she was there but unable to see the shame or desperation on my face gave me the strength to say what I needed to. "I really need a drink right now." I held my breath, imagining I could feel Jolene's disappointment radiating through the door.

It took a full minute before Jolene answered, her voice devoid of any condemnation. "Are you drinking again?"

I wanted to say *only socially*, but she would see it for the lie it was. "Yes."

She took a deep breath. "Nola, I'm not going to get you a drink. Because you're better than that, and because I'm your friend and I love you like a sister. But I will make you hot cocoa and fill half the mug with marshmallows and I will stay with you as long as you need me to and we can talk it all out. I'll bring a tissue box, the whole pecan pie with two forks, and a tube of color so I'll be ready to talk my lipstick off. Do you think that will help?"

I did smile this time. "Yeah. I think that will help a lot." My eyes stung and my throat constricted as warm tears began to slip down my face. Neither of us made a sound for a long time, just Mardi's snuffling audible as he changed sleep positions against the door. "Jolene?"

"I'm still here."

"Thank you. I'll have to get back to you about the shovel-and-trunk thing, but thanks for being here."

I could hear the smile in her voice. "That's what friends are for."

"So, are you going to tell me what happened with you and Jaxson that made you run home to Mississippi?"

She didn't answer right away. "If I tell you, you're going to have to come out of there. My knees are getting wrinkles. I'll get started on that hot cocoa and we can finally go through those hatboxes. We can do a fashion show!"

I managed another smile, my cheeks drawn and tight from the hot shower. "All right."

I listened as she settled herself into a more comfortable position. "Remember that night you went to Antoine's?"

"It's kind of hard to forget."

"Sorry. Just trying to establish the time frame. Anyway, that was the night we were supposed to spend together bingeing true-crime shows and going through the hatboxes, and I'd invited Jaxson since Carly was out of town, and I had planned to make a nice home-cooked dinner for the three of us. And even after I knew you weren't going to be here, I didn't disinvite Jaxson."

"Which shouldn't matter since you're friends, right?" I was listening eagerly, happy to focus on someone else's emotional turmoil. I seriously doubted I could offer any advice since I was apparently woefully ignorant in matters of the heart, but sometimes listening was all that was required.

"Right. That's what I thought, too. And everything was going fine until we were both sitting on the couch watching *Southern Fried Homicide* and he kissed me."

"Wait—what? That's a little disturbing."

"Don't be silly—where does your mind go, Nola? The episode was a little scary, so I sort of smooshed up against Jaxson by accident so we were sitting real close, and then . . . he kissed me."

"I see. And then what happened?"

"He jumped off the couch and apologized. And then told me that he'd already bought a ring for Carly but hadn't had a chance to propose yet. But he didn't want to lose me as a friend, so we agreed to pretend the kiss never happened."

"Ouch. I'm so sorry. Was it at least a good kiss?"

After a brief pause, she said, "The best I've ever had."

"Well, then. Looks like you'll need to fill half your mug with marshmallows, too. Or just bring the whole bag."

By seven o'clock, surrounded by the detritus of a six-hour true-crime binge-watching spree—including a half-eaten pecan pie still on the plate, two empty marshmallow bags, a pizza box with one lone slice remaining, and two empty mugs—I flipped off the television while we looked at each other in a sugar-induced euphoria.

"Feeling a little better?" Jolene asked, holding up the bottles of aspirin and antacids she'd brought to the feast.

I waved away the bottles and patted my stomach. "Yes, thank you. For now, anyway." I pulled at the elastic of my sweatpants. "Glad I wore these."

Jolene hadn't said anything when I'd emerged from my bedroom wearing a faded oversized College of Charleston sweatshirt, baggy sweatpants with holes in the knees, and fluffy socks that had been a gift from Melanie because she believed everyone had ice-cold feet throughout the year just like she did. Jolene's interpretation of casual was another color-coordinated athleisure outfit from Lululemon, her hair pulled back in a smooth and bouncy ponytail, yoga socks on her feet.

She stood and opened a drawer in the side table and pulled out a jumbo pack of sugarless gum. "This is my secret vice and if my mama found out I was chewing gum she'd jerk a knot in my tail. But I figure since chewing gum got Grandmama off of smoking those nasty cigarettes, maybe it could work for you with alcohol, too."

"Couldn't hurt to try." We each took a piece, and she put the pack on the coffee table. "Help yourself whenever you want one. I don't care how big the wad gets in your mouth—you won't offend me. The only rule is that you don't chew it in public. Otherwise I will deny that I even know you."

She picked up the pie plate and pizza box. "I'm going to clean up this mess while you drag those hatboxes in here. And just so you know, I have donated all the alcoholic beverages that were in the refrigerator to the frat house next door. I wasn't planning on it, figuring they didn't need it any more than we did, but they caught me putting the bottles in their garbage bin. My point being, don't go looking for it, because it's not here."

I nodded and began unwrapping another slice of gum, knowing from experience that this was only a start on a very long and bumpy road. But at least it was a start.

Jolene turned back. "Nola? You need to let Beau know that he was right about Michael."

"I know. I just can't stand to think of him gloating."

"From what I know about Beau Ryan, he's not into gloating. Especially where you're concerned. But he needs to know."

I didn't say anything as I watched her head into the kitchen. Leaving my phone on the coffee table, I brought all eight hatboxes into the living room area, along with the handful of dresses that Jolene had decided to hold back because she thought that one of us could wear them after a few modifications. Apparently, she was also a talented seamstress—of course—having taught herself as a child by making clothes for her dolls.

I began walking toward the kitchen to help with the cleanup, but Jolene called out, "I'm fine in here. Go ahead and text Beau. Or call him. It's important."

She also had eyes in the back of her head, apparently, and therefore would make a great mother. I should definitely let Jaxson know. "Whatever." I picked up my phone and opened the screen—no texts or calls from Michael, just a funny meme in a text chain with Alston and Lindsey. I opened up a new text and began typing.

You were right.

I hit SEND, then decided there were too many things Beau would want to claim to be right about.

About Michael.

I put my phone in my sweatpants pocket and had taken only two steps toward the kitchen when it rang with the opening bars of "Dancing Queen." I quickly answered it. "Hi, Melanie."

"Nola. It's so good to hear your voice. I've been thinking about you. Is everything all right?"

Alarm shot through me. "Why would you ask that?"

"I'm your mother. Aren't I allowed to check in and make sure everything's okay?"

"Yes. Sorry. It's just . . ." I considered telling her everything right then. But it wasn't something I could do over the phone and without my dad. It would have to wait until October when they visited. When I would hopefully already have put this episode behind me. I was afraid, too, that if I blurted out the whole sordid story now, she and Jack would be on the first plane to New Orleans and arrive with a plane ticket in hand to drag me back to Charleston. And I was far too stubborn to admit defeat so quickly. "I'm fine. Is everything okay there?"

"Yes. The twins are back in school, I just landed an amazing listing, and your dad's writing is going well. I was just calling because I, um, received a phone call."

I tasted marshmallows in the back of my throat and quickly swallowed. "From Grandmother Sarah?"

"Yes. It's always a little hard to understand her because—well, you know—but I'm pretty sure that she was telling me that . . ." She paused.

"That what?"

"That you're in danger. From the woman who scares you. Do you know who she's talking about?"

My heart hammered in my chest. "I'm not sure. Is she talking about Mimi?"

"Is Mimi dead?"

"No. She's very much alive."

"Then it's someone else. Someone who's lingering and doesn't want you disturbing . . . what's hidden. I think that's what Grandmother Sarah said."

I stared out the window at the darkening sky, seeing my reflection, and recalled the cold hands shoving me down the steps. The heavy scent of hair spray. "I . . . had an encounter. In my house. I was pushed. Not enough to hurt me, but enough to show me that I wasn't wanted. I thought it was the man whose pipe I smell all the time when I'm there."

I could hear the urgency and panic in Melanie's voice. "Do you need me to come to New Orleans right now?"

"No," I said quickly. "I've got everything under control."

"Are you sure? I can be there tomorrow."

"Absolutely not. I appreciate your offer," I hastily amended. "But I've got this. Really."

"Is Beau helping you?"

I opened my mouth to say something like *Hell no*, but stopped.

"Because whether or not he admits it, he can communicate with spirits. I've seen him in action. And I have a feeling that if you asked for his help, he'd be more than happy to give it."

"Would you by any chance want to ask for me?"

"Nola, what is going on? That is not like you. Really, I can buy my plane ticket—"

"Melanie, please don't. I need to handle this on my own, all right?"

"How about this—you reach out to Beau and tell him what I just said about my grandmother's phone call, and ask for his help with this angry woman. Otherwise, I'm on the next flight."

"Seriously? I'm an adult, you know."

"Then maybe you should start acting like one." To have Melanie say that to me was bad enough. But for her to be the second person to say that in as many days was even worse. "Sweetheart, asking for help doesn't mean you're weak. It means you're strong enough to know you can't handle it all on your own. Call Beau. Or text him—whatever it is that you Gen Zs do. Just do it today. Grandmother Sarah only calls when it's important."

"Fine," I said, deciding not to tell her about my own disconnected phone ringing in the closet. "I'll do it now."

"Good. And, Nola?"

"Yes?" I held my breath, not liking the tone of her voice.

"Is everything else okay? Are you staying—?"

"I've got to go—Jolene and I have a big night planned, going through old hatboxes and drinking hot cocoa. I'll call you back tomorrow, all right?"

She'd barely said good-bye before I disconnected the call. I looked down at my screen. Still no texts from Michael, or Beau. Not that I'd really been expecting to hear from either one of them. For a split second, I considered calling Beau. But I didn't want to give him the satisfaction. Instead, I opened the text screen and began to type.

Call me.

Right before I hit the SEND arrow, I added one more word.

Please.

Then I shoved the phone back in my pocket and began hoping that Beau would call almost as much as I hoped that he wouldn't.

CHAPTER 29

Less than an hour later, Jolene and I had opened six hatboxes and tried on eight dresses, mixing and matching to see which ones we liked best. The women's hats were mostly variations of the pillbox, along with one feathered cloche and a flower-petal capulet. After the first hats were tried on, we both agreed that neither one of us had correctly shaped heads for vintage hats, each selection more hilariously awful than the last.

I did, however, love the pale blue two-piece wool suit—very Jackie O according to Jolene—and had decided to keep it even though I had no idea where or when I'd wear it. But when Jolene plopped a flower-shaped beret on top of my head, the entire look was too ridiculous not to laugh.

Despite the trauma of the day, and the pangs I felt whenever I let my thoughts drift to Michael, the laughter—although a bit forced and a bit too loud—felt good. So good that after religiously checking my phone every five minutes to see if either Michael or Beau had responded, I'd flipped it over and put it on mute so I didn't have to think about it at all.

I picked up another hatbox. It was heavier than the others, and when I shook it something shifted from side to side, accompanied by an uneven roll of two separate objects. "I don't think this is a hat."

Jolene cleared the coffee table and I placed the box on top of it before lifting the lid. The odor of old cardboard and leather wafted toward us. I pulled back, aware of an odd mingling of tobacco and another scent. Floral. Something that smelled a lot like . . . hair spray.

"Look." Jolene reached inside.

"It's a pipe." I lifted it from her palm, feeling the smooth burled wood of the bowl, its size almost filling my palm, and I was surprised at the heft of it. But not by the particular scent of the tobacco that had once been smoked in this very pipe.

"You're looking at it like it's familiar."

"It is," I said, my finger slowly tracing the rim of the bowl. "I keep smelling a pipe when I'm at the house. And a few times I think I've seen . . . someone smoking one."

She leaned close enough that I could probably have counted the freckles on her nose. "Do you mean a *ghost*?" The last word was whispered loudly.

"I thought you were raised to not believe in ghosts."

"I was. But I'm not the one seeing them, so it's okay." She rubbed her lips together as if she were smoothing her lipstick. "I've smelled the smoke, too. I figured the house has a lot of memories, so I wasn't all that surprised."

"Yeah, well, that particular memory isn't by himself. There's a woman, too. One of them pushed me off the stairs."

Her eyes widened. "That's horrifying. Maybe we should ask Jorge to find us a priest."

"Not yet. From what I've learned, lingering spirits won't go away until we can figure out why they're still here and then send them on their way."

"You learned that from Melanie, didn't you?"

I turned to her with surprise.

Jolene shrugged. "I watched that episode of *Psychic Detectives* a while back that featured her work on that cold case about the missing family in Charleston. I recognized her as your stepmother. It must have been really cool living with her."

"That's one way to put it," I said. "Why didn't you mention this earlier?"

"I figured you'd tell me when you were ready to." She smiled brightly. "So, are you going to have her come here to help?"

I looked down, studying the pipe. "No. She said to ask Beau." My eyes met hers. "She believes he can communicate with the dead, too."

"Well, then. That makes a lot of sense, doesn't it? It's always those people who are most vocal with their denials who turn out to be the ones with the biggest reason to deny it, right?"

"Is that something else you learned from your grandmother?"

"Nope—I learned that from reading Nancy Drew mysteries."

"Yeah, well, sometimes Melanie gets phone calls from her dead grandmother Sarah. She got one today saying that I was in danger. From the woman I was afraid of. Someone who doesn't want me disturbing 'what's hidden.'"

Jolene's red eyebrows rose.

"Not Mimi—someone already dead. I think she meant the female spirit in the house. And I'm pretty sure it's Jeanne. Beau and I saw her—briefly. She looked exactly like a photo of Jeanne. I just have no idea why she would find me a threat."

Our gazes met, then slowly moved over the hatboxes, with their lids and contents spread across the room, before returning to the open one in front of us.

"What's this?" She reached into the bottom seam of the box and brought out a small metal object pinched between her index finger and thumb. Placing it on her palm, she said, "It looks like a man's tie clip. My granddaddy used to wear one, but I don't think they're popular anymore." Holding it closer to her face, she said, "It looks like it has some kind of a double snake-with-wings design on it."

I leaned closer to get a better look. "It's a caduceus. A symbol used by doctors."

Our eyes met. "Why would that be in here?"

Without answering, I lifted a black leather-bound notebook from the box. Flaking gold embossed lettering in the middle of the front cover read *Clientele*. On the bottom right, in the same lettering, was the name *Jeanne Broussard*. I opened the cover, exposing sheets of lined paper with the headers *Name*, *Address*, *Date*, and *Item(s)*, each column and line filled in with neat, precise handwriting in black ink.

I stared at the notebook, then raised my eyes to meet Jolene's. "Who would have put these things in a hatbox and locked them in the closet with the hats?"

Jolene rubbed her hands together as she plopped down on the couch. "I feel like Nancy Drew. She was a redhead, too, by the way." She patted the seat next to me. "Let's go through the clientele book. Maybe a name will jump out at us and tell us something."

"But tell us what? If we don't know what we're looking for, we're just wasting our time."

She looked at me with the patience a mother might give her toddler. "Did you never read Nancy Drew as a child? *Everything* is a potential clue. And sometimes you don't know what that might be until you look."

We spread the book on our laps, with Jolene reading the left side and me reading the right side, and starting with the A's. The first entry was made in 1962 with the name Berniece Adams.

Jeanne's cursive handwriting was neat, tidy, and extremely hard to read for those of us who were unaccustomed to cursive. Jolene and I each dragged an index finger down the name column on our respective page, looking for something that might jar a memory. Our enthusiasm had begun to wane by the time we made it to the R's, Jolene's voice waking me from my stupor. "Do you know of any woman in Beau's family whose first name starts with a C? The name C. Ryan keeps popping up. It's a common last name, but I thought it could mean something."

"I saw that, too," I said. "I can't say for sure, but the only females in his family I know of are Mimi, Adele, and Sunny—none of them with a C."

Jolene drummed her pink-tipped nails on the page. "Jeanne Broussard worked in the lingerie department, but the only things purchased by C. Ryan were gloves and pajamas. Lots and lots of gloves and pajamas. Not even a single bra or even stockings. Just seems odd."

"Agreed. And she was definitely Jeanne's best customer by far, since her name appears more than any other."

Jolene's head popped up. "Or not."

"What do you mean?"

"Think about it, Nola. Maybe C. Ryan isn't a she. Maybe C. Ryan is a he."

I blinked rapidly, the pieces and possibilities bouncing around my head like a ball in a pinball machine, each thought ricocheting off the sides. "Charles Ryan," I said. "He would have been a young man then."

"Maybe Mimi had an obsession with gloves. Although I can't really see her in pajamas. She's more of a flannel-nightgown person to me."

"True," I said. "Can you imagine her wearing a red bustier or anything sexy that a person might find in the lingerie department?"

"Maybe in her younger days," Jolene said, always trying to be fair.

We looked at each other, trying to imagine Mimi as a younger woman wearing a red bustier. "Or not," I said. "Although I can see her occasionally asking her husband to pick up something for her, or even him selecting a gift for her. Her husband's medical office was in the business towers on top of the Maison Blanche building, which meant that it would have been convenient for him to stop by and pick up the occasional item for her. But according to this clientele book, the purchases were made almost every week between July of 1963 and Jeanne's death in 1964."

"Maybe he was buying them for someone else?" Jolene asked.

I thought for a moment. "That frequently?" I thought about Jeanne's pregnancy, and her boyfriend's insistence that they'd never had sex. "What if his visits were only done so he'd have an excuse to visit Jeanne?"

We looked at each other, our mouths opening in silent O's of mutual understanding.

"I wonder if Mimi knew," I said.

I flipped through the rest of the pages, hoping to find something else that might explain why this book and its assortment of contents had been locked in the closet in my house. I held the covers open like a bird in flight and shook it. As if wishing could actually make things happen, a single strip of negative from a 35-millimeter camera fluttered to the ground like a feather along with a delicate hair ribbon, baby-fine blond hair still stuck in its knot.

"Hang on," Jolene said, jumping up from the couch and racing to her room. She returned a second later with a small square machine with a screen on the top. "It's one of those old slide viewers. My grand-daddy used it for his stamp collection and I asked for it when he died. Not because I have a stamp collection, but I thought it would be help-ful for showing me if something was navy or black."

I handed her the negative and she placed it on the coffee table. She flipped on a little switch on the side to turn on the light, then held the machine over the strip. We both looked into the screen, the nega-tive below it blown up to viewable proportions. The first two pictures showed different shots of someone's garden, of a pretty stone fountain surrounded by gladiolas and coneflowers. The next picture was blurred, as if the camera had moved while taking the photo. But the last picture, steady and clear, showed a black Mercedes pulled up at the curb, the Ryans' house visible behind it. A well-dressed woman was shown lift-ing a fair-haired little girl into the backseat of the car. It was almost as if the photographer had been distracted by what was happening across the street when they snapped the picture.

"Oh, my gosh," I said. "Christopher told me that the only witness to Sunny's disappearance was the neighbor. All she could remember was that Sunny was taken in a black car with Louisiana plates." I met Jolene's eyes. "She couldn't recall anything else."

"Then who took these photos, and how did they get in the closet with the rest of this stuff? It's almost as if they're all together here be-cause someone is trying to show a connection between Jeanne's death, Dr. Ryan, and Sunny's disappearance."

"Synchronicity," I said, absently stroking the yellow hair ribbon.

We both jumped at the sound of the doorbell, which started Mardi barking, as if to make sure we'd heard it.

I looked at the ancient digital clock on top of a bookshelf—another remnant from previous occupants. "It's after ten o'clock. Who would be coming by this late?"

We glanced at each other, quickly narrowing down the list to three people, then ran toward the now-empty—except for the Maison Blanche door—front room and peered out through the louvered window, immediately spotting a familiar truck parked behind Bubba.

"It's Beau," I said, feeling a stab of apprehension. "I'll answer it."

"But look what you're wearing! And you need to go put some color on first."

"I think that's the least of my worries right now." I grabbed my phone and backpack, shoving in the contents of the hatbox, including the negative and hair ribbon, and headed toward the stairs. "Please stay here with Mardi. I'll be back as soon as I can. Beau and I have an errand to run."

"Please text me to let me know what's going on!"

I waved my hand in the air to let her know I'd heard her, then began to carefully descend the stairs, clutching tightly to the banister since I still wore the fuzzy socks. I flung open the door just as Beau was reaching a finger out to press the doorbell again. He held a familiar Rouses shopping bag as he scanned me from head to toe and then back again. His lips twitched as he tried not to smile. "Did you get dressed up just for me?"

An odd feeling of relief washed over me as I looked at his familiar face, at his almost-smile, and focused on the fact that he had come because I'd asked him to. Regardless of everything else in my life, he was like the stone to hold on to in the middle of a strong current. Not that I would ever admit to actually thinking that, but there it was.

I looked at the bag. "Is that Mr. Bingle?"

"Yes. You said you wanted it back. And Jolene's shoes are in there, too. You left them at the sculpture garden last—"

I took the bag and put it inside the door before stepping outside and locking it. "Thank you." I could almost feel Melanie and Jolene prodding me in the back. "I really appreciate you bringing them, and coming by tonight."

He leaned close enough to sniff my breath. "Are you all right?"

I pulled back. "I'm fine. And the only thing you might smell on my breath is marshmallows and pizza." I began walking toward his truck. "Come on—let's go."

He didn't move. "Where are we going?"

At least he'd said *we*.

"To your house. We need to have a talk with Mimi."

CHAPTER 30

Beau and I drove down St. Charles Avenue, the street mostly deserted due to the late hour. I avoided looking toward the entrance to Audubon Place as we passed it. I had no idea how Michael was connected to any of this, but his disappearance proved that he was.

I thought about how my dad wrote his books, how he'd place all the questions on pieces of paper and pin them on a bulletin board, moving them around like pieces of a puzzle until everything fit. That's what I was doing now, gathering the pieces in an attempt to put them together. Except I had no idea where the missing pieces were or how they were supposed to fit. The only thing I knew for sure was that Mimi Ryan knew a lot more than she had been willing to tell me.

"So, what's so urgent that we need to speak to Mimi now instead of waiting until tomorrow?" Beau asked.

"Did Mimi ever mention to you that your grandfather might have been having an affair with Jeanne?"

His head jerked toward me. "What?"

A blaring horn from the adjacent lane forced his gaze back onto the street in front of him. "That can't be right. Mimi and Jeanne were best friends." He was silent for a moment. "But that could mean that the baby . . ." He stopped, and the car fell silent, as neither one of us wanted to finish the sentence.

"He was Jeanne's family's doctor, remember. And his office was in the Maison Blanche building. Jolene and I found Jeanne's clientele book in one of the hatboxes from the closet, and a C. Ryan was her most frequent customer through most of 1963 and the first part of '64 before she died. We know Jeanne had a mystery lover, so this clearly makes him a very good suspect."

"Hang on. Having an affair doesn't mean he's a murderer."

"It doesn't. Except we also found a few other things. One was a tie pin with a caduceus on it and another was a pipe."

He didn't say anything, but I could see his jaw tightening in the glow of the passing streetlights.

"The first time I smelled the pipe in my house, I asked Mimi if she knew of anyone associated with the house who smoked one, and she told me no."

It took Beau two tries to get out the right question. "Maybe because at the time she didn't know Charles was a frequent visitor to the house. I mean, if what you're saying is true, it's not likely that either Charles or Jeanne would have told her."

"Or maybe Mimi found out another way. Maybe after Jeanne's death. But whatever the reason, Mimi didn't want me to know that it could have been Charles. There was something else, too." I paused, trying to soften my words. "A strip of negatives from a roll of film. They were taken from across the street and showed a black Mercedes pulled up in front of your house, with a woman lifting a little girl into the backseat. Stuck inside the clientele book with the negative was a yellow ribbon. With long fair hair still stuck in the knot."

"Dear God," he said under his breath.

I touched his arm. "I have it with me. You and Mimi can tell us for sure if it's Sunny."

"Does that mean there's a connection? But how could there be? Jeanne was murdered in 1964, and Sunny disappeared forty-one years later."

"I don't know. I think we need to go right to the source and ask them."

"Ask who?"

"Charles and Jeanne. They're both at my house. I know because you and I have seen them."

"I'm not sure what you expect me to do—"

I cut him off. "No BS, okay? I'll admit that Michael is a lying, cheating scumbag who completely fooled me and turned me into a weak-willed idiot if you'll admit that you can talk to dead people. Melanie says you do and that I should ask for your help. There, see? I just asked you for help. I am capable of doing that."

We stopped at a traffic light, neither of us saying anything until it turned green. "You're wrong," Beau said.

"About what?"

"You're not weak-willed. Or an idiot. You're one of the strongest and smartest people I've ever met. Michael Hebert is a parasite who managed to find your one weakness and worm himself inside."

My eyes pricked with tears. Very quietly, I said, "Thank you." We drove another block. "It's your turn."

He rubbed his face with one of his hands, the raspy sound of his five-o'clock shadow loud inside the truck. "Fine. I see dead people."

"That's a start. Because according to Melanie, Jeanne doesn't want me to disturb what's hidden—although it's not clear what she's referring to. We already know about the baby. Maybe she wants to keep the baby's father a secret? But why? That's all in the past."

"Or is it?" Beau cut in. "This is somehow connected to Sunny. I just . . ." He shook his head, unable to finish. He put on his turn signal and took a right on Napoleon Avenue. "If what Uncle Bernie said about my grandfather ending the investigation into Sunny's disappearance has any truth in it, then there's our connection. I just can't see the why or the how, because it doesn't make any sense to me."

He turned onto Prytania, his truck slowing as he approached Mimi's darkened house. He parked the truck at the curb and turned off the ignition, the headlights still shining in front of us. We both looked at the house, only a dim hall light shining through the wavy glass of the front doors and sidelights, giving the impression of looking into a magic mirror.

Beau rubbed his hands over his face. "None of this explains why Michael's uncle wanted to buy your house, or why Michael insinuated himself into your life. There's a reason why he didn't tell you that Jeanne was his great-aunt. There's a connection somewhere that we're totally missing. And it is somehow related to Sunny's disappearance. It's like that song from the eighties where the chorus switches between lyrics about the Loch Ness Monster and some guy coming home to his family from a job he hated."

"'Synchronicity II' by the Police," we said in unison.

It was a game from our past, guessing the names of songs playing in the background in restaurants or at parties or at the grocery store. Music had always been the one thing we had in common. And I would almost say that it was coincidence that it was that song playing just now in the passing car as we sat in his truck.

Our eyes met in mutual understanding. "It's all about everything being linked by seemingly random connections that really aren't so random," I said. "Like Sunny's disappearance, Jeanne's murder, and Michael."

"I agree, but Michael? He's like the wild card."

"Think about it. Jaxson told me about the break-in last night, when you were out with Michael and he knew Jolene wasn't supposed to be home. I can't think that finding the intruder in the front room, where Michael knew you were storing the hatboxes and the Maison Blanche door, was a coincidence."

"Don't forget the break-in at the boutique where I'd sold most of the clothes from the attic. We'd already searched the pockets, so we know they couldn't have found anything there, and right after that, we had the break-in at the apartment."

"Definitely . . ." he began.

"Not a coincidence," we said in unison.

A car drove by with its windows down, an old song by Tom Petty blaring out into the night.

"'American Girl,'" Beau said.

"Two for two," I said, then took a deep breath. "So, how do you want to handle this? I'm fine coming right out and asking Mimi how much she knows and showing her the negative."

"Not knowing how much Mimi is already aware of, and because she's my grandmother, please let me take the lead. Although I will admit that you're very good at leaping with your eyes closed."

I felt my defensive hackles rise. "I don't—"

He held up his hand. "I meant that as a compliment. I think it's one of the things I like most about you. Too many of us think too long and then end up missing opportunities."

I looked at him and blinked, not sure how to respond.

"Yes. I just said something nice. Of course, sometimes—like your relationship with Michael—you land in the wrong place, but I don't mind coming in to rescue you. But I think that's how you and I work."

I glared at him. "There is no you and me, remember? I thought I made that clear in Charleston. And I don't need saving."

He surprised me with a small smile. "We all need saving, Nola. In one way or another."

To hide the sudden prick of heat in my eyes, I unsnapped my seat belt and opened my door.

As we approached the house, a thin shaft of light shone from an opening between the front doors. Beau stopped and put a hand on my arm. "Wait here," he said, and began moving forward.

I whipped out my phone, ready to dial 9-1-1, and began following him. He turned around and looked at me. After sighing heavily, he proceeded to walk up onto the front porch with me close behind.

He stopped in front of the doors. "Can you stay here while I make sure everything's okay? If you hear me shout, call the police. Otherwise, wait until I call you or come get you."

"What about a weapon?" I whispered.

We both looked through the opening between the doors, our gazes landing on the same bronze candelabra on the vestibule table. Beau nodded once, then walked inside, picking up the candelabra as he passed it before he disappeared into the house.

I nervously shifted my feet and checked my phone for exactly three minutes before deciding I couldn't wait outside for another second. I stepped inside the vestibule, leaving the door cracked just in case we needed to make a quick exit. Feeling inordinately glad that I hadn't worn shoes over my fuzzy socks, I moved soundlessly forward into the foyer, listening for Beau or Mimi. Or someone else. The *tick*ing and *tock*ing of antique clocks throughout the house was the only sound of habitation, the Hitchcockian sound unnerving enough to coat my arms with goose bumps.

I crossed the foyer to peer into the front parlor and the dining room—both deserted—before retreating to the foyer and the single burning lamp on the hall table, unsure what else to do. I was afraid to begin wandering, afraid to get lost again.

I peered up the staircase, recalling the creepy room upstairs with the weird assortment of items from other people's lives. I held my breath, listening for voices or footsteps, but hearing only the infernal ticking of clocks.

I put a foot on the bottom step, telling myself I was going to go only to the top and determine if I could hear or see anything, and then come right back down to wait for Beau, but I hesitated. The hairs on the back of my neck stood on end, a sure indication that someone was looking at me. Someone, or some*thing*.

Turning slowly, I found myself facing the dark gaze of the man in the portrait. Dr. Charles Ryan. Fighting my instincts to either run up the stairs or bolt out the front door, I took a step closer to the painting, studying his face. Trying to uncover its secrets. Except it looked the same as it had when I'd first visited the house.

Same navy blue suit and wide tie that I remembered, along with the thick light brown hair with streaks of gray atop the handsome, strong-boned face. But it was his eyes, then as now, that drew my attention. Blue and piercing, they followed me as I walked closer, drawn to stand in front of the portrait, allowing that blue gaze to bore into me. It was almost as if he were trying to say something to me, something I felt I needed to hear.

As if being prodded, I allowed my gaze to drift down to the man's chest, to the striped tie. To the silver tie pin. The tie pin with the caduceus emblazoned on it. My gaze dropped to the jacket pocket with just the top edge of a white handkerchief protruding from the top. And the tip of the slender stem of a pipe sticking out of the corner.

I'd been too mesmerized by the eyes to notice those two small details before. But now I could see only them as I stared at the portrait. I backed away, my gaze drawn to the eyes again. The light in them seemed to have changed. They no longer appeared to be challenging. It now looked as if the subject might have been asking for forgiveness.

"Nola?"

I dropped my phone at the sound of Beau's voice. He stood on the stairs, his face unreadable in the dim light. I quickly retrieved my phone, relieved to see it still worked, with only a new crack across the screen cover.

"Is everything okay?" I asked, my voice cracking.

"We need you to come up here."

We. "All right." I looked behind me, then at the stairs, as if choosing between a hungry alligator and a pack of rabid dogs, before slowly climbing the steps. I didn't turn around, regardless of the doctor's eyes I felt following me.

CHAPTER 31

I followed Beau to the top of the stairs, then stopped. A single door sat open in the middle of the hallway, a wedge of light cutting into the darkness. I looked up at him, hoping he could guess the words I was too polite to say out loud.

"Mimi's in there. She's been waiting for you."

With a hand on my arm he indicated that I should walk ahead of him, but he knew better than to propel me forward, knew that would be the one thing that would make me bolt.

Gripping my phone, I headed toward the door, then paused at the threshold. The room was much like I'd last seen it, with the rows of shelves and the curio cabinet filled with Frozen Charlottes. Except this time Mimi sat in the Queen Anne chaise in the middle of the room, the Murano glass chandelier above dusting her with pale blue light. On the low table in front of her sat a little girl's jewelry box, just like the one my little sister, Sarah, had on her dressing table. When the lid was opened, a ballerina in a tutu twirled in a circle while "The Blue Danube" played.

Mimi's hair was down, lying in a single gray braid over her shoulder, a dark lavender flannel housecoat tied over a high-necked white nightgown. As I entered she smiled, as if this were a normal room and I was coming for tea, her odd dual-colored eyes watching me intently.

"Hello, Nola. Have a seat." She indicated the two cane-backed chairs for Beau and me to sit in.

I carefully sat on the edge of the chair closest to the door. "I hope you weren't sleeping."

She smiled sadly. "I'm afraid I don't sleep much, so no worries."

I slid a glance to Beau, but he was looking closely at a baseball glove on the shelf nearest us, snapping the rubber band on his arm. Remembering how the room had been locked when I'd discovered it, I'd wanted to ask him if Mimi allowed him inside. Then I remembered Melanie, and how she avoided places like cemeteries and antiques shops and just about any place where dead people might congregate and bombard her with requests. Places like this room, stuffed with the remnants of so many different lives. And if forced to come inside, she would have been singing an ABBA tune at the top of her lungs.

I looked down at my own rubber band on my wrist, recalling what Beau had told me about why he wore his. *I snap it when I need to be reminded that fear can't win. That whether or not I'm afraid isn't important. What matters is that I don't allow it to get between me and my objective. And then I remind myself that the rain always stops.* He raised his gaze in an unasked question, and I snapped my rubber band in response in unspoken solidarity.

About a thousand questions flipped through my brain like cards in the old-fashioned Rolodex my grandmother kept on her desk at Trenholm Antiques. Except mine weren't filed alphabetically, and most of the cards were half empty. I randomly settled on the first two. "What is this room? And why was my hairbrush in here? I know it was mine, and then you put it back in my backpack so I would think I'd just misplaced it. But I know what I saw."

"You're right," Mimi said. "I did borrow your hairbrush. For the same reason I have my granddaughter's music box here. For the same reason all of these objects are in here."

I looked at Beau, wondering if he knew what she was talking about. But his face was drawn, his eyes serious. His fingers plucking faster at the band on his wrist.

"Don't worry," Mimi continued. "Beau didn't know, either. He's always thought this was a storage room for the shop's inventory overflow and was happy to avoid it. Except these items will never be sold in our store. Most will be returned to their owners. Like your hairbrush."

I looked up at the shelves again, spotting the baseball glove, a set of headphones. A pair of roller skates. I turned to see the back of the room, the corner near the Mardi Gras gown, and my blood froze. A mangled tricycle with red, white, and blue streamers on the handles and a flattened front wheel lay on its side next to a small yellow cardigan. The sweater had been folded neatly, making visible an embroidered puppy on the front left, just above a jagged hole and a crusty brown stain.

I faced Beau, remembering the first episode I'd listened to of his podcast, *Bumps in the Night and Other Improbabilities*. He'd been denouncing a psychic ability. I couldn't remember the exact name, but I remembered that it was the ability to touch an object to gain insight about the person associated with that object. Beau had given it zero ghosties in flat refusal that such a thing was possible. I clenched my eyes as an icy shiver shook my body.

"It was a hit-and-run," Mimi said quietly. "Her parents were hoping I could see the car or a face through their little girl's eyes. Unfortunately, sometimes the channels of communication are too blurry and I have to keep trying, sometimes even over a period of years. But I will keep an object as long as the family members wish me to hold on to it so I can keep trying."

"Psych—" I stopped, unable to remember the rest of it.

"Psychometry," Mimi finished for me. "That's the official term. I've just known it as the special gift I was given at birth. My family tree is festooned with generations of relatives with different psychic powers.

It always presents itself in various ways. We had two ancestors burned at the stake as witches, so who knows what their gifts actually were? My son, Beauregard—Buddy—had the same gift. It could have been as strong as mine but he spent a lifetime fighting it and pretending it wasn't there, so it faded over time. And of course, there's Beau."

She smiled at him. "As I'm sure you are already aware, he has a very powerful psychic gift. One that he has been denying for most of his life because it frightens him. Beau has never learned how to channel to his heart and head his access to lost souls, or even to winnow out the ones he doesn't want to allow in. So he's learned instead to deny his gift completely."

Beau frowned, keeping his focus on the snapping of his rubber band.

"So, why did you take my hairbrush?" I had another realization. "And Thibaut's hammer—Christopher was there the day that it disappeared. Did he help you?"

"Christopher understands and appreciates my gift. He helps me when I need him. I wanted to make sure that Thibaut was a good person—and he is. And you, Nola, are a strong person, with a good heart and an open mind. But I know of your struggles. I smelled the gin when I held your hairbrush. I needed to make sure that we could welcome you into our inner circle."

"I never said I wanted to be let inside—"

Mimi held up her hand. "You didn't have to. I could see your loneliness the first day I met you. Even standing in a crowded room, you were like a little girl with her nose pressed against a store window, looking at all the things you couldn't have."

I stood, bristling with righteous anger and ready to leave. Beau grabbed my hand, holding me back. "Please don't leave. We both need to hear this."

He gave me an encouraging smile, his eyes pleading. Reluctantly, I sat down again. "What about Mr. Bingle?" I asked. "Did you 'borrow' him, too?"

"Of course. He must have belonged to Louise, because all I got from him was the smells of Christmas and the happy feeling of a child on Christmas morning. I gave it back to you, didn't I? I thought you could use the happy vibrations from it."

I quickly opened my backpack and pulled out the clientele book, placing it on the table next to the jewelry box. Then, one by one, I placed the pipe and the tie pin, the pipe rolling over with a small clunk. "Maybe you can tell us who these things belonged to, and why they were locked in the closet of my house."

She gave us an odd smile. "You're thinking my husband and Jeanne were having an affair, aren't you?"

"It seems pretty obvious," Beau said. "Weren't they?"

Mimi folded her hands in her lap and smiled. "From the outside, it does seem logical. But there's nothing logical or natural about any of this. I will tell you everything I know, but I need you to understand that none of it will be easy to hear. And when I'm done, you need to promise that you won't do the one thing you will feel compelled to do."

"I can't promise you anything right now, Mimi. You've kept me in the dark my whole life and I don't know why. And if Jeanne and Grandfather and all of the rest of it are somehow connected to Sunny, I want—need—to know everything. And then you will have to trust me to make my own decisions."

Mimi's unusual eyes settled on me. "What about you, Nola? Are you willing for Beau to risk his life? And yours?"

My hands shook, my nerves jumping across my skin. I turned and met Beau's gaze. "Look, this all sounds very dramatic. Can you just tell us what you know and let us decide for ourselves?"

Mimi took a deep breath, then settled back into the chaise. "All right. Charles did love Jeanne. But not like that. He loved her like a daughter. He was the family doctor, and it became clear, not long after he took over the practice from their old doctor, that Jeanne's feelings for Charles weren't those of a daughter for a father.

"He used to laugh about it, tell me how she would flirt so outrageously with him, and how she would try to shock him by deliberately taking off her clothes when she came to see him for a sore throat. She would also tell him . . . confidences . . . that he wouldn't share with me, saying they were too personal. But I knew they upset him." Her chest rose and fell. "I can't tell you how much I later wished that I had forced him to tell me. Because then everything would have been different."

"Everything?" Beau asked.

Mimi nodded. "Jeanne was my best friend. She was the one who introduced me to Charles. I actually loved that they were friends. I had such dreams of Charles and me and Jeanne and Angelo being friends forever. Raising our children and spending holidays together. I was so young and naïve.

"For the record, I had no idea Jeanne was pregnant. I know she and Angelo were not sleeping together. She said she wasn't attracted to him 'that way,' that she liked older men. Someone more mature. She was so much more worldly than I was, so I assumed she must have met someone at Maison Blanche, but she never mentioned anyone.

"I was devastated when she was murdered, and I believed along with everyone else that it had been a random murder. And I continued to believe that until 1997."

I sat up, the year ringing a bell in my memory, but I didn't know why.

"That's the year that they began remodeling the upper floors of the Maison Blanche building to convert them to the Ritz Hotel," Beau said, his voice almost a monotone. "When my grandfather had to move his medical office, and a lot of architectural and other remnants were either discarded, scavenged, or sold."

My eyes widened. "And that's where my door came from. But how?"

Mimi nodded. "Because it had a connection to my husband's office, I wanted to reuse it as the door for my storage room at the Past Is Never Past."

"But you didn't."

"I sent my son, Buddy, to go retrieve it since I knew it was too heavy for me and he had a truck." She pressed her lips together. "I can't tell you how many times I wish I had gone, because then I would have known to never allow that thing anywhere near me."

Beau leaned toward her. "Let me get you some water."

She shook her head. "No. Because if I stop, I don't think I'll have the courage to start again."

Beau stood and took the box from her and replaced it on the table before sitting next to her on the chaise. He placed her hand in his.

"What happened?" I asked.

"He put the door in the back room at the shop. He and Adele were there when I went to go see it. The door was already 'speaking' to Buddy, and he was exhausted from fighting it, so I knew that whatever it wanted to tell us was powerful. I wish I could go back in time and leave that damned door where it was and allow it to be consigned to a dump." She shook her head. "But we didn't. And Adele and Buddy were there to witness me laying my hands on it."

She pressed her forehead into Beau's shoulder as his arm went around her. "Please stop, Mimi. If this is too hard . . ."

She straightened, took a deep breath. "It's time. I've been holding on to this for too long. I need to let it go."

Unable to sit and watch Mimi struggle without helping, I left the room to get a cup of water from the bathroom next door. Mimi took it gratefully.

"What did you see?" I asked gently.

Mimi closed her eyes, her gaze turned inward. "I saw Charles. And Jeanne. In his office. They were fighting. Or she was fighting, and he was trying to calm her. She was in trouble—what we used to call unwanted pregnancies in those days—and she was begging Charles to get rid of the baby, and he was telling her no. That he would go talk to the baby's father and sort it all out. And she hit him. He was bleeding from the nose and his mouth and she was laughing and laughing and I could hear it, but there was no joy. It was . . . fear." Mimi paused to take a long drink of water. "And then she said"—she took another deep breath—"that the baby was her own uncle's, and that's why she needed to get rid of it. And if Charles didn't help her, she'd tell her father that the baby was his."

My stomach churned and Beau's breathing became harsh, like that of a man being held back from a fight.

"What did he do?" I asked, my voice barely audible.

Mimi began to shake and Beau moved to the chaise to put his arm around her.

"I don't know. He must have told her no. Because then I saw Jeanne again, and she was showing me this . . . this horrible scene. She was on the stairs of your house, with her father. Antoine. And she was telling him that she was pregnant. That Charles was the baby's father. And then, and then . . ." She let out a choking sob and pressed her face against Beau's arm.

"No, no, no." I shook my head, wondering if I might get sick. I pressed my fingers to my temples to make the urge to vomit go away. "So her father killed her, believing that Charles had made her pregnant."

"Yes. But we had no proof—not that anyone would believe me— but we knew from that moment on that our lives would never be the same. Because everyone knew that Antoine Broussard always de-manded payback and that sooner or later he would exact his revenge on us."

"But he killed his own daughter," Beau said. "And her uncle sexu-ally abused her. Even if Charles *had* gotten her pregnant, surely that's the lesser crime?"

Mimi's face softened as she looked at her grandson. "To us, of course. But to men like Antoine Broussard, it's not. He believed Charles had defiled his daughter, and that was all he cared about. He lived by his own warped code, and we had inadvertently offended his sense of honor." She took Beau's hand.

"After that, we found a way to live with the fear of the unknown. Then Beau came along, which helped us a great deal. And then sweet Sunny was born. As she grew from babyhood into a little girl, it be-came harder for Adele to find peace with what had happened to Jeanne, and how Antoine had gotten away with murder. Adele was always concerned about fairness, and right and wrong. It bothered all of us, of course, but especially her.

"Then one day Paulette Broussard—Jeanne's mother—walked into the shop while Adele was working. Adele knew who she was, of course.

She'd become obsessed with the Broussards, reading everything about them in the papers—which wasn't hard, because they were at every society event and were involved in every community organization. But that's all it took. Adele told Paulette what her husband had done to Jeanne all those years ago. To a mother, of course, there is no time limit to the grief of losing a child."

"Was Antoine arrested?"

Mimi laughed, a dry choking sound. "Of course not. We will never know what he said to his wife to extricate himself from the guilt, but nothing happened. Not right away, at least. He was like a cat playing with his prey. We spent sleepless nights wondering when we would get the knock on our door. Or the bullet through a car window." She reached over and squeezed Beau's hand. "We never blamed your mother. She had done the one thing we had not been brave enough to do. Yet the days went on, and nothing happened, and we began to relax. Maybe Paulette hadn't believed Adele. Or maybe Antoine had told his own lie and Paulette believed him.

"Finally, Charles couldn't take it anymore and paid a call to Antoine at his office. He was finally ready to confront him, to tell him that he had never laid a finger on Jeanne. And then, despite me begging him not to, he told Antoine that he knew he'd killed his own daughter— that I had seen it in a vision when I touched that door.

"Antoine laughed in his face and had him escorted out of his office, and then we waited, knowing there would be no reprieve that time. And there wasn't. A week later, Sunny was gone."

I stood and began walking around the room, just like my dad did when he was figuring out plot points in his books. So many answers were easily clicking into their slots, but there were others still floating around without any indication of where they went. I felt like we were working an all-white double-sided puzzle where everything and nothing looked like it went together. I caught sight of my backpack and hurried over to it with excitement, then retrieved the hair bow and negative. "But we have proof. I think this was taken by the neighbor who saw the Mercedes pull up and a woman step out and take Sunny."

I slid the negative over to her along with the hair ribbon. "Look at these—touch them! This might be the evidence you need to go to the police. Maybe it's not too late to get justice. Or to find Sunny, if she's still out there."

Mimi opened the top of the jewelry box, the music silenced and the ballerina frozen in position. She reached inside and pulled out a matching yellow ribbon. "I retrieved this from the street. I suppose that's where yours came from, too. I've had this for years. I held the ribbon and saw them take her. And Christopher showed me the negative years ago. But we already knew who was responsible, and my evidence wouldn't really count in a court of law anyway, so none of it mattered. All I could do was be at police headquarters every day asking for updates, trying to find out what the police were doing to find my sweet grandbaby. Buddy and Adele were beside themselves with grief. We were all walking ghosts, unable to eat or sleep. But the Broussards weren't done with us yet."

Mimi's chest rose and fell, her breathing more labored. "Antoine was the one who made sure Sunny's case was closed much sooner than it should have been. He made sure that the police files indicated that they were pressured by Charles. And then he told Charles that if we didn't stop with the private investigation, then . . ." She stopped, grabbed hold of Beau's hand. "Then Beau would disappear, too. I'd already lost one grandchild; we couldn't stand to lose another." She brought Beau's hand to her lips. "Saving you became our priority. That was our choice. Sunny was gone, but we still had you."

Beau continued to hold her hand, his face now expressing as much devastation as hers. "That's why so many doors were shut in my face when I tried to investigate, isn't it? Dear God. If she's alive, then she's out there somewhere. And she has no idea who she is."

Mimi nodded, wet tears soaking her cheeks. "But you can't look for her, do you understand? Promise me, please. Antoine is dead, but that doesn't matter. His reach continues beyond the grave."

The incessant sound of clicking pendulums echoing throughout the large house interrupted the heavy silence. I felt as if I'd run ten miles, my limbs rubbery with exhaustion. "That's why they wanted the door, and anything else that might allow you to connect Antoine to the murder. He's long dead, but he's still family."

"Then we need to get rid of the door, and make sure they know it," Beau said. "Because I wouldn't be the only one in danger."

I sat up. "So, who put all of the evidence in the closet in my house?"

"I told Buddy to get rid of it all," Mimi said. "I wanted nothing left behind that might be used later to hurt Beau. He must have locked it all inside, knowing I'd never go in there to look—but knowing it was the only connection to his missing daughter."

"Except for the music box and the ribbon," I said.

She nodded. "Adele kept the music box. I found it years later on the top shelf of her closet." Smiling softly, she said, "It's as if we've all been busy trying to save each other, and look where we are."

My phone vibrated in my hands, startling all three of us. I looked at it, the caller's name shooting a feeling of foreboding through me. "It's Ernest from across the street," I explained as I stood and slid my thumb across the screen to read his text.

Someone with a flashlight is in your house. Should I call the police?

The text was followed with about twenty emojis that I didn't have the time to figure out. To Beau, I said, "There's someone at my house with a flashlight. I need to go find out who it is." I quickly texted back that I would take care of it.

Beau's eyes met mine. "Michael?"

"Who else would it be? He knew the neighbors would call me if they saw a light on in the house, because that's what they've done twice before already. He must be wanting to talk to me alone."

"No," Beau said, standing. "You're not going alone."

I bristled. "I'm not asking for you to come. I can do this on my own."

"I know you can. But I want to help. I won't even make you ask. I think it's time to see if I can live up to Mimi's faith in my abilities."

He turned to his grandmother. "Will you be okay alone for a little bit? I promise to come back as soon as I can. I'll set the alarm when I leave."

Mimi managed a small smile. "I'll be fine. I think I'll watch a little television in my bedroom and then turn in. We'll talk more tomorrow."

Beau bent to kiss her cheek. To me he said, "You ready?"

I said good-bye to Mimi with a squeeze of her hand, then followed Beau out of the house. We rode in silence on our way to Dauphine Street, both of us sporadically snapping the rubber bands on our wrists in a primal rhythm meant to scatter the restless spirits that haunted more than just buildings.

CHAPTER 32

When we pulled up in front of my house, there was no sign of Ernest, Bob, or Belle across the street, but their outside lights glinted off the Christmas trees beginning their transition from Labor Day to Halloween in their front yard. Small white laminated paper ghosts hung from branches, fluttering like moths and creating a strobe-light effect.

I recognized the handful of cars lined up against the curb as belonging to my neighbors, with no sign of Michael's car. We climbed out of the truck, the unmistakable scent of pipe tobacco drifting over to us.

"Do you see your grandfather?" I whispered.

"No. Not yet. Or Jeanne."

"She might put up a fight. Melanie said Jeanne wanted to keep things hidden. Maybe we just need to tell her that we know everything and she can move on."

"Yeah. If you believe in that kind of thing."

I rolled my eyes. "I think that horse left the stable long ago."

He smiled, but it wobbled.

"Are you nervous?" I asked.

I couldn't say for sure since the light was dim, but I thought he might have rolled his eyes. "Are you?" he asked.

"Touché."

We both looked up at the darkened windows. Just as I took a step forward, a beam of light in an upstairs dormer shone through the glass.

"Your guess," Beau said. "Charles, Jeanne, or . . ."

"Michael," we finished together.

"It might not be him," Beau said quietly. "Because Michael is weaselly enough to send someone else."

"It's him." I didn't need to explain that the feelings I'd felt between Michael and me had been real. I knew that, just as much as I knew it was Michael in the house. Softly, I asked, "Are you ready?"

"Do I have a choice?"

"We always have a choice, Beau."

He nodded slowly. "We know why Jeanne's still here—she thinks she still needs to hide her secret. That should be easy, then, right? Just tell her we know and then that's it."

I sighed. "According to Melanie, ghosts are all different and never easy. Mostly, I think you need to understand her motivation for staying, and explain that it doesn't need to hold her back anymore."

"So what's her motivation?"

"It might be the oldest motivation in the world."

Beau's eyebrows rose. "Money?"

I rolled my eyes. "Love. She might have really loved your grandfather. Or thought she did. Maybe she needs to know that he loved her like a daughter and would want her to find peace."

He looked at me with a quizzical expression.

I shrugged. "I'm pretty intuitive about love and matters of the heart from watching Melanie and Jack over the years. Trust me—it was a learning experience." Quietly, I added, "And I read romance novels in secret."

"Wow. So there *is* something I didn't know about Nola Trenholm."

"Funny. What I wanted to say is that I think Charles is here because she is like a daughter to him. He wants to make sure that she crosses safely before he can." I looked at my phone. "Oh, great. It's midnight."

"The witching hour."

Nodding, I gritted my teeth and stepped up onto the porch. The wind chime swung violently, much harder than the breeze warranted. I put my hand on it, making it stop.

"Do you have the key?" Beau asked, just as the door opened on its own, the hinges conspicuously squeaky.

We looked at each other. "Do you know what to do?" I asked.

"With the ghosts, or with Michael?"

"I can handle Michael. I was just wondering if you want me to FaceTime with Melanie so she can walk you through this."

This time he was close enough that I could definitely see his eye roll. "That won't be necessary. Just as long as there aren't any hangers-on who want to follow me home afterwards, I'm good to go."

He stepped over the threshold and I hurried to squeeze through the doorway at the same time. "You shouldn't go first," I explained when he sent me an annoyed breath expulsion. "We're in this together. Besides, it's my house."

Floorboards above us creaked as stealthy footsteps moved across the floor upstairs. Beau held a finger to his lips as he grabbed a hammer that had been left on the bottom step.

"Is that really necessary?" I whispered loudly.

"Not if whoever is up there is only armed with a water gun."

"Good point." I flipped on my phone light, partially hiding the bright beam with my hand and aiming it in the direction of the staircase, knowing I wasn't going to be particularly thrilled to see any one of the three candidates. I couldn't help remembering the odd smile on Jeanne's face when I'd seen her in the flash of a lightning strike.

I headed toward the stairs, but Beau grabbed my elbow. "I really should go first."

I hated to admit that he was right, but whether the intruder was flesh and blood or . . . not, Beau was better equipped to deal with all possibilities. Reluctantly, I stepped aside and waited until he'd climbed two steps before following close behind. We'd reached the middle of the stairs before I noticed the drop in temperature, goose bumps marching like tiny mice down my arms and back. My lips stung from exhaling, my tongue dry and sticking to the roof of my mouth. The nearly overpowering smell of pipe tobacco suddenly descended on us, making me cough.

"He's here," I whispered. "Charles."

"I know. He's been watching us climb the stairs from the upstairs hallway. Jeanne's here, too. Watching him." He climbed another step and stood silently for a long moment, his face partially illuminated by the house lights across the street shining in through the dormer. "He's heading toward the other room."

Beau ascended to the top of the stairs, with me only one step behind. He quickly walked in the direction of the large room that was slated to become two bedrooms. Eventually. I took a step behind him, but stopped at the soft sound of an exhale coming from the closet. I wanted to call Beau back, but he'd disappeared into the dark room and I didn't want to shout and alert whoever it was in the closet that I was alone. I moved my shaking fingers off the flashlight on my phone and shone it into the blackened chasm of the closet.

I opened my mouth to scream as the outline of a man emerged from the back of the closet. Clutching my chest and wondering if I was too young to be having a heart attack, I stared at Michael.

"Nola," he said, reaching a hand toward me.

I took a step back, my emotions riding a roller coaster and hitting every curve. I was sure only that I definitely didn't want him to touch me. As usual, I selected the most random question of all of the ones I had floating on the tip of my tongue. "How did you get in here?" Even I wanted to shake me.

He held up a key. "It was Jeanne's."

I glared at him. "I imagine you've been laughing at me behind my back this whole time. Why, Michael? Why did you lie to me?"

He lifted his hands again, but, on seeing the look on my face, immediately dropped them. "I'm sorry, Nola. I know that's not enough. All I can say is that it wasn't meant to go so far. I was just supposed to get to know you. I wasn't supposed to fall in love with you."

"Don't say that. I can't believe anything you tell me anymore. You lied to me. This whole relationship was a lie. Why would you do that?"

"You wouldn't understand unless you came from a family like mine. They . . . tell you to do things, and you do them. It was my job. I just didn't think it would be so hard to keep my personal feelings out of it."

"I'm a real person, Michael. With real feelings. And to know that it was all a lie . . ." I stopped, unable to continue, my throat too tight to speak, but I was desperate not to show him any tears.

"I know. I know. I was falling for you in a big way, and I hoped that once I'd found what my uncle needed, we could see each other for real."

"Were you planning on telling me then? That it was all some kind of a setup at first? Did you think that as soon as you acquired the door and whatever else they thought was here, you could just continue our relationship? I don't know who's a bigger idiot—you or me."

He reached for me again, and I took another step backward, the banister pressing into my spine.

"Don't make another move toward her"—Beau stood in the doorway, the hammer raised in his hand—"or I will shove this down your throat. Try explaining that to your uncle."

Michael held up his hands. "I'm not here to hurt anyone." He glanced at Beau. "Could you put that down, please, so I can explain?"

"Just do it quickly, because I'm short on patience where you're concerned."

I wanted to resent Beau for taking charge, but there was also a sense of relief that I wasn't alone facing the enemy. At that moment I felt nothing but gratitude. My resentment would no doubt emerge tomorrow.

"Why are you here?" I asked, proud that my voice didn't wobble.

"I wanted to say I'm sorry."

"Oh, please." Beau took a step toward him, and Michael stood his ground. "In the middle of the night?"

"Nobody can know that I was here. I knew that if the neighbors across the street saw a flashlight, they would call Nola and she would come. They're easily annoyed." He glanced at Beau, who adjusted his hold on the hammer before focusing on me. "I needed to warn you. About not searching for Sunny. You're better off believing that she's dead."

"So you know that she's not?" Beau's eyes went wide, the street-lights making them glitter.

"I don't know anything—I swear. I only know that this house or something in it is connected to her disappearance. That's it. My uncle told me that I was supposed to get the door and anything else in this house that was connected to Jeanne and Charles. He didn't tell me why. But then I overheard him talking on the phone to someone, and he said Sunny's name." His gaze moved to Beau's face before settling on mine again. "And then he said, 'Broken bone for broken bone, eye for eye, tooth for tooth.'"

"Leviticus," Beau said.

Michael nodded. "Chapter twenty-four, verse twenty. I Googled it. Anyway, I put two and two together and figured out that my family might be involved with Sunny's disappearance. And it's somehow connected to what happened to Jeanne in this house more than forty years before." He held up his hand as if he were about to take an oath. "But I swear that's all I know."

A cold breeze blew through the upstairs hallway, strong enough to make my hair sway and tickle my neck. I took a deep breath, the events of the last few weeks rushing through my memory. "You're the one who's been snooping around here after dark. And orchestrated the break-in at the used-clothing boutique." It wasn't a question. "And made sure I was out of the house when someone broke into my apartment."

"Yes." He at least met my eyes. "Nobody was supposed to get hurt. I'm sorry Jolene was there."

"It's a good thing she wasn't hurt," Beau said. "Because I don't think I could be responsible for my actions right now."

Michael faced Beau, and I heard him swallow. "I don't blame you."

"But that doesn't explain why your uncle would need those things, or even know about them," I said, the myriad questions swirling around my head, colliding with one another before bouncing back in the opposite direction.

"One of the workers you had on the site doing the demo does a lot of work for the Sabatier Group. My uncle asked him to let him know if there was anything unusual in the house. That's how he found out about the door and the locked closet. If Mimi had just let him buy the property to begin with, we wouldn't have had a problem."

"Oh, no you don't. Don't you *dare* try to blame your criminal activity on someone else. Your whole family should be locked away somewhere. Including you for breaking in. Did your uncle tell you why he wants those things?"

"No. And I was told not to ask. I've learned that when someone in my family says that, I listen."

"So what do you know about Sunny?"

Michael held out his hands, palms up. "I swear—I don't know anything. All I know is that anyone poking their noses into her disappearance is in grave danger."

Beau tightened his grip on the hammer. "And all this time, you didn't think this information would have been helpful? That maybe you didn't need to mess with Nola's emotions just to be your uncle's minion?"

"Please believe me—I didn't know the whole story until Nola texted me asking me if I knew that I was related to Jeanne. I knew that part, of course, but after Nola's text I asked my uncle if I could tell her that I knew, and he told me to pack my bags, that we were going into the mountains, and not to say another word about it." He closed his eyes for a moment. "I only did it so I could have time to think. To prepare for what I needed to tell Nola. I know it's hard to believe. But I really need you to, because it's the truth."

"Of all the bull—" Beau didn't get to finish his sentence. Michael stepped to the side to avoid Beau's punch and I moved backward to get away from Michael, forgetting that I was already pressed against the banister. Beau and Michael didn't see me teetering on the top step until I'd already begun my backward descent over the railing toward the floor below.

Everything seemed to narrow in clarity and move in slow motion—a blade of blurred light on the peeling wallpaper of the stairwell, the black round hole in the ceiling getting smaller, and the surprised faces of Michael and Beau as they peered over the stairwell, their arms reaching for me in futility as I continued my free fall. I braced for landing and closed my eyes, picturing my mother's face one last time.

I waited for impact. And waited. But instead of my body breaking as it slammed onto the cypress floors, strong arms wrapped around me, holding me briefly before gently settling me on the floor. I turned, expecting to see Beau or Michael, but they were still on the landing above me, looking down with horrified expressions. The pungent scent of pipe tobacco swirled around me, thick enough that I expected to see smoke rings rising toward the ceiling. But all was as it should be, except for the smell of smoke and the freezing temperature that chilled the lining of my nose.

Michael began running down the stairs. "Nola—are you okay? What just happened?"

"I'm not exactly sure. . . ." My voice drifted away as I turned toward Beau, who'd moved toward the bottom of the stairs, his arms stretched across the width of the stairwell as if blocking the way from someone trying to climb up them. Except there was no one there. No one I could see. But it was clear that Beau saw someone.

"Jeanne, it's time for you to go."

Once again, the flash of light from nonexistent fixtures brightened and dimmed in quick succession. The temperature continued to plummet, a soft breeze blowing ice onto the bare skin of my face and neck.

"You have no more secrets, Jeanne. We know the truth about what happened to you. We know about your baby." The breeze swirled harder around our legs, blowing dust into our faces. "We know that you loved Charles. And Charles loved you—like a daughter."

The air vibrated with an electric force as fixtures without bulbs blazed with light, then flickered off. Beau took a step backward, his arms still stretched wide and his chest caving slightly as if an unseen force was pushing him back up the stairs. Despite the chilly temperature, sweat beaded on his forehead and cheeks.

Undaunted, he straightened and reached out a hand. "Take my hand, Jeanne. I'll lead you toward the light. You did nothing wrong. You don't need to stay here to protect secrets that aren't yours. Take my hand."

Beau's body was shoved hard enough that he was bent over the banister. I screamed, running toward him, ready to break his fall. His hair stood on end as if he were being electrocuted, his head jerking back as if slapped before he managed to right himself.

Looking up the stairs, he once again extended his hand. "Take my hand, Jeanne. And Charles will take the other one. He's ready to go. He's waiting for you."

A piercing wail began in the centers of the walls before spreading upward toward the roof in a deafening roar. I placed my hands over my ears, feeling the despair deep in my core as the house was plunged into utter darkness, even the lights from outside obliterated by dark shadows. My blood trembled with my bones, my breath sucked out of my lungs in fear.

"*Nooooooooo!*" came the wailing sound again, a woman's voice of utter despair.

"Yes!" Beau's voice rattled the walls with its sheer force. "Yes, you will. Take his hand and move toward the light. There is nothing left for you to do here. Go!"

Static electricity jerked through my body from my toes to the top of my head, making my hair stand on end. A low buzz swam around my ears as lights flickered on and off, the acrid scent of burned ions filling my nostrils. I held my breath as an eerie quiet descended for a brief moment. Splintering glass shattered the silence as windows exploded onto the wooden floors in an unholy symphony.

Beau's voice had quieted to a low whisper. "Good-bye, Granddad. Thank you for saving the life of someone I care about very much."

A moment later, the house settled again into silence, only the lingering scent of pipe tobacco and hair spray letting me know that I hadn't imagined anything.

Michael was already outside, staring back at the house, when Beau led me off the porch. "What the hell was that?" His question was directed at either Beau or me, or both. Either way, neither of us was prepared to answer.

Beau staggered toward Michael. "We didn't get to finish our conversation, did we?"

Without another word, Beau pulled back his fist and hit Michael square in the jaw, knocking him down on the grass. As Michael writhed on the ground, holding his face, Beau leaned over him. "That's for Nola. And tell your uncle or whoever wants to know, I'm not done looking for Sunny. If she's out there, I'm going to find her and bring her home."

Beau took my arm and led me back to the truck, but not before I'd seen the set of footprints leading from the house and down the front walk, the lights across the street reflected in the small arcs of water heading toward Beau's truck.

CHAPTER 33

"Ta-da!" Jolene emerged from the kitchen, carrying a large platter, on top of which rested a gray and white cake shaped like a dog's head that looked alarmingly like Mardi's. "Happy Gotcha Day," she said to Mardi, who was propped up in the wooden high chair Jolene had found in someone's trash and had refinished in bright blue and painted paw prints all over. If I didn't love Jolene so much, it would have been very easy to hate her.

Everyone assembled in our small apartment clapped, and Jaxson, with a surprisingly strong tenor voice, began to sing "For He's a Jolly Good Fellow," quickly joined by the rest of the guests with varying musical talent.

It had been Jolene's idea to have a party to celebrate Mardi's formal adoption, claiming that her hostess skills were getting rusty and she needed an excuse to use her fine china. She'd even invited Thibaut and Jorge as the afternoon's entertainment, and although they were at first cautious around Mardi—no doubt remembering when they'd first met him—the dog was soon licking their hands and stealing the tennis balls they'd brought for their juggling act.

Jolene set the cake on the table, decorated with a tablecloth on which she'd embroidered dog bones and fire hydrants all along the hem. Three blue candles stood in the middle of the cake, and I preferred to think they looked like a crown instead of three sticks impaling a head. Since we didn't know how old Mardi was, Jolene said three candles symbolized the past, the present, and the future.

Having survived a collision of the past and present two weeks prior when Beau cleansed my house of spirits, I didn't question Jolene's wisdom. It was usually doled out with a heavy Southern accent and using words not strung together in other parts of the country, but Jolene was most definitely the wisest person I knew.

Mardi barked at the cake, either in recognition of another dog or because he wanted a snack. Or both. We had discovered that he had a sweet tooth that rivaled my own, making us wonder where he'd come from and who had taught him to love sweets. After a month with no responses to any of the flyers we'd passed out and posted, and discovering that he had no chip, I'd made it official. I had to keep reminding Jolene that I was his mom, but she continued to pretend not to hear my protests when I found Mardi in another sweater or playing with a new toy. I figured there were worse things in this world than spoiling a dog.

"I hope that tastes better than it looks," Carly said. She caught me frowning at her. "I mean, because it looks so real."

"I want the pink tongue!" Jaxson called out, earning a sour glance from Carly.

"I'll take one of the ears. And any leftovers." Uncle Bernie winked at me. He was already sitting at the table, a napkin tucked into the collar of his shirt, holding two empty plates. He'd come alone and had assigned himself to Mimi, bringing her food and drinks and making her laugh with his stories of growing up in New Orleans at the same time as she had.

Jolene began to slice pieces and put them on plates while I handed them out to guests. Without being asked, Beau took over the music selection, and right now Ella Fitzerald was singing "Can't We Be Friends?" I gave a quick glance toward Jolene, but she was too busy handing out cake to notice.

"What are you going to do with the Maison Blanche door?" Christopher asked, taking the plate I offered. It was a bit of a floppy ear but mostly the back of the head.

"It broke my heart, but Beau drove it out to Manchac Swamp and threw it in. I hope it never rises to the surface."

"And the other things?"

I raised my finger to my lips. "I'm keeping them in a very special place. Just in case."

"'Just in case'?"

"I don't believe in coincidence, but I do believe in 'just in case.' You never know when something from your past might come in handy."

Trevor walked by with a plate of cookies, either intended for his own consumption or to convince Thibaut and Jorge to juggle them. I hoped they would be mature enough to say no, because I doubted any of them would be volunteering to vacuum up the mess.

"Like a flask?"

I looked sharply at Christopher. "Did Trevor tell you about that?"

"He did. He randomly mentioned all the things he's acquired for you and that was one of them."

"He's very resourceful, isn't he?"

His odd eyes assessed me carefully. "Yes, he definitely is."

"For the record, I don't even remember where I put it."

Christopher smiled, then excused himself to join Mimi and Uncle Bernie. Beau and Sam approached, holding hands. I had met Samantha for the first time that afternoon, and I liked her. I might have liked her a whole lot more if she weren't Beau's girlfriend, but that was something I wasn't quite ready to examine.

"Good job, you two," she said. "Eliminating two restless spirits and one weasel all in one shot. Congratulations."

I smiled. "Thank you. Although it was all Beau's doing."

"Well, for the record, I think the two of you make an amazing team."

"Don't say that too loudly," I said, "or you'll have to change the name of your podcast."

"Yeah," Beau said, taking a sip of his alcohol-free beer. "Baby steps. I've got other things I'm working on right now anyway." His eyes met mine, and I knew we were both thinking about Sunny.

Sam reached across and plucked the rubber band on my wrist. "Hey, Beau has one, too."

I looked at her, surprised to find her own wrist empty. "Yeah," I said. "It keeps my anxiety in check."

She nodded, but I could feel Beau's gaze on me. "Will you excuse me? I need to see if Jolene needs help in the kitchen."

I walked quickly toward the kitchen, where Jolene was arranging a plate of bone-shaped cookies on a serving platter. "Need any help?"

"I think you'd be more like a third arm, Nola. Not as helpful as you might think."

"Got it," I said as I moved toward the door leading into my back-room sanctuary. My music stand stood next to my untouched guitar, and the unplugged pink princess phone sat on the edge of my desk. I was tired of hearing it ringing in the middle of the night, so I'd moved it in there in the hopes of getting a good night's sleep.

I picked up the guitar and plucked a few notes, each more jarring than the one before. I closed my eyes, waiting for the notes to speak to me, waiting for the music to take me someplace else. But nothing came to me at all. I slid my palm across the strings, listening to the angry discord with an odd satisfaction.

Beau stuck his head around the door. "Everything okay in here?"

"Fine," I said, replacing my guitar on the stand. That had become my standard answer every time Jolene asked. Her response was usually a tight-lipped frown, followed by a plate of lemon bars or brownies or whatever new concoction she was baking that she'd hoped would magically shake me from my current state of *fine*.

Beau apparently thought it was an invitation to come in and sit down on one of two armchairs Jolene said I needed in there. She'd included two throw pillows with my monogram, claiming that if something couldn't be monogrammed, it wasn't worth having. Beau immediately took one of the pillows from behind his back and dropped it on the floor.

"I'm starting to think you're avoiding me. I've called you a few times about resuming your driving lessons, but you never called me back."

"Yeah. Sorry. Jolene's volunteered, so I think I'm good for now."

His eyebrows shot up. "Jolene?" He rubbed his hand over his chin. "Isn't that like asking Wile E. Coyote how to catch a roadrunner?"

"Funny. It's definitely a learning experience, but at least she doesn't act like she's doing me a favor."

"I never did that, Nola, and you know it. But if you prefer Wreck-It Ralph as your driving instructor, that's fine. At least you're learning defensive driving. Just remember that I'm always available."

"Thank you," I said. I shifted a bit in my seat. "I've been thinking of ways to thank you for doing what you did in my house." I'd actually been procrastinating, because I didn't want to remind him about what he said after I'd taken the free fall over the banister. He'd been thanking his grandfather for saving my life. *For protecting someone who means a lot to me.* "I know it wasn't easy for you."

"No. It wasn't. But I found it oddly . . . satisfying." He frowned. "Having you there somehow made it easier. I think Sam is right. We do make a good team."

"Yes, well, one and done. I think we can rest on our laurels and retire from, well, whatever that was. I don't think my heart could take another dive over a second-story banister."

"Not all spirit cleansings are that dangerous, you know."

"Right. Some of them just involve burning down a house."

"They're all not like that. And I'm not even sure this is really a direction I want to move in. In the past, whenever I got involved with restless spirits, I couldn't block them out and I ended up letting too many of them inside my head. I couldn't stop them. So I just avoided them until I got better at blocking them. But something about you being there . . ." He shrugged. "You gave me something else to focus on—emotionally, anyway. It allowed me to concentrate on just my grandfather and Jeanne so I wasn't a beacon to all the other lost spirits I know are roaming around the Marigny."

"You should bring Sam next time."

His gaze met mine before drifting away. "Yeah, maybe."

Suddenly nervous, I quickly switched the conversation. "Jorge still wants to have the house blessed by a priest. Jaxson said he'd ask his brother."

"Father Luke? That should be fun. Jaxson, Luke, and I were like the Three Musketeers growing up. He could throw a left punch even better than Jaxson. When he went into the seminary, all the girls cried."

"I haven't met him yet, but Jolene refers to him as 'Father What-a-Waste.' She says he's hotter than doughnut grease, which I personally find disturbing."

"Because he's a priest?"

"No, because that means she probably knows how to make dough-nuts. Is there nothing that woman can't do?"

Beau grinned. "Before Luke moved parishes, he and I used to take long motorcycle trips together."

"Wait—he's a good-looking priest on a motorcycle?"

"Yeah. He's like a sitcom waiting to happen. I mean, they had *The Flying Nun*, so why not?"

I didn't say anything about Beau's being a fan of old television sit-coms, if only because I was one, too. "I'm sure Jolene will let you know when the house blessing is going to be, as she's planning on throwing a little party and she'll want you to be there. The roof should be fin-ished by then, so at least we won't get rained on. I'm not even going to plan on having electricity or water, because every time I plan on something, a wrench always seems to get thrown in the machine."

"'The best laid plans of mice and men . . .'" Beau quoted.

"Yeah," I said. "Pretty much."

A scratch on the door announced Mardi's presence. Beau stood and opened the door, allowing in the guest of honor, who immediately pounced into my lap. His kisses smelled like frosting, which I hoped was from the special vet-approved dog cupcakes that Jolene had baked just for him.

"Not that my opinion matters, but I like Sam. She's really nice."

"'Nice' sounds a lot like 'fine.' You're just full of descriptive adjectives today, aren't you?"

I set Mardi on the floor to let Beau know I was done with our conversation. "Was there anything in particular that you wanted to see me about?"

"Yes, actually. Have you heard from Michael?"

Hearing the name made me take in a sudden breath. Since the episode at my house, everyone who knew me had been careful not to mention Michael's name in my presence. Beau's saying it now felt like a shock to my system, like stepping on a down escalator and going up instead. "No. And I hope he knows better than to try to get in touch."

Beau looked at his hands clasped between his knees. "I don't blame you. But I was hoping that maybe I could ask for your help."

"My help?"

"It's a huge ask, and I wouldn't blame you for saying no. But I was hoping that maybe your need for a little revenge and to beat Michael at his own game would override your need to never see him again."

"What are you suggesting?"

He was silent for a beat, as if reconsidering, then spoke quickly. "I would need you to pretend you've forgiven Michael and say you want to start over. Any sane person would see it as completely ridiculous, but he doesn't seem to be particularly sane. At least, he doesn't seem to think like the rest of us. It would be just for a short time, until he trusts you enough to let you inside his family circle."

"You can't be serious. If you are, you're more crazy than he is."

"I get it. I do. But Michael might be the key to finding Sunny, and you're my only in with the Broussards."

I wanted to help him find his sister—but in any other way than what he was proposing. "Absolutely not," I said sharply, making Mardi look up at me. "I'm sure there are other ways to find out what happened to Sunny. Because I don't ever want to see Michael again. He reminds me of . . ." I'd been about to say *what a horrible judge of character I am*, but stopped. Because Beau already knew that.

"I'm just asking that you think about it. It could be the best kind of revenge, to beat him at his own game."

With Mardi trotting behind me, I walked to the door, eager to end the conversation. "I thought you should know. That night—at my house. I saw those wet footprints again. I think it might be your mother."

He remained seated, his eyes darkening. "It is."

"Can you not communicate with her?"

Beau didn't answer right away. "I can. I just don't want to listen to what she has to say."

I wasn't sure how to respond, so I remained silent. Maybe one day I'd tell him about how Melanie finally sent my mother into the light. At the time, I'd told her that I forgave her, but I was still angry. I realized now that the anger had long faded, and that all I felt when I thought of my mother was the cold ache of loss, and a blossom of love that had once almost been erased by all the anger. If anything, it proved that growth and change were possible. Even for me.

He stood. "There's something else I've been meaning to ask you. Remember that night when I slept on your couch?"

I pretended to think. "Vaguely. You were sick or something."

"Really? Because I remember it pretty vividly. And I definitely remember you kissing me."

"Oh, no," I said, pointing a finger at him. "You kissed me first."

He didn't smile. "I know. I was just making sure it wasn't a dream. I was thinking that we should probably talk about that at some point."

The princess phone rang on the corner of my desk, its dangling cord lying unplugged on the floor.

We both stared at it for a moment. Then I picked up Mardi and opened the door. "It's for you." I paused long enough to see him lift the receiver, then closed the door behind me.

I carried Mardi through the door to the stairway that led out to the backyard. I sat on the steps, watching the last of the sun bleed from the sky, my thoughts running through my conversation with Beau about using Michael to help find Sunny, and Beau's reluctance to talk to his mother. And the memory of our kiss.

I had come to New Orleans for a new chance, for a change. I should have known that a person couldn't become someone new just by changing zip codes. Dr. Wallen-Arasi had given me a book when I graduated from grad school—*Wherever You Go, There You Are*. I hadn't read it yet; maybe that was the problem. But I remembered the title now as one of life's little truths. Yet I still felt no wiser.

My adopted city of New Orleans was shaped by the meandering Mississippi, its curves a false embrace of the Crescent City, her people thriving in their vulnerability. It's how their *laissez les bon temps rouler* and laissez-faire attitudes evolved from the unpredictability of the tiger sleeping outside the door.

I had come here believing that was the sort of attitude toward life I was meant to have. My nightmarish childhood had evolved into an ideal and cherished Charleston adolescence. In my quest to find a new identity, I had chosen the Big Easy as my home. My life over the past few months had begun to make me question my choice. And my ability to change.

I buried my face again in Mardi's soft fur, so grateful that he had found us. Wherever I decided my home would be, it wouldn't be a home without a dog. I stuck my hands under his T-shirt that read STILL LIVES AT HOME WITH MOM—a gift from Jolene—to feel the warm sweetness that is dog, and missed my General Lee as much as I had the day he'd gone to sleep in the garden behind our house on Tradd Street and had silently crossed over the rainbow bridge.

"Hello?"

Mardi and I both jerked to attention at the sound of the voice coming from the driveway. A young girl in her early twenties stood looking at us, a bright smile on her face, her eyes hidden by large sunglasses. She had shoulder-length sun-streaked blond hair and coltishly long arms and legs despite being past adolescence. A fleur-de-lis tattoo decorated the inside of her wrist, visible when she flicked her hair behind her shoulders.

Mardi didn't growl at the newcomer, nor did he leap toward her, asking for attention. He just looked at her, as seemingly surprised to see her as I was. "May I help you?"

"Yeah. I'm looking for Beau Ryan? Some lady named Lorda said I could find him here." Her accent seemed oddly familiar, but I couldn't place it. Definitely not Southern, nor was she a native New Orleanian, despite the tattoo.

I stood, setting Mardi on the ground. He sat next to me, still unsure of the stranger.

"Sure," I said. "I'll go get him. Who should I say is looking for him?"

She smiled even wider. "Sunny Ryan. I'm his sister."

ACKNOWLEDGMENTS

A huge thanks to dear friends Nancy Mayer Mencke and Lynda Ryan for sharing with me your native city, for showing me the best place to get my king cake, and for always being up for a frozen daiquiri—even if it doesn't come from a drive-through window. Thanks, Lynda, for allowing me to borrow the name for Mardi from your sweet dog who crossed the rainbow bridge many years ago but who will always live on in our hearts.

Special thanks go to Patricia Casey, a great friend and New Orleans native (and now a professional tour guide), for your excellent tour of the Marigny in the heat of a summer morning and for sharing your insight to help me make this book as accurate as possible. Thanks for allowing me to put you in the book!

Last, but not least, thank you to all of my readers, whose enthusiasm for the stories and characters in my Tradd Street books led to the creation of this spin-off series. I hope you enjoy Nola and her experiences as we venture into a new setting that is familiar yet fresh, and into another great Southern city full of history, beautiful architecture, and—of course—plenty of ghosts!

Happy reading,
Karen

THE
SHOP ON
ROYAL STREET

KAREN WHITE

Questions for Discussion

1. Why do you think Nola wanted to own the house so much? Do you think there is truth to the idea of being connected to a house?

2. Do you think Beau has a sixth sense, as Melanie (if you are familiar with the Tradd Street series!) does? Why do you think he is not yet ready to deal with the prospect?

3. What do you think of Nola's potential romantic suitors? Is there one you like better than the other?

4. Jolene is a contrast to Nola in many ways; why do you think their friendship works the way it does? Do you have someone like a Jolene or Nola in your life?

5. What makes the setting of New Orleans so special for this book? Do you think it could have been set anywhere else in the United States?

6. What do you make of Beau's grandmother Mimi? Do you think she has other secrets she is hiding?

7. Are there any characters from the Tradd Street series whom you would like to have appear in the new series?

8. What do you think is next in store for Nola? Where do you see this series going?

Keep reading for an excerpt from the
second book in the Royal Street series,

THE HOUSE ON PRYTANIA

The Crescent City, with its long and tangled history, its glorious architecture and subtropical allure, along with its inarguably dark past and requisite restless spirits, is a forgiving place. A city with accepting arms for society's lost and hungry souls, and a haven for people like me who'd stumbled and fallen yet managed to pull themselves back up. People who were brave enough to try again in a place known for its extremes, or simply too hardheaded to admit defeat.

I listened to the clanging and jangling of the St. Charles streetcar I'd just exited as it waddled its way down the tracks toward the river bend. It had become the soundtrack of my life in a new city, much as the church bells chiming their holy chorus in my hometown of Charleston once were.

Slowly walking down Broadway, I enjoyed the afternoon air of an early October Saturday. The oppressive humidity of summer had lifted, giving us a reprieve, and although the temperature was nowhere near what anybody up north would call cold, it was still cool enough that I wore a sweater over my usual T-shirt. Even my fingers felt chilled as they gripped the straps of my backpack.

I considered slipping on the gloves that my stepmother, Melanie, had sent me—along with typed instructions on how to care for them. I was due a visit from my family—my parents and my twelve-year-old half siblings, Sarah and JJ—the following week, and I didn't want to register Melanie's disappointment at seeing my dirty gloves. Exactly the reason why I wasn't wearing them. Because absolutely nobody in real life had the patience to clean their gloves to Melanie's specifications. Unless they were Melanie.

I lived on Tulane University's so-called fraternity row, my upstairs town house apartment sandwiched between two fraternity houses, so I was prepared to dodge the street football being played as I made my way down the street. The days were shorter now, the rose-tinted dusk sky hovering over me as I walked, the growing dimness darkening the shadows between houses and behind unlit windows. Not for the first time, I was grateful that I had only five senses and couldn't see anything within the shadows. Nor did I have a close connection to those who could make me quicken my steps. Just because I couldn't see anything didn't mean nothing was there.

I climbed the steps to my apartment, enjoying the scents drifting down the stairwell of something spicy and pumpkin-y baking in the oven. Being greeted by fresh baked goods was just one of the perks of having the Southern version of Martha Stewart as my roommate. A version that sported flame red hair and had a skill set that included all things domestic as well as the ability to change a tire while wearing high heels, and had an accent as thick as the Delta mud from her home state of Mississippi.

Jolene McKenna was a force of nature whose turns of phrase could be simultaneously head-scratching and profound, and whose sweet nature hid a backbone of steel mixed with concrete. Jolene had been my roommate during my abbreviated tenure at Tulane University, and when we'd run into each other in New Orleans seven years later, I had needed a roommate, and she'd needed an apartment. It had seemed serendipitous.

As soon as I opened the French door at the top of the stairwell and threw off my backpack, I was attacked by a small gray-and-white fur ball with two dark button eyes and a matching nose and a wildly waving plumed tail. He was also wearing yet another fall-themed dog sweater courtesy of his favorite aunt, Jolene. Although Mardi was technically *my* rescue dog, Jolene had taken over all of his accessorizing, something only my stepmother, Melanie, could appreciate. I had drawn the line at mono-gramming, but little by little I'd noticed MLT (Mardi Lee Trenholm) appearing on bowls, bedding, and his dog-sized bathrobe.

At the tap-tap sound of approaching high heels, Mardi and I looked up from our spots on the floor to see Jolene. As usual, her hair and makeup were perfect, and she wore a *The Wizard of Oz*–themed apron over a cocktail dress. At her look of disappointment, something clicked in the back of my mind. "Oh, no. Did I forget . . . ?"

"Yes. Tonight is the big welcome-home party for Sunny Ryan. I've been texting you for the last hour, but you didn't respond." Her eyes widened as they settled on my unruly hair, which had had only a glan-cing blow from a brush earlier that morning, before I'd left for work. "I'm not sure if we have enough time to make you presentable, but I've never been called a quitter."

She lifted Mardi from my lap so I could stand. "Sorry—I was catch-ing up on Beau's podcast and my battery died. Really, Jolene, there's no reason for me to get all gussied up." I used one of her words to pla-cate her. "It's just a small gathering of family and close friends."

Jolene grabbed my wrist and began pulling me toward the bath-room. "I've already drawn your bath. It's grown cool, but that means you won't lollygag. And of course you should get gussied up. Beau will be there."

I blinked at her. My relationship with Beau Ryan was complicated. Which was a lot like saying the levee system in New Orleans might have a few flaws. I hadn't the energy or the time to hash it all out now. Instead I said, "Well, Beau is Sunny's brother, so it would be strange if he wasn't. And I'm sure his girlfriend will be there, too. Besides, I haven't heard from Beau since Sunny showed up the night of Mardi's gotcha party. He's obviously moved on now that he doesn't need my help finding his sister."

Jolene stopped at the threshold of the bathroom and pulled off my baggy cardigan before gently pushing me inside. "For someone so smart, you sure can be ignorant. Now hop in the tub and do the best you can with that shampoo. You have exactly five minutes, and I'm timing you. Starting now." She tapped the screen of her smart watch before closing the door in my face.

One hour and fifteen minutes later, we were in Jolene's relic of a car—named Bubba by its owner—and heading down Broadway on our way to the Ryans' historic family home on Prytania in the Garden District. Mardi, wearing a celebratory yellow kerchief that matched his sweater, sat dutifully in his car seat in the back, the air from the vent blowing his fur from his face like in a shampoo commercial. The heater in the old car apparently had only two settings: off and full blast. I wanted to crack open my window to let in fresh air but was scolded by Jolene, who warned me that the three layers of Aqua Net she'd applied to my hair could go only so far.

A silver platter filled with Jolene's pumpkin nut muffins sat on my lap. Apparently, she had the hearing of a bat, because despite the volume of the heater and the rumbling of the tires passing over the ubiquitously uneven paving of New Orleans's streets, she heard me carefully lifting the plastic wrap to grab a pinch of one, and she slapped my hand.

"You're worse than Mardi," she scolded.

"I'm starving. I've been cutting bathroom floor tiles all afternoon. Thibaut is teaching me and he's very patient, but it takes forever. I didn't want to take a food break and disappoint him."

Jolene swerved around a giant pothole in the middle of the road, causing me to grab the platter of muffins to keep them from sliding off my lap. "You do know that Thibaut works for you, right?"

"Yeah, that. I keep forgetting." Thibaut Kobylt was a master of all things construction-related and led the two-man crew—including another jack-of-all-trades, Jorge—helping me restore my first home, a Creole cottage in the Marigny neighborhood. He was talented, smart, funny, and patient. His only flaw was that he'd done time in jail for the manslaughter of his wife. I'd left out that little detail when telling my parents about Thibaut. There were some things they were probably better off not knowing.

Regardless, I was lucky to have Thibaut on my crew, which was a very small one, owing to the not-unfounded rumor that my house wasn't "right." Meaning it was either haunted, possessed, or cursed. Or maybe just possessed or cursed, since it shouldn't still be haunted. With the help of a reluctant Beau Ryan, who still hadn't reconciled himself to the idea that he could communicate with ghosts, we had eradicated two spirits bound to the house—those of Beau's grandfather and his grandmother's best friend, Jeanne, who'd been murdered in the house in 1964 by her own father.

But in the weeks since, it had become clear even to me that things were still not right with my house. Judging from the fact that neighbors and most workmen continued to refuse to set foot inside, and from the regular delivery of gris-gris bags to my front porch, I wasn't the only person who thought so. Even when the house was empty, the atmosphere was like that of a suspended breath, the air thick with the sort of tension that precedes the whistling of a teakettle.

I had even thought I'd smelled a hint of pipe tobacco, the telltale sign that Beau's grandfather was nearby. But he couldn't be. Beau had sent him to the light. Maybe he just wanted to hang on for a little while longer to get to see Beau. Or maybe they didn't allow smoking in heaven. Anything except for the nagging thought that Charles Ryan still had something to tell us.

"How long do you think we need to stay?"

Jolene sighed as she turned onto Prytania, rolling over the curb and jostling the platter on my lap. "Don't you want to meet Beau's long-lost sister and find out where she's been for the past couple of decades? I mean, the last time they saw her she was just a baby and had been abducted by strangers. That's a lot to go over."

"I agree. And I'm interested in hearing her story. From what she's already told us, all she knows is that she was adopted when she was a toddler and raised by a loving family in Edina, Minnesota. Curiosity about her birth parents brought her back to New Orleans."

"So, what's bothering you?" Jolene asked.

"I didn't say something was bothering me."

"You didn't have to. You're snapping that rubber band on your wrist, which is something you've started doing when you've got something stewing inside your head."

"It's just that, don't you think it odd that Sunny showed up when she did? Right after we'd uncovered the truth about Antoine Broussard and his connection to the kidnapping?"

"But now that Sunny's shown up, none of that matters anymore," Jolene said as she slid into a driveway and flipped down the car's visor—bravely hanging on to the ceiling with duct tape and a prayer—and began reapplying her lipstick.

"Exactly," I said.

She carefully closed the visor, then slid her gaze to meet mine. "What are you saying?"

I shrugged, not really sure what I was saying. "I don't know. It just seems like such a . . . coincidence."

"And there's no such thing as coincidence," she said slowly, echoing my father, Jack Trenholm's, oft-repeated mantra. He was an international bestselling author of true-crime books, and it was something he'd discovered in his research that had been proven time and time again.

Jolene shifted in her seat so that she faced me. "Sometimes, Nola, we are handed miracles disguised as coincidences. For over twenty years, Sunny had no idea that she had a family looking for her, and that family had no idea that she was even alive. Then suddenly, for reasons beyond our comprehension, all the stars aligned and the pieces fell into place and Sunny and her family are together again. I don't think it's fair for us to question it. I think all we need to do is rejoice in this miracle."

When I didn't respond, Jolene squeezed my hand where it rested on the seat. "I don't blame you for questioning it. It's your nature to question things. I'm sure you can't help but compare Sunny's story with your own and how you had no one looking for you after your mama died, because they didn't know you existed." She squeezed my hand again, then sat back in the seat. "But now you are loved to pieces by your family and friends, so none of that matters. Even if that little green face of jealously pops up every once in a while, you can just whack it on the head with the full knowledge that you are deeply loved and cherished."

"You're right," I said, my eyes open, but seeing nothing except my thirteen-year-old self on a cross-country bus from California to South Carolina, with all my hopes and fears confined to a single piece of paper crumpled in my pocket, on which my mother had scribbled the name of the father I had never met.

"And I know you don't want to talk about it, but I think your heart is still hurting because of Michael. He's a weasel and he betrayed your trust, but it takes the heart a lot longer than the brain to get over that kind of hurt. Just thank your stars that it was short-lived, and you didn't have to eat the whole egg to know it's rotten." She gave me a sympathetic smile to soften her words. "I think that might be the reason why you can't feel the kind of happy you should at Sunny's reunion with her family."

The mention of Michael Hebert shook me out of my reverie. I widened my eyes, finally registering where Jolene had parked the car. "Where are we? This isn't the Ryans' house."

"I know that. I just didn't want anyone seeing me fixing my makeup."

By "anyone," I knew she meant Jaxson Landry, a local lawyer and the object of her unrequited love. He was dating her friend Carly. She had told me that Jaxson had bought a ring for Carly, and I didn't want to rub salt in the wound. Pressing hard on the pedal, Jolene backed out of the driveway, oblivious to the blaring horn of an oncoming car.

"Maybe I need to stop looking at everything like a crime novel and just be happy for Beau and his family," I said.

"I think that's a very good plan. Besides, Sunny looks like Beau and is cute as a button. Except for the blond hair. It's completely the wrong shade."

"What do you mean? You think she highlights it?"

Jolene pulled up onto the curb before coming to rest on the street behind a line of cars parked in front of the Ryan's Italianate house. With an aggrieved sigh, she put the car in park. "Nola, I thank my lucky stars that we found each other again. There is so much I need to teach you. Sunny, despite her name, is no more a natural blond than Dolly Parton is. And I adore Dolly, so you know that I'm not throwing shade on anyone's character."

"Of course not. And dying your hair isn't a crime."

"Although in some cases it should be. From the pictures we've seen, Sunny was blond as a little girl and it just darkened over time. It happens a lot—both ways. My second cousin twice removed on my mama's side was born with a whole head of jet-black hair, and let me tell you that all that tongue-wagging almost did that poor baby's mama in. Luckily, it all fell out when she was two. Or maybe it was three, but it all grew back just as blond as can be. We think it's because her granddaddy was part I-talian. . . ."

I made a big show of unbuckling my seat belt and gathering my backpack, eager to distract Jolene before she gave me another lesson about her family tree. Jolene pushed open her door with a soft grunt before walking around the car to open my door. She took the platter of muffins. "I think these will be safer with me until we get them inside. You can bring Mardi."

Mardi pulled at his leash as we headed toward the gate with the hourglass in the middle. It was a nod to the Ryans' antiques shop, called the Past Is Never Past, on Royal Street in the Quarter. I held the gate open for Jolene, doing my best to restrain Mardi on his leash. I wasn't sure whether he was excited about the muffins or if he loved visiting Beau's grandmother. They had bonded at his gotcha party, and Mimi Ryan had included Mardi's name on the invitation to Sunny's welcome home party. I just hoped no food would be left on low tables, because Mardi's name should have been Hoover.

Despite Mardi's hard tugging on the leash, I slowed my walk, never tired of seeing the glorious architecture of what I thought was one of the prettiest houses in a neighborhood famed for its beautiful houses. As we approached the marble steps and arched colonnade of the front porch, the massive wooden double doors opened and Christopher Benoit, a longtime Ryan family friend and employee, stood in the entranceway with a welcoming smile.

I'd started to greet him when Mardi gave one more tug, pulling the leash from my hand. He raced around Jolene—who mercifully didn't drop the muffins—and up the steps. After briefly and enthusiastically greeting Christopher, he ran behind him into the foyer. I hurried to catch up, expecting to hear the sounds of crashing china and crystal, but by the time I'd reached the foyer, all I could hear was Mardi's soft whimpers of pleasure coming from the front parlor. I stopped abruptly on the threshold, taking in at a single glance the small gathering of familiar faces, along with a few new ones, and Sunny Ryan sitting between Mimi and Beau on the sofa while my dog—previously known as my fierce protector—rested his head on Sunny's chest, licking the bottom of her pixie-like chin while staring up at her adoringly.

"See?" Jolene whispered in my ear. "Would Mardi steer us wrong?"

I recalled how Mardi had never liked Michael, and would greet him with bared fangs. Albeit fangs that resembled tiny pillows, but the intent had been clear. My shoulders relaxed as I looked at the glowing, happy people assembled in the Ryans' parlor. It reminded me of my last birthday party in Charleston, where I'd been surrounded by the family and friends who loved me unconditionally. Even with the lopsided and barely edible cake that Melanie had made for me with her own hands, I'd felt cherished. The same emotion I now recognized on the pink and now slightly wet face of Sunny Ryan as my traitorous dog continued to bathe her with affection.

I had the sudden feeling someone was watching me intently from behind. Slowly, I turned to find I was in the direct line of sight of the large portrait of Dr. Charles Ryan hanging in the foyer, the end of his pipe sticking out from his jacket pocket, and the light and shadows of the painting made the eyes seem to follow me. Turning back toward the roomful of people, my attention was drawn to two small puddles of water in front of Beau that were in the distinctive shape of a pair of a woman's feet.

Jerking my gaze away, I looked up to discover Sam, Beau's girlfriend and podcast partner, looking at me, a curious expression on her face. She motioned for me to stay where I was, as if she had the intention of speaking with me. I wasn't sure what it was she wanted to say to me, but I was fairly certain it had something to do with Beau. I pretended I hadn't seen her and I stepped backward into the small crowd, hoping to disappear long enough to call an Uber and leave.

I had made it into the dining room, where the table sat covered with all kinds of food on platters and in bowls, including Jolene's muffins, which she had already dusted with powdered sugar from the little dispenser she'd brought in her purse (because Jolene). I'd hit the Order button on my Uber app when I heard Sam call my name.

I gave a quick wave in her direction as I headed toward the door. "My Uber's here—I've got to go."

Jolene sent me a questioning look and I held my hand up to my head like an old-fashioned telephone—something I'd seen Melanie do frequently—to let her know I'd call later.

Sam followed me out the door, then stopped on the porch as I jogged down the path toward the gate, silently hoping that the approaching car actually was my Uber.

"We need to talk," she shouted as I clanged the gate shut behind me. "I'll text you."

I forced a grin as I opened the car door, pausing briefly to verify that I was actually in the correct Uber, then slid inside. I wasn't sure if Sam wanted to talk about the footprints or Beau—or both. I wasn't interested in discussing either topic with anyone, especially Sam, for reasons I couldn't explain even to myself.

I shut the car door without glancing back, feeling her gaze on me long after I lost sight of the house on Prytania.

Photo by Marchet Butler

Karen White is the *New York Times* bestselling author of more than thirty novels, including the Tradd Street series, *The Last Night in London*, *Dreams of Falling*, *The Night the Lights Went Out*, *Flight Patterns*, *The Sound of Glass*, *A Long Time Gone*, and *The Time Between*. She is the coauthor of *The Lost Summers of Newport*, *All the Ways We Said Goodbye*, *The Glass Ocean*, and *The Forgotten Room* with *New York Times* bestselling authors Beatriz Williams and Lauren Willig. She grew up in London but now lives with her husband and a spoiled Havanese dog near Atlanta, Georgia.

CONNECT ONLINE

Karen-White.com
🅕 KarenWhiteAuthor
🐦 KarenWhiteWrite
📷 KarenWhiteWrite